image comics presents

created by John Layman & Rob Guillory

"International Flavor"

written & lettered by
John Layman
drawn & coloured by
Rob Guillory

IMAGE COMICS, INC.

Robert Kirkman - chief operating officer
Erik Larsen - chief financial officer
Todd McFarlane - president
Marc Silvestri - chief executive officer
Jim Valentino - vice-president

Eric Stephenson - publisher
Joe Keatinge - sales & licensing coordinator
Betsy Gomez - pr & marketing coordinator
Branwyn Bigglestone - accounts manager
Sarah deLaine - administrative assistant
Tyler Shainline - production manager
Drew Gill - art director
Jonathan Chan - production artist
Monica Howard - production artist
Vincent Kukua - production artist

www.imagecomics.com

International Rights Representative: Christine Jensen (christine@gfloystudio.com)   ISBN: 978-1-60706-260-8

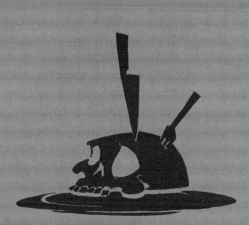

Dedications:

JOHN: To BattytheCat and Lux Interior. Fallen heroes.

ROB: To Thomas and Harold. Coolest uncles ever. And to the show LOST and the movie Commando.

Thanks:

Lisa Gonzales and Steven Struble, for the color flats.
Tom B. Long, for the logo.
Comicbookfonts.com, for the fonts.

And More Thanks:

The incredible Image crew of Kirkman, Stephenson, Shainline, Keatinge, Bigglestone & Gill. Plus: Kim Peterson, April Hanks, Brit Nowlin, Mike Heisler, Kody Chamberlain and Richard Starkings. And You, dear reader.

Chapter 1

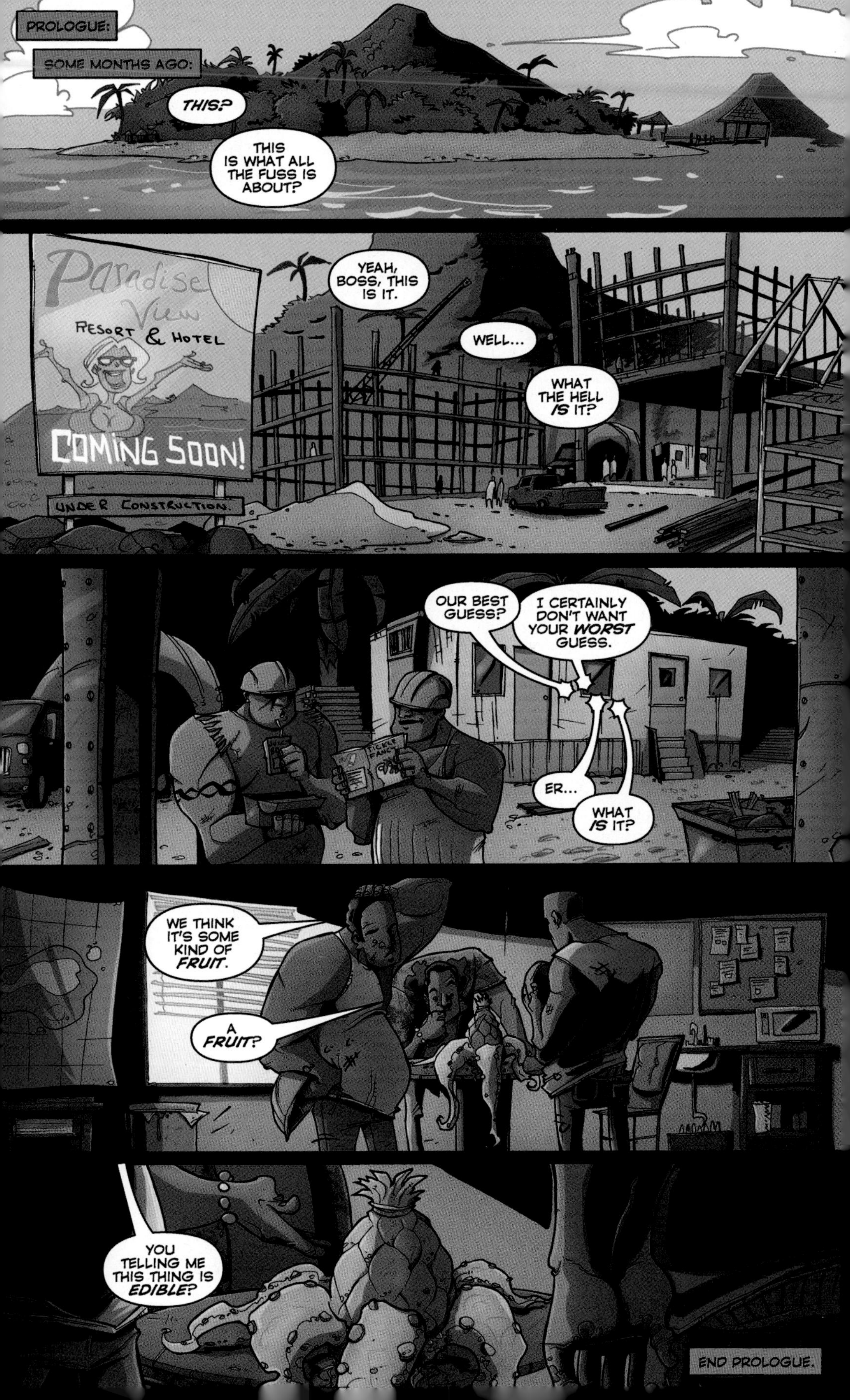
PROLOGUE:
SOME MONTHS AGO:
THIS?
THIS IS WHAT ALL THE FUSS IS ABOUT?
Paradise View
RESORT & HOTEL
COMING SOON!
UNDER CONSTRUCTION
YEAH, BOSS, THIS IS IT.
WELL...
WHAT THE HELL *IS* IT?
OUR BEST GUESS?
I CERTAINLY DON'T WANT YOUR *WORST* GUESS.
ER...
WHAT *IS* IT?
WE THINK IT'S SOME KIND OF *FRUIT*.
A *FRUIT*?
YOU TELLING ME THIS THING IS *EDIBLE*?
END PROLOGUE.

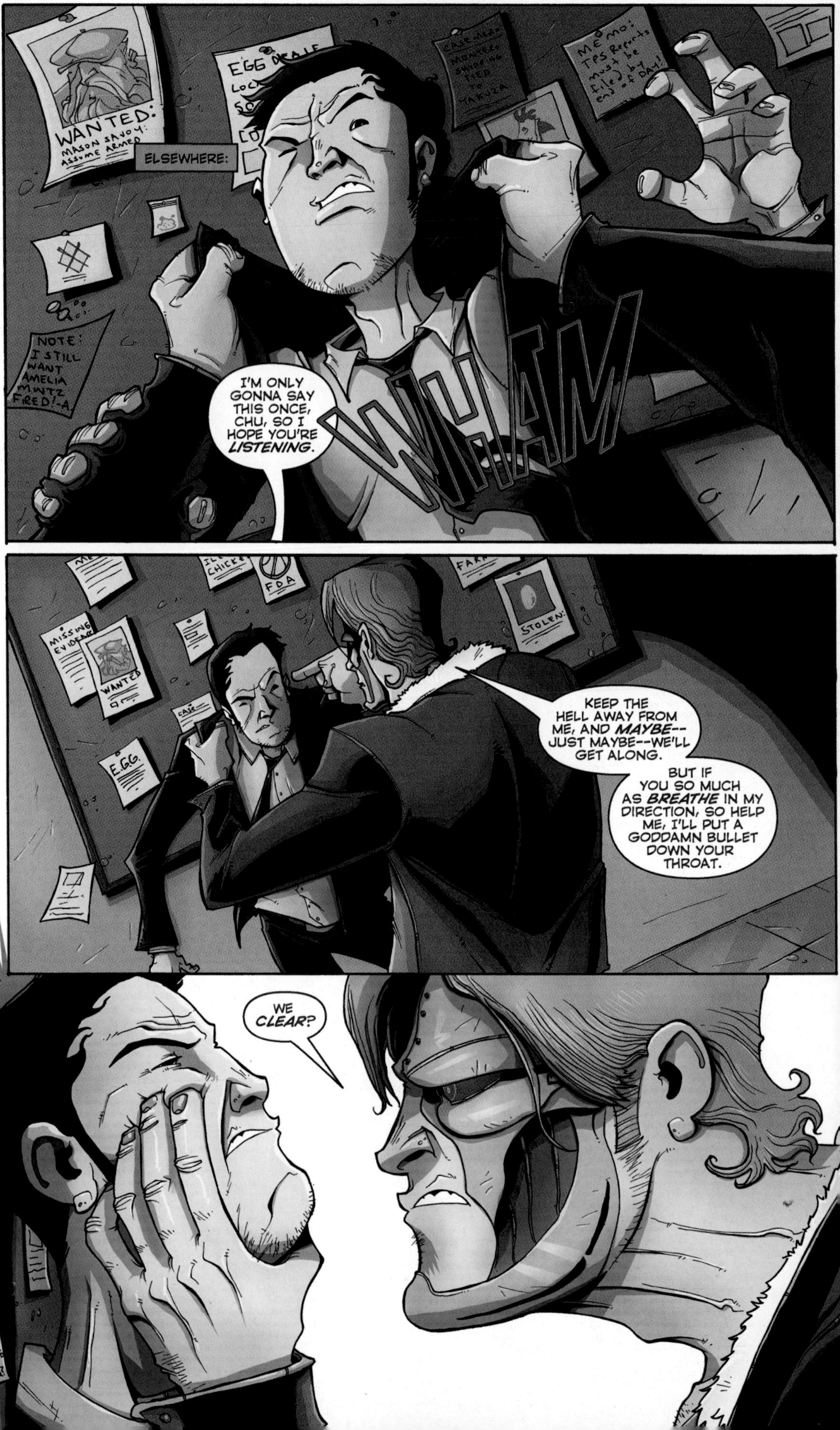

ELSEWHERE:
WANTED: MASON SAVOY: ASSUME ARMED
NOTE: I STILL WANT AMELIA MINTZ FIRED!-A
ME MO: TPS Reports must be filed by end of DAY!
I'M ONLY GONNA SAY THIS ONCE, CHU, SO I HOPE YOU'RE *LISTENING*.
WHAM
MISSING EVIDENCE
WANTED
FDA
STOLEN!
E.G.G.
KEEP THE HELL AWAY FROM ME, AND *MAYBE*-- JUST MAYBE--WE'LL GET ALONG.
BUT IF YOU SO MUCH AS *BREATHE* IN MY DIRECTION, SO HELP ME, I'LL PUT A GODDAMN BULLET DOWN YOUR THROAT.
WE *CLEAR*?
E.GG TERROR LINKED TO IRAQ?

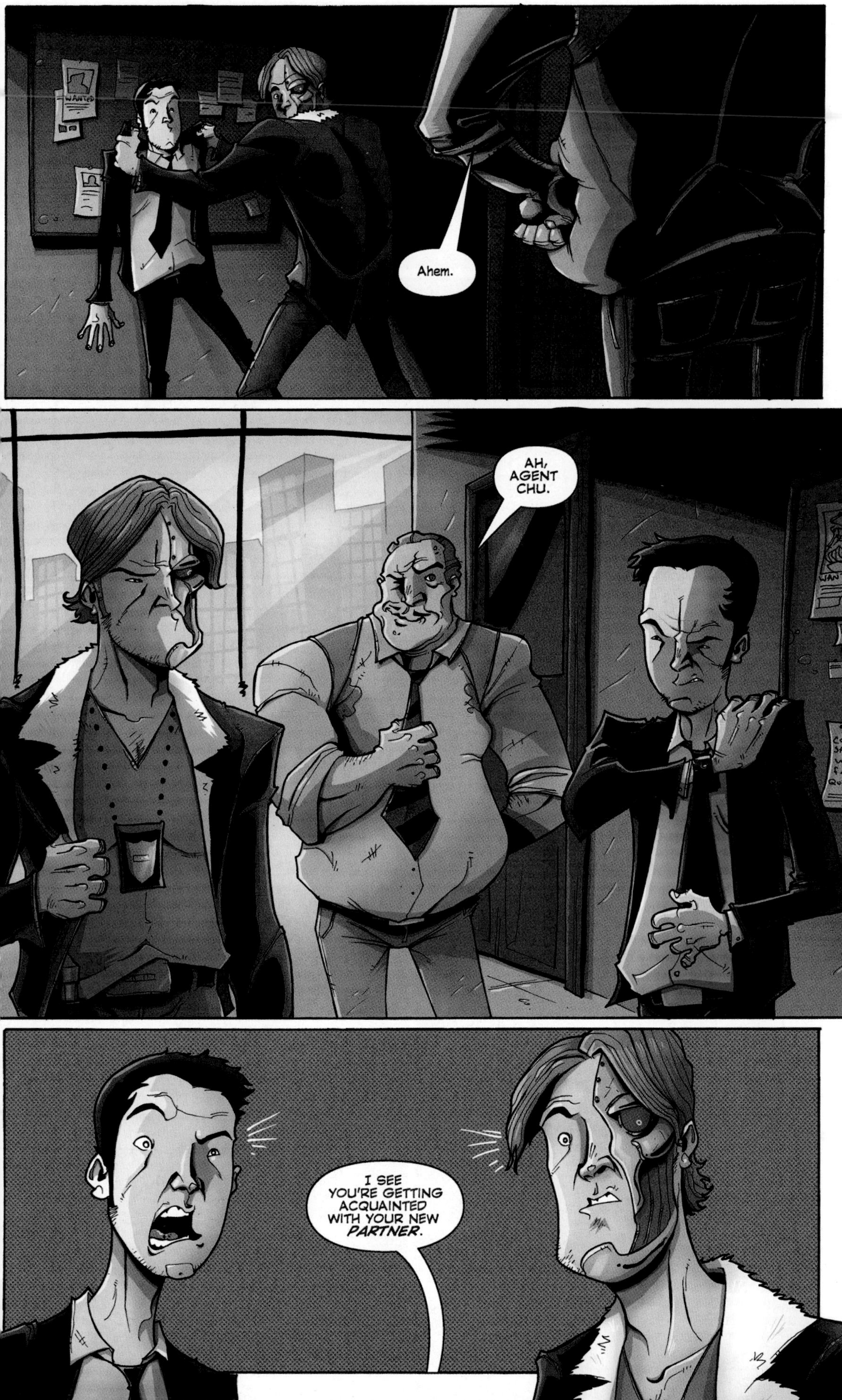
WANTED
Ahem.
AH, AGENT CHU.
I SEE YOU'RE GETTING ACQUAINTED WITH YOUR NEW *PARTNER*.

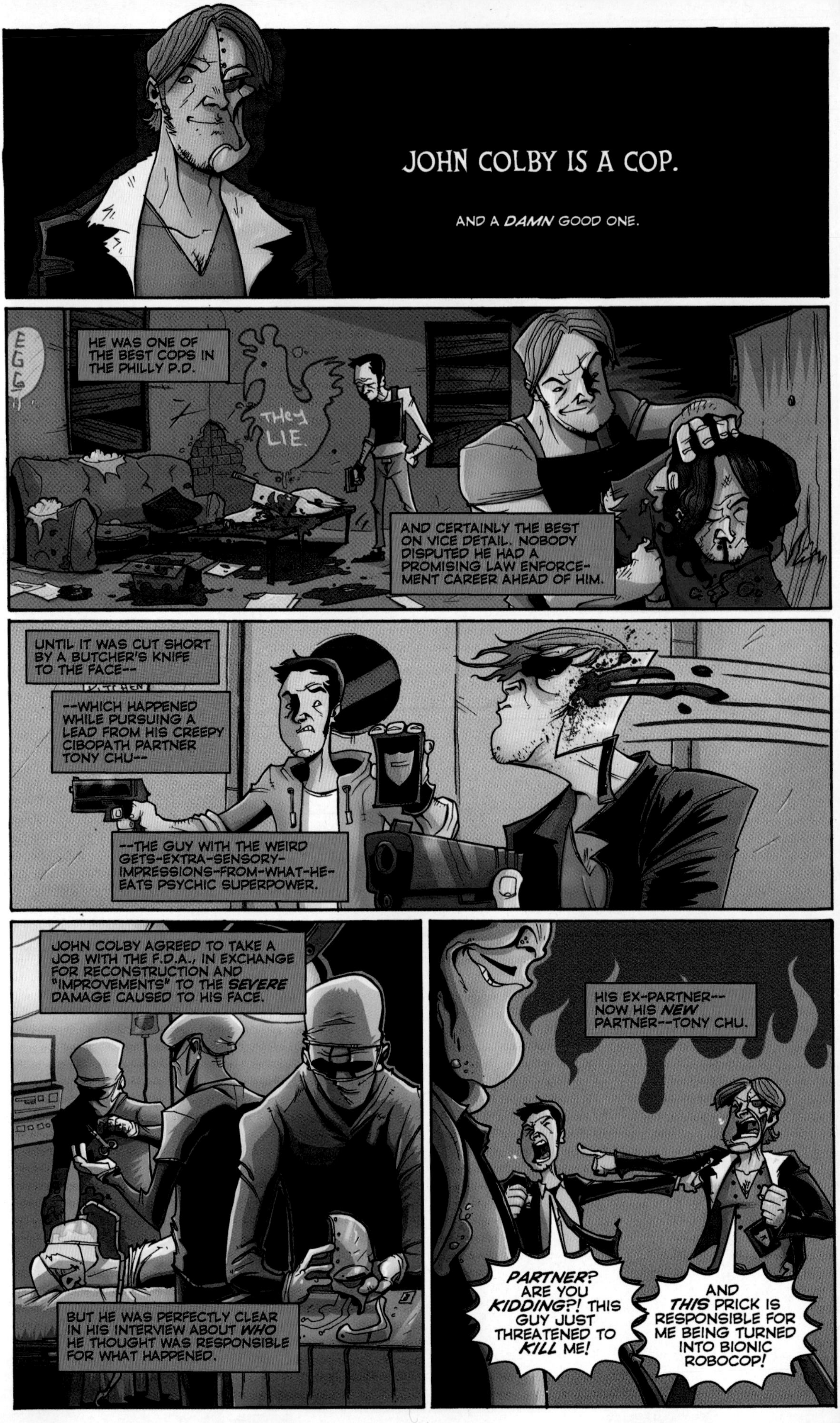
JOHN COLBY IS A COP.
AND A *DAMN* GOOD ONE.
EGGS
HE WAS ONE OF THE BEST COPS IN THE PHILLY P.D.
They LIE.
AND CERTAINLY THE BEST ON VICE DETAIL. NOBODY DISPUTED HE HAD A PROMISING LAW ENFORCEMENT CAREER AHEAD OF HIM.
UNTIL IT WAS CUT SHORT BY A BUTCHER'S KNIFE TO THE FACE--
--WHICH HAPPENED WHILE PURSUING A LEAD FROM HIS CREEPY CIBOPATH PARTNER TONY CHU--
--THE GUY WITH THE WEIRD GETS-EXTRA-SENSORY-IMPRESSIONS-FROM-WHAT-HE-EATS PSYCHIC SUPERPOWER.
JOHN COLBY AGREED TO TAKE A JOB WITH THE F.D.A., IN EXCHANGE FOR RECONSTRUCTION AND "IMPROVEMENTS" TO THE *SEVERE* DAMAGE CAUSED TO HIS FACE.
BUT HE WAS PERFECTLY CLEAR IN HIS INTERVIEW ABOUT *WHO* HE THOUGHT WAS RESPONSIBLE FOR WHAT HAPPENED.
HIS EX-PARTNER--NOW HIS *NEW* PARTNER--TONY CHU.
PARTNER? ARE YOU *KIDDING*?! THIS GUY JUST THREATENED TO *KILL* ME!
AND *THIS* PRICK IS RESPONSIBLE FOR ME BEING TURNED INTO BIONIC ROBOCOP!

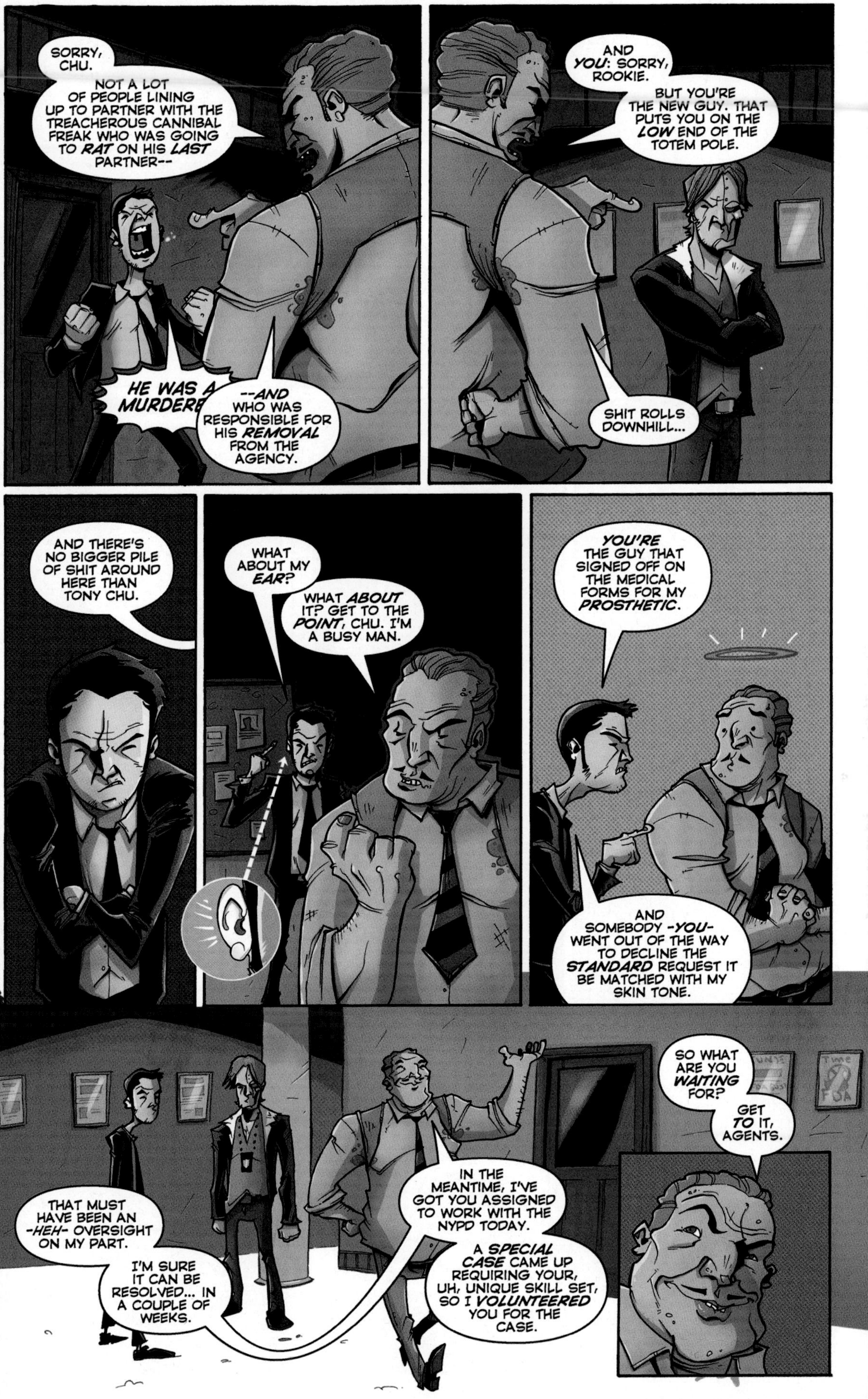
SORRY, CHU.
NOT A LOT OF PEOPLE LINING UP TO PARTNER WITH THE TREACHEROUS CANNIBAL FREAK WHO WAS GOING TO RAT ON HIS LAST PARTNER--
HE WAS A MURDERER
--AND WHO WAS RESPONSIBLE FOR HIS REMOVAL FROM THE AGENCY.
AND YOU: SORRY, ROOKIE.
BUT YOU'RE THE NEW GUY. THAT PUTS YOU ON THE LOW END OF THE TOTEM POLE.
SHIT ROLLS DOWNHILL...
AND THERE'S NO BIGGER PILE OF SHIT AROUND HERE THAN TONY CHU.
WHAT ABOUT MY EAR?
WHAT ABOUT IT? GET TO THE POINT, CHU. I'M A BUSY MAN.
YOU'RE THE GUY THAT SIGNED OFF ON THE MEDICAL FORMS FOR MY PROSTHETIC.
AND SOMEBODY -YOU- WENT OUT OF THE WAY TO DECLINE THE STANDARD REQUEST IT BE MATCHED WITH MY SKIN TONE.
THAT MUST HAVE BEEN AN -HEH- OVERSIGHT ON MY PART.
I'M SURE IT CAN BE RESOLVED... IN A COUPLE OF WEEKS.
IN THE MEANTIME, I'VE GOT YOU ASSIGNED TO WORK WITH THE NYPD TODAY.
A SPECIAL CASE CAME UP REQUIRING YOUR, UH, UNIQUE SKILL SET, SO I VOLUNTEERED YOU FOR THE CASE.
SO WHAT ARE YOU WAITING FOR?
GET TO IT, AGENTS.

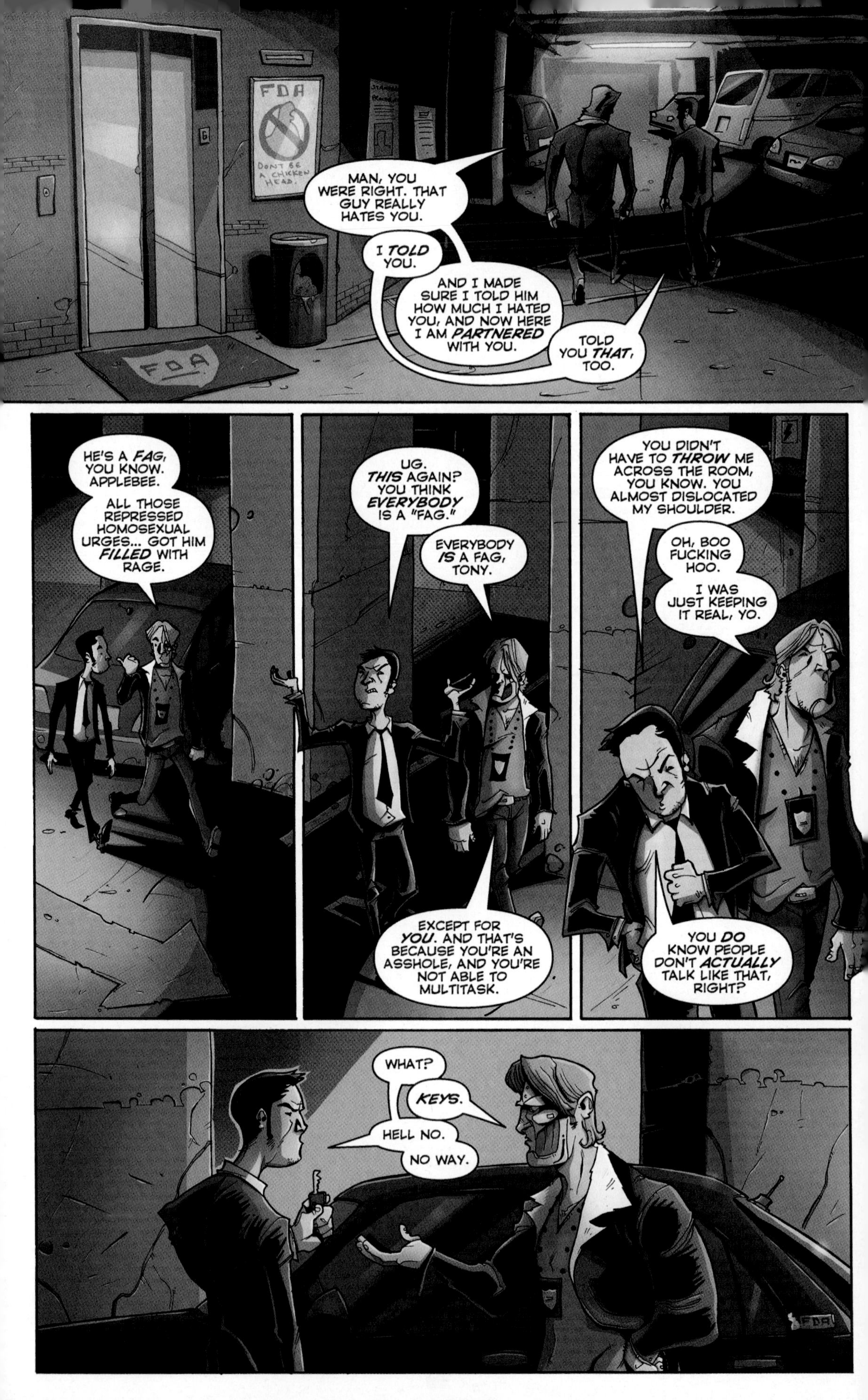
FDA
DONT BE A CHIKKEN HEAD.
MAN, YOU WERE RIGHT. THAT GUY REALLY HATES YOU.
I TOLD YOU.
AND I MADE SURE I TOLD HIM HOW MUCH I HATED YOU, AND NOW HERE I AM PARTNERED WITH YOU.
TOLD YOU THAT, TOO.
FDA
HE'S A FAG, YOU KNOW. APPLEBEE.
ALL THOSE REPRESSED HOMOSEXUAL URGES... GOT HIM FILLED WITH RAGE.
UG. THIS AGAIN? YOU THINK EVERYBODY IS A "FAG."
EVERYBODY IS A FAG, TONY.
EXCEPT FOR YOU. AND THAT'S BECAUSE YOU'RE AN ASSHOLE, AND YOU'RE NOT ABLE TO MULTITASK.
YOU DIDN'T HAVE TO THROW ME ACROSS THE ROOM, YOU KNOW. YOU ALMOST DISLOCATED MY SHOULDER.
OH, BOO FUCKING HOO.
I WAS JUST KEEPING IT REAL, YO.
YOU DO KNOW PEOPLE DON'T ACTUALLY TALK LIKE THAT, RIGHT?
WHAT?
KEYS.
HELL NO.
NO WAY.
FDA

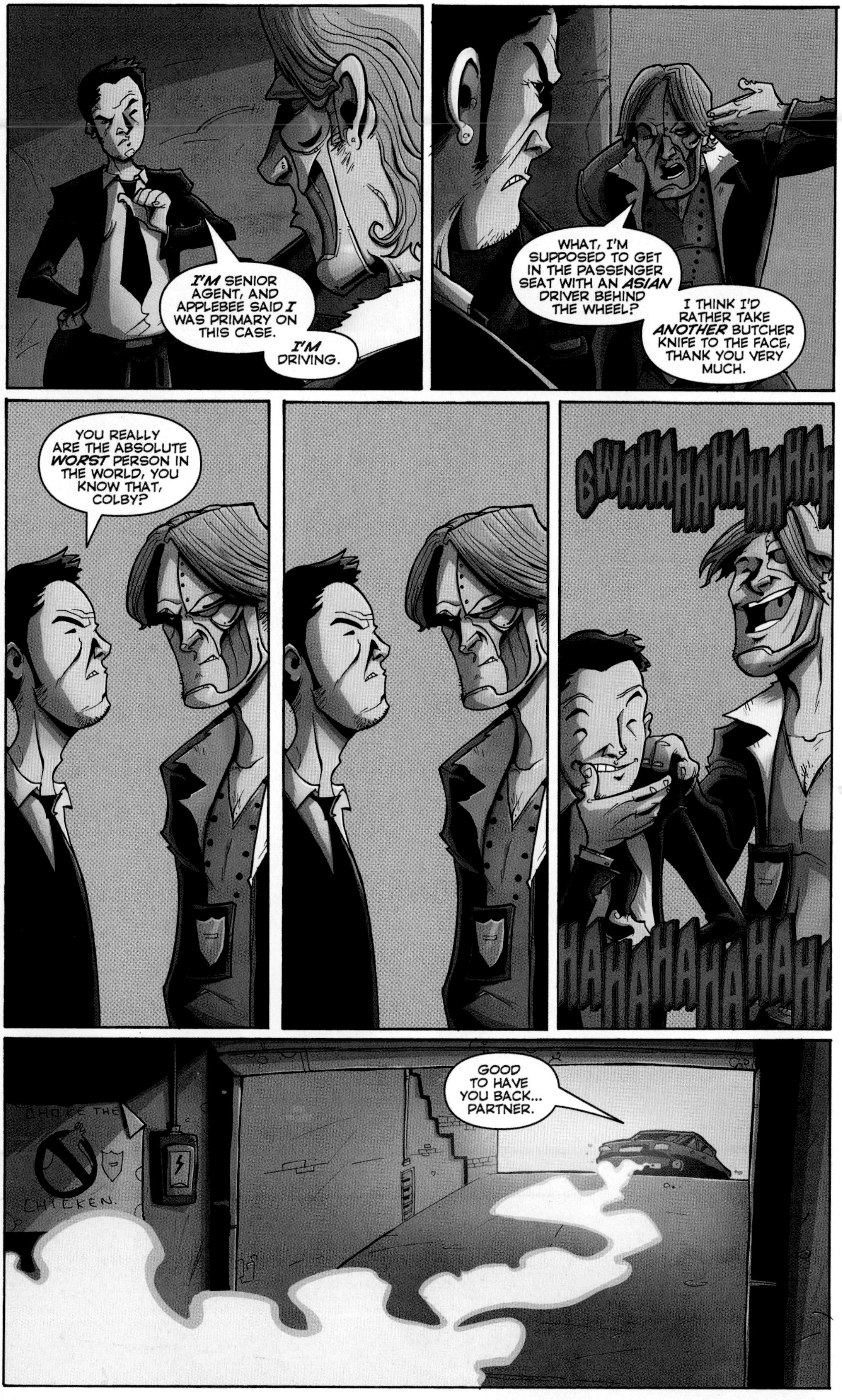
I'M SENIOR AGENT, AND APPLEBEE SAID I WAS PRIMARY ON THIS CASE.
I'M DRIVING.
WHAT, I'M SUPPOSED TO GET IN THE PASSENGER SEAT WITH AN ASIAN DRIVER BEHIND THE WHEEL?
I THINK I'D RATHER TAKE ANOTHER BUTCHER KNIFE TO THE FACE, THANK YOU VERY MUCH.
YOU REALLY ARE THE ABSOLUTE WORST PERSON IN THE WORLD, YOU KNOW THAT, COLBY?
BWAHAHAHAHAHAHAH
HAHAHAHAHAHAHA
GOOD TO HAVE YOU BACK... PARTNER.
CHOKE THE CHICKEN.

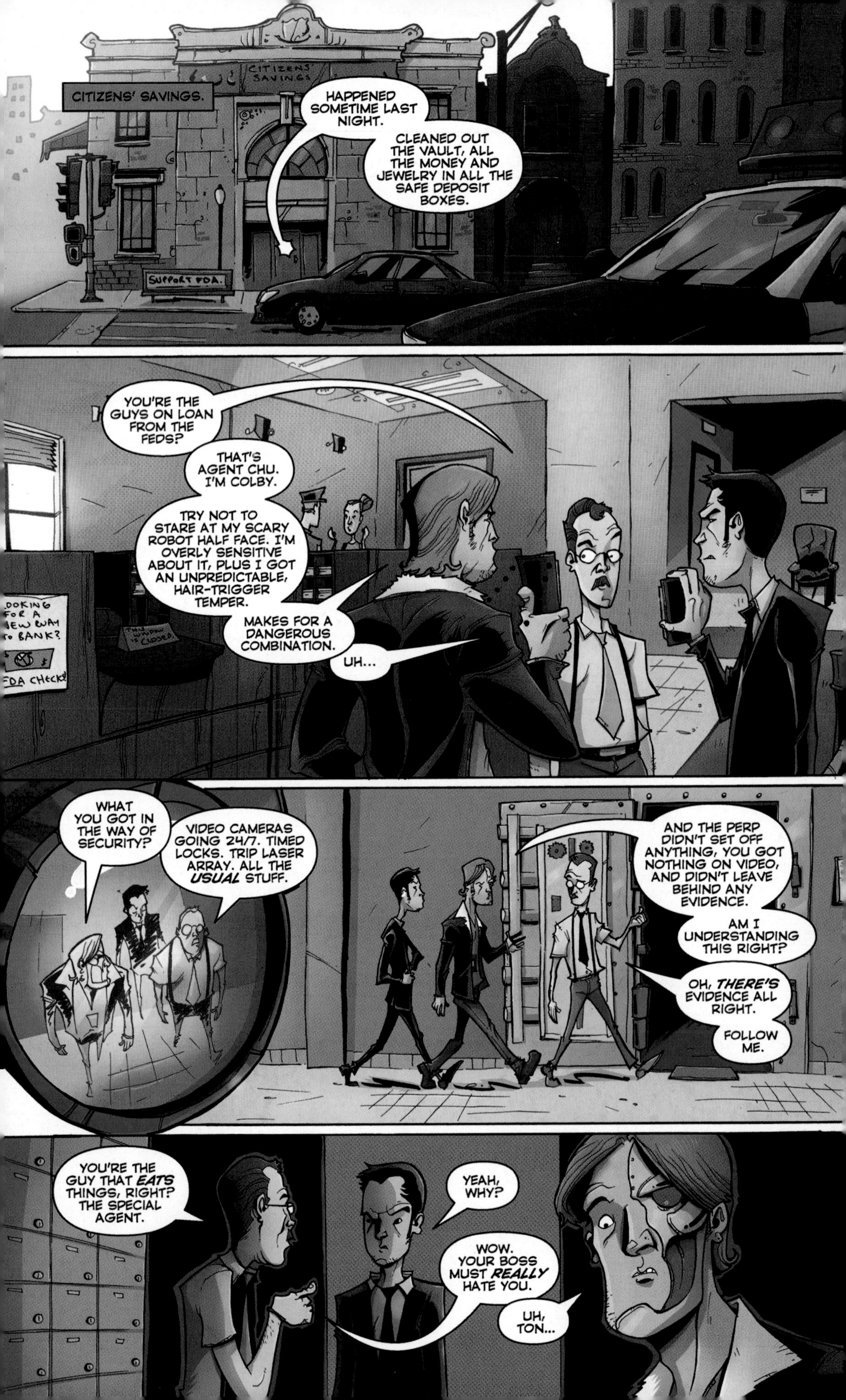

CITIZENS' SAVINGS.
CITIZENS' SAVINGS
SUPPORT FDA.
HAPPENED SOMETIME LAST NIGHT.
CLEANED OUT THE VAULT, ALL THE MONEY AND JEWELRY IN ALL THE SAFE DEPOSIT BOXES.
YOU'RE THE GUYS ON LOAN FROM THE FEDS?
THAT'S AGENT CHU. I'M COLBY.
TRY NOT TO STARE AT MY SCARY ROBOT HALF FACE. I'M OVERLY SENSITIVE ABOUT IT, PLUS I GOT AN UNPREDICTABLE, HAIR-TRIGGER TEMPER.
MAKES FOR A DANGEROUS COMBINATION.
UH...
LOOKING FOR A NEW WAY TO BANK?
FDA CHECK!
WHAT YOU GOT IN THE WAY OF SECURITY?
VIDEO CAMERAS GOING 24/7. TIMED LOCKS. TRIP LASER ARRAY. ALL THE *USUAL* STUFF.
AND THE PERP DIDN'T SET OFF ANYTHING, YOU GOT NOTHING ON VIDEO, AND DIDN'T LEAVE BEHIND ANY EVIDENCE.
AM I UNDERSTANDING THIS RIGHT?
OH, *THERE'S* EVIDENCE ALL RIGHT.
FOLLOW ME.
YOU'RE THE GUY THAT *EATS* THINGS, RIGHT? THE SPECIAL AGENT.
YEAH, WHY?
WOW. YOUR BOSS MUST *REALLY* HATE YOU.
UH, TON...

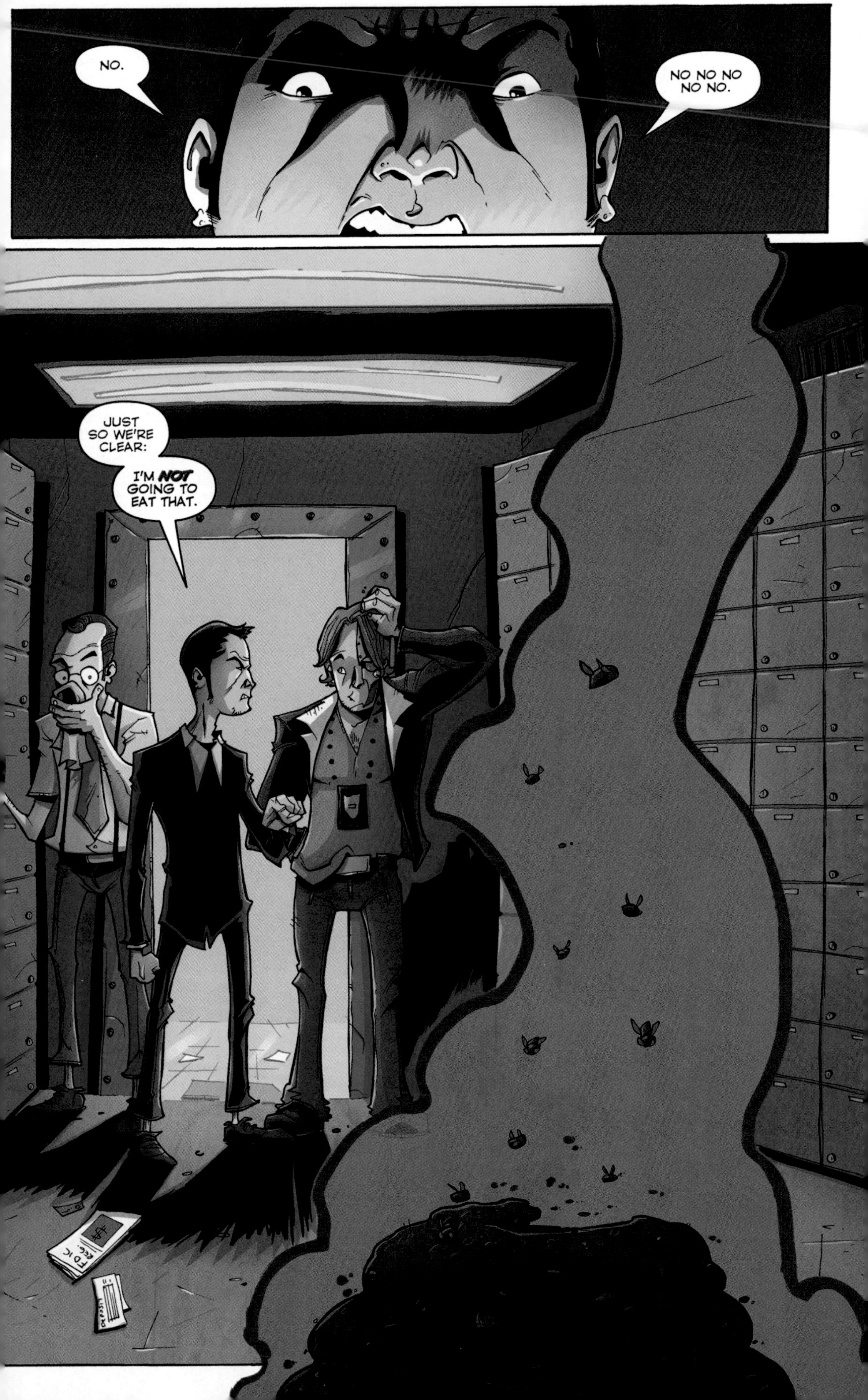
NO.
NO NO NO NO NO.
JUST SO WE'RE CLEAR:
I'M **NOT** GOING TO EAT THAT.

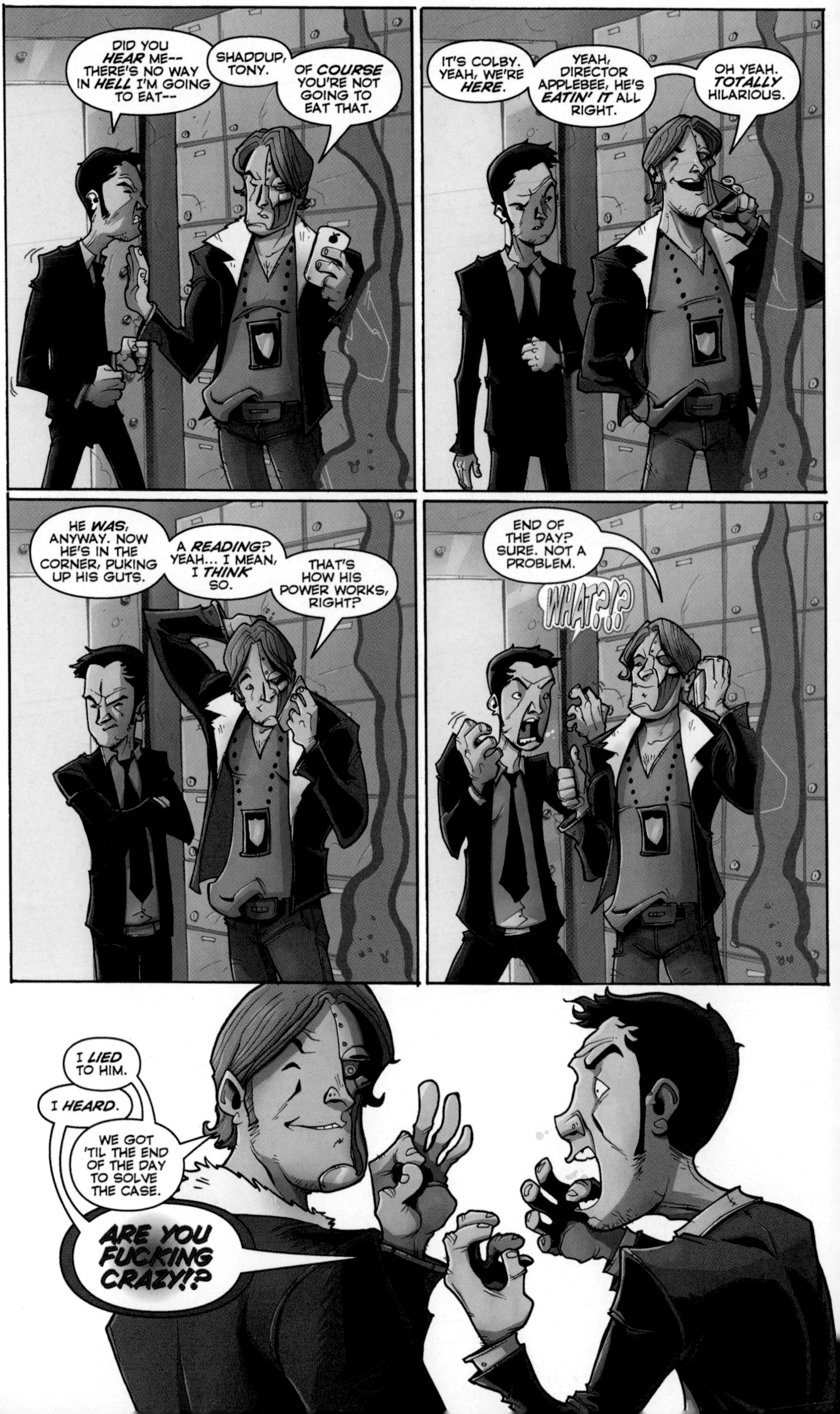
DID YOU HEAR ME-- THERE'S NO WAY IN HELL I'M GOING TO EAT--
SHADDUP, TONY.
OF COURSE YOU'RE NOT GOING TO EAT THAT.
IT'S COLBY. YEAH, WE'RE HERE.
YEAH, DIRECTOR APPLEBEE, HE'S EATIN' IT ALL RIGHT.
OH YEAH. TOTALLY HILARIOUS.
HE WAS, ANYWAY. NOW HE'S IN THE CORNER, PUKING UP HIS GUTS.
A READING? YEAH... I MEAN, I THINK SO.
THAT'S HOW HIS POWER WORKS, RIGHT?
END OF THE DAY? SURE. NOT A PROBLEM.
WHAT?!?
I LIED TO HIM.
I HEARD.
WE GOT 'TIL THE END OF THE DAY TO SOLVE THE CASE.
ARE YOU FUCKING CRAZY!?

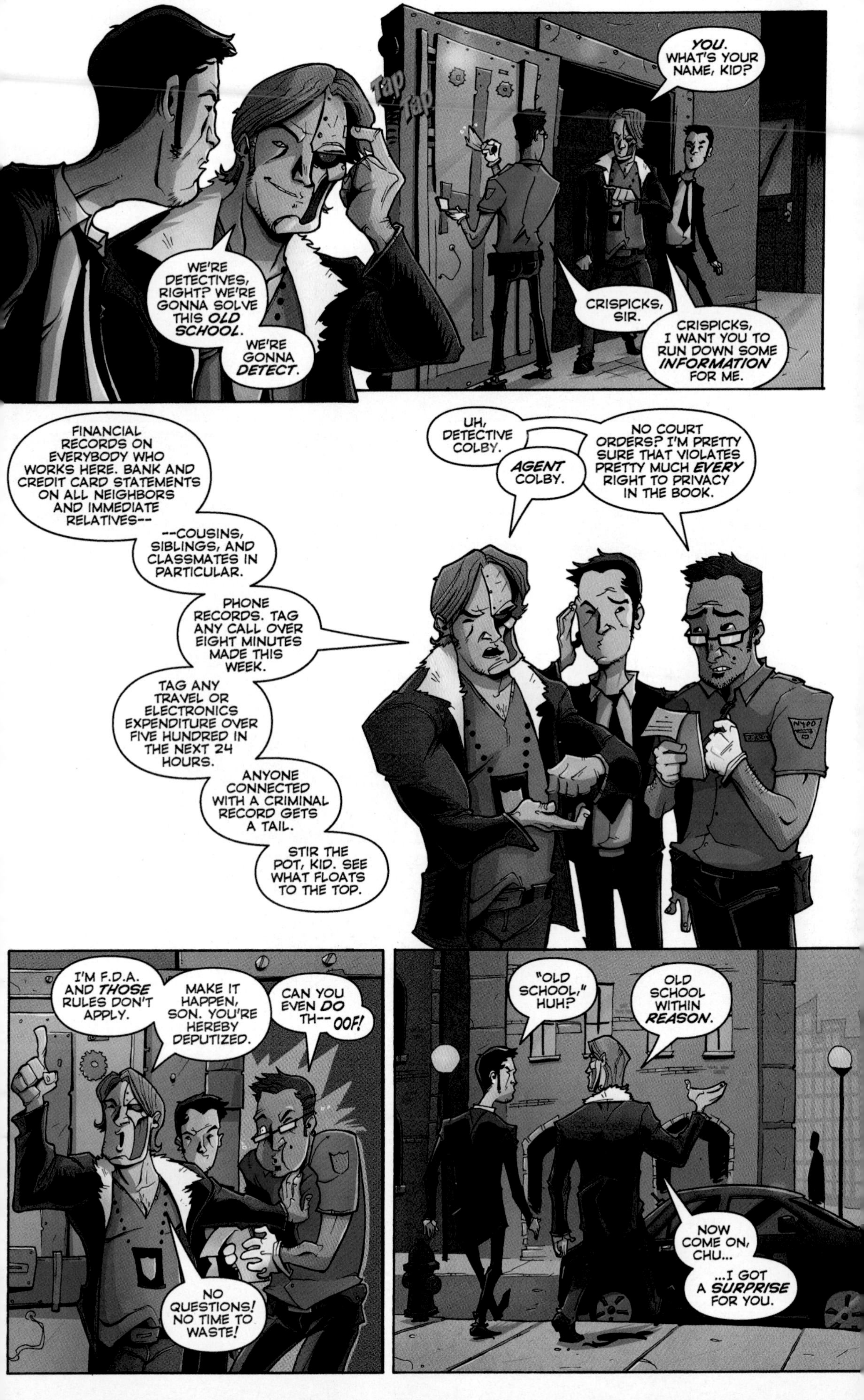
WE'RE DETECTIVES, RIGHT? WE'RE GONNA SOLVE THIS OLD SCHOOL.
WE'RE GONNA DETECT.
TAP TAP
YOU. WHAT'S YOUR NAME, KID?
CRISPICKS, SIR.
CRISPICKS, I WANT YOU TO RUN DOWN SOME INFORMATION FOR ME.
FINANCIAL RECORDS ON EVERYBODY WHO WORKS HERE. BANK AND CREDIT CARD STATEMENTS ON ALL NEIGHBORS AND IMMEDIATE RELATIVES--
--COUSINS, SIBLINGS, AND CLASSMATES IN PARTICULAR.
PHONE RECORDS. TAG ANY CALL OVER EIGHT MINUTES MADE THIS WEEK.
TAG ANY TRAVEL OR ELECTRONICS EXPENDITURE OVER FIVE HUNDRED IN THE NEXT 24 HOURS.
ANYONE CONNECTED WITH A CRIMINAL RECORD GETS A TAIL.
STIR THE POT, KID. SEE WHAT FLOATS TO THE TOP.
UH, DETECTIVE COLBY.
AGENT COLBY.
NO COURT ORDERS? I'M PRETTY SURE THAT VIOLATES PRETTY MUCH EVERY RIGHT TO PRIVACY IN THE BOOK.
I'M F.D.A. AND THOSE RULES DON'T APPLY.
MAKE IT HAPPEN, SON. YOU'RE HEREBY DEPUTIZED.
CAN YOU EVEN DO TH-- OOF!
NO QUESTIONS! NO TIME TO WASTE!
"OLD SCHOOL," HUH?
OLD SCHOOL WITHIN REASON.
NOW COME ON, CHU...
...I GOT A SURPRISE FOR YOU.

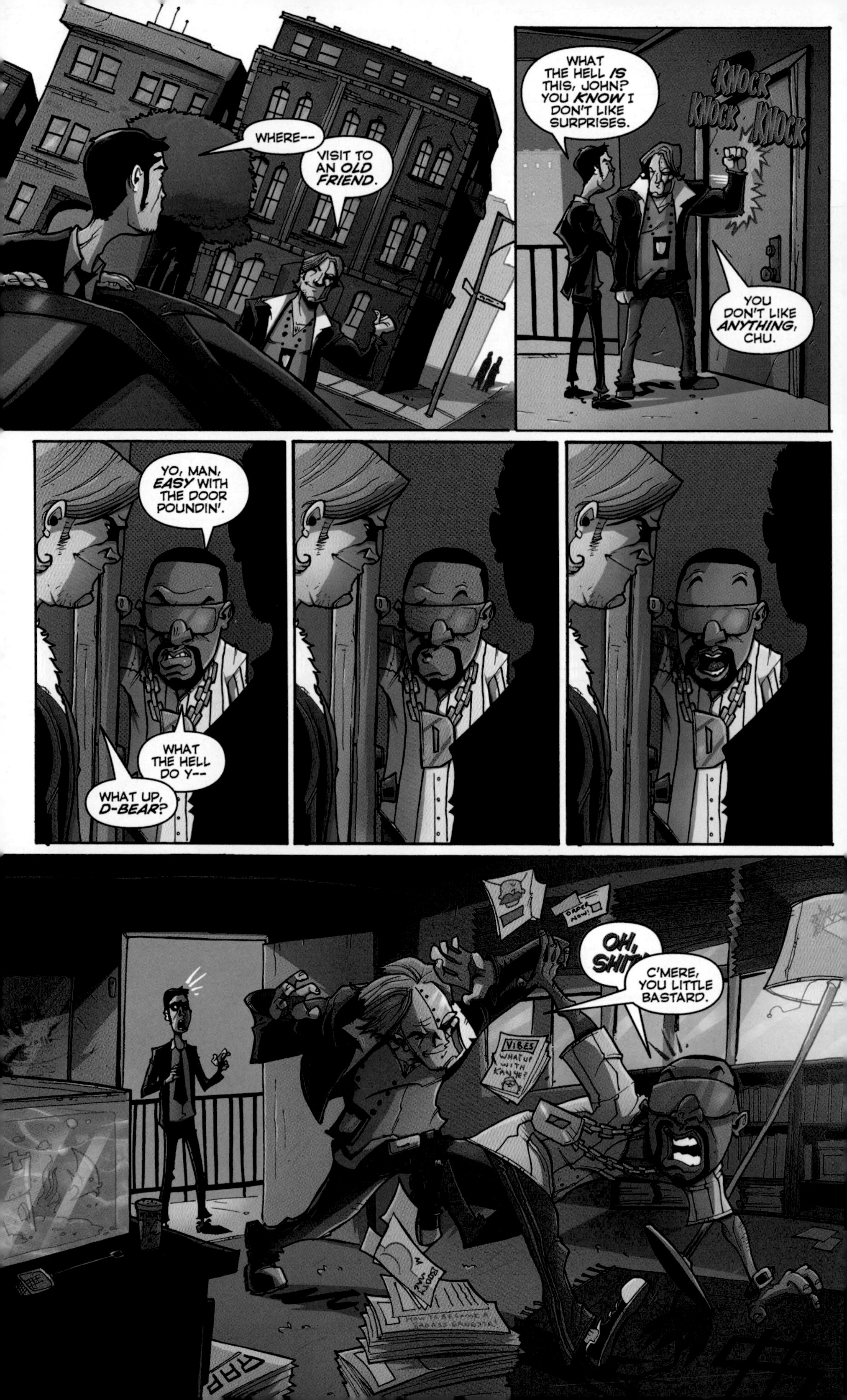
WHERE--
VISIT TO AN OLD FRIEND.
WHAT THE HELL IS THIS, JOHN? YOU KNOW I DON'T LIKE SURPRISES.
KNOCK KNOCK KNOCK
YOU DON'T LIKE ANYTHING, CHU.
YO, MAN, EASY WITH THE DOOR POUNDIN'.
WHAT THE HELL DO Y--
WHAT UP, D-BEAR?
ORDER NOW!
OH, SHIT!
C'MERE, YOU LITTLE BASTARD.
VIBES
WHAT UP WITH KANYE!

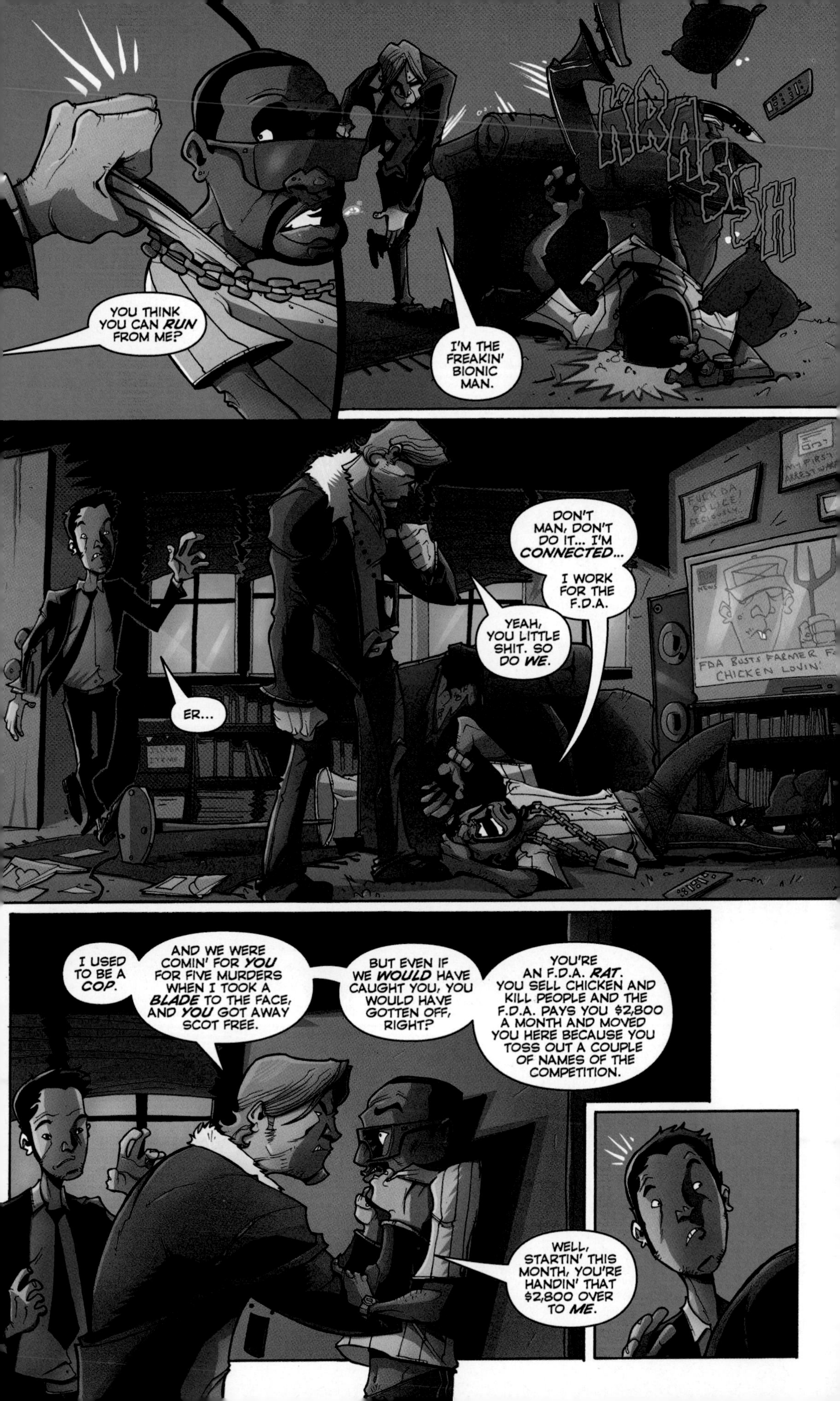
KRASH
YOU THINK YOU CAN RUN FROM ME?
I'M THE FREAKIN' BIONIC MAN.
DON'T MAN, DON'T DO IT... I'M CONNECTED...
I WORK FOR THE F.D.A.
YEAH, YOU LITTLE SHIT. SO DO WE.
ER...
FDA BUSTS FARMER
CHICKEN LOVIN'
I USED TO BE A COP.
AND WE WERE COMIN' FOR YOU FOR FIVE MURDERS WHEN I TOOK A BLADE TO THE FACE, AND YOU GOT AWAY SCOT FREE.
BUT EVEN IF WE WOULD HAVE CAUGHT YOU, YOU WOULD HAVE GOTTEN OFF, RIGHT?
YOU'RE AN F.D.A. RAT. YOU SELL CHICKEN AND KILL PEOPLE AND THE F.D.A. PAYS YOU $2,800 A MONTH AND MOVED YOU HERE BECAUSE YOU TOSS OUT A COUPLE OF NAMES OF THE COMPETITION.
WELL, STARTIN' THIS MONTH, YOU'RE HANDIN' THAT $2,800 OVER TO ME.

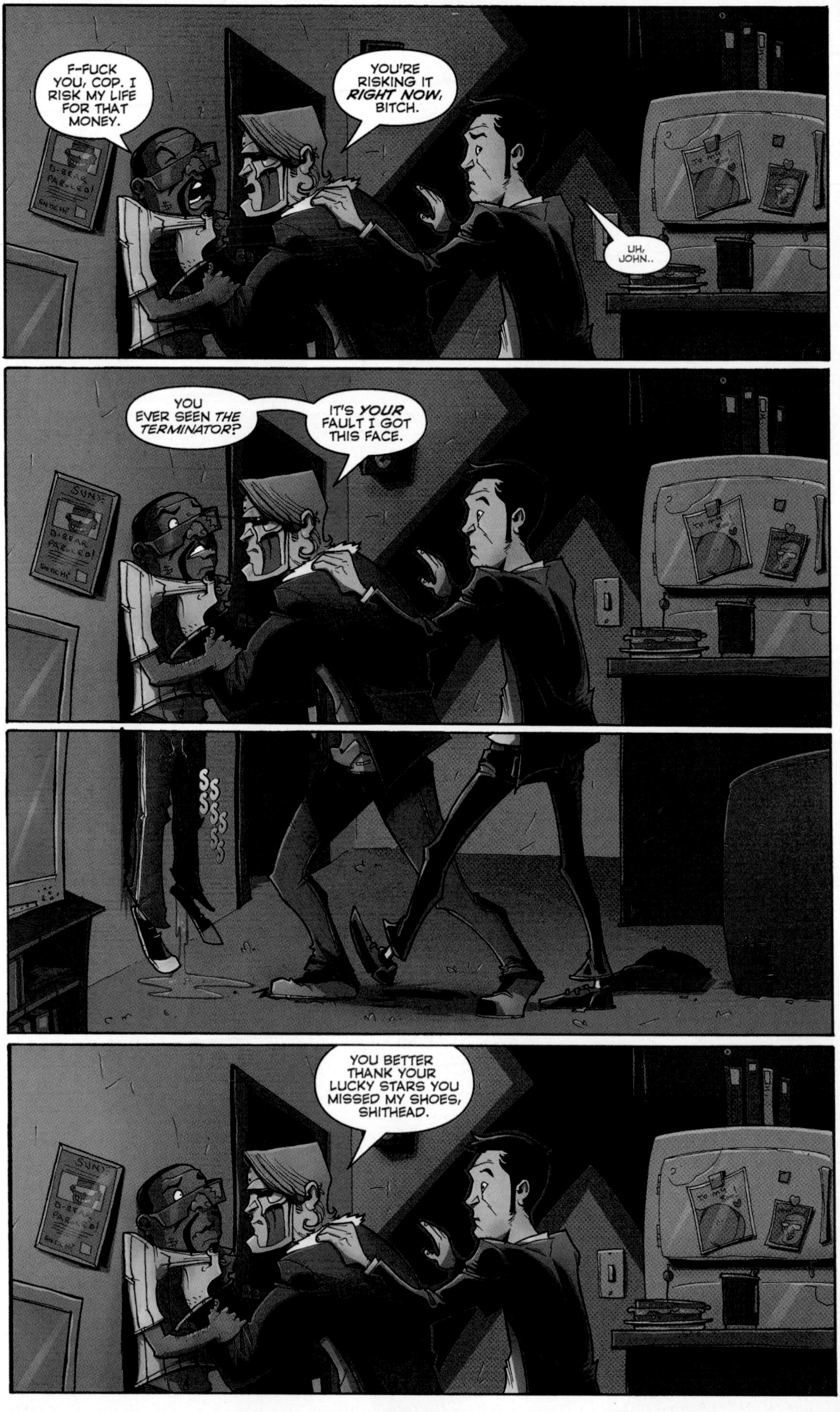
F-FUCK YOU, COP. I RISK MY LIFE FOR THAT MONEY.
YOU'RE RISKING IT *RIGHT NOW,* BITCH.
UH, JOHN..
YOU EVER SEEN *THE TERMINATOR*?
IT'S *YOUR* FAULT I GOT THIS FACE.
YOU BETTER THANK YOUR LUCKY STARS YOU MISSED MY SHOES, SHITHEAD.

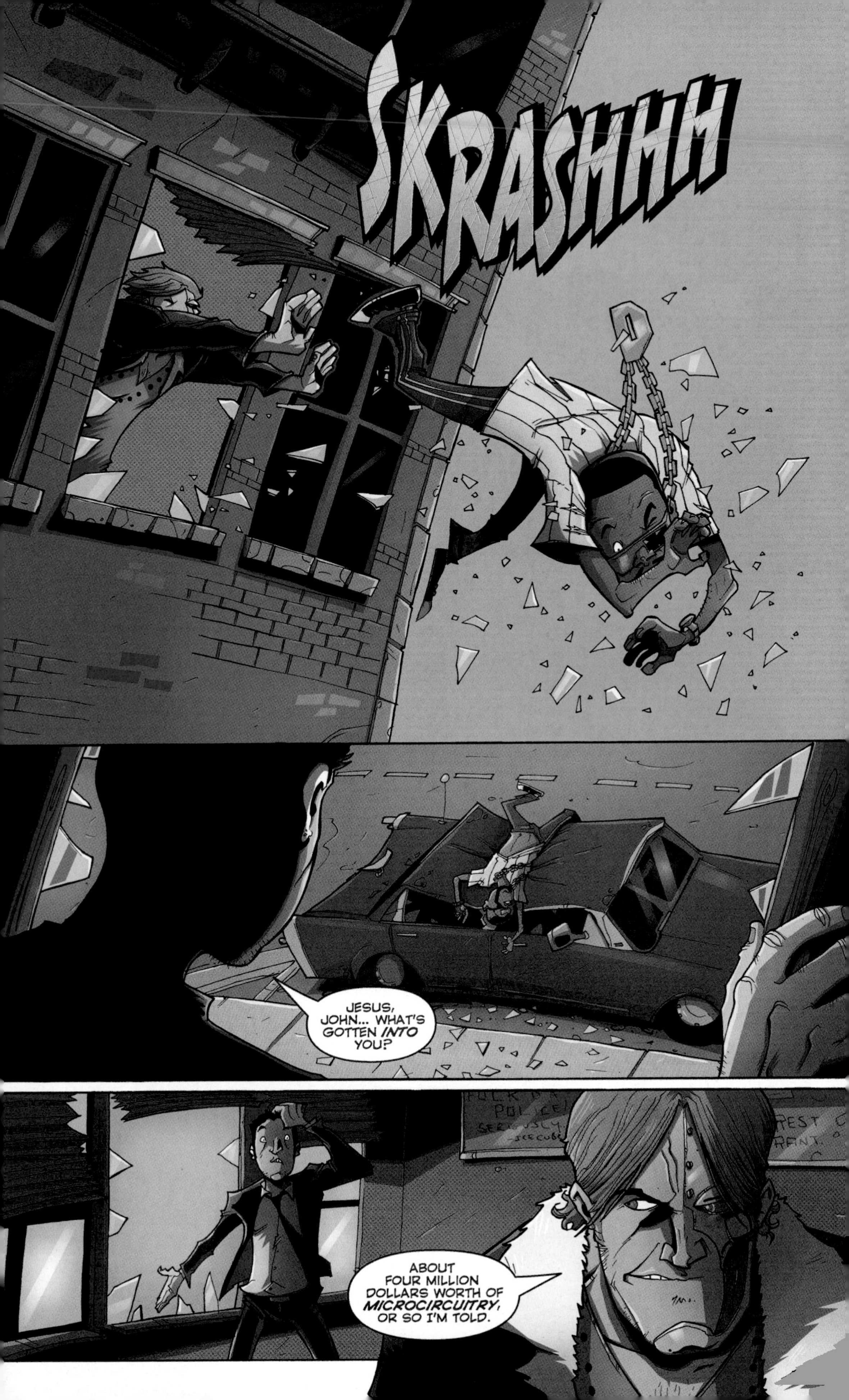
SKRASHHH
JESUS, JOHN... WHAT'S GOTTEN *INTO* YOU?
ABOUT FOUR MILLION DOLLARS WORTH OF *MICROCIRCUITRY*, OR SO I'M TOLD.

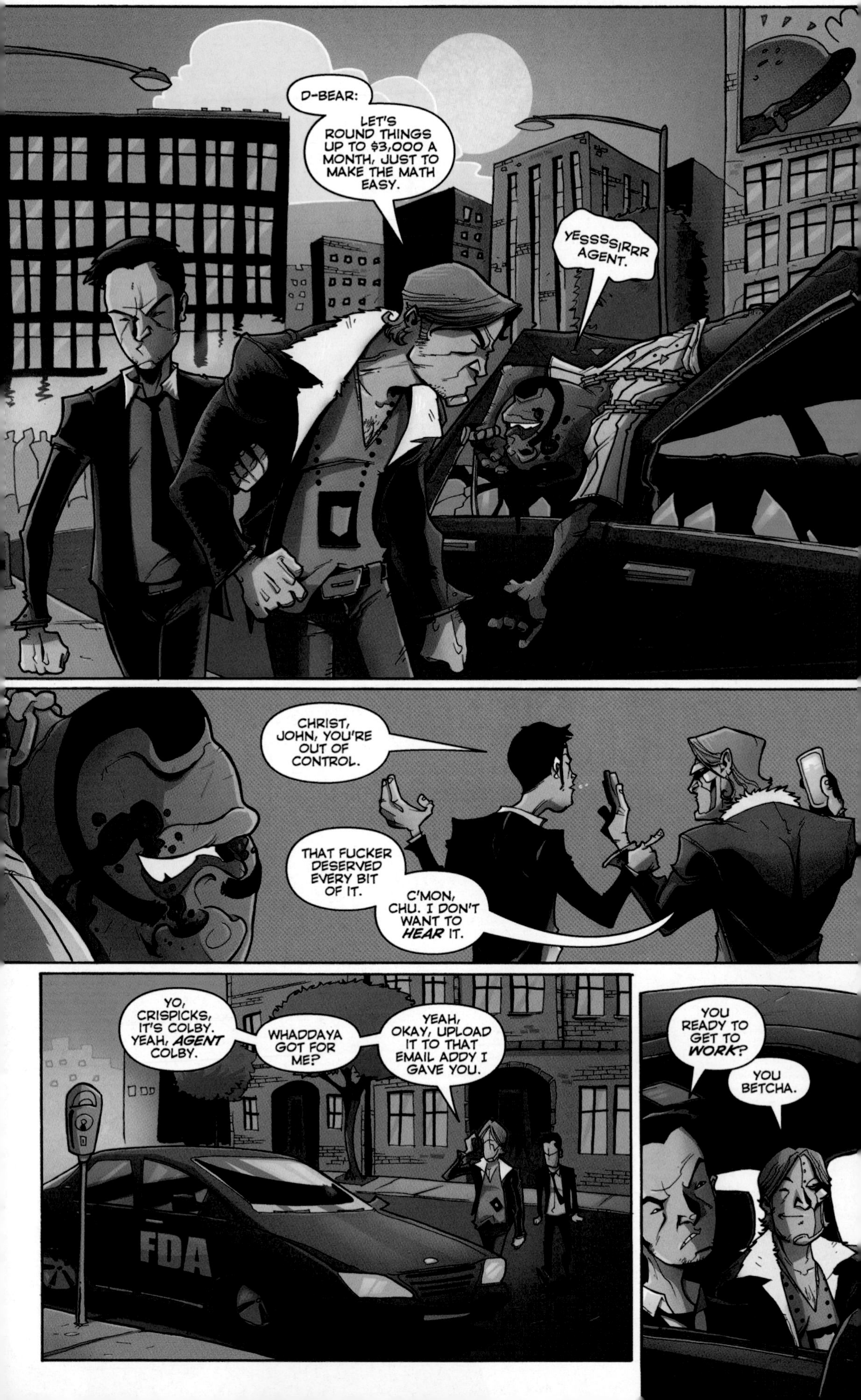

D-BEAR:
LET'S ROUND THINGS UP TO $3,000 A MONTH, JUST TO MAKE THE MATH EASY.
YESSSSIRRR AGENT.
CHRIST, JOHN, YOU'RE OUT OF CONTROL.
THAT FUCKER DESERVED EVERY BIT OF IT.
C'MON, CHU. I DON'T WANT TO HEAR IT.
YO, CRISPICKS, IT'S COLBY. YEAH, AGENT COLBY.
WHADDAYA GOT FOR ME?
YEAH, OKAY, UPLOAD IT TO THAT EMAIL ADDY I GAVE YOU.
FDA
YOU READY TO GET TO WORK?
YOU BETCHA.

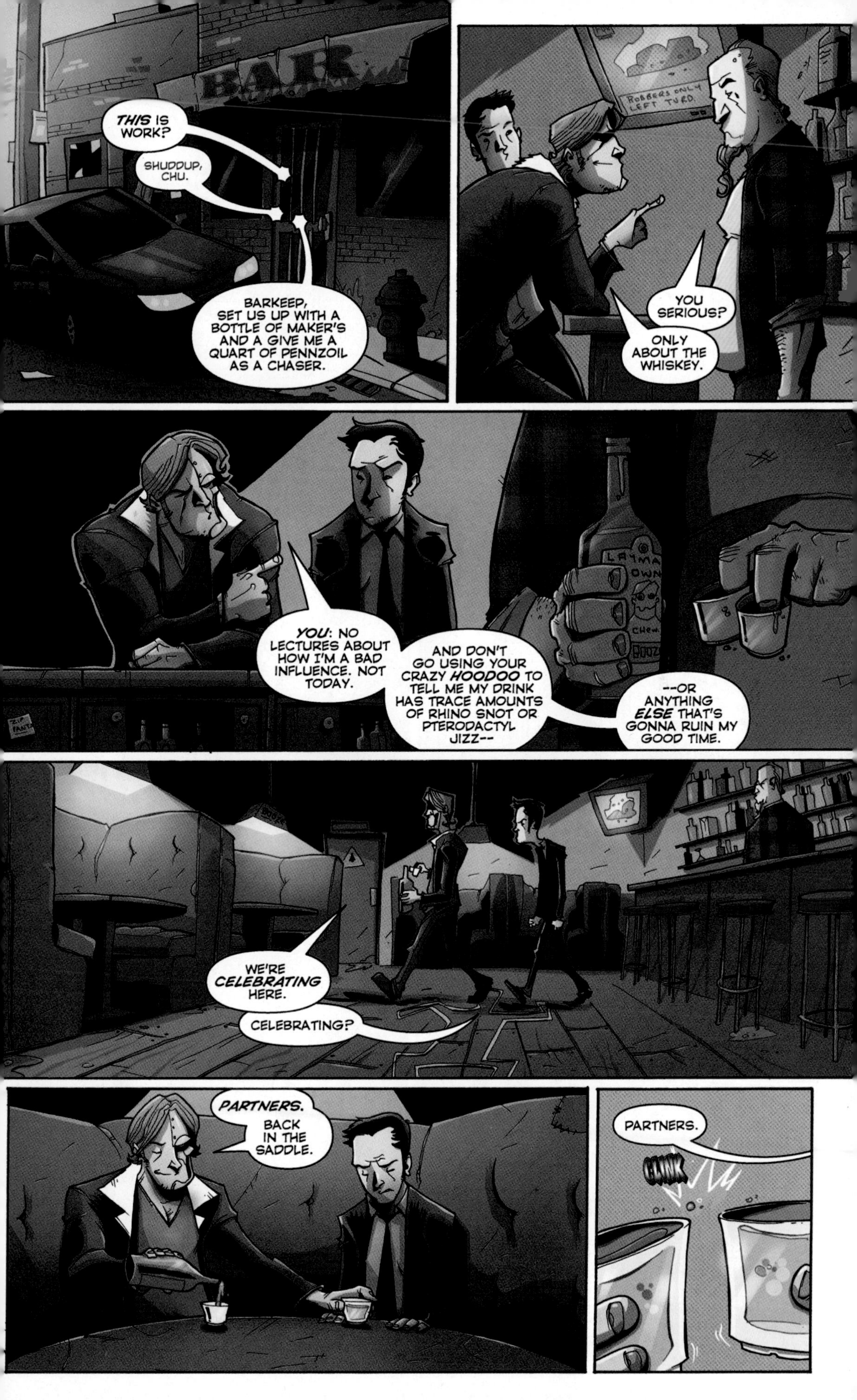
BAR
THIS IS WORK?
SHUDDUP, CHU.
BARKEEP, SET US UP WITH A BOTTLE OF MAKER'S AND A GIVE ME A QUART OF PENNZOIL AS A CHASER.
ROBBERS ONLY LEFT TURD.
YOU SERIOUS?
ONLY ABOUT THE WHISKEY.
YOU: NO LECTURES ABOUT HOW I'M A BAD INFLUENCE. NOT TODAY.
AND DON'T GO USING YOUR CRAZY HOODOO TO TELL ME MY DRINK HAS TRACE AMOUNTS OF RHINO SNOT OR PTERODACTYL JIZZ--
--OR ANYTHING ELSE THAT'S GONNA RUIN MY GOOD TIME.
WE'RE CELEBRATING HERE.
CELEBRATING?
PARTNERS. BACK IN THE SADDLE.
PARTNERS.
CLINK

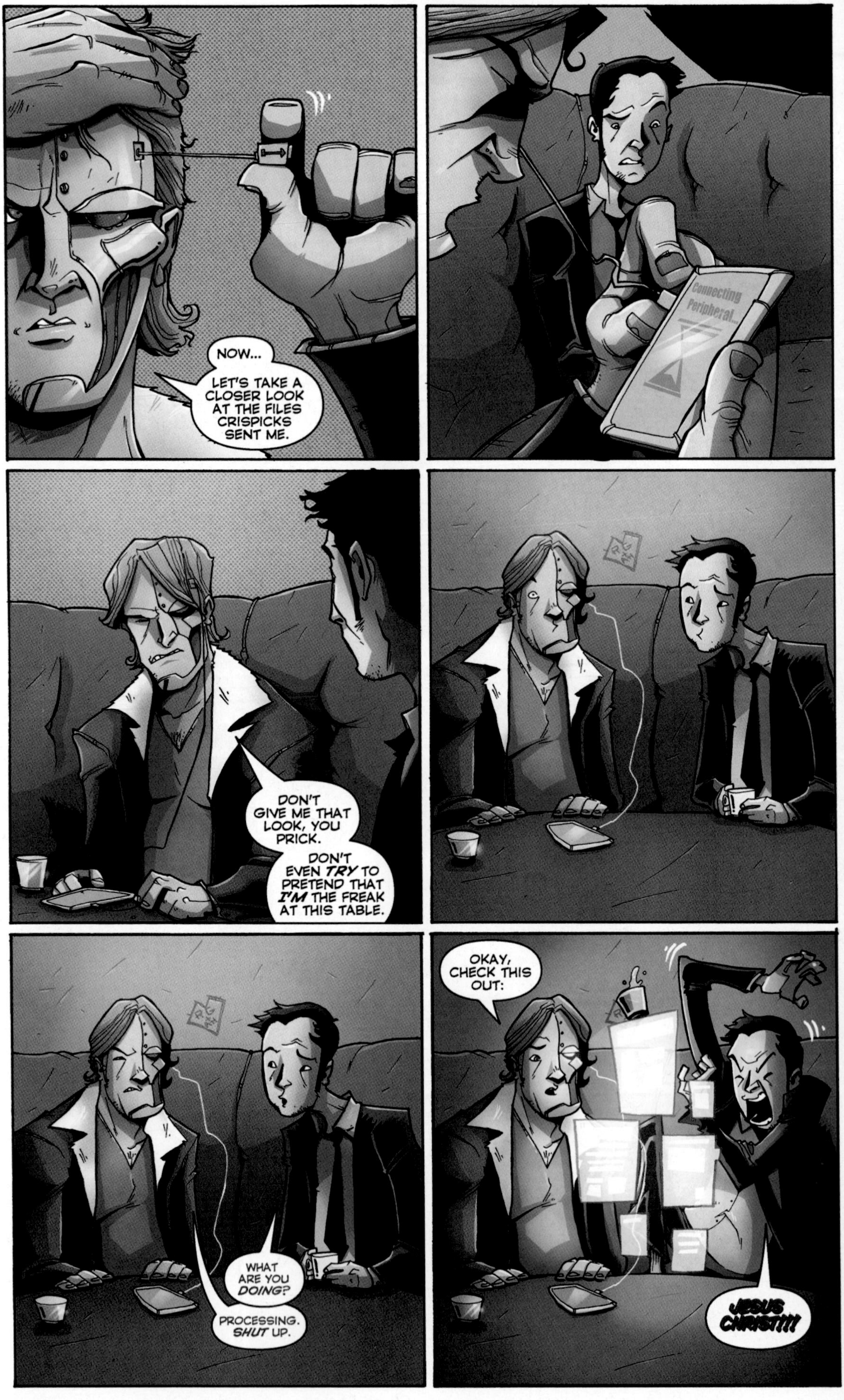
NOW...
LET'S TAKE A CLOSER LOOK AT THE FILES CRISPICKS SENT ME.
Connecting Peripheral...
DON'T GIVE ME THAT LOOK, YOU PRICK.
DON'T EVEN TRY TO PRETEND THAT I'M THE FREAK AT THIS TABLE.
WHAT ARE YOU DOING?
PROCESSING. SHUT UP.
OKAY, CHECK THIS OUT:
JESUS CHRIST!!!

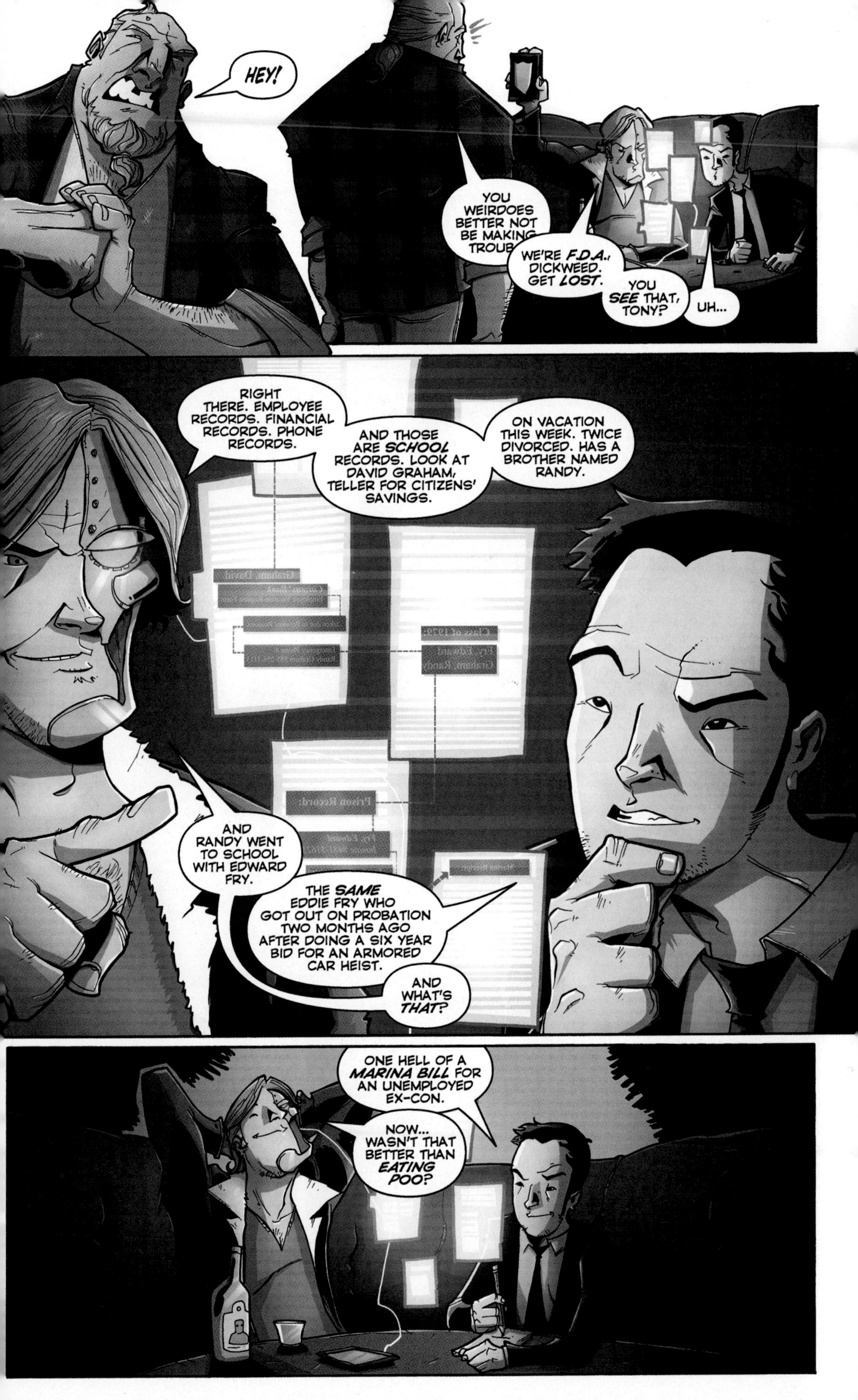
HEY!
YOU WEIRDOES BETTER NOT BE MAKING TROUB
WE'RE F.D.A., DICKWEED. GET LOST.
YOU SEE THAT, TONY?
UH...
RIGHT THERE. EMPLOYEE RECORDS. FINANCIAL RECORDS. PHONE RECORDS.
AND THOSE ARE SCHOOL RECORDS. LOOK AT DAVID GRAHAM, TELLER FOR CITIZENS' SAVINGS.
ON VACATION THIS WEEK. TWICE DIVORCED. HAS A BROTHER NAMED RANDY.
AND RANDY WENT TO SCHOOL WITH EDWARD FRY.
THE SAME EDDIE FRY WHO GOT OUT ON PROBATION TWO MONTHS AGO AFTER DOING A SIX YEAR BID FOR AN ARMORED CAR HEIST.
AND WHAT'S THAT?
ONE HELL OF A MARINA BILL FOR AN UNEMPLOYED EX-CON.
NOW... WASN'T THAT BETTER THAN EATING POO?

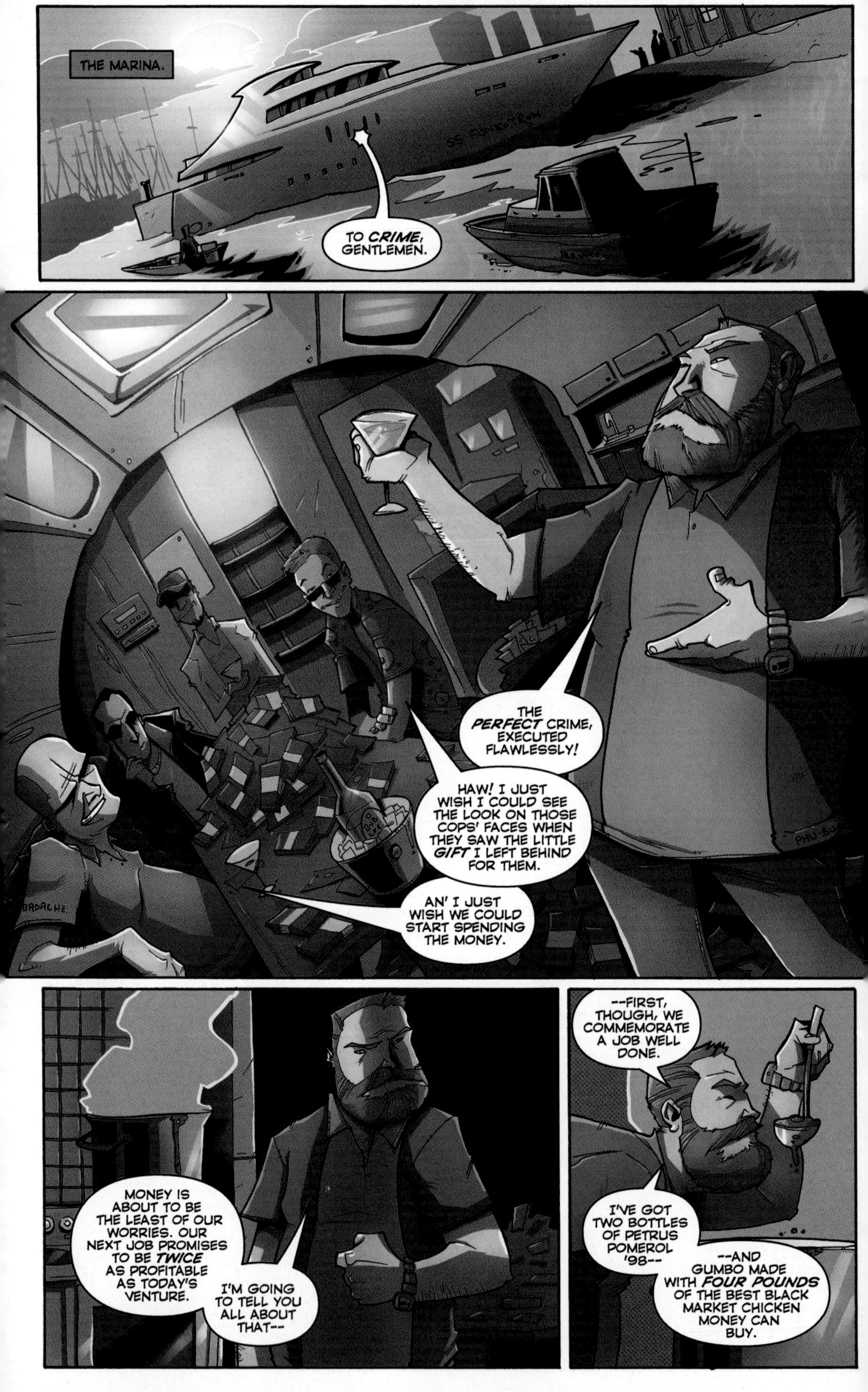
THE MARINA.
TO *CRIME*, GENTLEMEN.
THE *PERFECT* CRIME, EXECUTED FLAWLESSLY!
HAW! I JUST WISH I COULD SEE THE LOOK ON THOSE COPS' FACES WHEN THEY SAW THE LITTLE *GIFT* I LEFT BEHIND FOR THEM.
AN' I JUST WISH WE COULD START SPENDING THE MONEY.
MONEY IS ABOUT TO BE THE LEAST OF OUR WORRIES. OUR NEXT JOB PROMISES TO BE *TWICE* AS PROFITABLE AS TODAY'S VENTURE.
I'M GOING TO TELL YOU ALL ABOUT THAT--
--FIRST, THOUGH, WE COMMEMORATE A JOB WELL DONE.
I'VE GOT TWO BOTTLES OF PETRUS POMEROL '98--
--AND GUMBO MADE WITH *FOUR POUNDS* OF THE BEST BLACK MARKET CHICKEN MONEY CAN BUY.

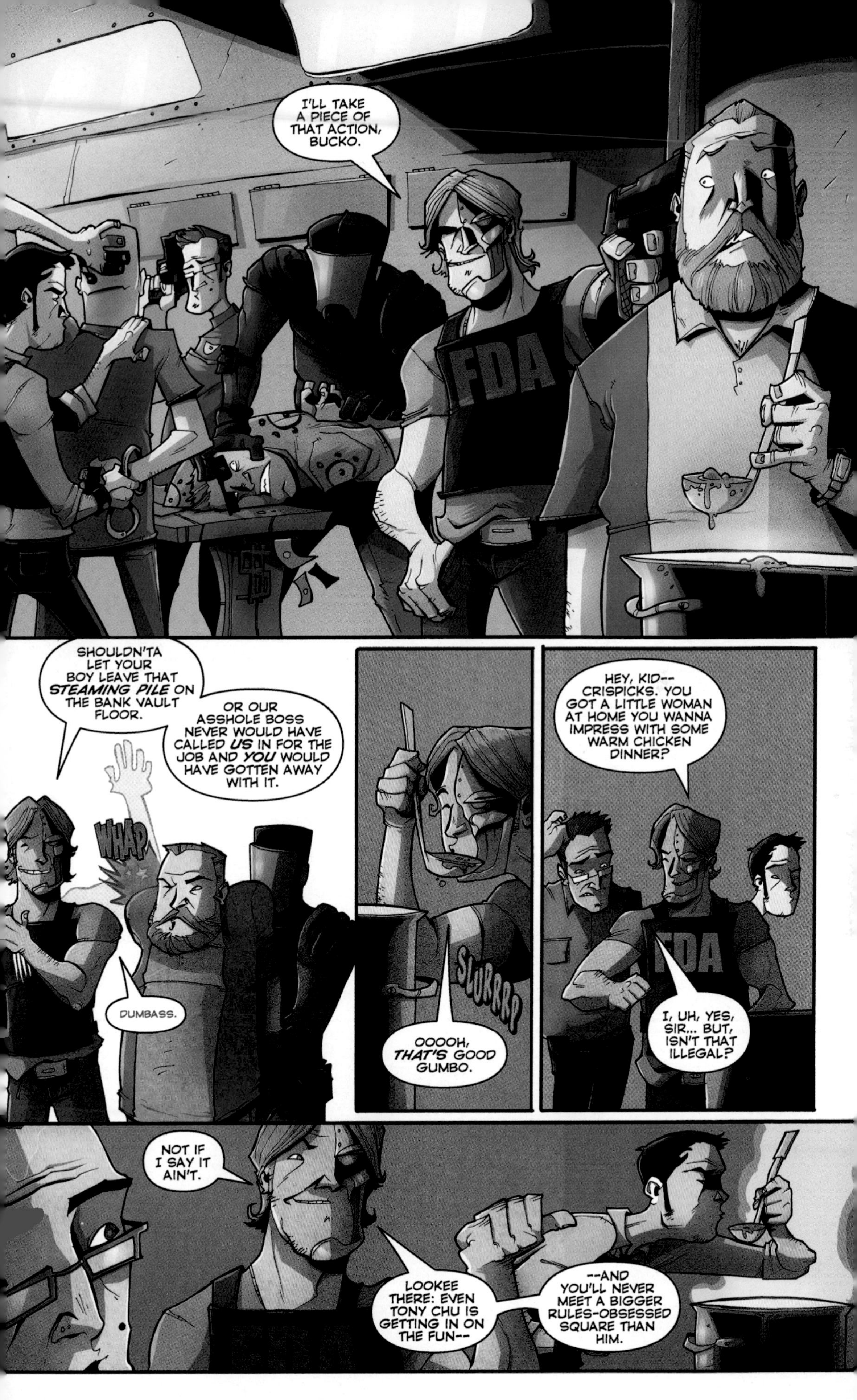
I'LL TAKE A PIECE OF THAT ACTION, BUCKO.
FDA
SHOULDN'TA LET YOUR BOY LEAVE THAT *STEAMING PILE* ON THE BANK VAULT FLOOR.
OR OUR ASSHOLE BOSS NEVER WOULD HAVE CALLED *US* IN FOR THE JOB AND *YOU* WOULD HAVE GOTTEN AWAY WITH IT.
WHAP
DUMBASS.
SLURRRP
OOOOH, *THAT'S* GOOD GUMBO.
HEY, KID-- CRISPICKS. YOU GOT A LITTLE WOMAN AT HOME YOU WANNA IMPRESS WITH SOME WARM CHICKEN DINNER?
FDA
I, UH, YES, SIR... BUT, ISN'T THAT ILLEGAL?
NOT IF I SAY IT AIN'T.
LOOKEE THERE: EVEN TONY CHU IS GETTING IN ON THE FUN--
--AND YOU'LL NEVER MEET A BIGGER RULES-OBSESSED SQUARE THAN HIM.

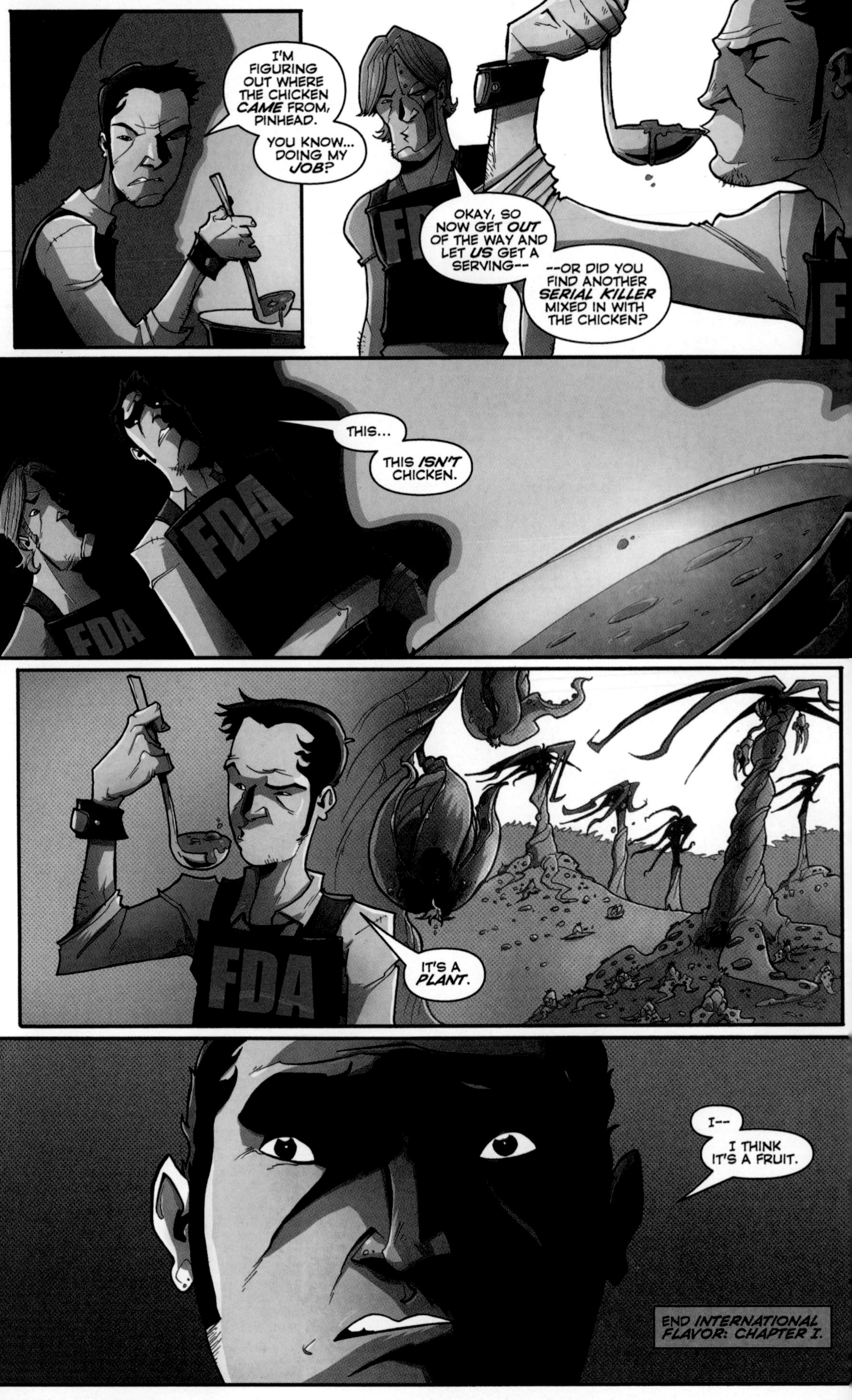
I'M FIGURING OUT WHERE THE CHICKEN CAME FROM, PINHEAD.
YOU KNOW... DOING MY JOB?
OKAY, SO NOW GET OUT OF THE WAY AND LET US GET A SERVING--
--OR DID YOU FIND ANOTHER SERIAL KILLER MIXED IN WITH THE CHICKEN?
FDA
THIS...
THIS ISN'T CHICKEN.
FDA
FDA
FDA
IT'S A PLANT.
I--
I THINK IT'S A FRUIT.
END INTERNATIONAL FLAVOR: CHAPTER I.

Chapter 2

USDA
ROB!

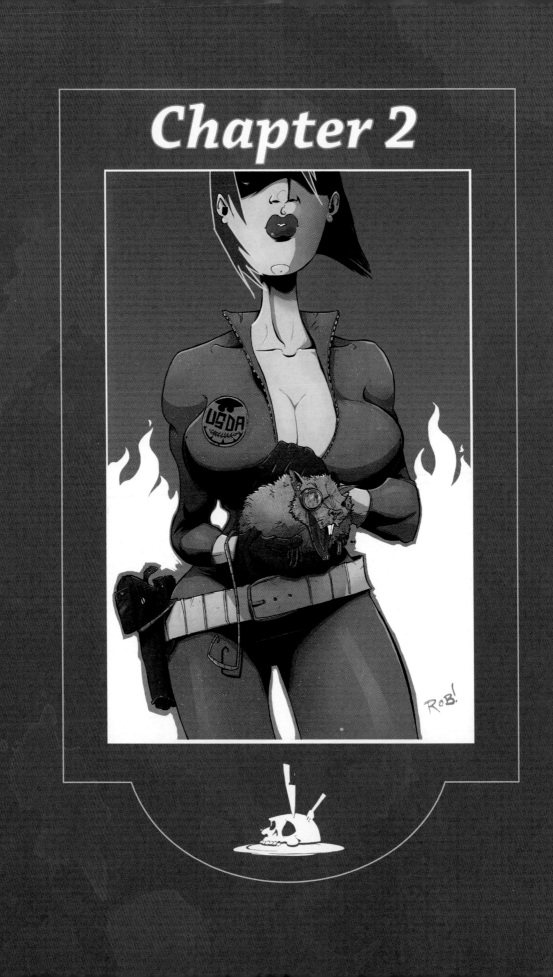

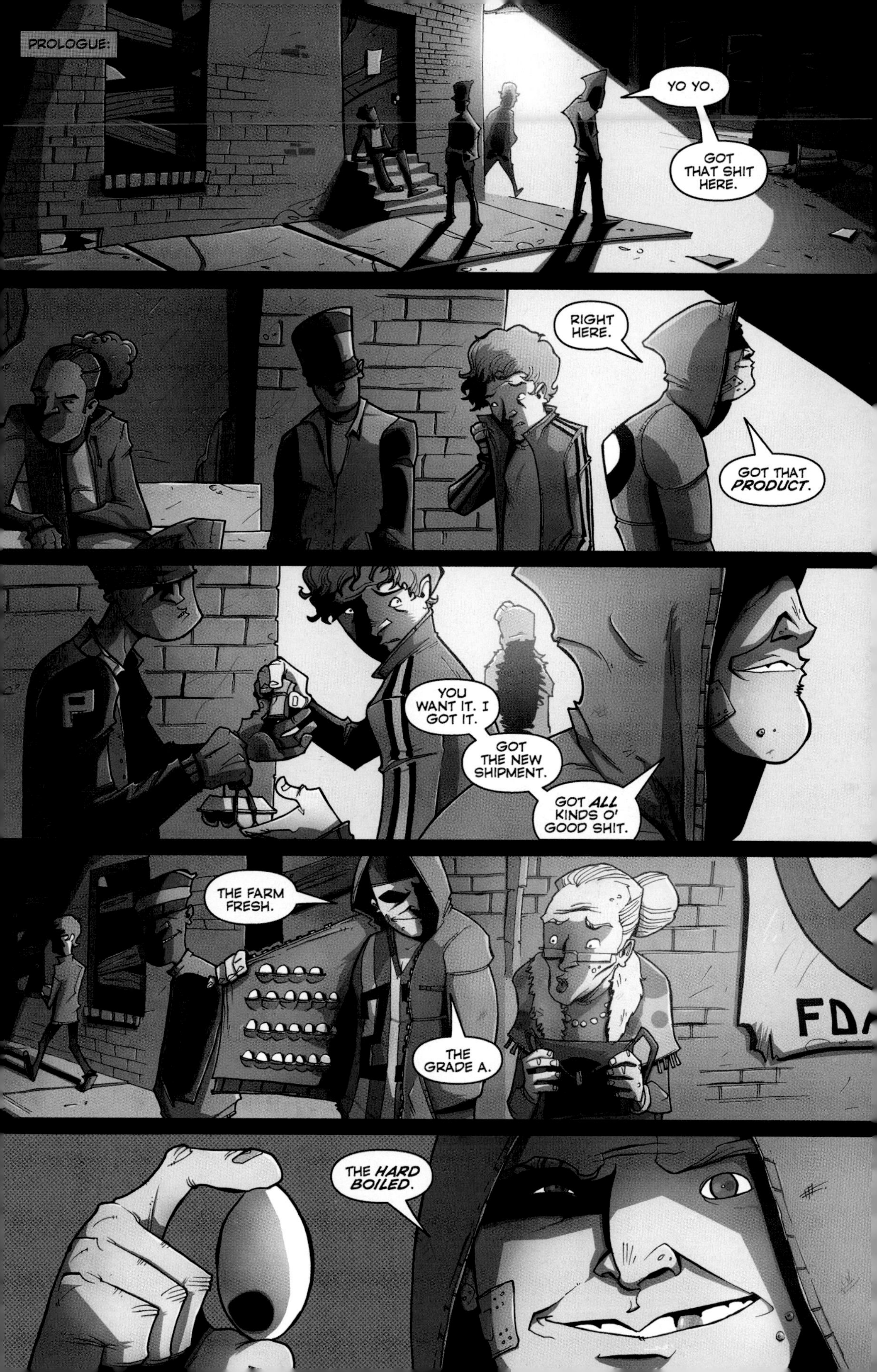
PROLOGUE:
YO YO.
GOT THAT SHIT HERE.
RIGHT HERE.
GOT THAT *PRODUCT*.
YOU WANT IT. I GOT IT.
GOT THE NEW SHIPMENT.
GOT *ALL* KINDS O' GOOD SHIT.
THE FARM FRESH.
THE GRADE A.
FDA
THE *HARD BOILED*.

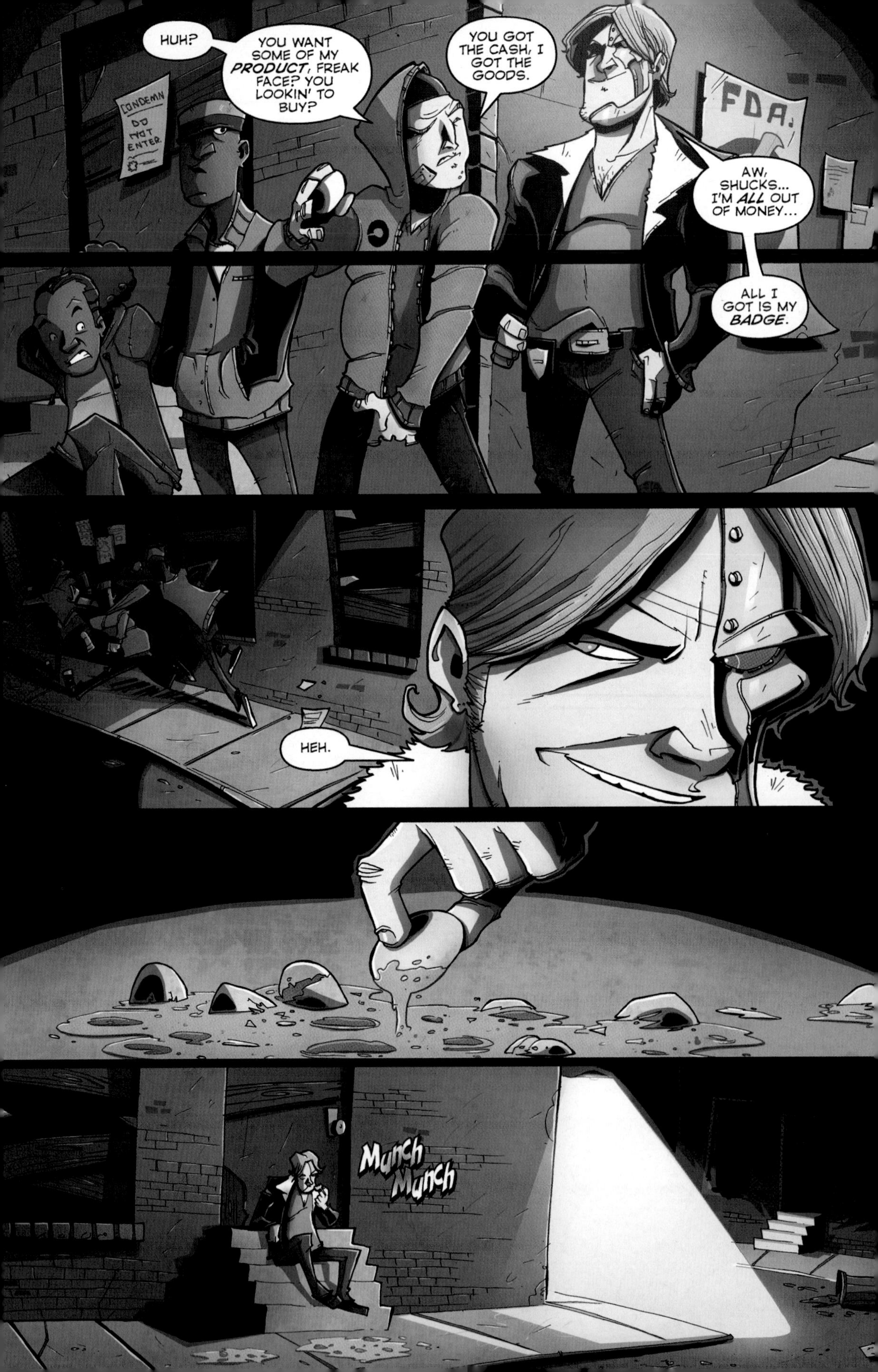
HUH?
YOU WANT SOME OF MY *PRODUCT*, FREAK FACE? YOU LOOKIN' TO BUY?
YOU GOT THE CASH, I GOT THE GOODS.
CONDEMN
DO NOT ENTER.
FDA
AW, SHUCKS... I'M *ALL* OUT OF MONEY...
ALL I GOT IS MY *BADGE*.
HEH.
Munch
Munch

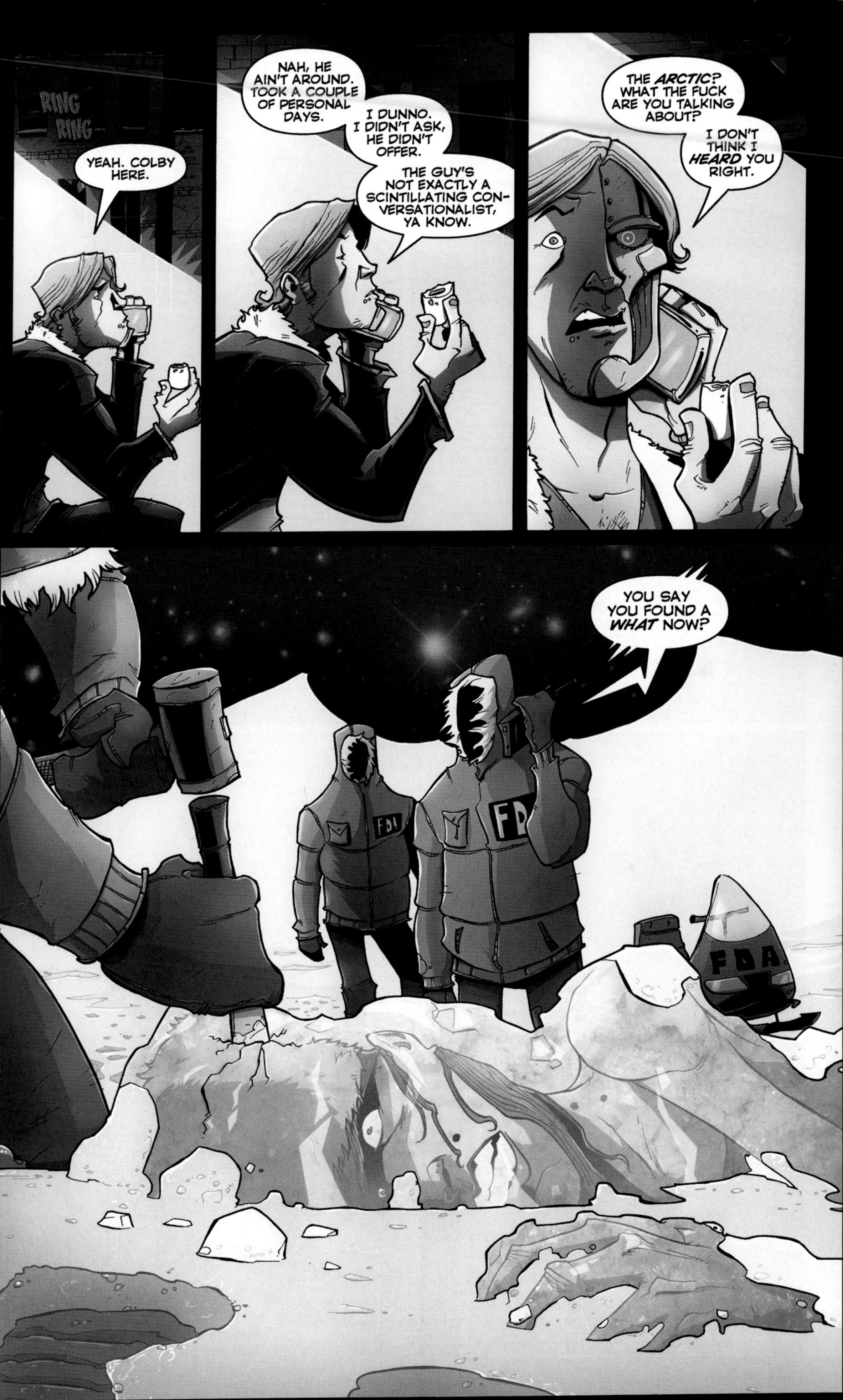

RING RING
YEAH. COLBY HERE.
NAH, HE AIN'T AROUND. TOOK A COUPLE OF PERSONAL DAYS.
I DUNNO. I DIDN'T ASK, HE DIDN'T OFFER.
THE GUY'S NOT EXACTLY A SCINTILLATING CON-VERSATIONALIST, YA KNOW.
THE *ARCTIC*? WHAT THE FUCK ARE YOU TALKING ABOUT?
I DON'T THINK I *HEARD* YOU RIGHT.
YOU SAY YOU FOUND A *WHAT* NOW?
FDA
FDA
FDA

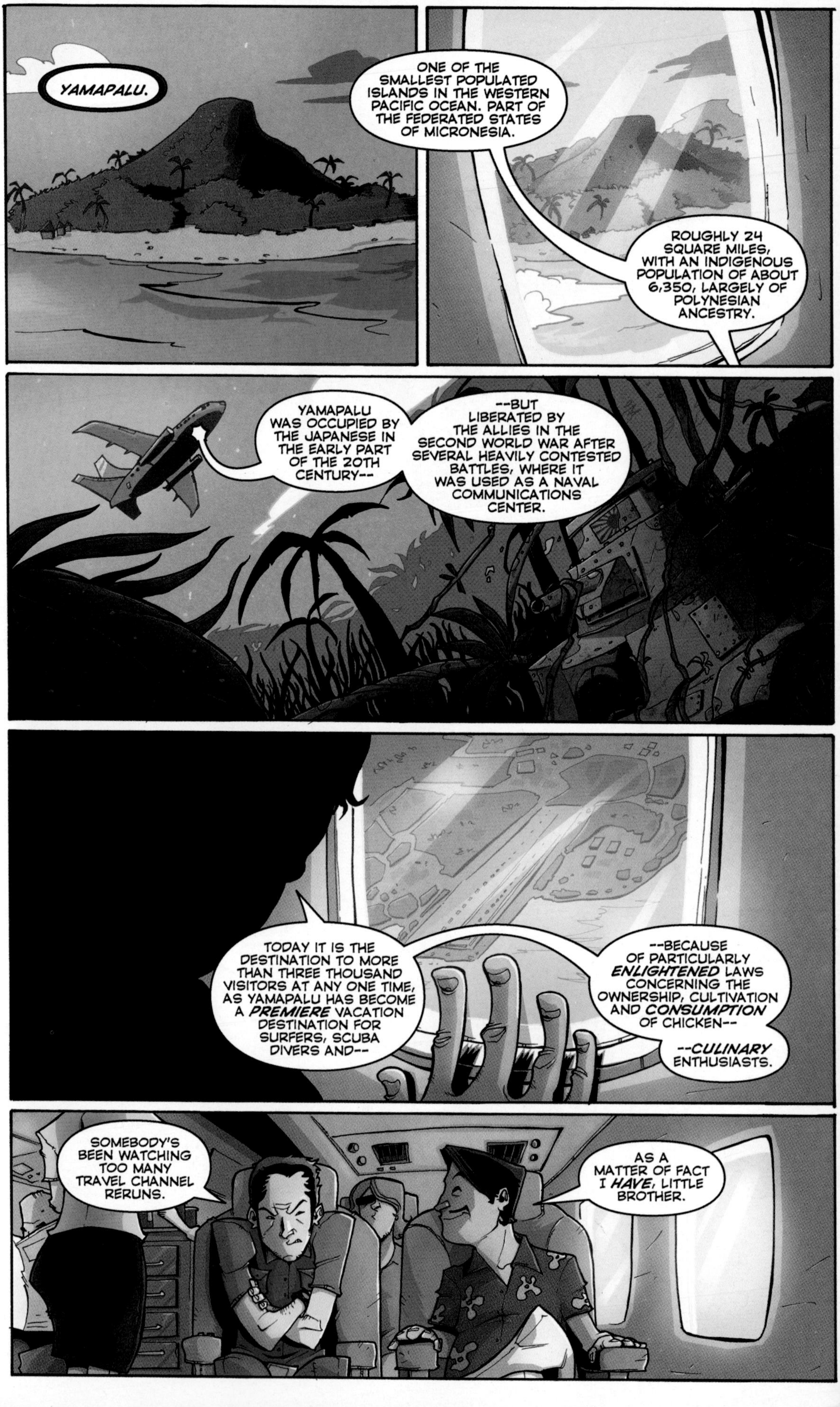
YAMAPALU.
ONE OF THE SMALLEST POPULATED ISLANDS IN THE WESTERN PACIFIC OCEAN. PART OF THE FEDERATED STATES OF MICRONESIA.
ROUGHLY 24 SQUARE MILES, WITH AN INDIGENOUS POPULATION OF ABOUT 6,350, LARGELY OF POLYNESIAN ANCESTRY.
YAMAPALU WAS OCCUPIED BY THE JAPANESE IN THE EARLY PART OF THE 20TH CENTURY--
--BUT LIBERATED BY THE ALLIES IN THE SECOND WORLD WAR AFTER SEVERAL HEAVILY CONTESTED BATTLES, WHERE IT WAS USED AS A NAVAL COMMUNICATIONS CENTER.
TODAY IT IS THE DESTINATION TO MORE THAN THREE THOUSAND VISITORS AT ANY ONE TIME, AS YAMAPALU HAS BECOME A PREMIERE VACATION DESTINATION FOR SURFERS, SCUBA DIVERS AND--
--BECAUSE OF PARTICULARLY ENLIGHTENED LAWS CONCERNING THE OWNERSHIP, CULTIVATION AND CONSUMPTION OF CHICKEN--
--CULINARY ENTHUSIASTS.
SOMEBODY'S BEEN WATCHING TOO MANY TRAVEL CHANNEL RERUNS.
AS A MATTER OF FACT I HAVE, LITTLE BROTHER.

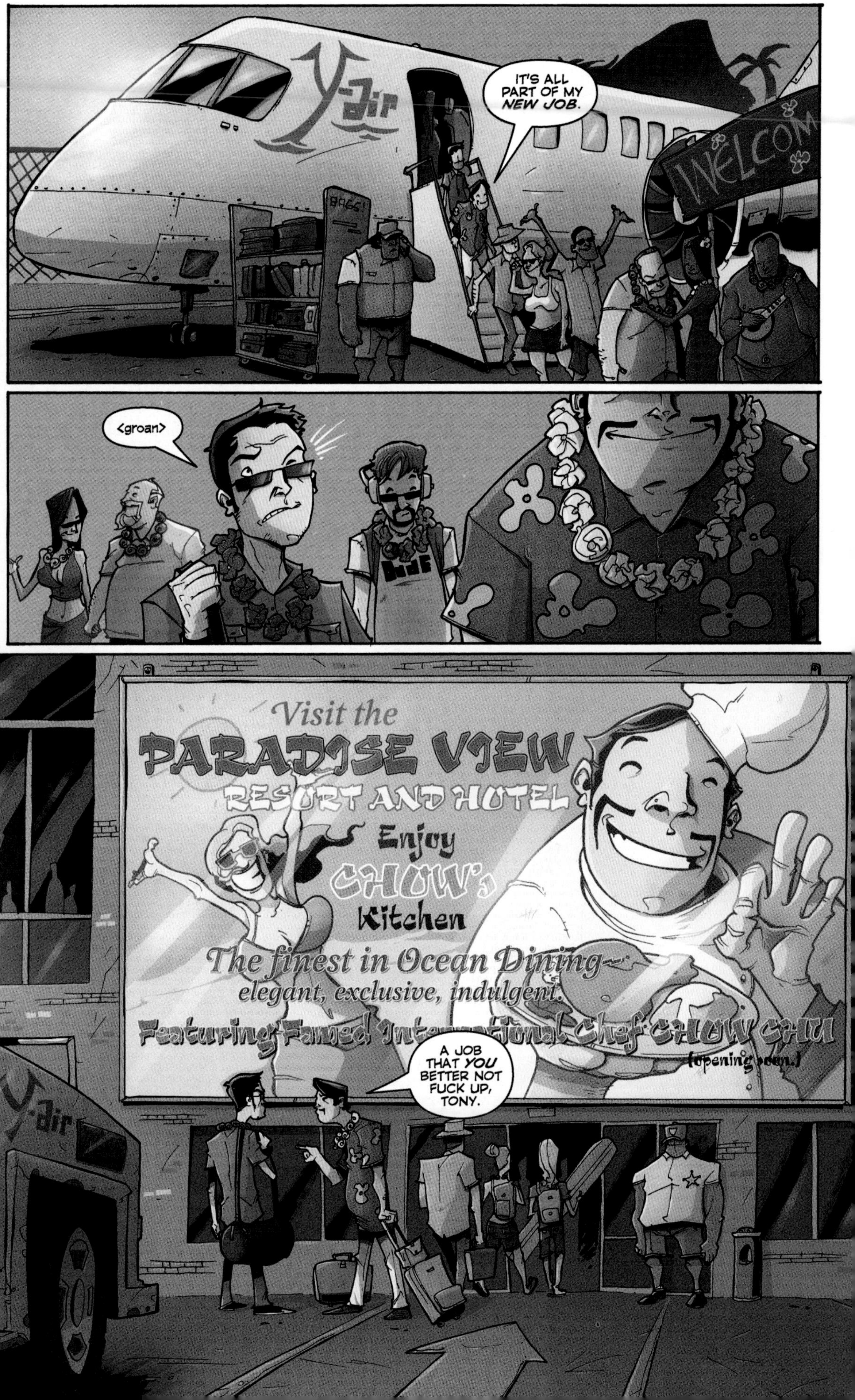
Y-air
IT'S ALL PART OF MY NEW JOB.
WELCOM
<groan>
Visit the
PARADISE VIEW
RESORT AND HOTEL
Enjoy
CHOW's
Kitchen
The finest in Ocean Dining–
elegant, exclusive, indulgent.
Featuring Famed Inte tional Chef CHOW CHU
A JOB THAT YOU BETTER NOT FUCK UP, TONY.
Y-air

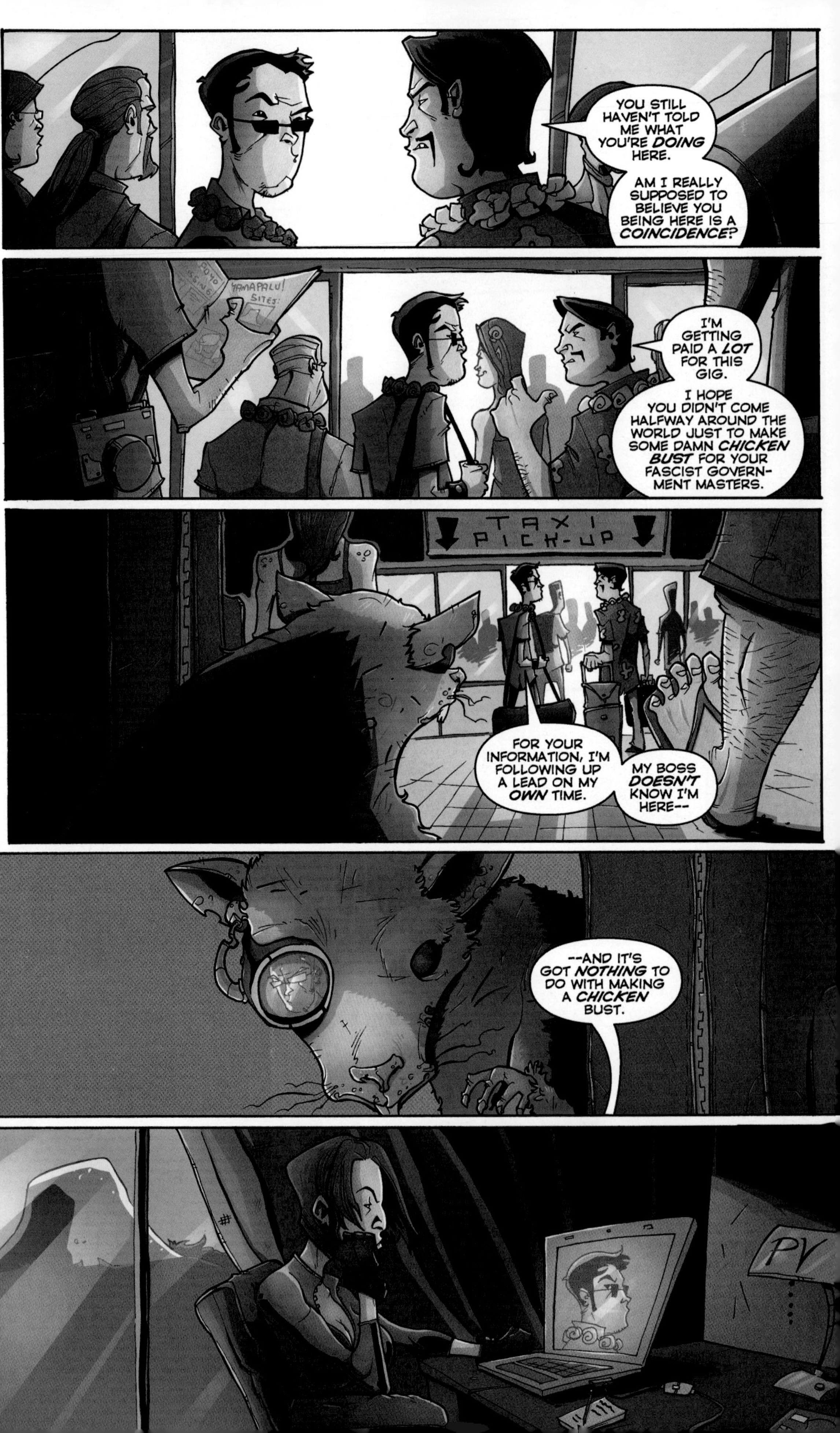
YOU STILL HAVEN'T TOLD ME WHAT YOU'RE DOING HERE.
AM I REALLY SUPPOSED TO BELIEVE YOU BEING HERE IS A COINCIDENCE?
YAMAPALU! SITES:
I'M GETTING PAID A LOT FOR THIS GIG.
I HOPE YOU DIDN'T COME HALFWAY AROUND THE WORLD JUST TO MAKE SOME DAMN CHICKEN BUST FOR YOUR FASCIST GOVERNMENT MASTERS.
TAXI PICK-UP
FOR YOUR INFORMATION, I'M FOLLOWING UP A LEAD ON MY OWN TIME.
MY BOSS DOESN'T KNOW I'M HERE--
--AND IT'S GOT NOTHING TO DO WITH MAKING A CHICKEN BUST.
PV

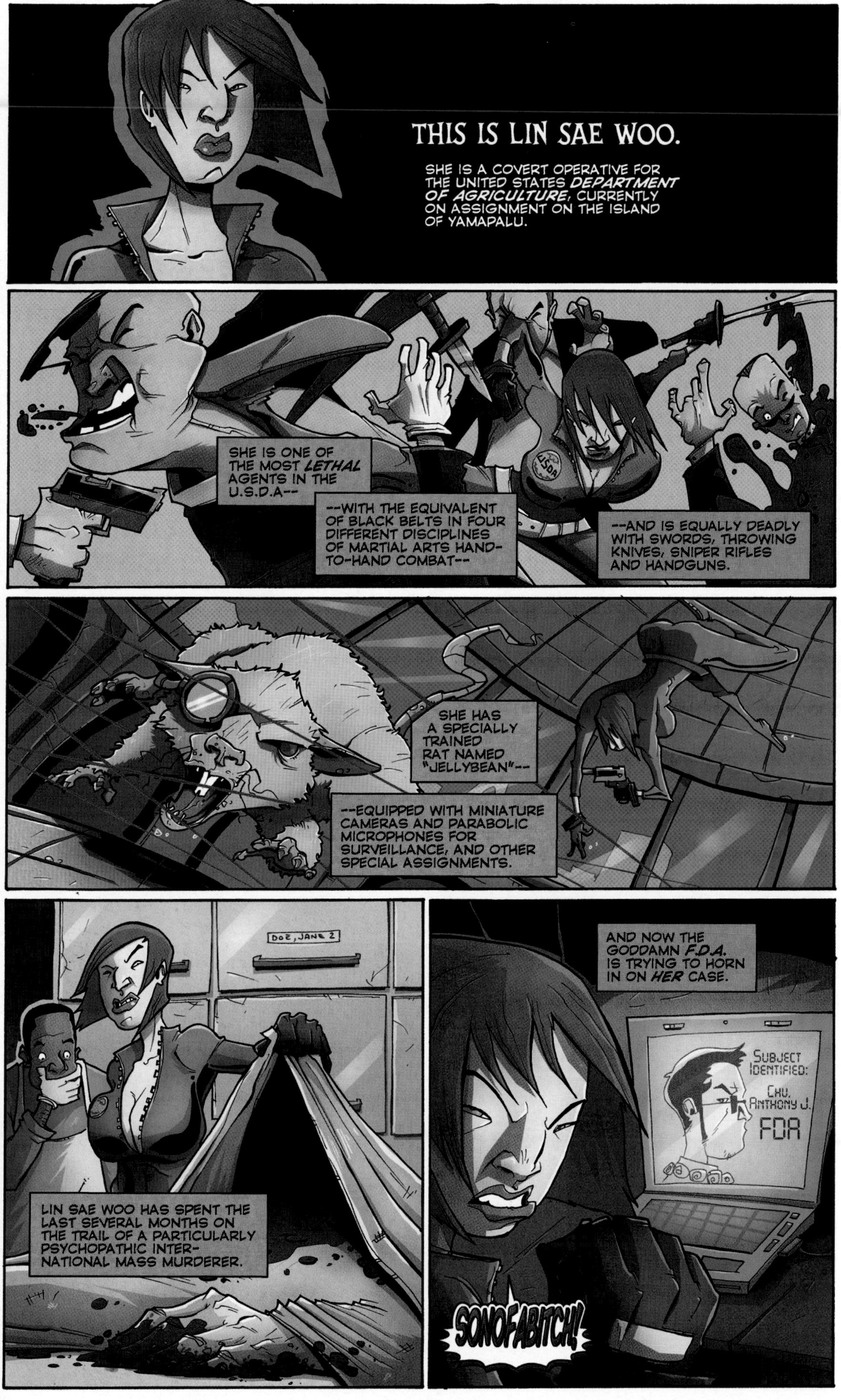
THIS IS LIN SAE WOO.
SHE IS A COVERT OPERATIVE FOR THE UNITED STATES DEPARTMENT OF AGRICULTURE, CURRENTLY ON ASSIGNMENT ON THE ISLAND OF YAMAPALU.
SHE IS ONE OF THE MOST LETHAL AGENTS IN THE U.S.D.A--
USDA
--WITH THE EQUIVALENT OF BLACK BELTS IN FOUR DIFFERENT DISCIPLINES OF MARTIAL ARTS HAND-TO-HAND COMBAT--
--AND IS EQUALLY DEADLY WITH SWORDS, THROWING KNIVES, SNIPER RIFLES AND HANDGUNS.
SHE HAS A SPECIALLY TRAINED RAT NAMED "JELLYBEAN"--
--EQUIPPED WITH MINIATURE CAMERAS AND PARABOLIC MICROPHONES FOR SURVEILLANCE, AND OTHER SPECIAL ASSIGNMENTS.
DOE, JANE 2
LIN SAE WOO HAS SPENT THE LAST SEVERAL MONTHS ON THE TRAIL OF A PARTICULARLY PSYCHOPATHIC INTERNATIONAL MASS MURDERER.
AND NOW THE GODDAMN F.D.A. IS TRYING TO HORN IN ON HER CASE.
SUBJECT IDENTIFIED:
CHU, ANTHONY J.
FDA
SONOFABITCH!

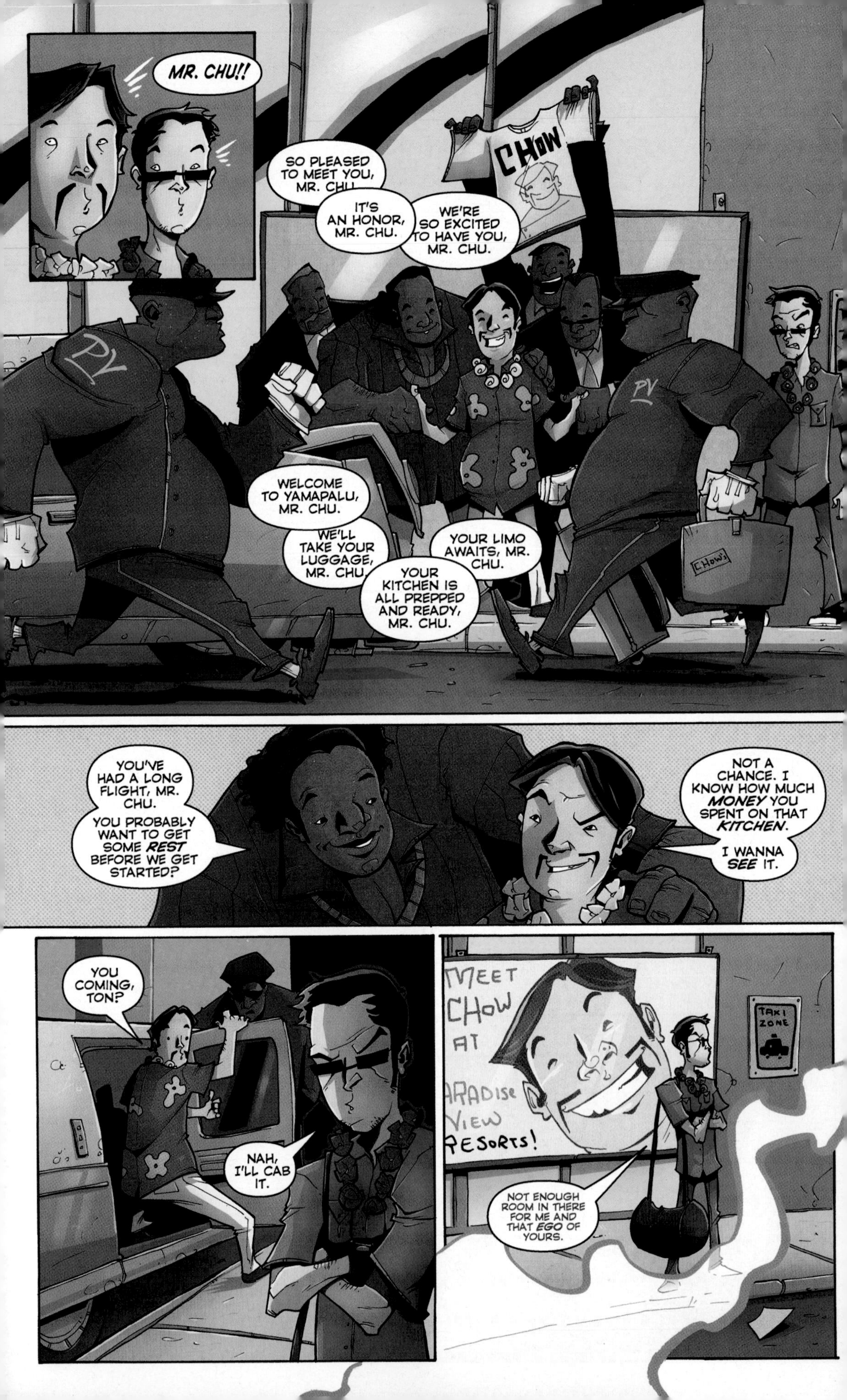
MR. CHU!!
SO PLEASED TO MEET YOU, MR. CHU.
IT'S AN HONOR, MR. CHU.
WE'RE SO EXCITED TO HAVE YOU, MR. CHU.
CHOW
WELCOME TO YAMAPALU, MR. CHU.
WE'LL TAKE YOUR LUGGAGE, MR. CHU.
YOUR LIMO AWAITS, MR. CHU.
YOUR KITCHEN IS ALL PREPPED AND READY, MR. CHU.
CHOW'S
PV
YOU'VE HAD A LONG FLIGHT, MR. CHU.
YOU PROBABLY WANT TO GET SOME REST BEFORE WE GET STARTED?
NOT A CHANCE. I KNOW HOW MUCH MONEY YOU SPENT ON THAT KITCHEN.
I WANNA SEE IT.
YOU COMING, TON?
NAH, I'LL CAB IT.
MEET CHOW AT ARADISE VIEW RESORTS!
TAXI ZONE
NOT ENOUGH ROOM IN THERE FOR ME AND THAT EGO OF YOURS.

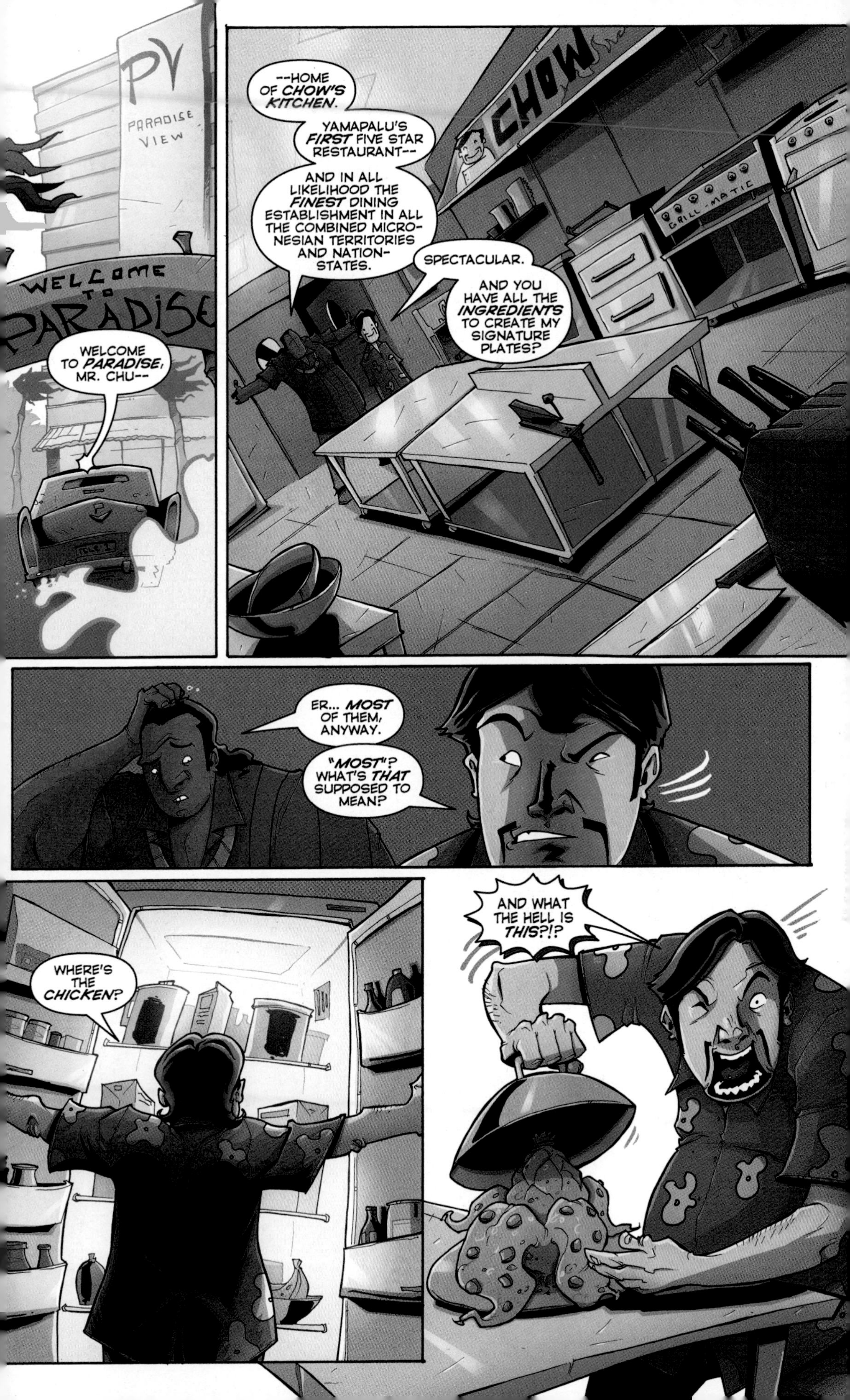

PV
PARADISE VIEW
WELCOME TO PARADISE
WELCOME TO PARADISE, MR. CHU--
--HOME OF CHOW'S KITCHEN.
YAMAPALU'S FIRST FIVE STAR RESTAURANT--
AND IN ALL LIKELIHOOD THE FINEST DINING ESTABLISHMENT IN ALL THE COMBINED MICRONESIAN TERRITORIES AND NATION-STATES.
CHOW
GRILL-MATIC
SPECTACULAR.
AND YOU HAVE ALL THE INGREDIENTS TO CREATE MY SIGNATURE PLATES?
ER... MOST OF THEM, ANYWAY.
"MOST"? WHAT'S THAT SUPPOSED TO MEAN?
WHERE'S THE CHICKEN?
AND WHAT THE HELL IS THIS?!?

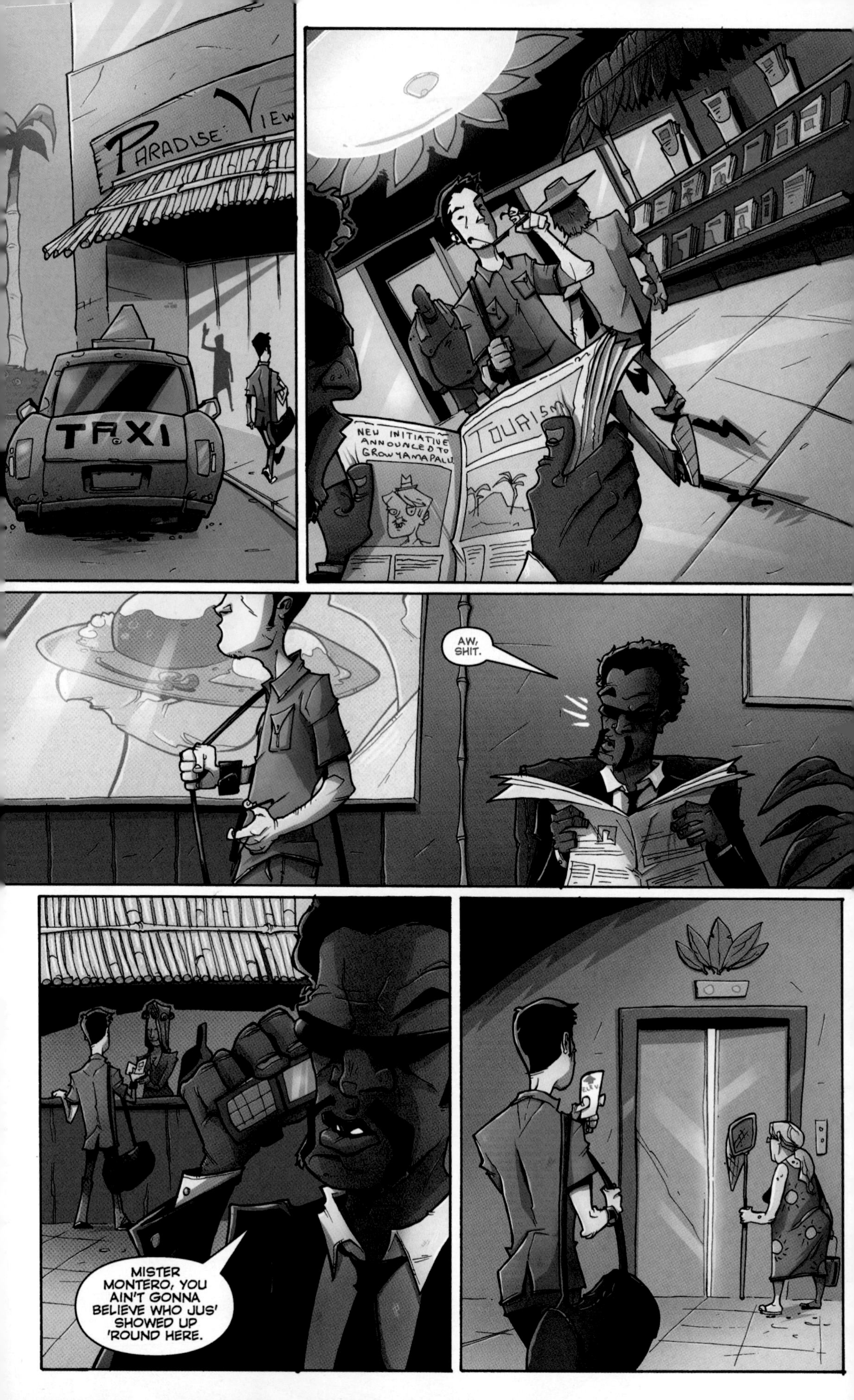
PARADISE
TAXI
NEW INITIATIVE ANNOUNCED TO GROW YAMAPALU
AW, SHIT.
MISTER MONTERO, YOU AIN'T GONNA BELIEVE WHO JUS' SHOWED UP 'ROUND HERE.

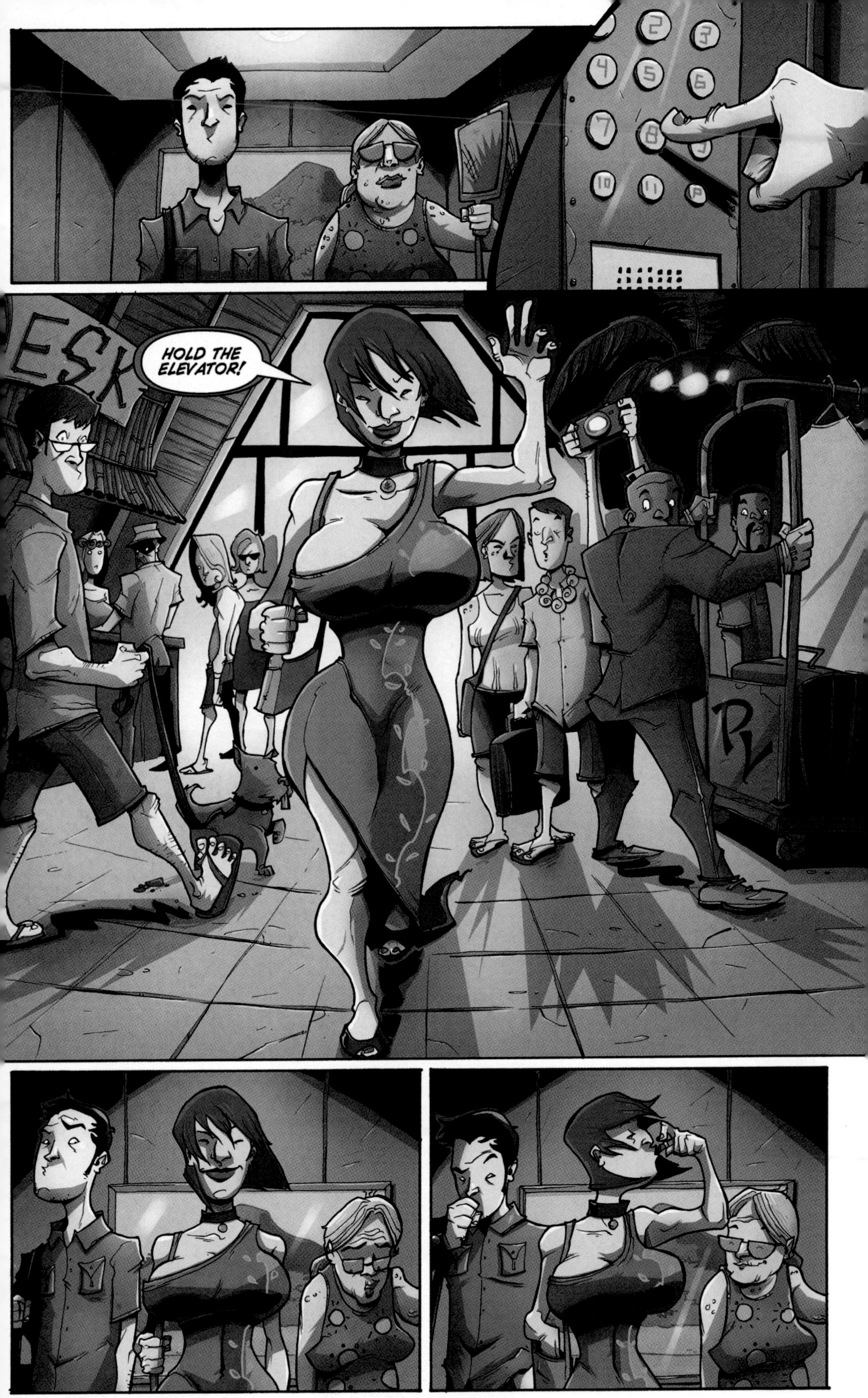
HOLD THE ELEVATOR!

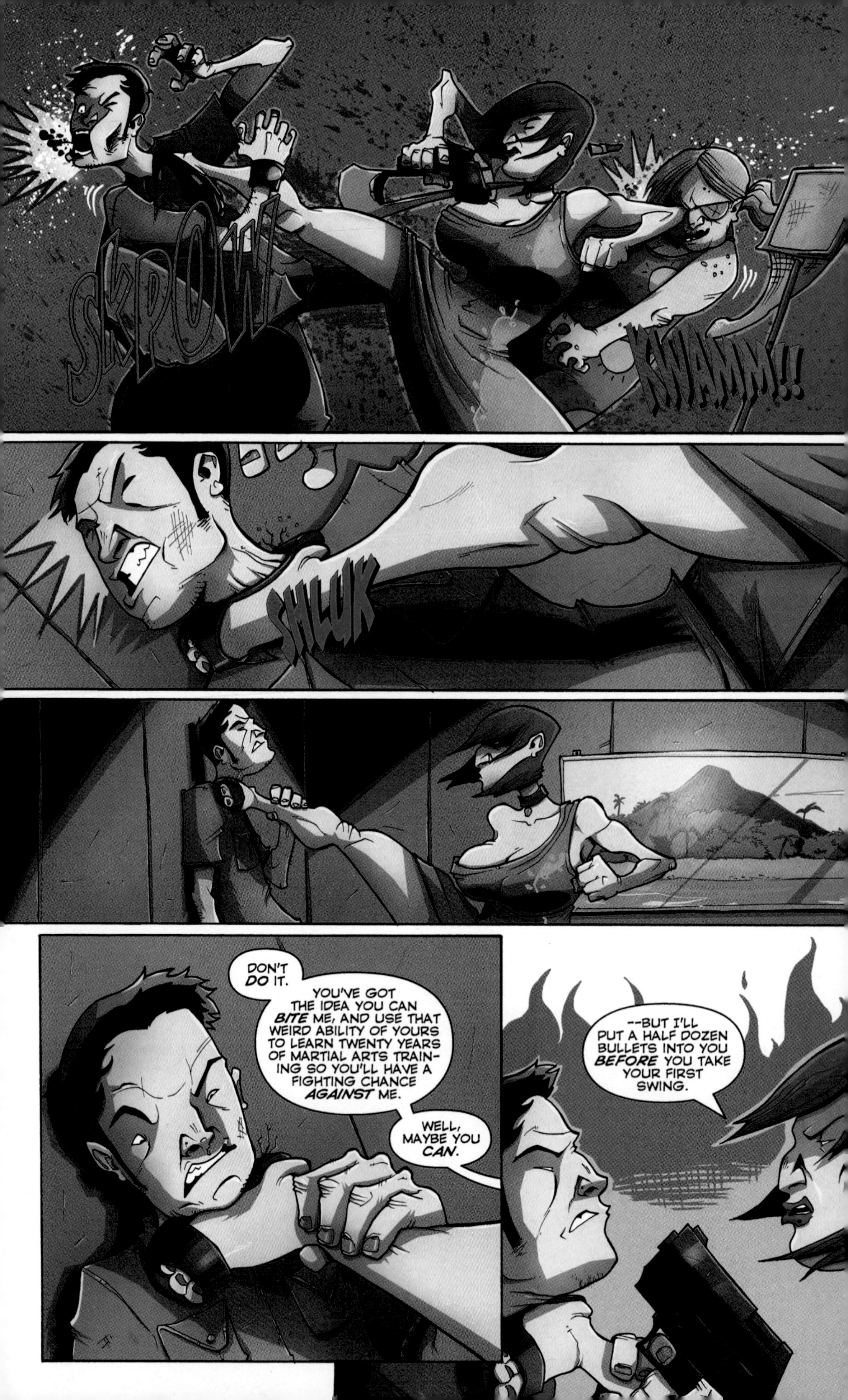

SKPOW!
KWAMM!!
SHLUK
DON'T DO IT.
YOU'VE GOT THE IDEA YOU CAN BITE ME, AND USE THAT WEIRD ABILITY OF YOURS TO LEARN TWENTY YEARS OF MARTIAL ARTS TRAINING SO YOU'LL HAVE A FIGHTING CHANCE AGAINST ME.
WELL, MAYBE YOU CAN.
--BUT I'LL PUT A HALF DOZEN BULLETS INTO YOU BEFORE YOU TAKE YOUR FIRST SWING.

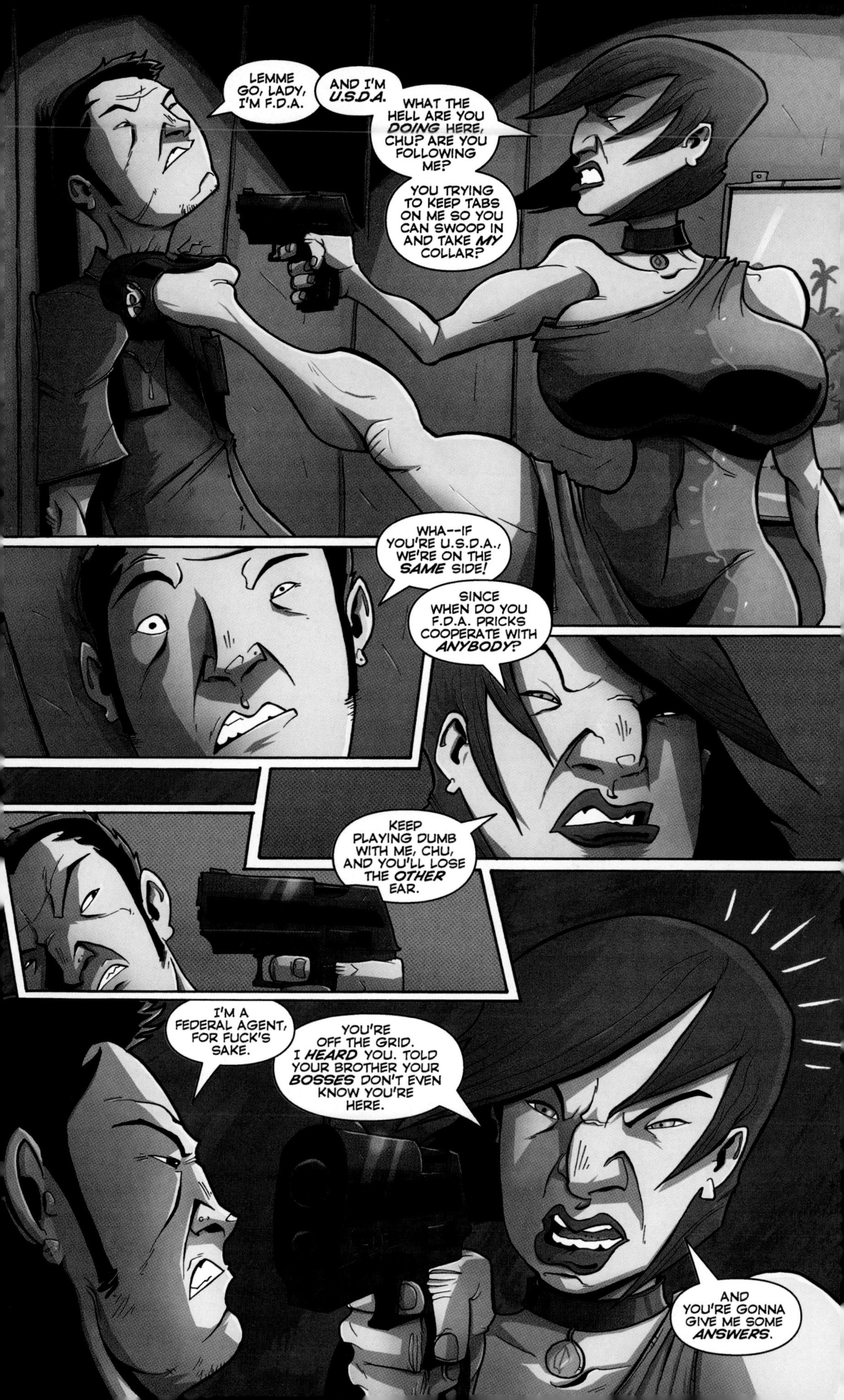
LEMME GO, LADY, I'M F.D.A.
AND I'M *U.S.D.A.*
WHAT THE HELL ARE YOU *DOING* HERE, CHU? ARE YOU FOLLOWING ME?
YOU TRYING TO KEEP TABS ON ME SO YOU CAN SWOOP IN AND TAKE *MY* COLLAR?
WHA--IF YOU'RE U.S.D.A., WE'RE ON THE *SAME* SIDE!
SINCE WHEN DO YOU F.D.A. PRICKS COOPERATE WITH *ANYBODY*?
KEEP PLAYING DUMB WITH ME, CHU, AND YOU'LL LOSE THE *OTHER* EAR.
I'M A FEDERAL AGENT, FOR FUCK'S SAKE.
YOU'RE OFF THE GRID. I *HEARD* YOU. TOLD YOUR BROTHER YOUR *BOSSES* DON'T EVEN KNOW YOU'RE HERE.
AND YOU'RE GONNA GIVE ME SOME *ANSWERS*.

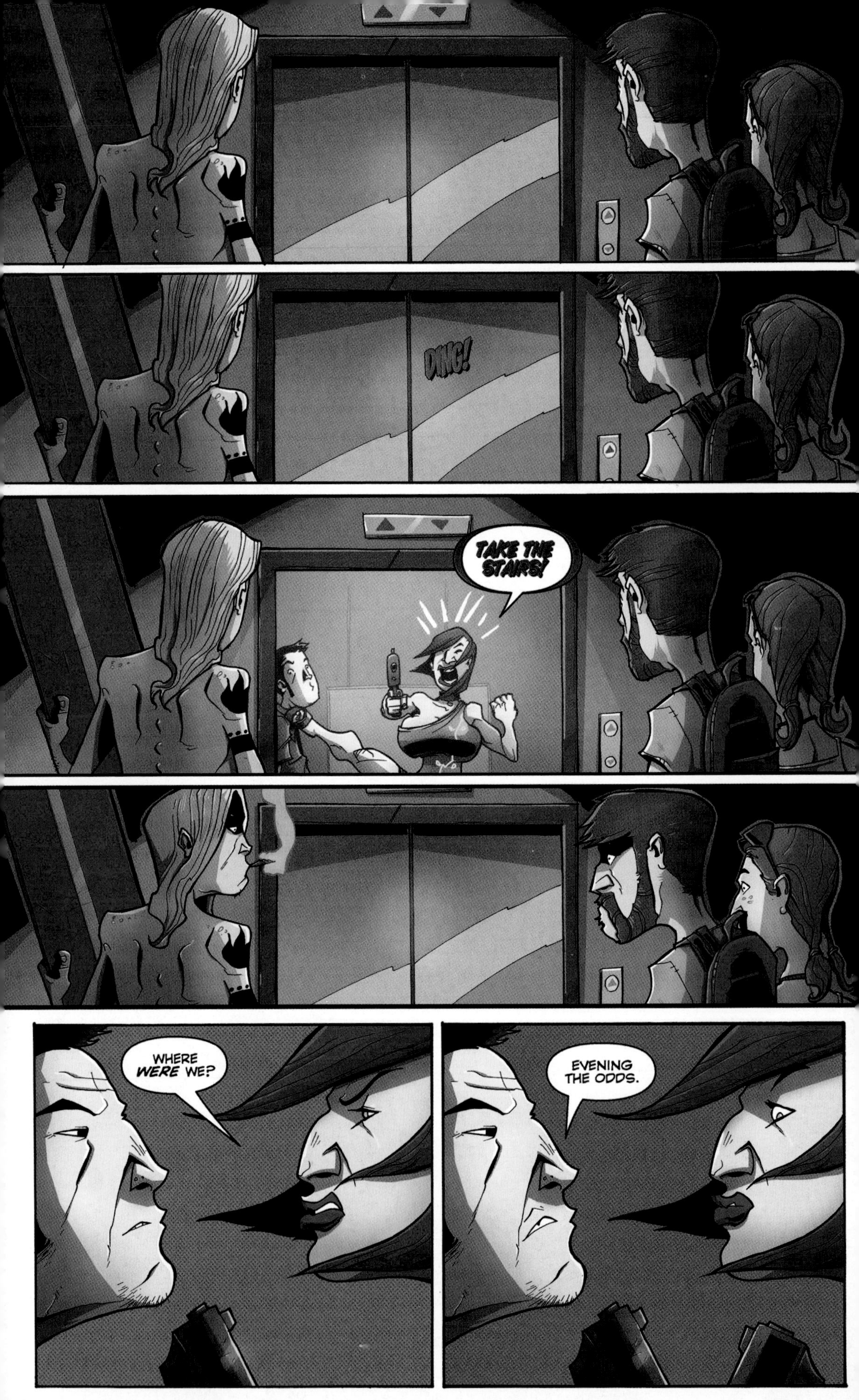
DING!
TAKE THE STAIRS!
WHERE *WERE* WE?
EVENING THE ODDS.

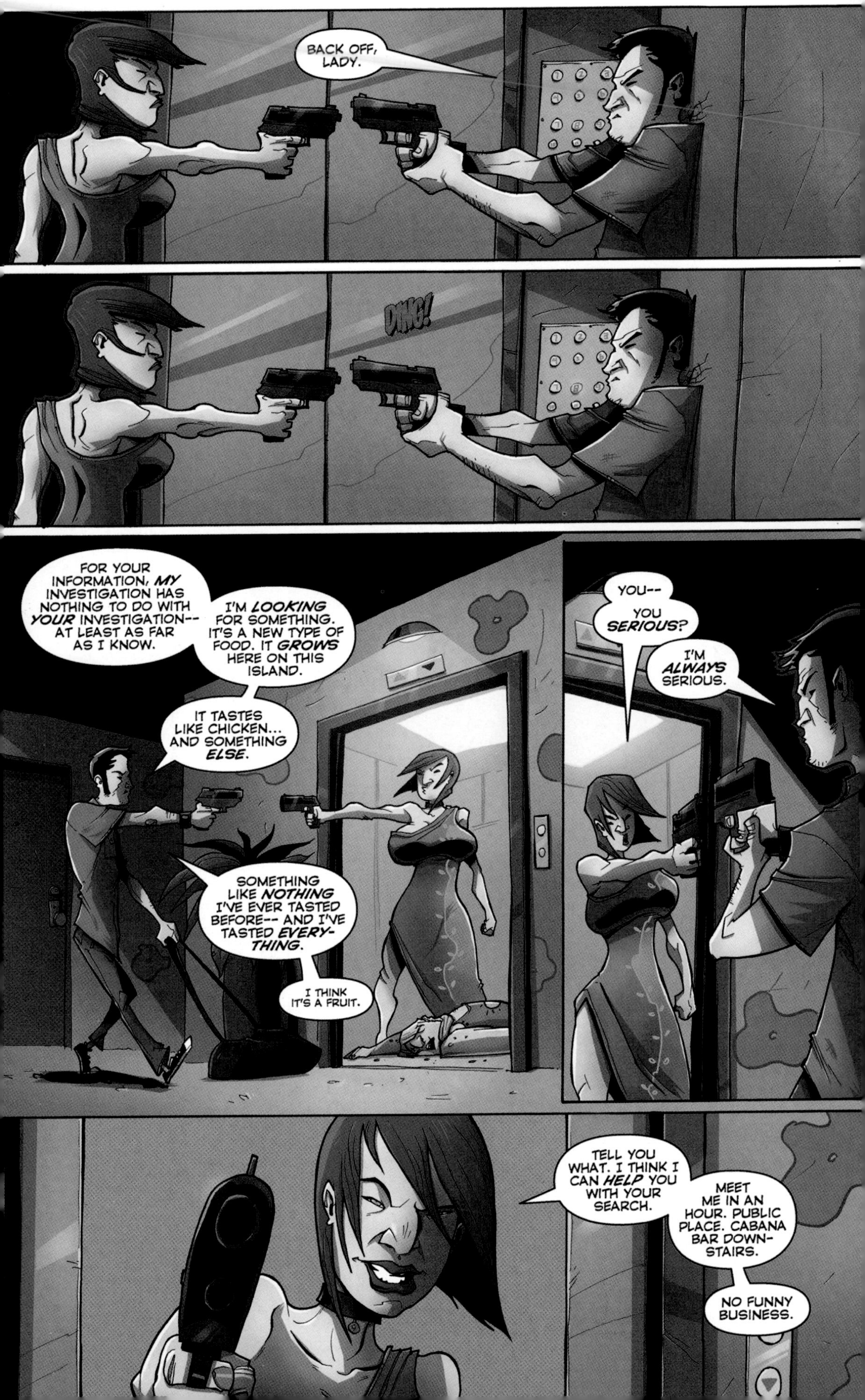
BACK OFF, LADY.
DING!
FOR YOUR INFORMATION, MY INVESTIGATION HAS NOTHING TO DO WITH YOUR INVESTIGATION-- AT LEAST AS FAR AS I KNOW.
I'M LOOKING FOR SOMETHING. IT'S A NEW TYPE OF FOOD. IT GROWS HERE ON THIS ISLAND.
IT TASTES LIKE CHICKEN... AND SOMETHING ELSE.
SOMETHING LIKE NOTHING I'VE EVER TASTED BEFORE-- AND I'VE TASTED EVERY-THING.
I THINK IT'S A FRUIT.
YOU--
YOU SERIOUS?
I'M ALWAYS SERIOUS.
TELL YOU WHAT. I THINK I CAN HELP YOU WITH YOUR SEARCH.
MEET ME IN AN HOUR. PUBLIC PLACE. CABANA BAR DOWN-STAIRS.
NO FUNNY BUSINESS.

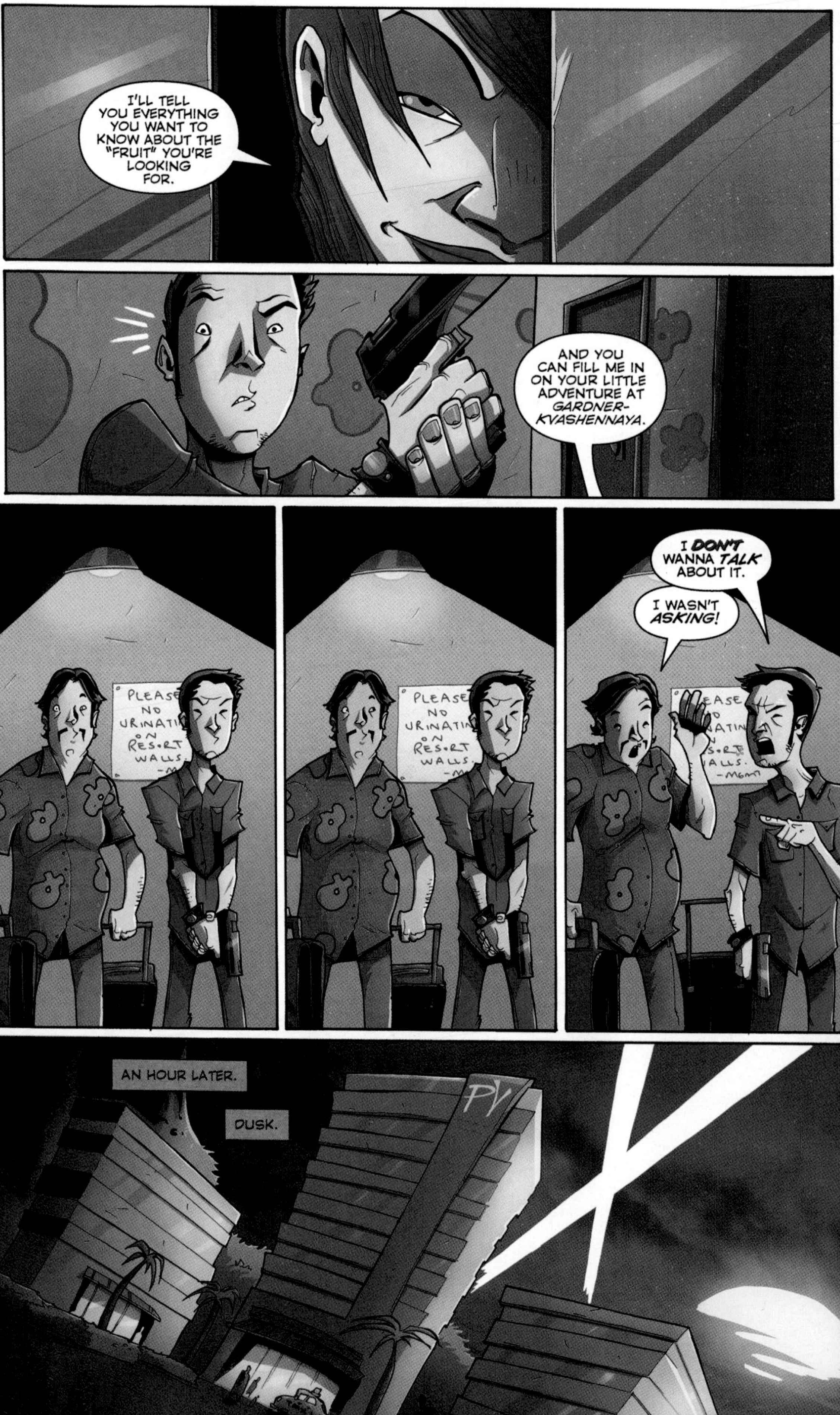
I'LL TELL YOU EVERYTHING YOU WANT TO KNOW ABOUT THE "FRUIT" YOU'RE LOOKING FOR.
AND YOU CAN FILL ME IN ON YOUR LITTLE ADVENTURE AT *GARDNER-KVASHENNAYA*.
PLEASE NO URINATIN ON RESORT WALLS. -MGMT
I ***DON'T*** WANNA *TALK* ABOUT IT.
I WASN'T *ASKING*!
AN HOUR LATER.
DUSK.

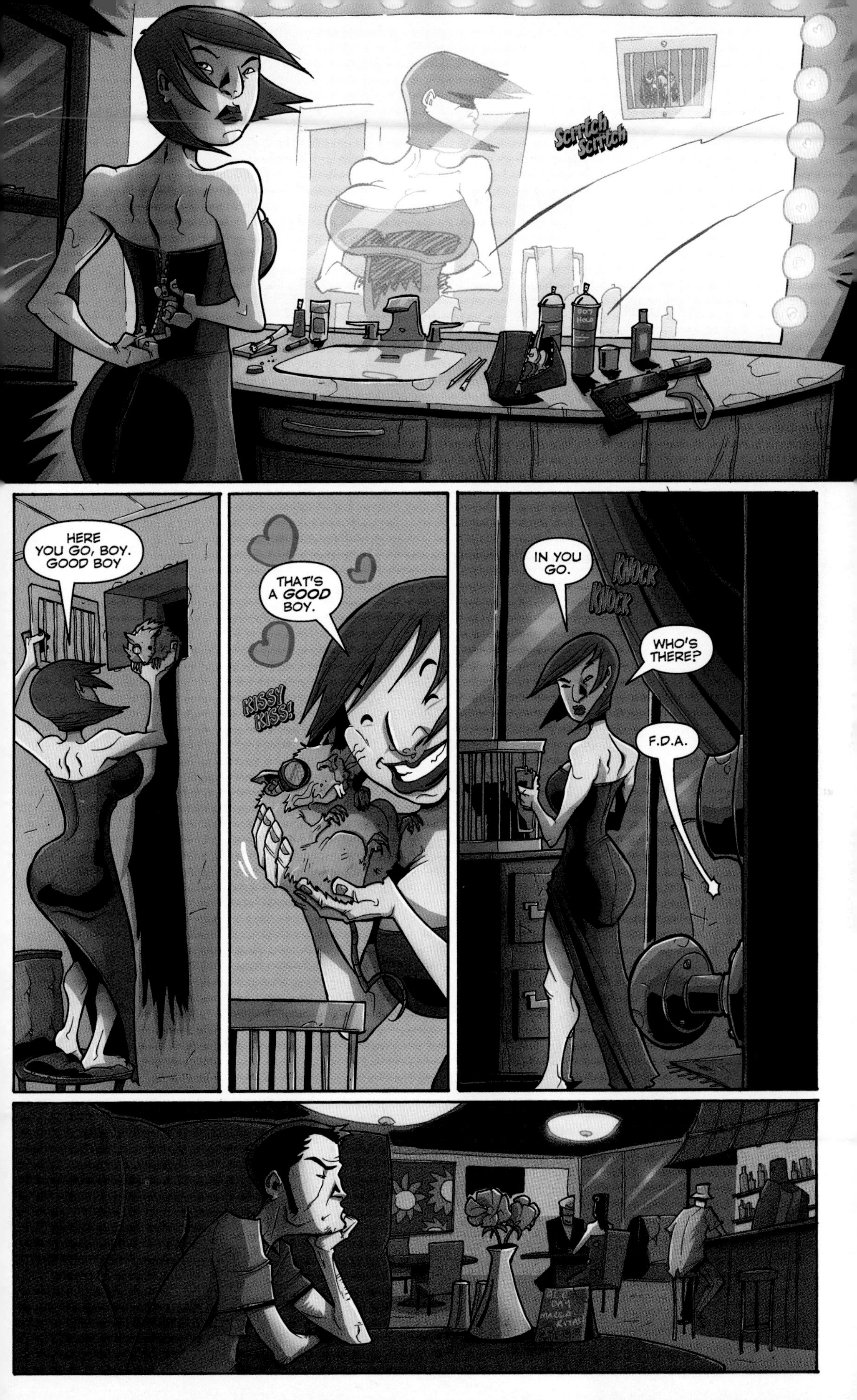
Scrritch Scrritch
HERE YOU GO, BOY. GOOD BOY
THAT'S A *GOOD* BOY.
KISSY KISS!
IN YOU GO.
KNOCK KNOCK
WHO'S THERE?
F.D.A.
ALL DAY MARGA RITAS!

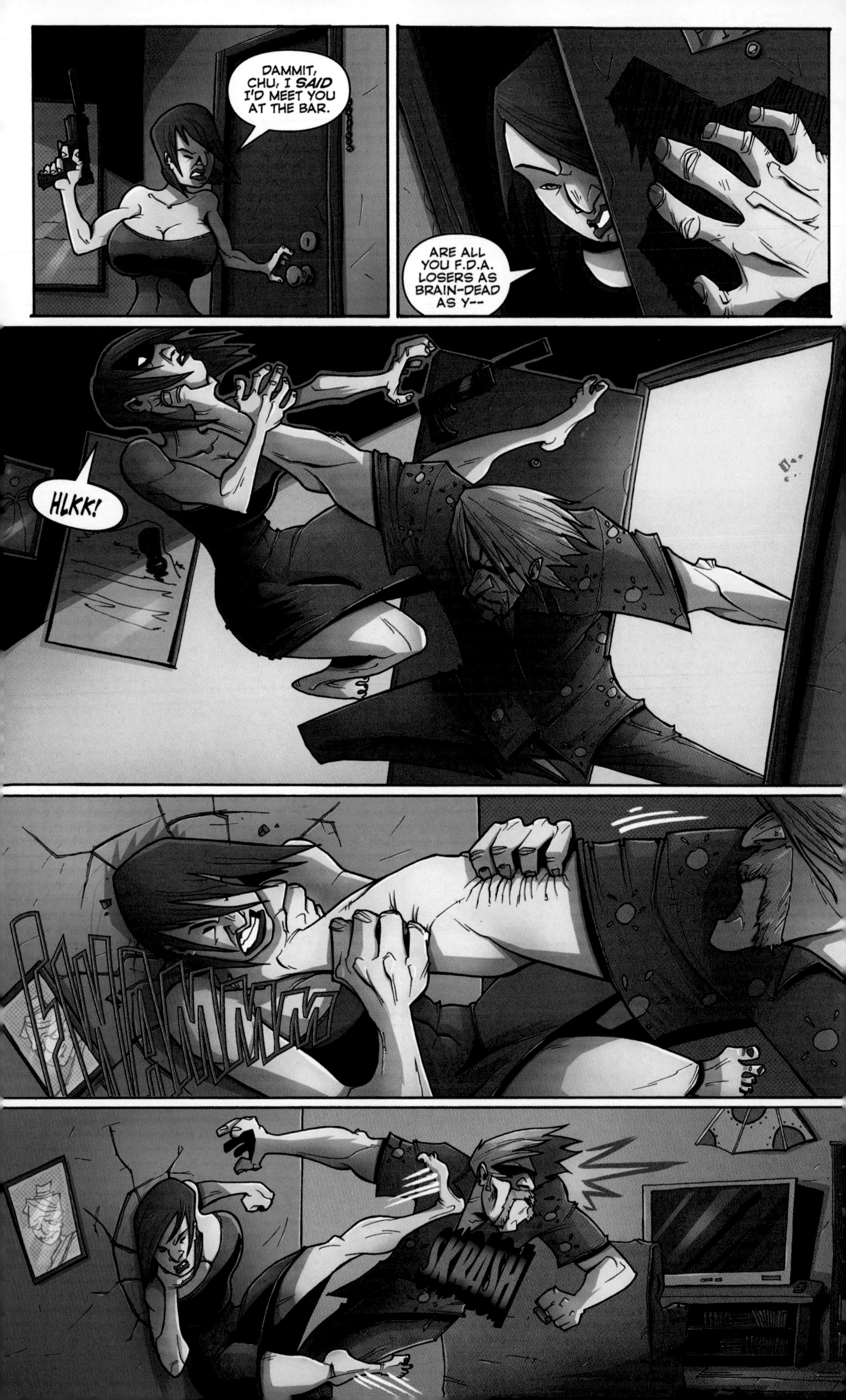
DAMMIT, CHU, I *SAID* I'D MEET YOU AT THE BAR.
ARE ALL YOU F.D.A. LOSERS AS BRAIN-DEAD AS Y--
HLKK!
SKRASH

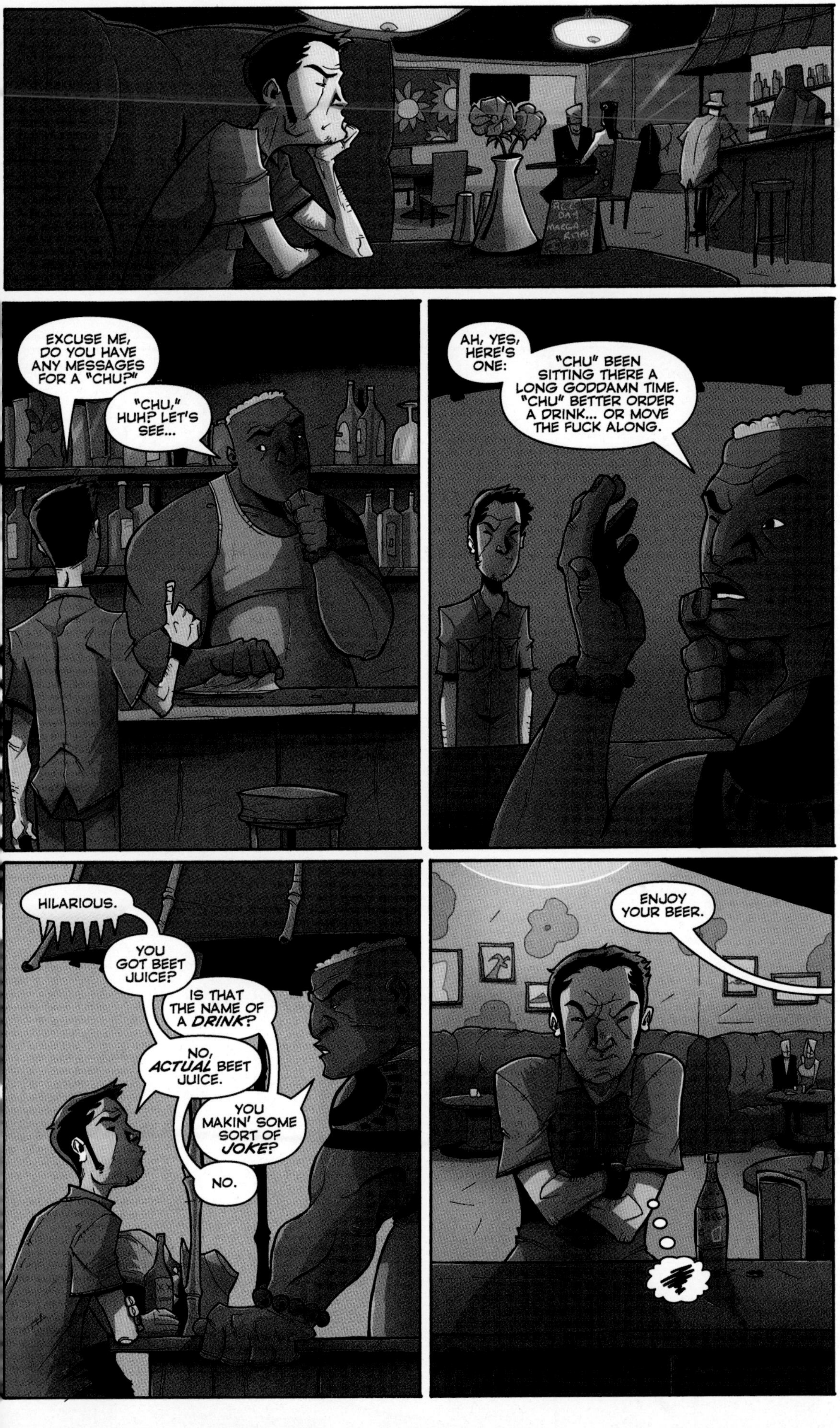
ACE DAY MARGA-RITAS!
EXCUSE ME, DO YOU HAVE ANY MESSAGES FOR A "CHU?"
"CHU," HUH? LET'S SEE...
AH, YES, HERE'S ONE:
"CHU" BEEN SITTING THERE A LONG GODDAMN TIME. "CHU" BETTER ORDER A DRINK... OR MOVE THE FUCK ALONG.
HILARIOUS.
YOU GOT BEET JUICE?
IS THAT THE NAME OF A *DRINK*?
NO, *ACTUAL* BEET JUICE.
YOU MAKIN' SOME SORT OF *JOKE*?
NO.
ENJOY YOUR BEER.

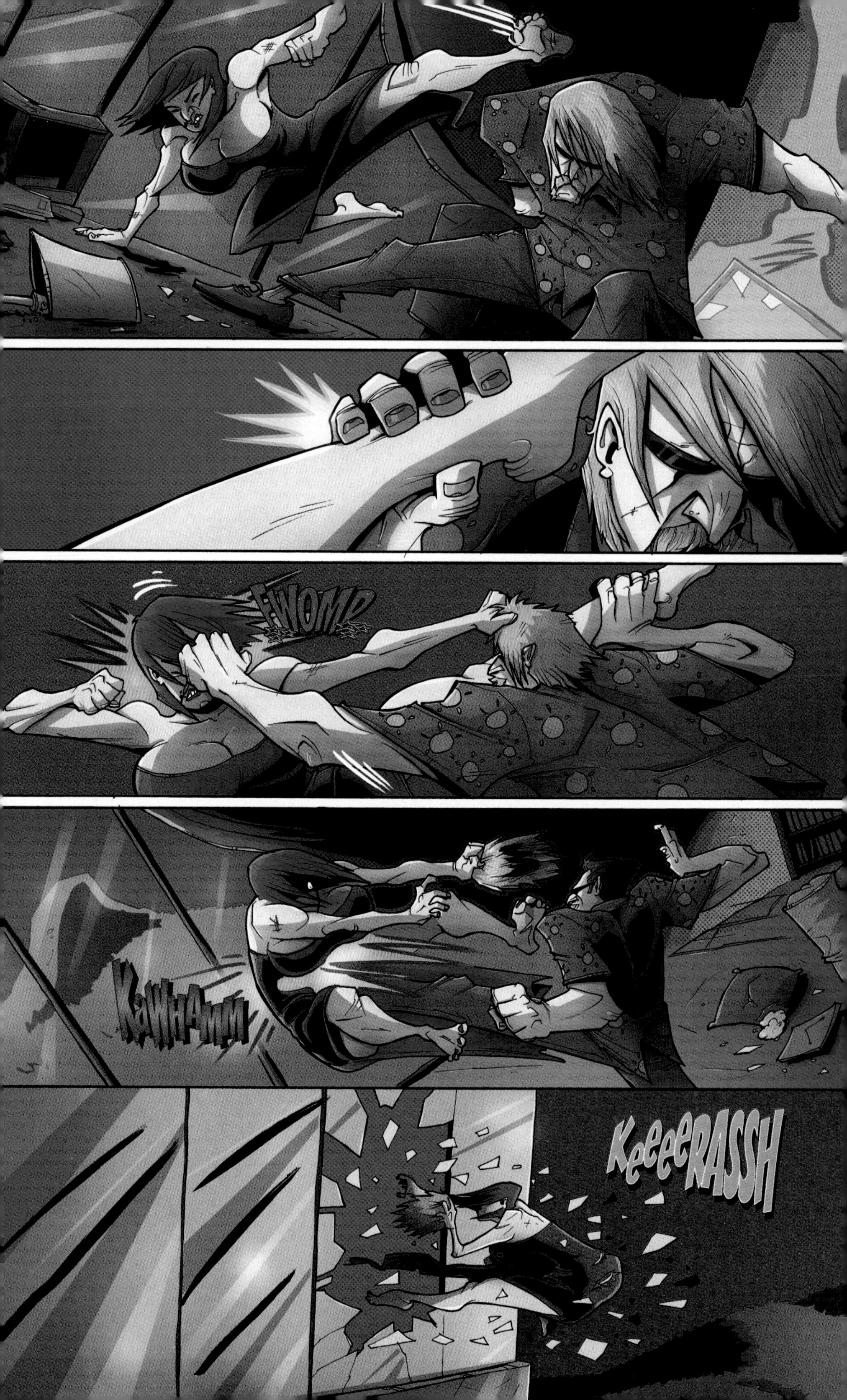
FWOMP
KaWHAMM
KeeeeRASSH

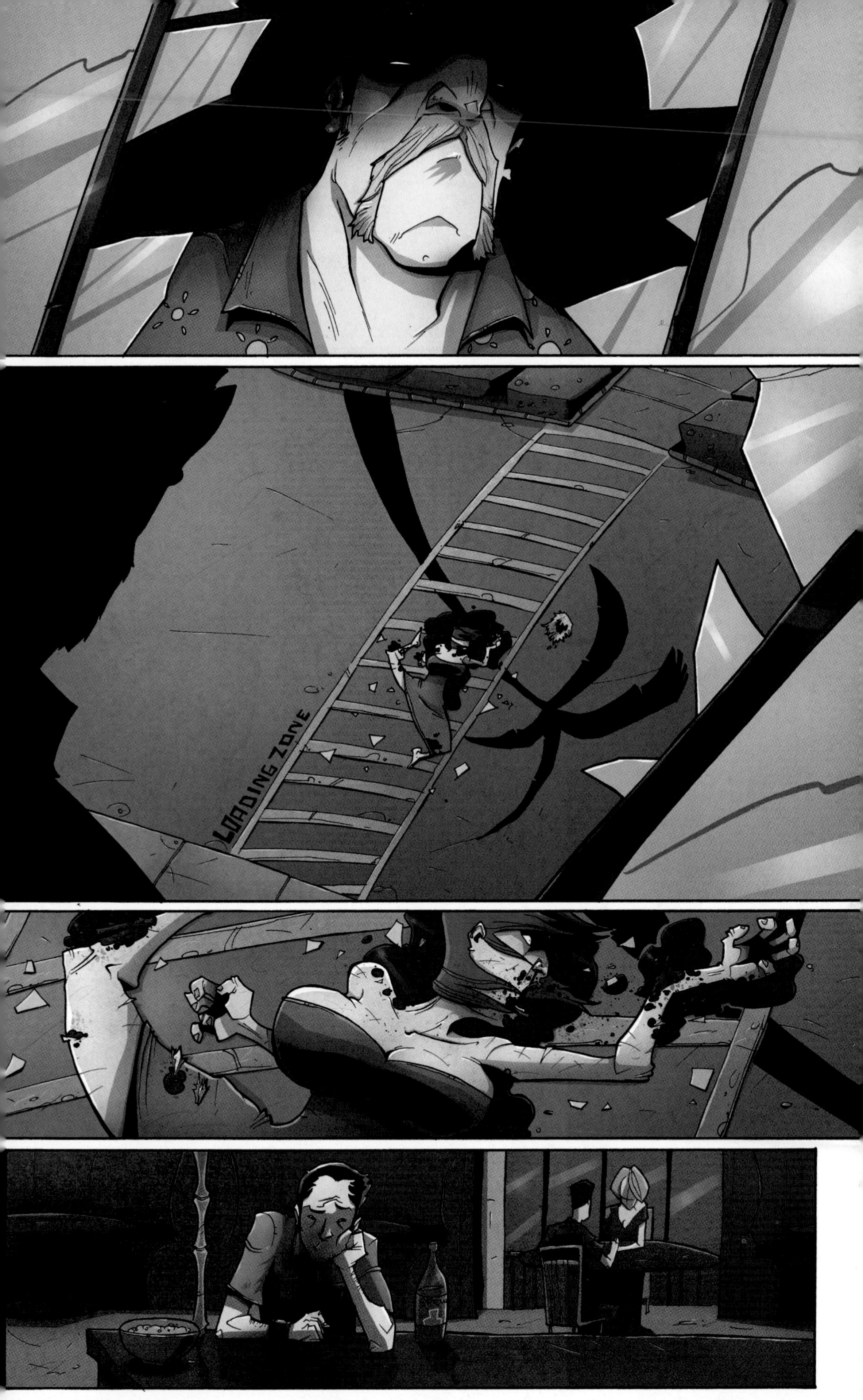
LOADING ZONE

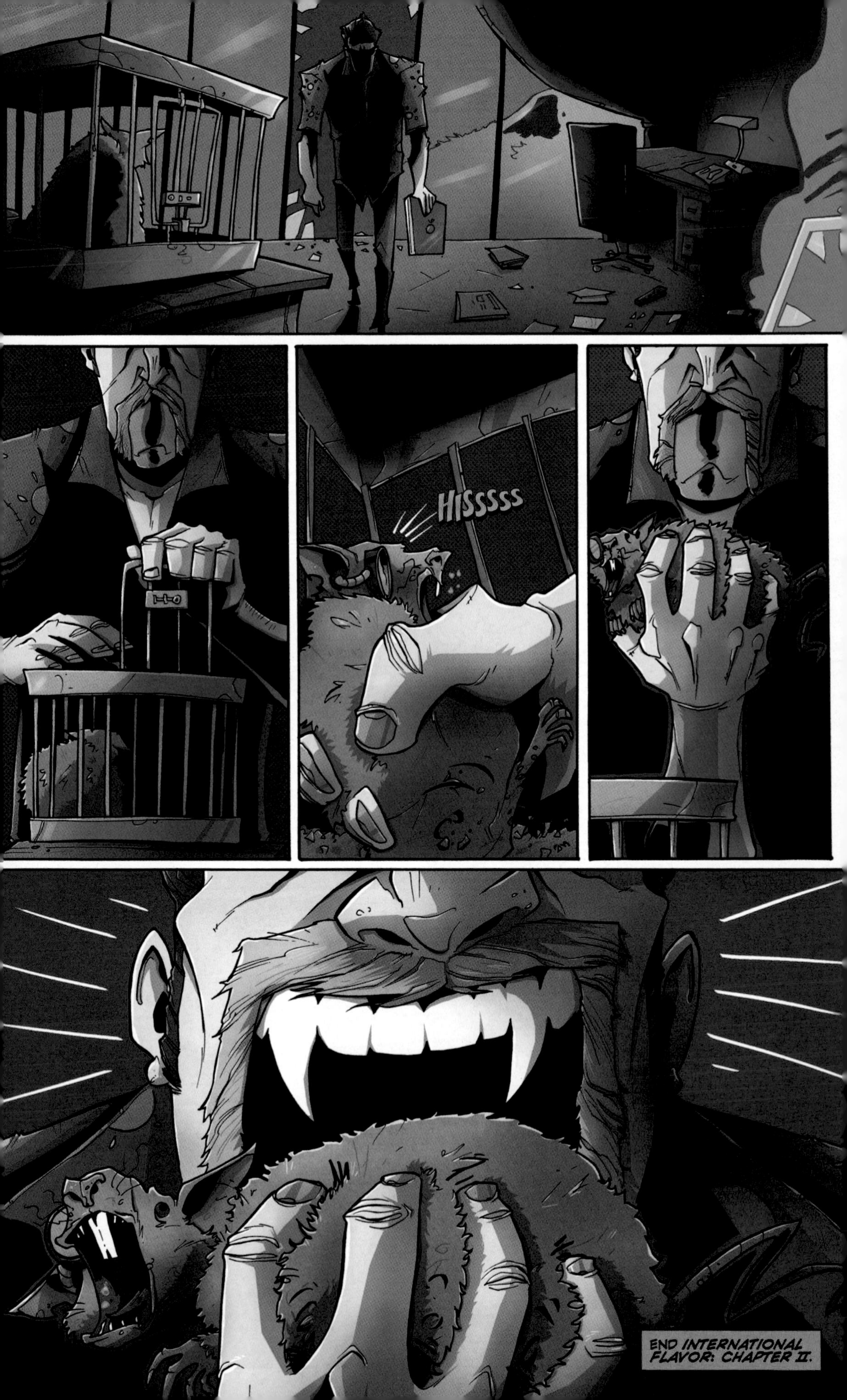
HISSSSS
END INTERNATIONAL FLAVOR: CHAPTER II.

Chapter 3

MISSING:
POYO
KING OF COCKS.

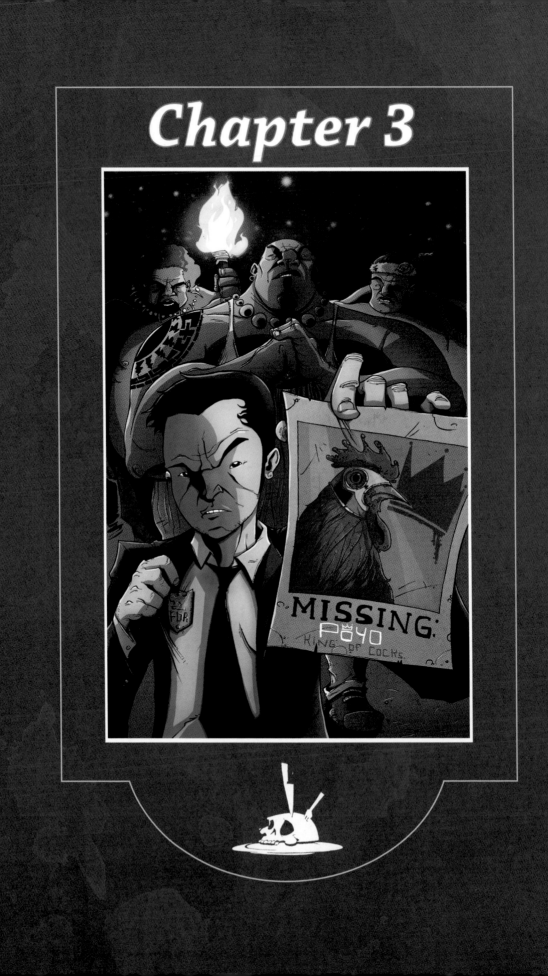

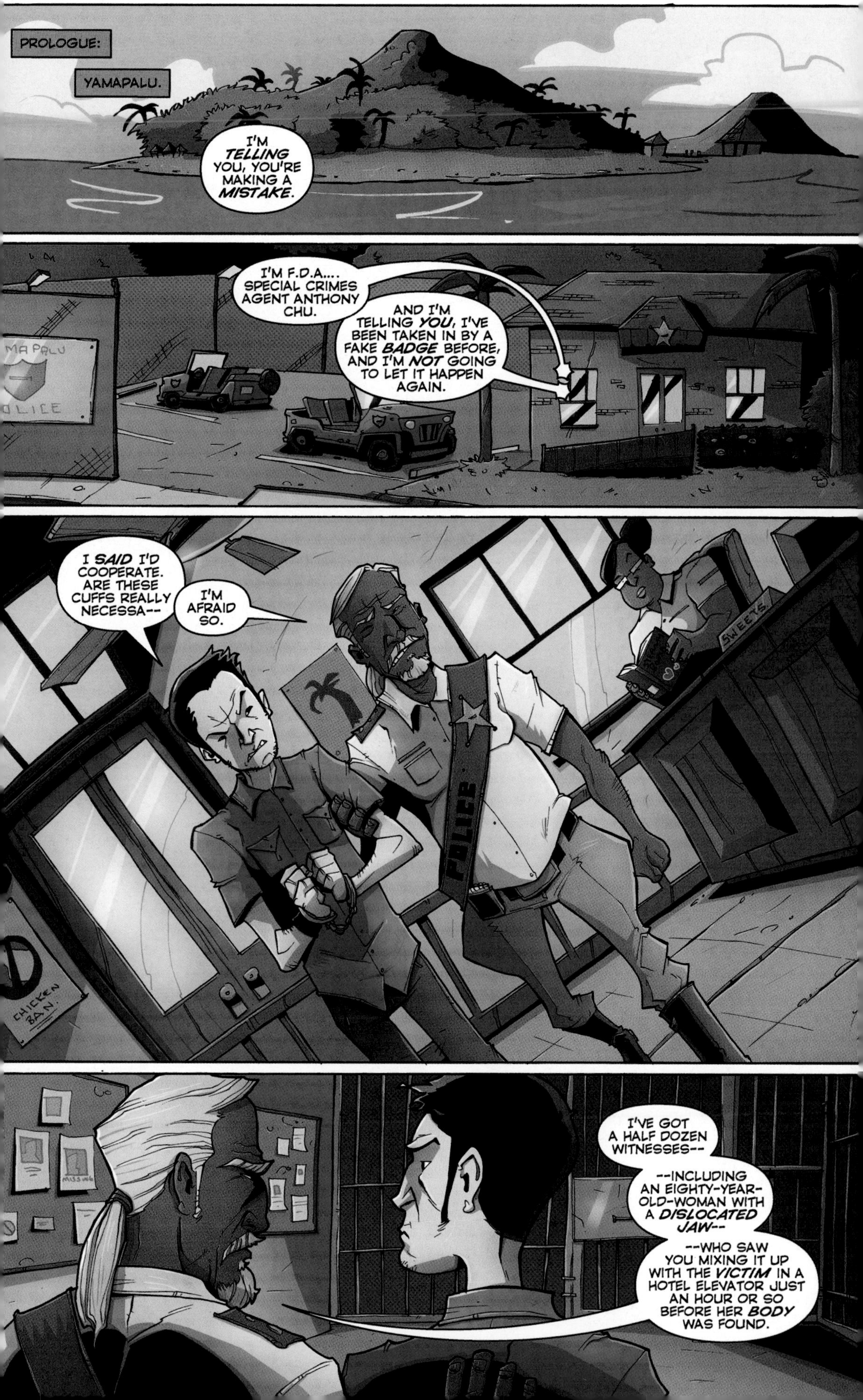
PROLOGUE:
YAMAPALU.
I'M TELLING YOU, YOU'RE MAKING A MISTAKE.
I'M F.D.A.... SPECIAL CRIMES AGENT ANTHONY CHU.
AND I'M TELLING YOU, I'VE BEEN TAKEN IN BY A FAKE BADGE BEFORE, AND I'M NOT GOING TO LET IT HAPPEN AGAIN.
I SAID I'D COOPERATE. ARE THESE CUFFS REALLY NECESSA--
I'M AFRAID SO.
SWEETS
POLICE
CHICKEN BAN
I'VE GOT A HALF DOZEN WITNESSES--
--INCLUDING AN EIGHTY-YEAR-OLD-WOMAN WITH A DISLOCATED JAW--
--WHO SAW YOU MIXING IT UP WITH THE VICTIM IN A HOTEL ELEVATOR JUST AN HOUR OR SO BEFORE HER BODY WAS FOUND.

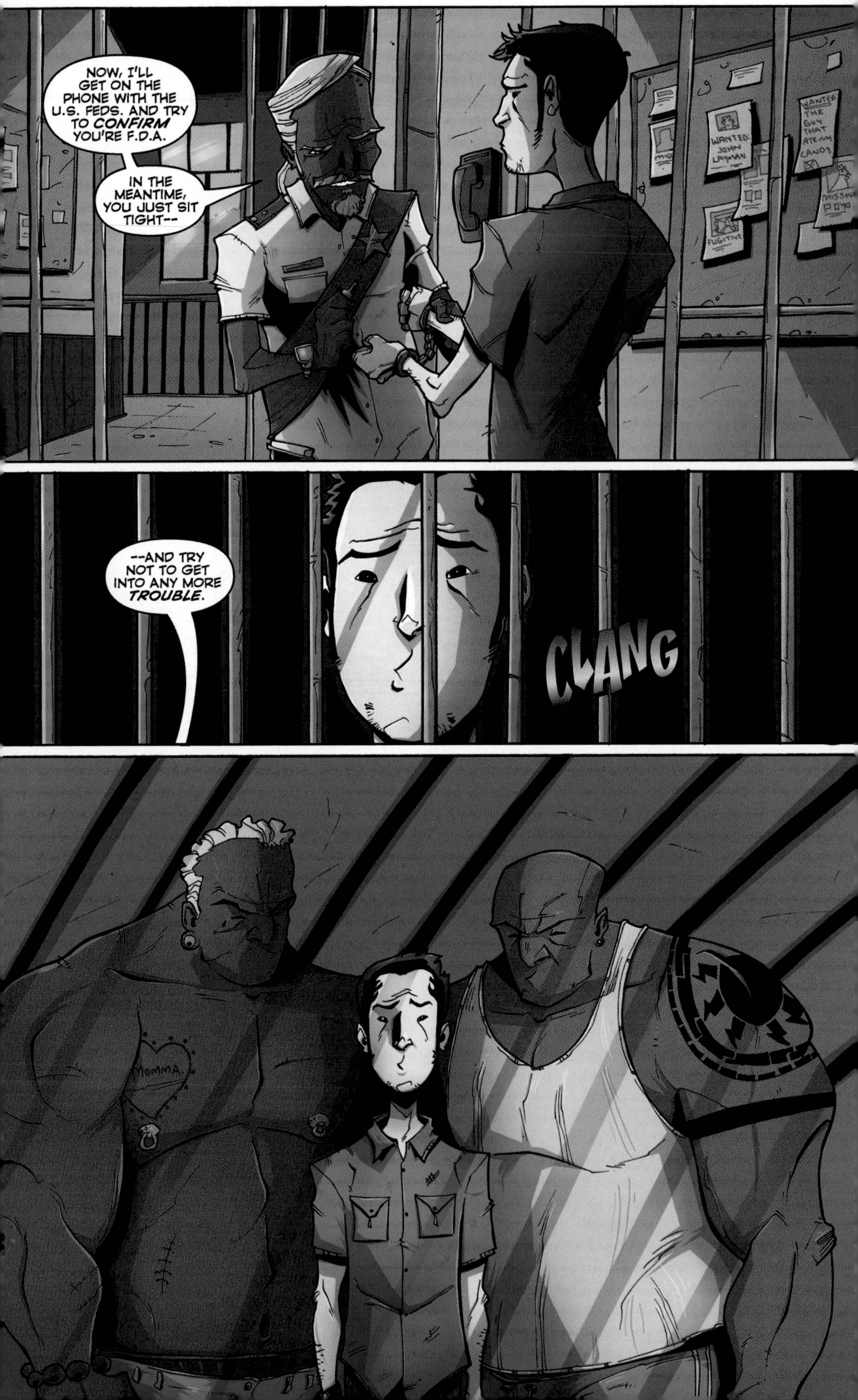
NOW, I'LL GET ON THE PHONE WITH THE U.S. FEDS. AND TRY TO *CONFIRM* YOU'RE F.D.A.
IN THE MEANTIME, YOU JUST SIT TIGHT--
WANTED: JOHN LAYMAN
WANTED THE GUY THAT ATE MY CANDY
FUGITIVE
--AND TRY NOT TO GET INTO ANY MORE *TROUBLE*.
CLANG
MOMMA

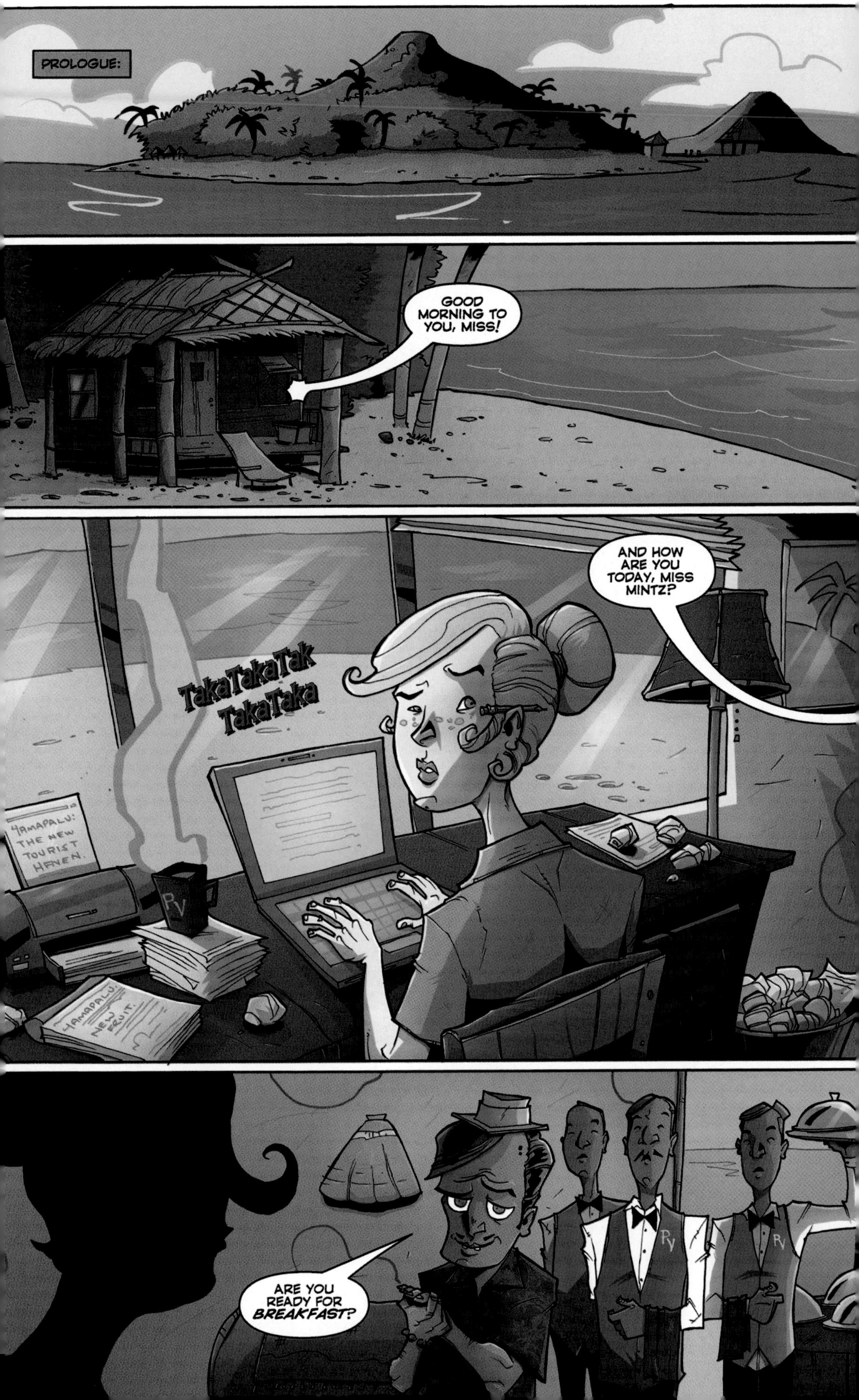
PROLOGUE:
GOOD MORNING TO YOU, MISS!
AND HOW ARE YOU TODAY, MISS MINTZ?
TakaTakaTak TakaTaka
YAMAPALU: THE NEW TOURIST HAVEN.
YAMAPALU. NEW FRUIT.
ARE YOU READY FOR BREAKFAST?

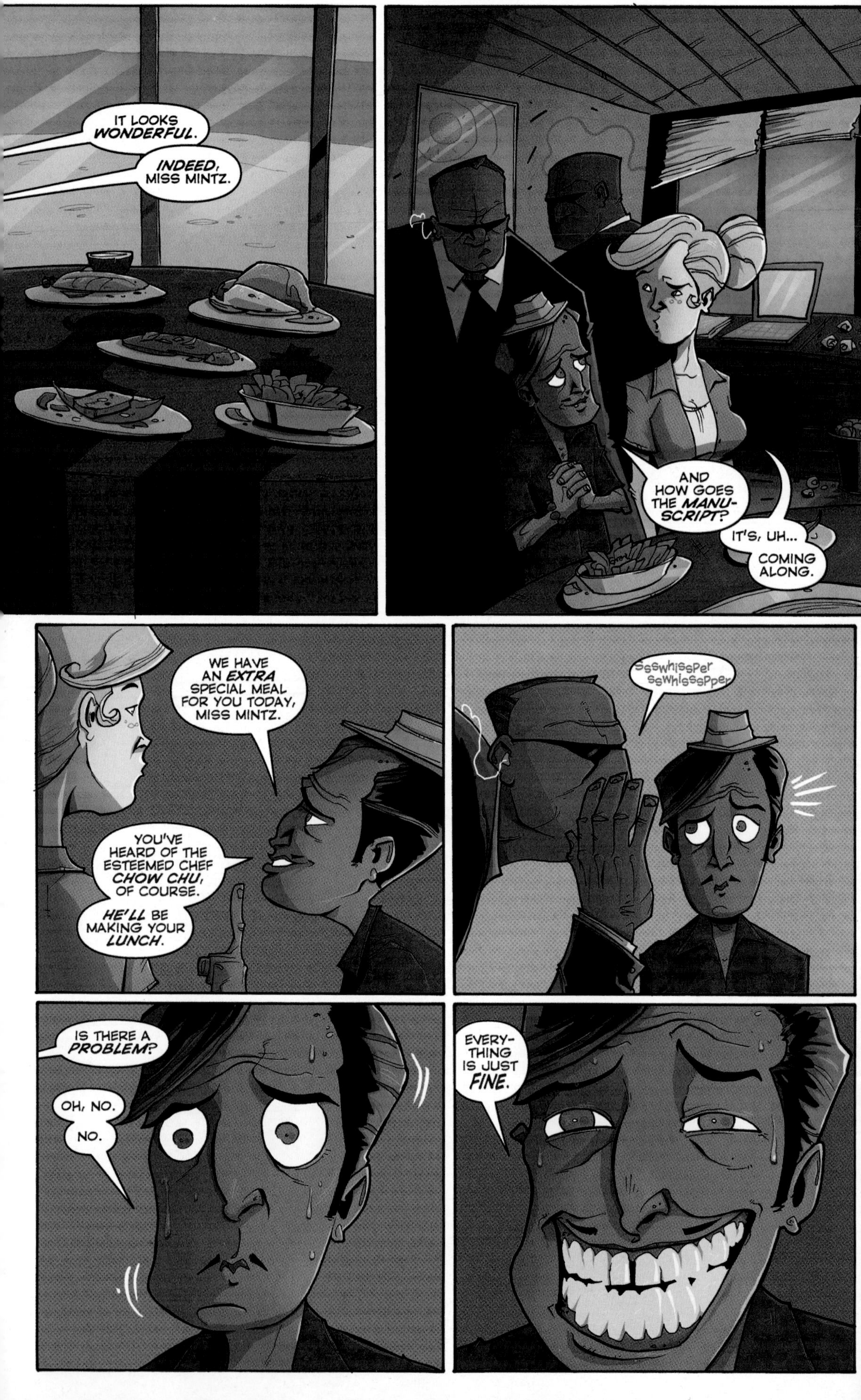
IT LOOKS WONDERFUL.
INDEED, MISS MINTZ.
AND HOW GOES THE MANU-SCRIPT?
IT'S, UH...
COMING ALONG.
WE HAVE AN EXTRA SPECIAL MEAL FOR YOU TODAY, MISS MINTZ.
YOU'VE HEARD OF THE ESTEEMED CHEF CHOW CHU, OF COURSE.
HE'LL BE MAKING YOUR LUNCH.
Sswhissper sswhisssper
IS THERE A PROBLEM?
OH, NO.
NO.
EVERY-THING IS JUST FINE.

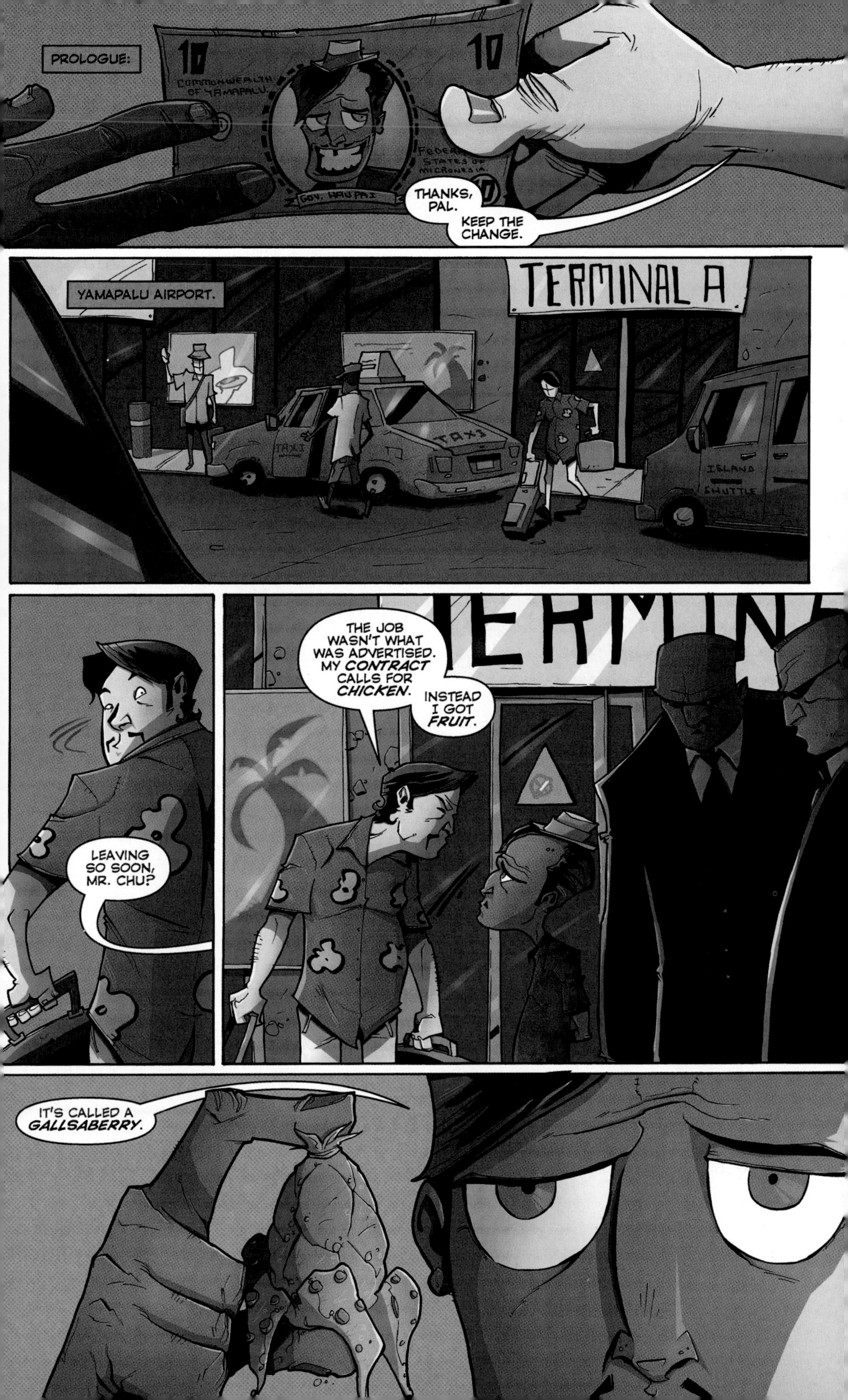
PROLOGUE:
10
COMMONWEALTH OF YAMAPALU
GOV. HAUPAI
STATES OF MICRONESIA
THANKS, PAL.
KEEP THE CHANGE.
YAMAPALU AIRPORT.
TERMINAL A
TAXI
ISLAND SHUTTLE
LEAVING SO SOON, MR. CHU?
THE JOB WASN'T WHAT WAS ADVERTISED. MY CONTRACT CALLS FOR CHICKEN.
INSTEAD I GOT FRUIT.
IT'S CALLED A GALLSABERRY.

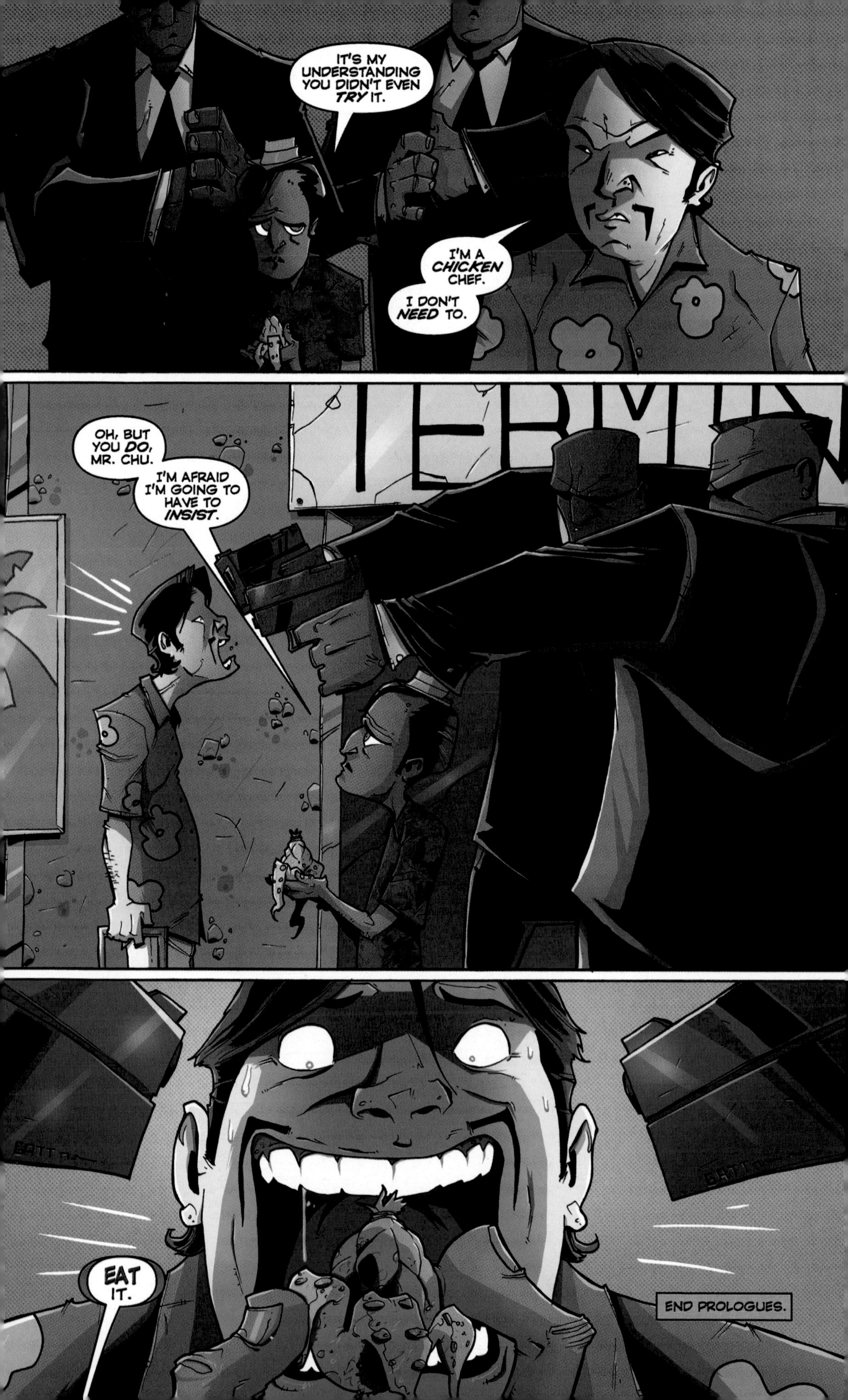
IT'S MY UNDERSTANDING YOU DIDN'T EVEN *TRY* IT.
I'M A *CHICKEN* CHEF.
I DON'T *NEED* TO.
OH, BUT YOU *DO*, MR. CHU.
I'M AFRAID I'M GOING TO HAVE TO *INSIST*.
EAT IT.
END PROLOGUES.

THIS IS THE GALLUS SAPADILLO.

SOMETIMES REFERRED TO AS "GALLSABERRY," IT IS A FRUIT UNIQUE TO THE ISLAND OF YAMAPALU.

THE MEAT OF THE FRUIT TASTES REMARKABLY LIKE CHICKEN. IN FACT, AFTER IT IS COOKED, IT TASTES *EXACTLY* LIKE CHICKEN.

EIGHT MONTHS AGO, NOBODY ON YAMAPALU HAD HEARD OF OR SEEN THE GALLUS SAPADILLO, MUCH LESS TASTED IT.

NOW IT GROWS WILD ON THE MOUNTAIN PLAINS OF YAMAPALU...

...AND *FARMING* THE GALLSABERRY HAS ALMOST OVERTAKEN TOURISM AS THE PRIMARY INDUSTRY ON THE SMALL ISLAND NATION.

ONCE AN ISLAND RENOWN FOR ITS LIBERAL NATIONAL POLICY REGARDING THE OWNERSHIP, CULTIVATION AND CONSUMPTION OF CHICKENS--

--THE GOVERNMENT OF YAMAPALU HAS RECENTLY INSTITUTED LAWS MIRRORING THE POULTRY PROHIBITION ENACTED AND ENFORCED BY THE UNITED STATES OF AMERICA.

NO POULTRY!

NATURALLY, THOSE YAMAPALUVIANS WHO ONCE PROSPERED IN THE CHICKEN INDUSTRY ARE *GREATLY* DISPLEASED ABOUT THESE RECENT EVENTS.

AS THE NEWLY-INCARCERATED AGENT TONY CHU HAS THE UNFORTUNATE LUCK OF DISCOVERING.

YOU'RE AMERICA F.D.A., HUH?

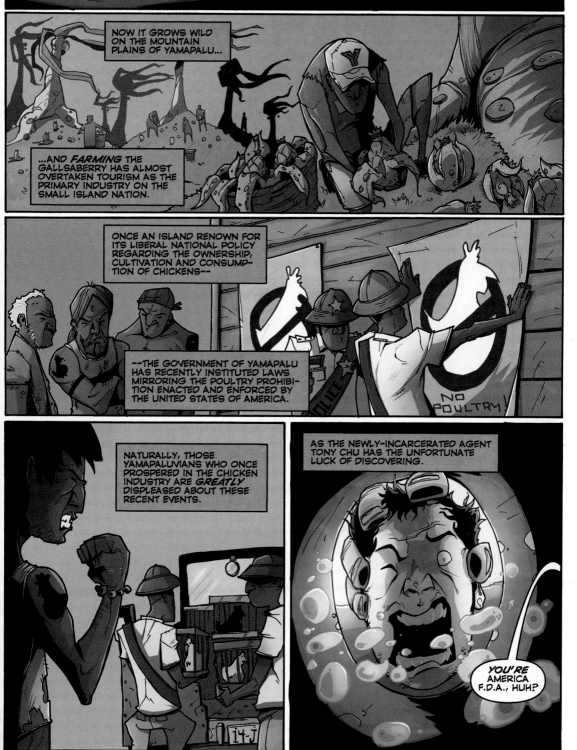

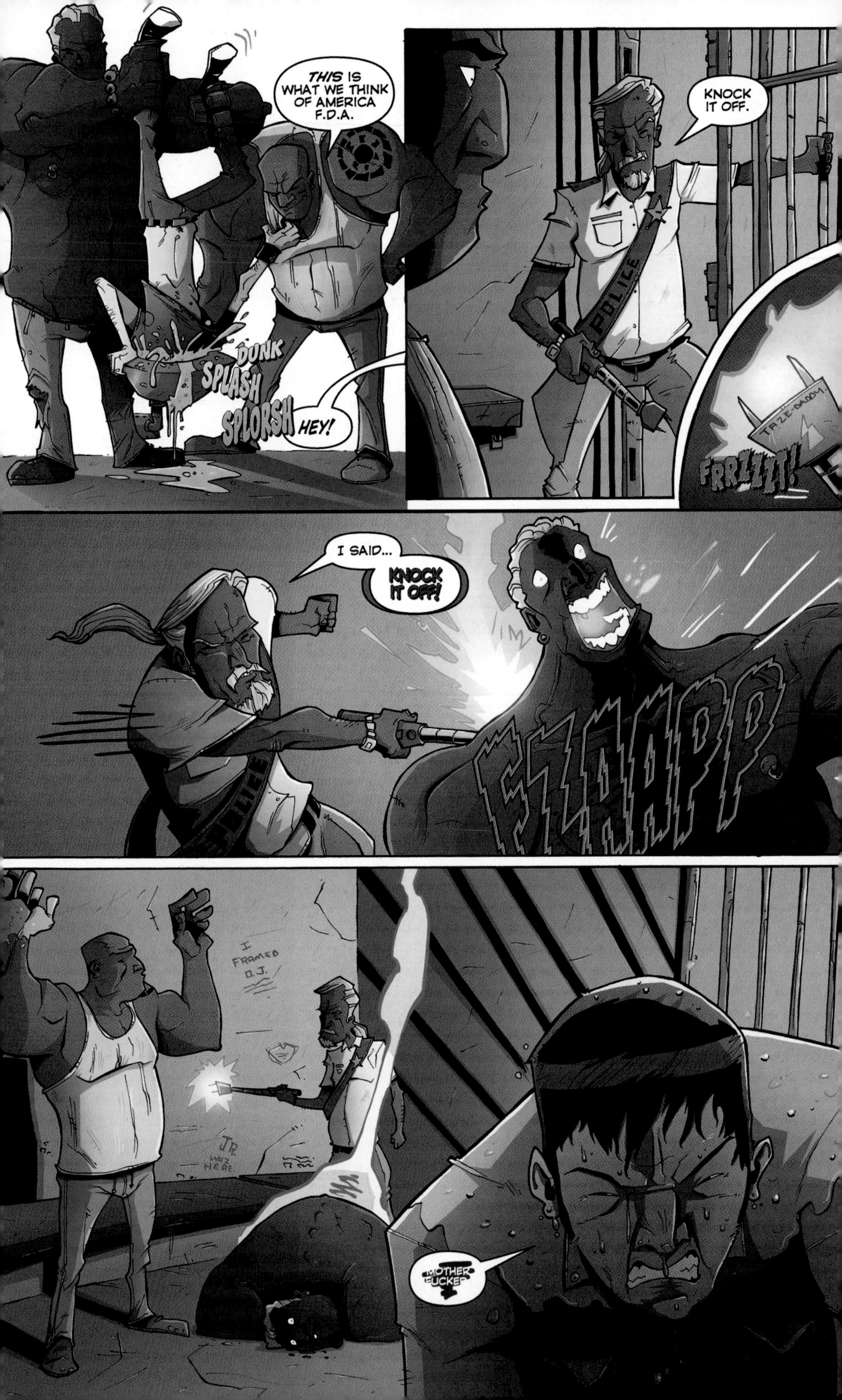
THIS IS WHAT WE THINK OF AMERICA F.D.A.
DUNK
SPLASH
SPLORSH
HEY!
KNOCK IT OFF.
TAZE-DADDY
FRRZZZT!
I SAID...
KNOCK IT OFF!
SZAPP
I FRAMED O.J.
JR. WUZ HERE
MOTHER FUCKER

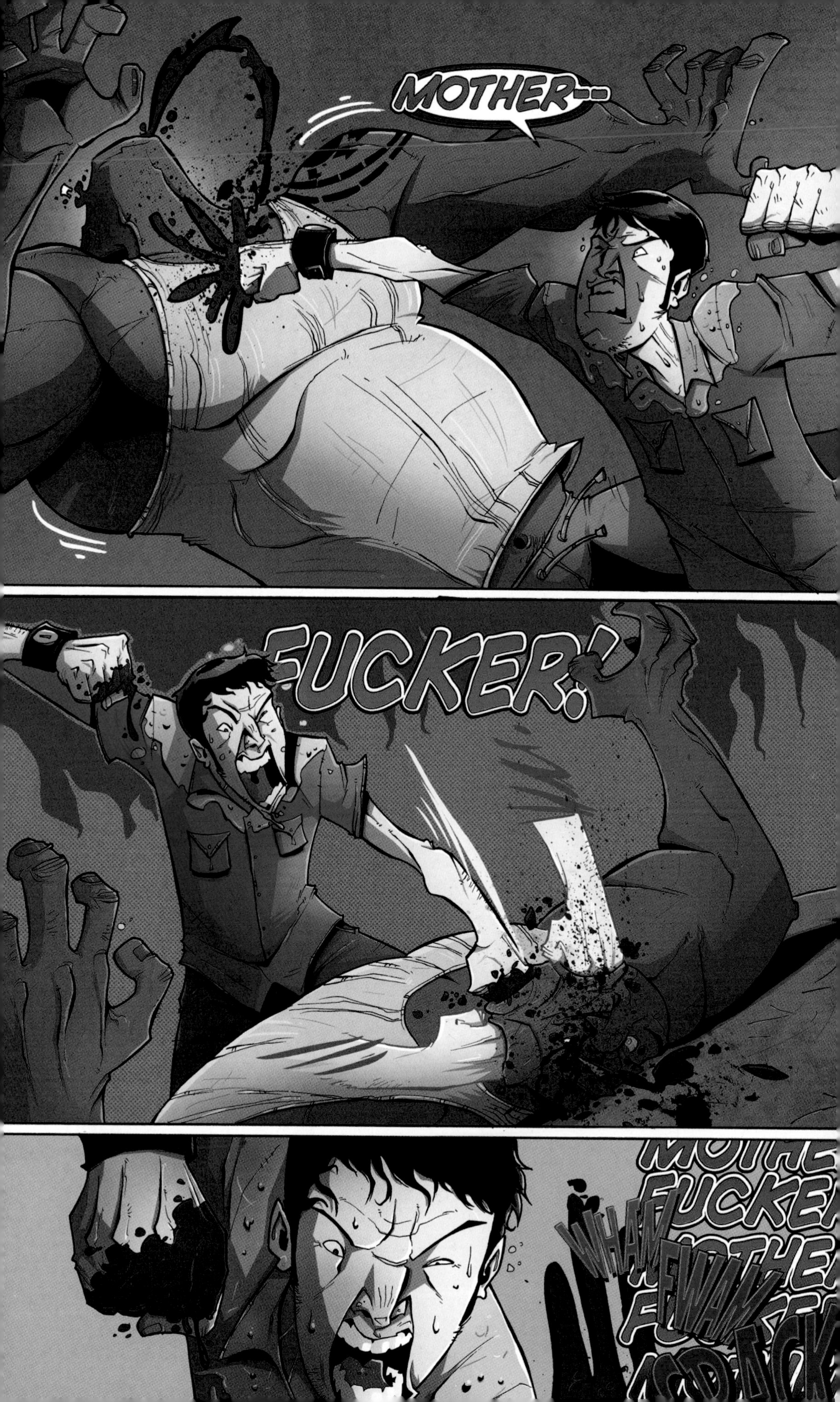
MOTHER--
FUCKER!
WHAM

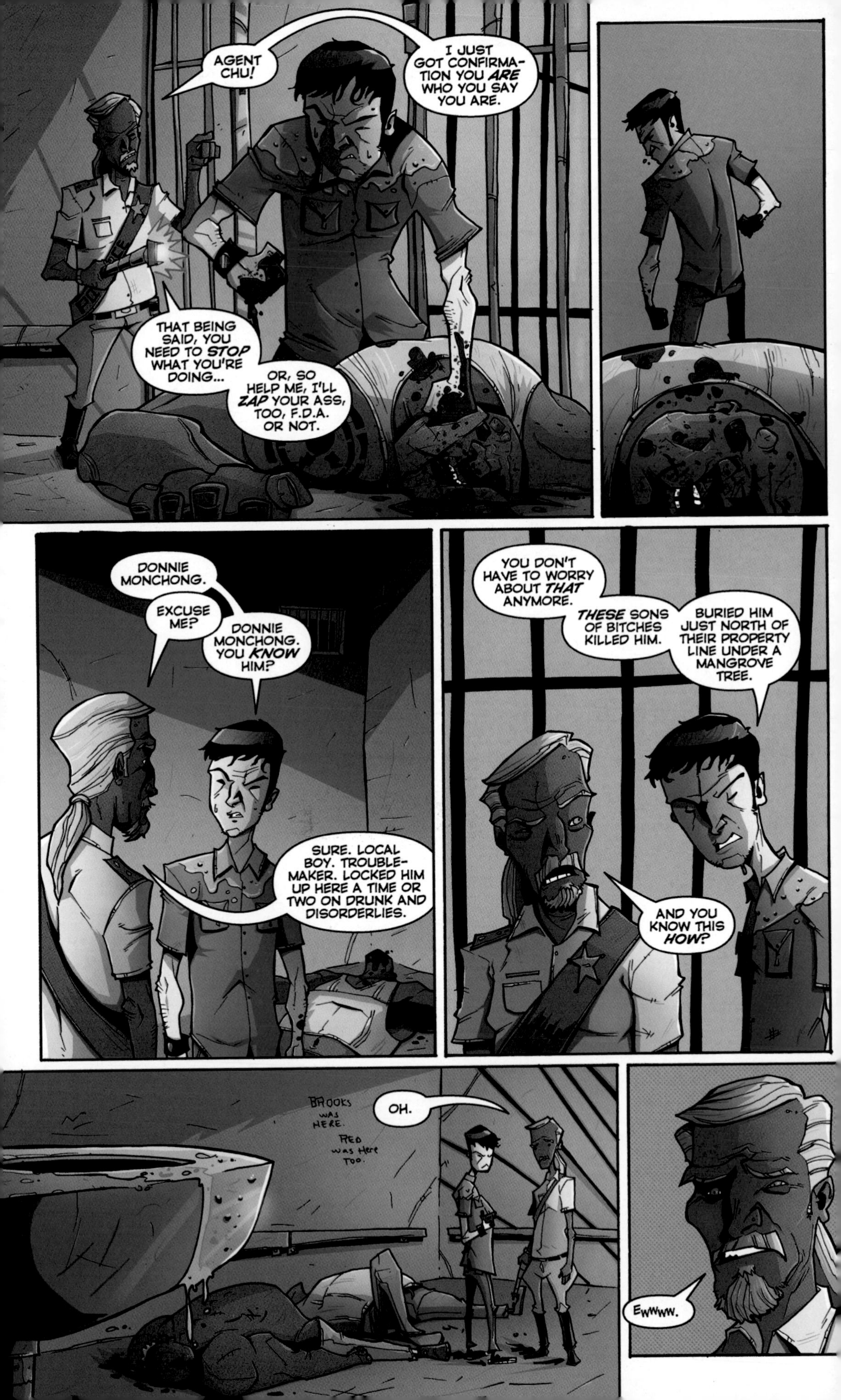
AGENT CHU!
I JUST GOT CONFIRMATION YOU *ARE* WHO YOU SAY YOU ARE.
THAT BEING SAID, YOU NEED TO *STOP* WHAT YOU'RE DOING...
OR, SO HELP ME, I'LL *ZAP* YOUR ASS, TOO, F.D.A. OR NOT.
DONNIE MONCHONG.
EXCUSE ME?
DONNIE MONCHONG. YOU *KNOW* HIM?
SURE. LOCAL BOY. TROUBLE-MAKER. LOCKED HIM UP HERE A TIME OR TWO ON DRUNK AND DISORDERLIES.
YOU DON'T HAVE TO WORRY ABOUT *THAT* ANYMORE.
THESE SONS OF BITCHES KILLED HIM.
BURIED HIM JUST NORTH OF THEIR PROPERTY LINE UNDER A MANGROVE TREE.
AND YOU KNOW THIS *HOW*?
BROOKS WAS HERE.
RED WAS HERE TOO.
OH.
EWWWW.

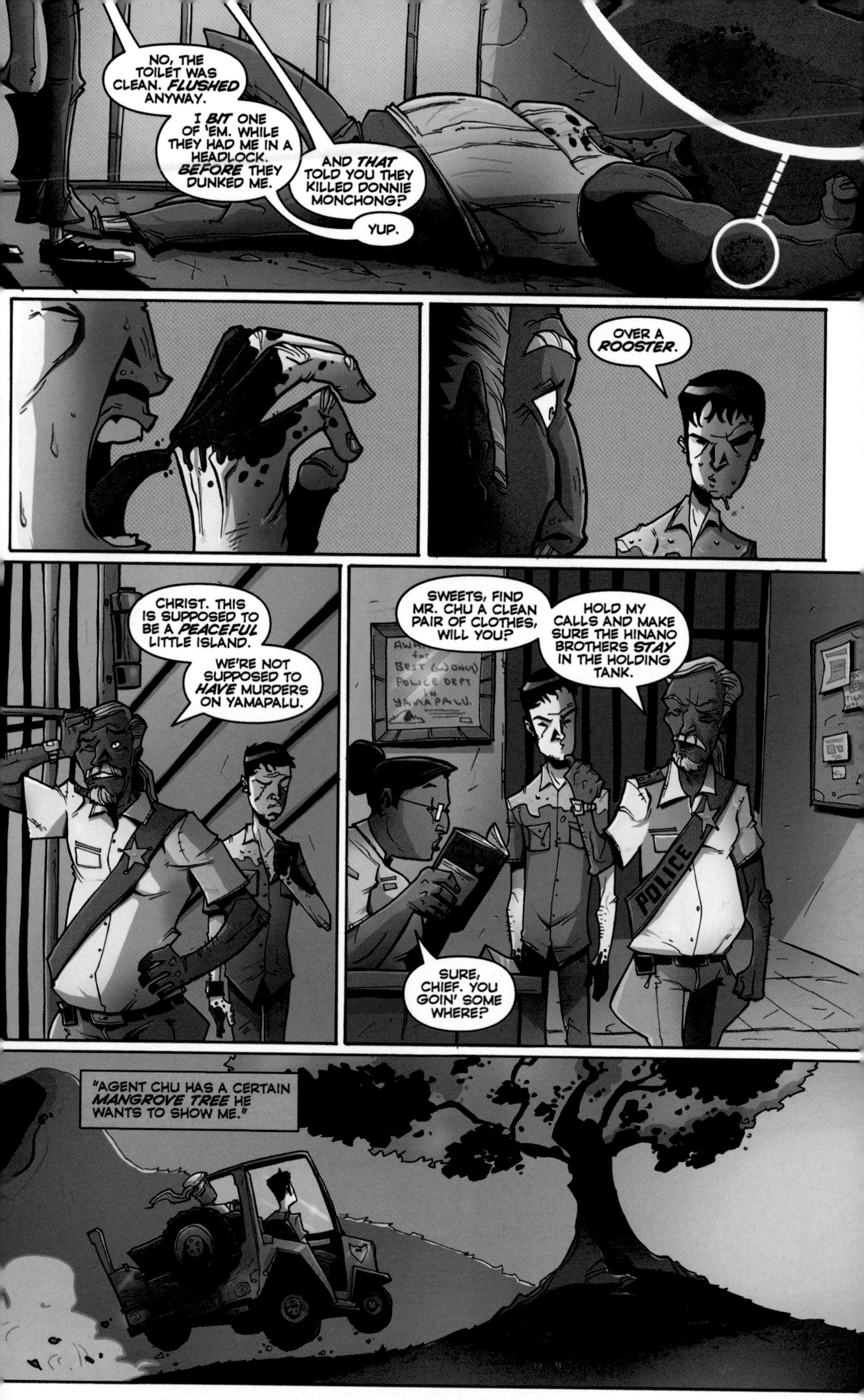
NO, THE TOILET WAS CLEAN. FLUSHED ANYWAY.
I BIT ONE OF 'EM. WHILE THEY HAD ME IN A HEADLOCK. BEFORE THEY DUNKED ME.
AND THAT TOLD YOU THEY KILLED DONNIE MONCHONG?
YUP.
OVER A ROOSTER.
CHRIST. THIS IS SUPPOSED TO BE A PEACEFUL LITTLE ISLAND.
WE'RE NOT SUPPOSED TO HAVE MURDERS ON YAMAPALU.
SWEETS, FIND MR. CHU A CLEAN PAIR OF CLOTHES, WILL YOU?
HOLD MY CALLS AND MAKE SURE THE HINANO BROTHERS STAY IN THE HOLDING TANK.
POLICE
SURE, CHIEF. YOU GOIN' SOME WHERE?
"AGENT CHU HAS A CERTAIN MANGROVE TREE HE WANTS TO SHOW ME."

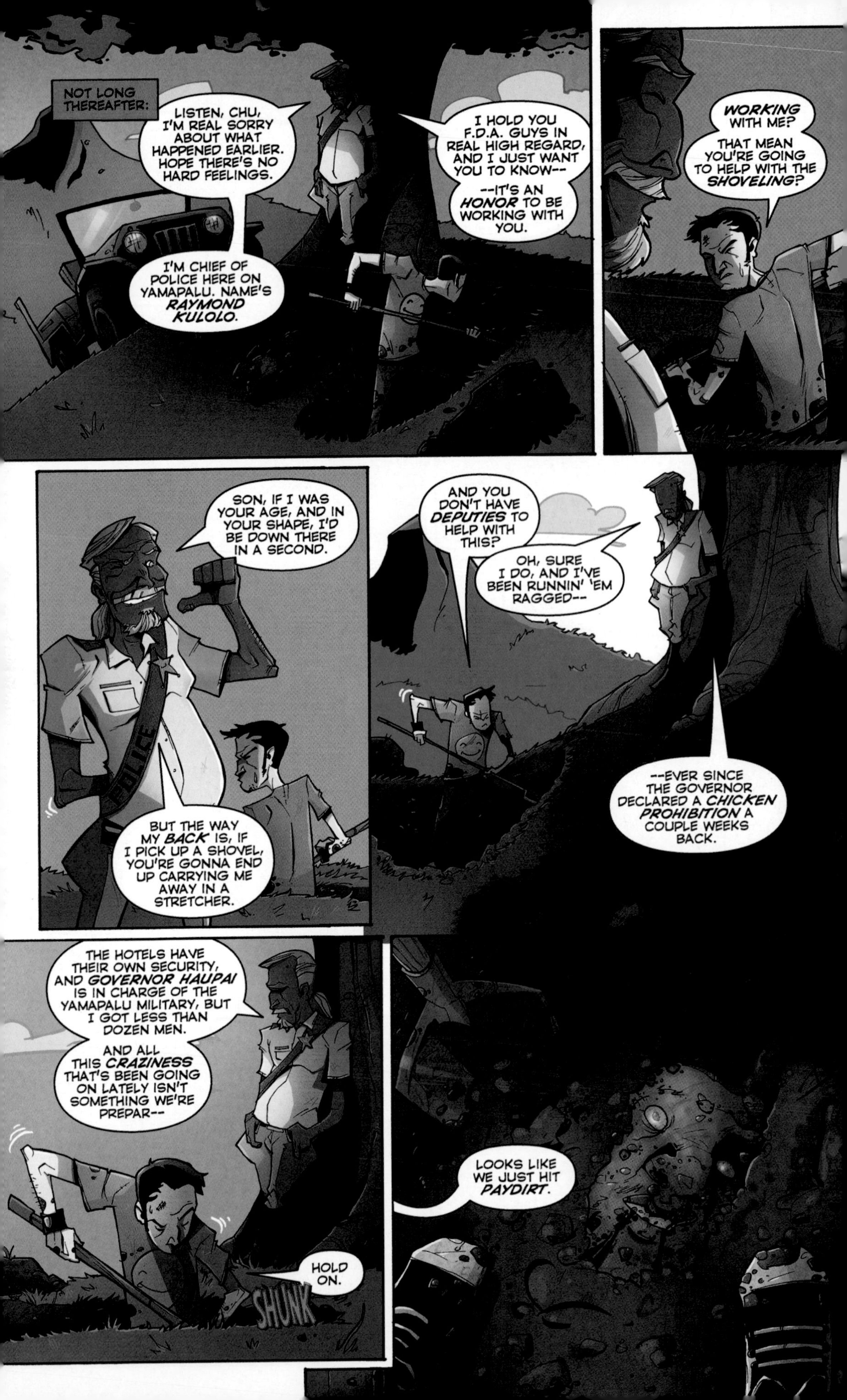
NOT LONG THEREAFTER:
LISTEN, CHU, I'M REAL SORRY ABOUT WHAT HAPPENED EARLIER. HOPE THERE'S NO HARD FEELINGS.
I'M CHIEF OF POLICE HERE ON YAMAPALU. NAME'S RAYMOND KULOLO.
I HOLD YOU F.D.A. GUYS IN REAL HIGH REGARD, AND I JUST WANT YOU TO KNOW--
--IT'S AN HONOR TO BE WORKING WITH YOU.
WORKING WITH ME?
THAT MEAN YOU'RE GOING TO HELP WITH THE SHOVELING?
SON, IF I WAS YOUR AGE, AND IN YOUR SHAPE, I'D BE DOWN THERE IN A SECOND.
BUT THE WAY MY BACK IS, IF I PICK UP A SHOVEL, YOU'RE GONNA END UP CARRYING ME AWAY IN A STRETCHER.
POLICE
AND YOU DON'T HAVE DEPUTIES TO HELP WITH THIS?
OH, SURE I DO, AND I'VE BEEN RUNNIN' 'EM RAGGED--
--EVER SINCE THE GOVERNOR DECLARED A CHICKEN PROHIBITION A COUPLE WEEKS BACK.
THE HOTELS HAVE THEIR OWN SECURITY, AND GOVERNOR HAUPAI IS IN CHARGE OF THE YAMAPALU MILITARY, BUT I GOT LESS THAN DOZEN MEN.
AND ALL THIS CRAZINESS THAT'S BEEN GOING ON LATELY ISN'T SOMETHING WE'RE PREPAR--
HOLD ON.
SHUNK
LOOKS LIKE WE JUST HIT PAYDIRT.

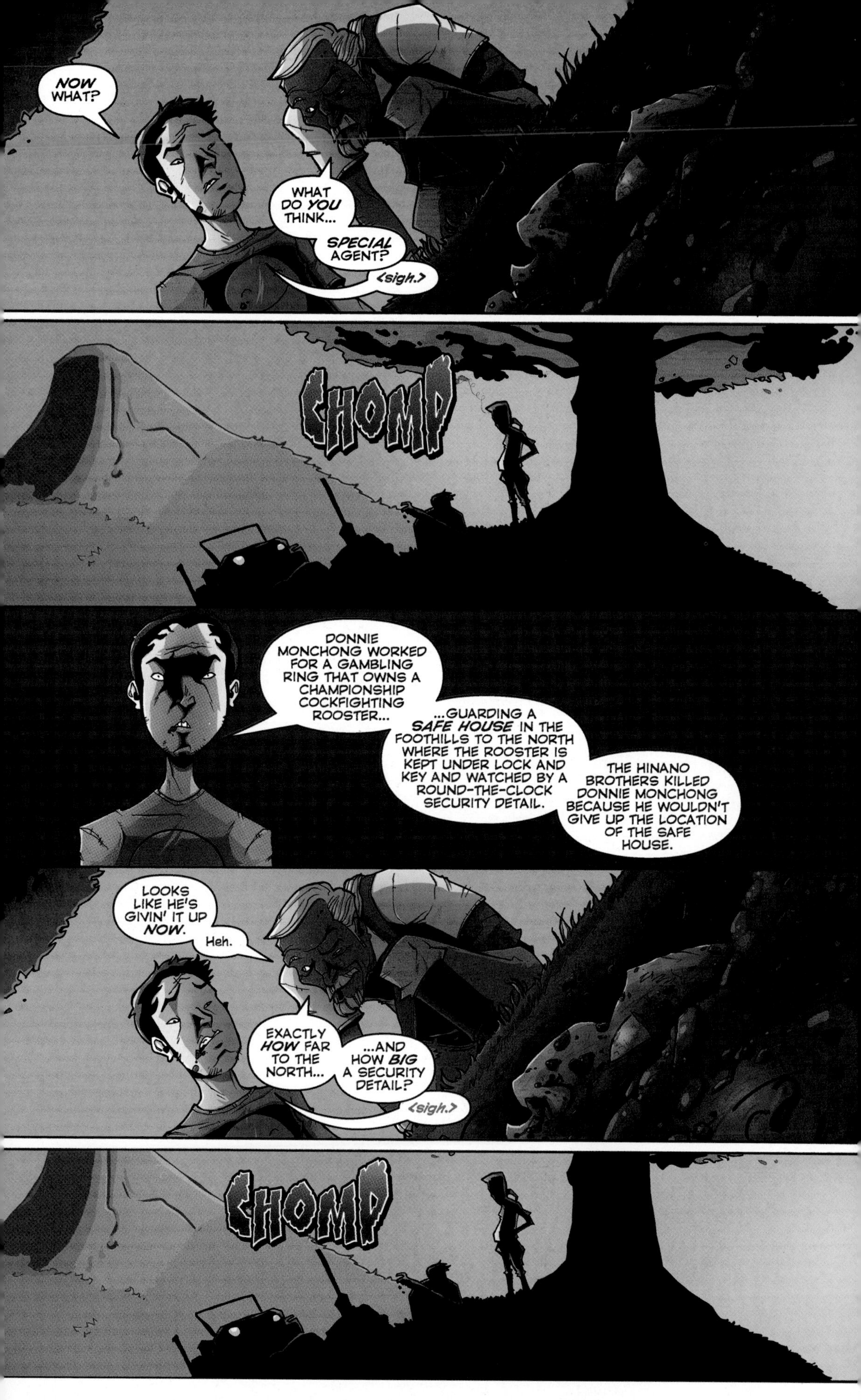
NOW WHAT?
WHAT DO YOU THINK...
SPECIAL AGENT?
<sigh.>
CHOMP
DONNIE MONCHONG WORKED FOR A GAMBLING RING THAT OWNS A CHAMPIONSHIP COCKFIGHTING ROOSTER...
...GUARDING A SAFE HOUSE IN THE FOOTHILLS TO THE NORTH WHERE THE ROOSTER IS KEPT UNDER LOCK AND KEY AND WATCHED BY A ROUND-THE-CLOCK SECURITY DETAIL.
THE HINANO BROTHERS KILLED DONNIE MONCHONG BECAUSE HE WOULDN'T GIVE UP THE LOCATION OF THE SAFE HOUSE.
LOOKS LIKE HE'S GIVIN' IT UP NOW.
Heh.
EXACTLY HOW FAR TO THE NORTH...
...AND HOW BIG A SECURITY DETAIL?
<sigh.>
CHOMP

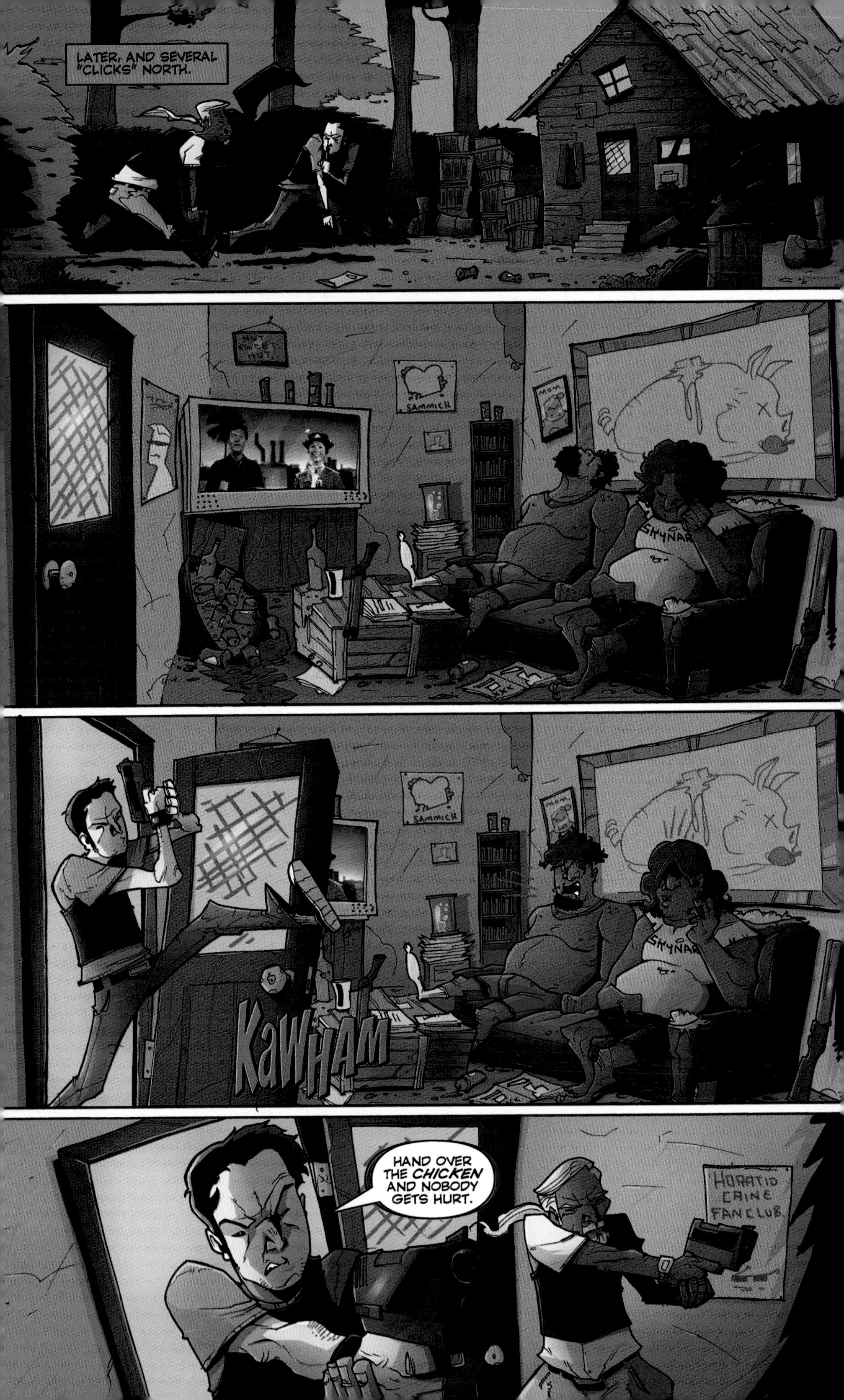
LATER, AND SEVERAL "CLICKS" NORTH.
HUT SWEET HUT
SAMMICH
MOM.
KaWHAM
HAND OVER THE *CHICKEN* AND NOBODY GETS HURT.
HORATIO CAINE FAN CLUB.

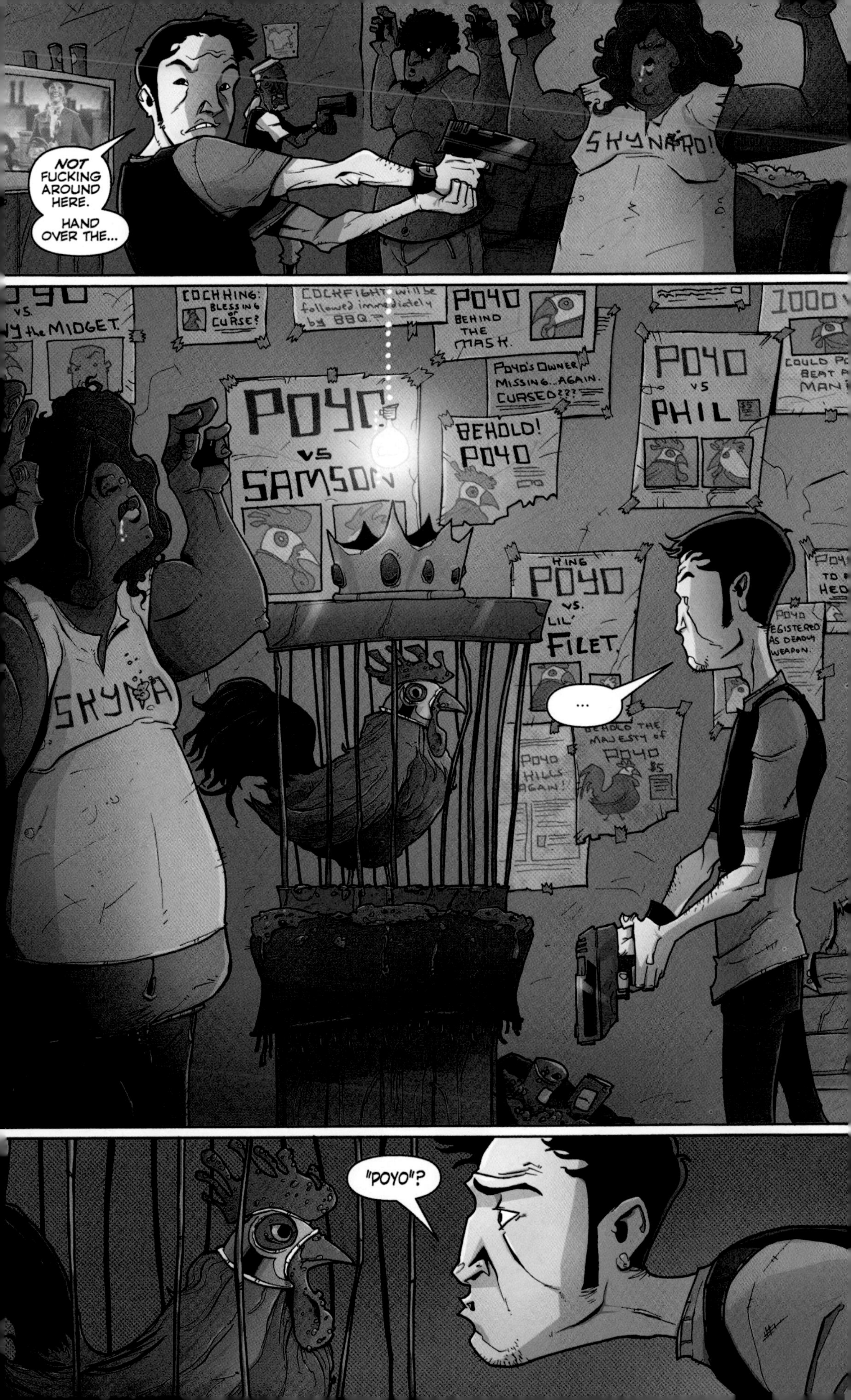
NOT FUCKING AROUND HERE.
HAND OVER THE...
SKYNARD!
COCKKING: BLESSING or CURSE?
COCKFIGHT will be followed immediately by BBQ.
POYO BEHIND THE MASK.
POYO vs SAMSON
BEHOLD! POYO
Poyo's OWNER MISSING...AGAIN. CURSED???
POYO vs PHIL
KING POYO vs. LIL' FILET
BEHOLD THE MAJESTY of POYO $5
POYO KILLS AGAIN!
POYO REGISTERED AS DEADLY WEAPON.
...
"POYO"?

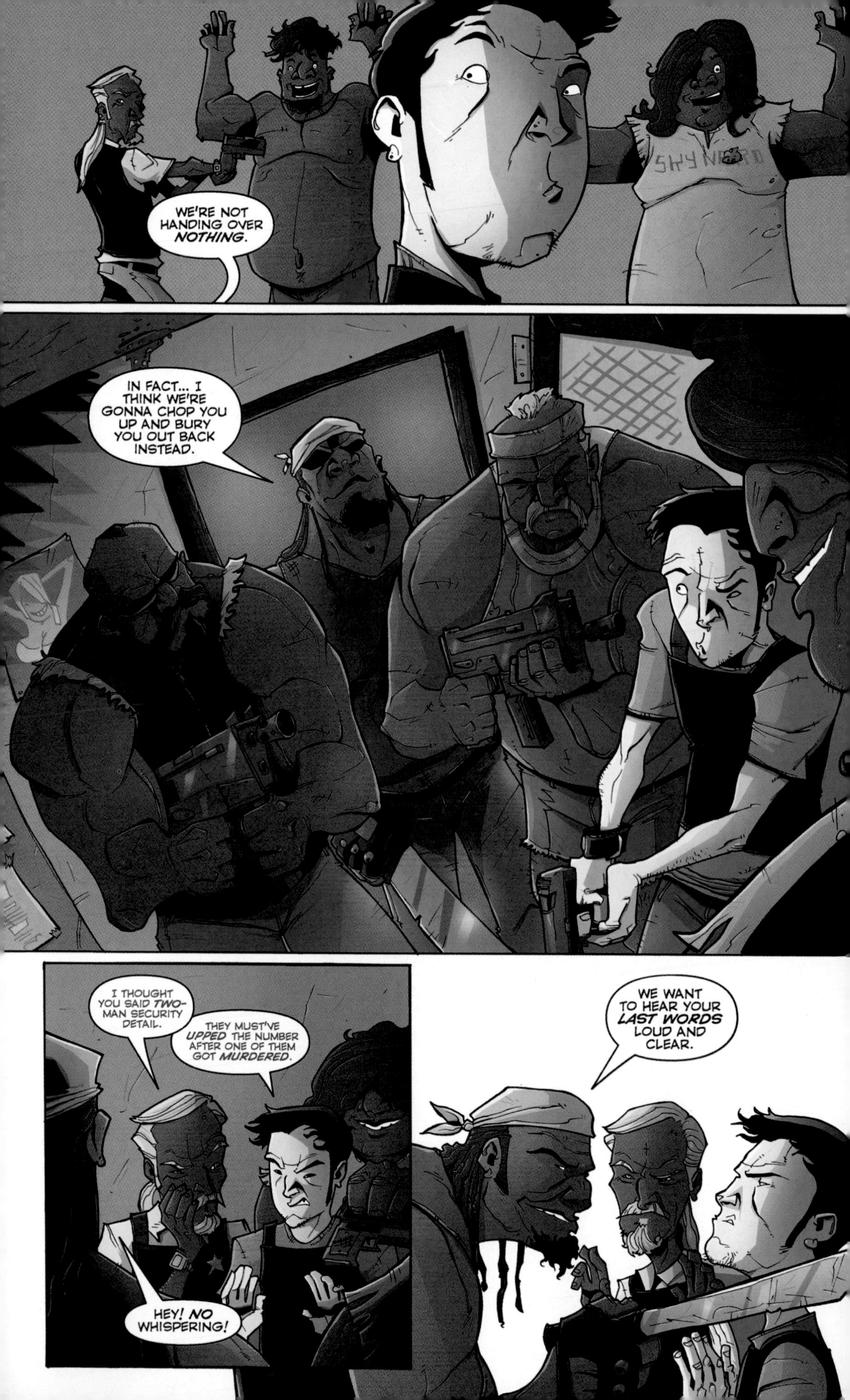
WE'RE NOT HANDING OVER *NOTHING*.
IN FACT... I THINK WE'RE GONNA CHOP YOU UP AND BURY YOU OUT BACK INSTEAD.
I THOUGHT YOU SAID *TWO*-MAN SECURITY DETAIL.
THEY MUST'VE *UPPED* THE NUMBER AFTER ONE OF THEM GOT *MURDERED*.
HEY! *NO* WHISPERING!
WE WANT TO HEAR YOUR *LAST WORDS* LOUD AND CLEAR.
SKYNERD

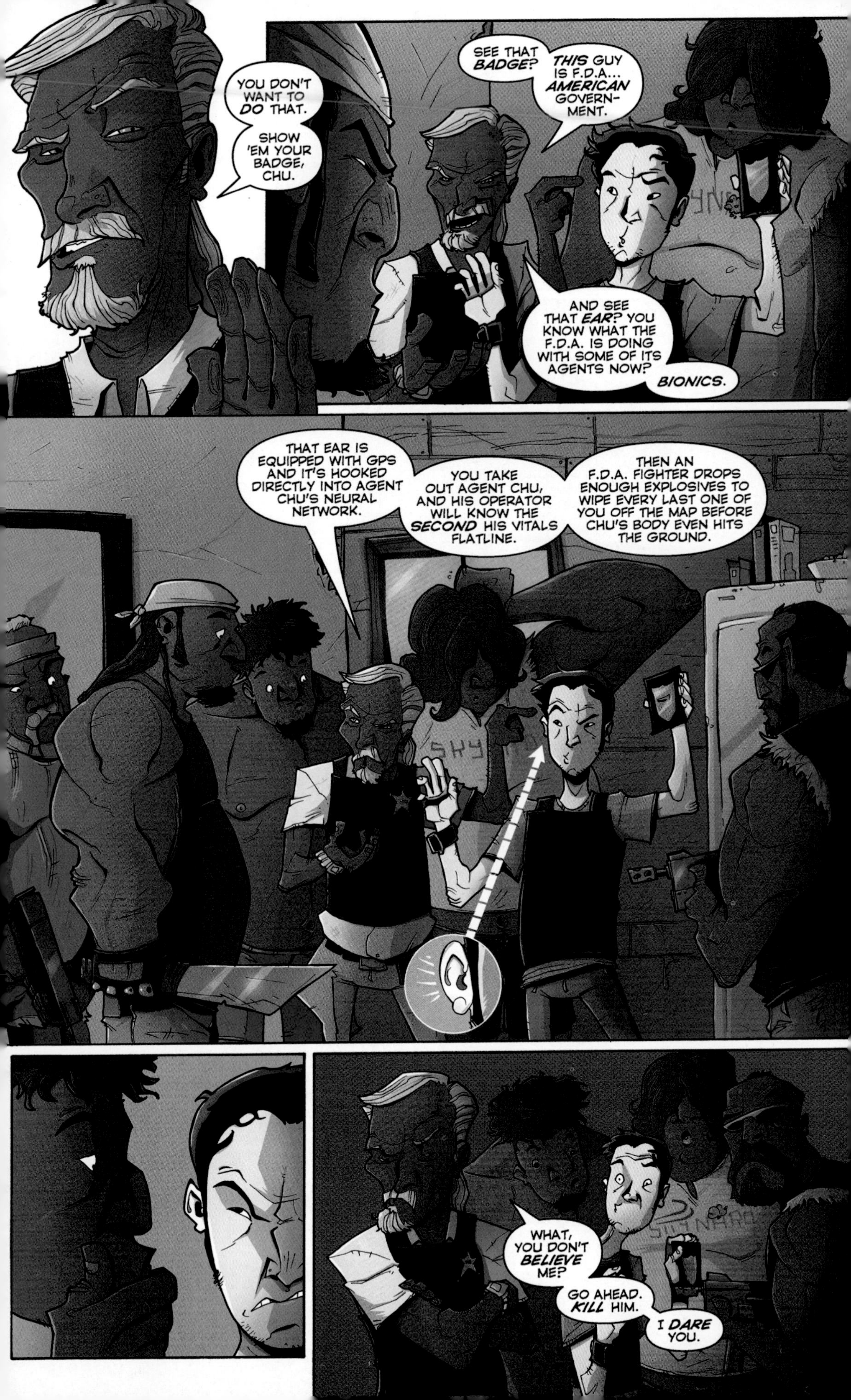
YOU DON'T WANT TO DO THAT.
SHOW 'EM YOUR BADGE, CHU.
SEE THAT BADGE?
THIS GUY IS F.D.A... AMERICAN GOVERNMENT.
AND SEE THAT EAR? YOU KNOW WHAT THE F.D.A. IS DOING WITH SOME OF ITS AGENTS NOW? BIONICS.
THAT EAR IS EQUIPPED WITH GPS AND IT'S HOOKED DIRECTLY INTO AGENT CHU'S NEURAL NETWORK.
YOU TAKE OUT AGENT CHU, AND HIS OPERATOR WILL KNOW THE SECOND HIS VITALS FLATLINE.
THEN AN F.D.A. FIGHTER DROPS ENOUGH EXPLOSIVES TO WIPE EVERY LAST ONE OF YOU OFF THE MAP BEFORE CHU'S BODY EVEN HITS THE GROUND.
WHAT, YOU DON'T BELIEVE ME?
GO AHEAD. KILL HIM.
I DARE YOU.

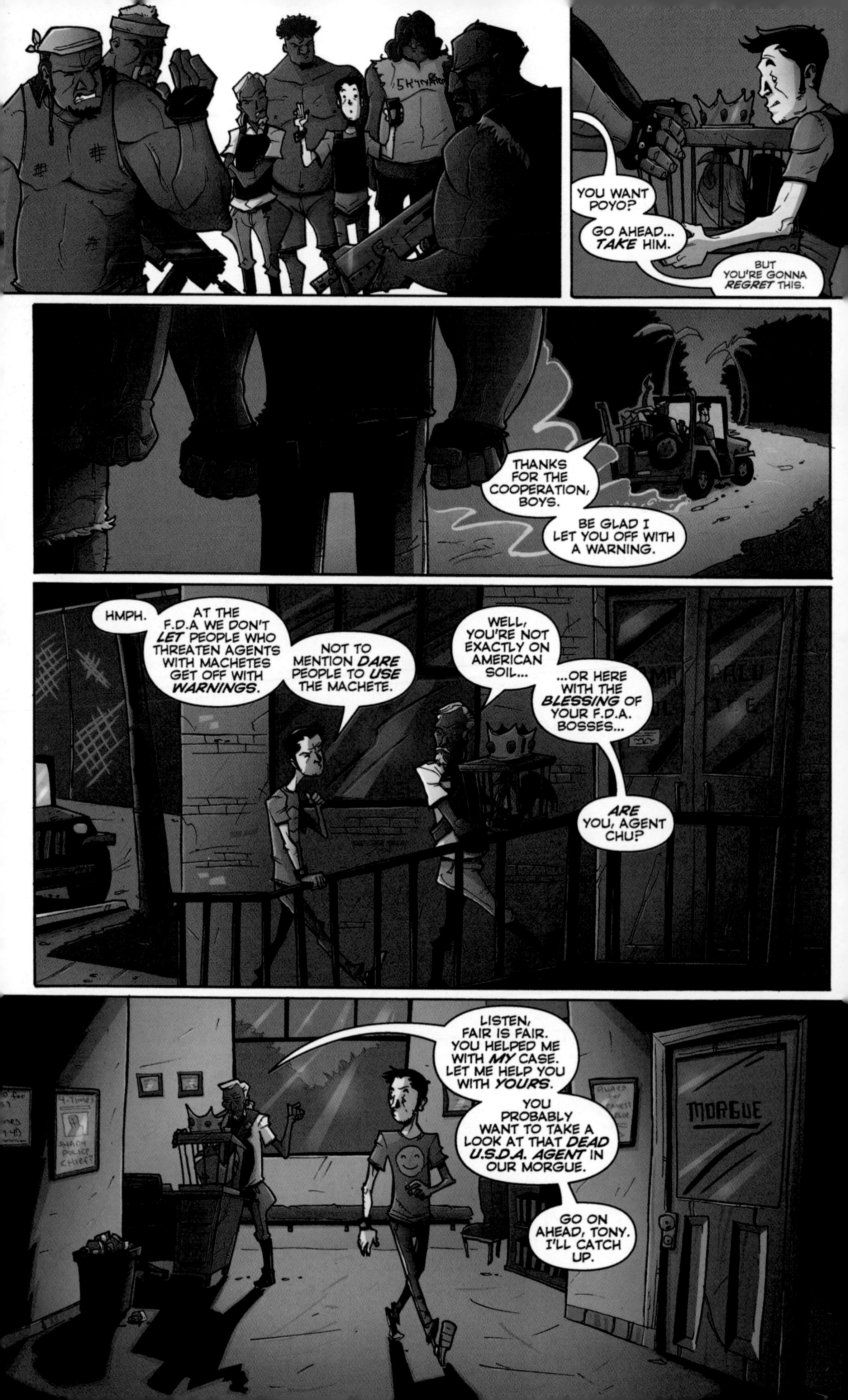
YOU WANT POYO?
GO AHEAD... TAKE HIM.
BUT YOU'RE GONNA REGRET THIS.
THANKS FOR THE COOPERATION, BOYS.
BE GLAD I LET YOU OFF WITH A WARNING.
HMPH.
AT THE F.D.A WE DON'T LET PEOPLE WHO THREATEN AGENTS WITH MACHETES GET OFF WITH WARNINGS.
NOT TO MENTION DARE PEOPLE TO USE THE MACHETE.
WELL, YOU'RE NOT EXACTLY ON AMERICAN SOIL...
...OR HERE WITH THE BLESSING OF YOUR F.D.A. BOSSES...
ARE YOU, AGENT CHU?
LISTEN, FAIR IS FAIR. YOU HELPED ME WITH MY CASE. LET ME HELP YOU WITH YOURS.
YOU PROBABLY WANT TO TAKE A LOOK AT THAT DEAD U.S.D.A. AGENT IN OUR MORGUE.
GO ON AHEAD, TONY. I'LL CATCH UP.
MORGUE

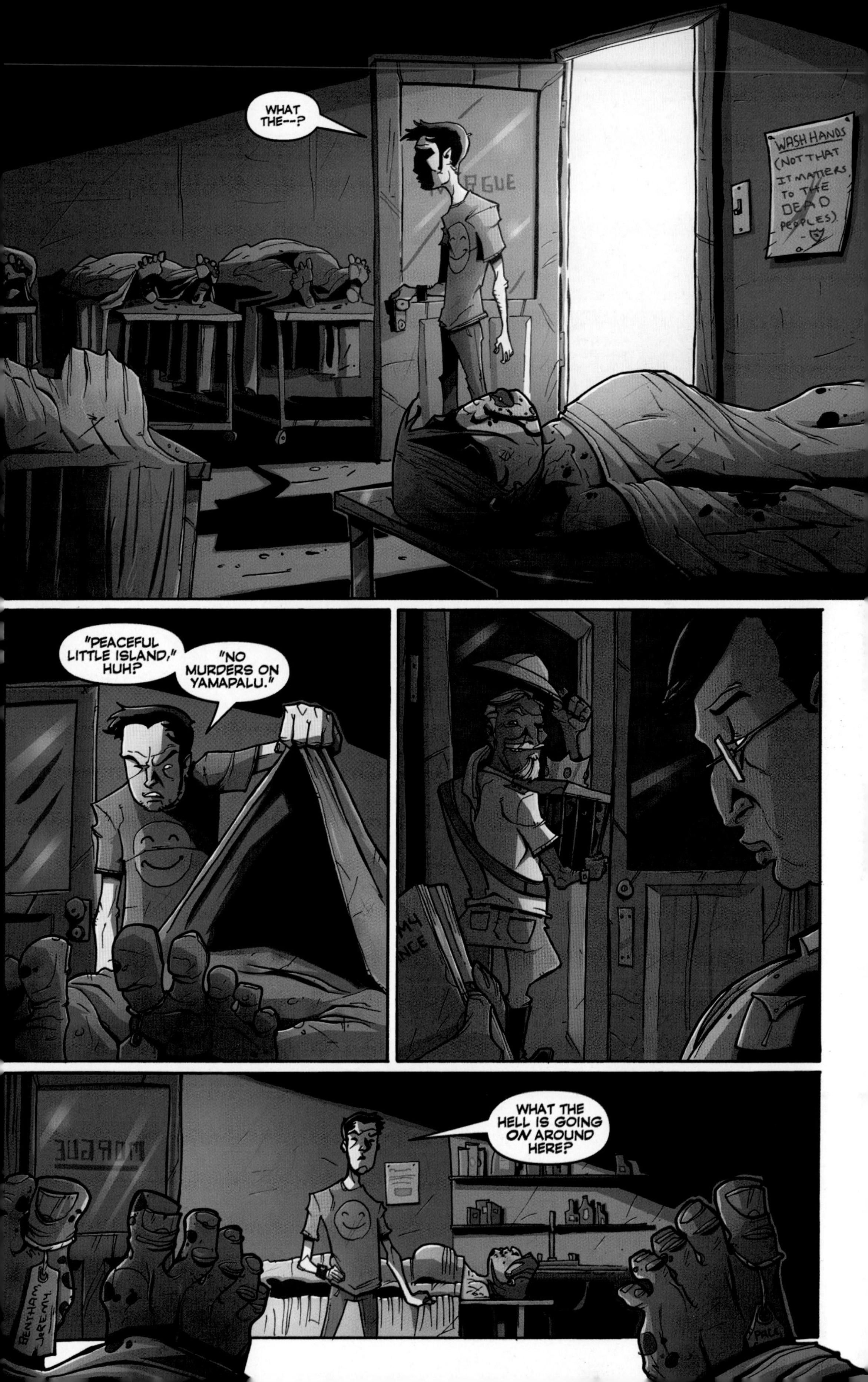

WHAT THE--?
WASH HANDS (NOT THAT IT MATTERS TO THE DEAD PEOPLES)
"PEACEFUL LITTLE ISLAND," HUH?
"NO MURDERS ON YAMAPALU."
WHAT THE HELL IS GOING ON AROUND HERE?
BENTHAM, JEREMY

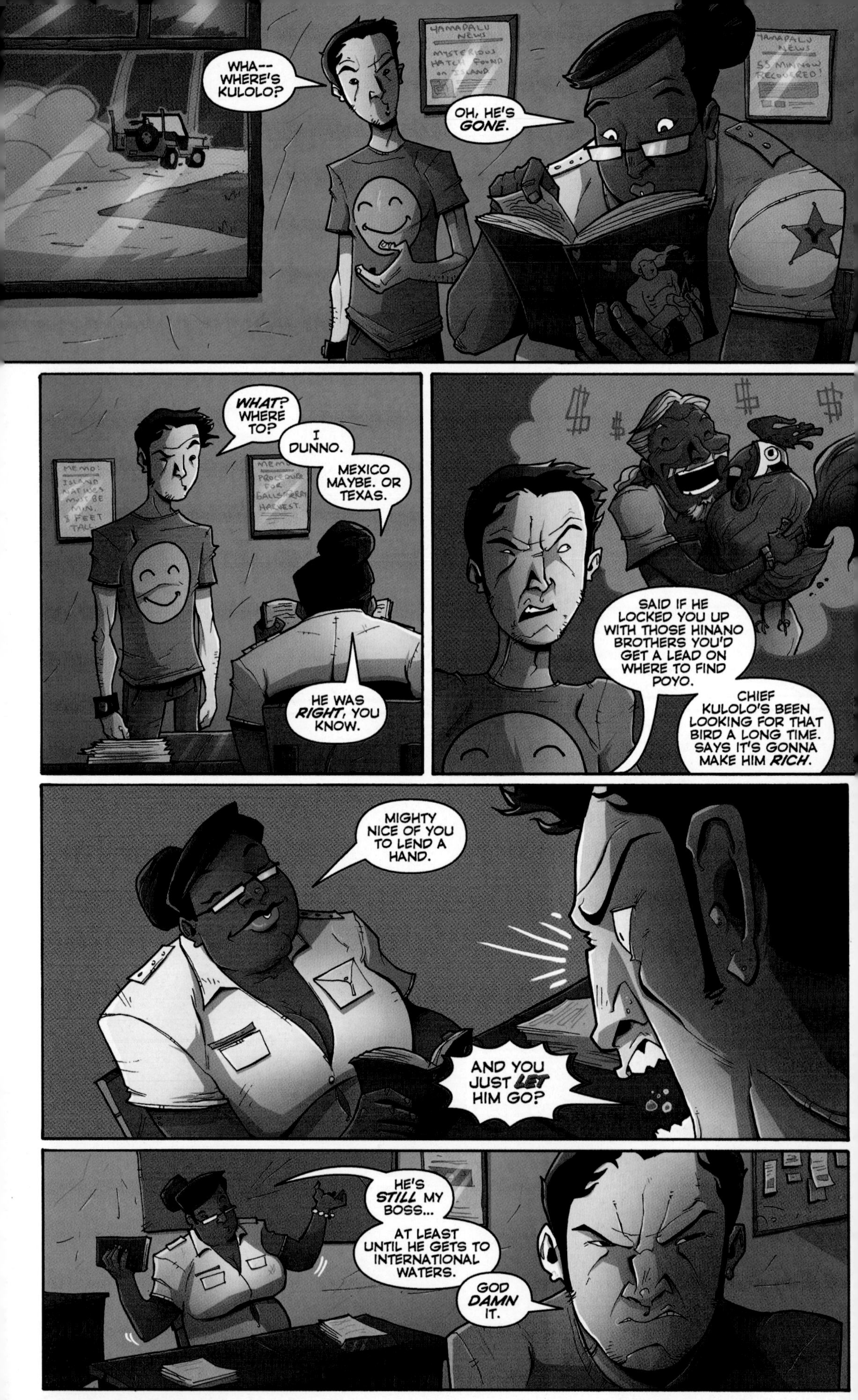

WHA-- WHERE'S KULOLO?
OH, HE'S GONE.
WHAT? WHERE TO?
I DUNNO.
MEXICO MAYBE. OR TEXAS.
HE WAS RIGHT, YOU KNOW.
SAID IF HE LOCKED YOU UP WITH THOSE HINANO BROTHERS YOU'D GET A LEAD ON WHERE TO FIND POYO.
CHIEF KULOLO'S BEEN LOOKING FOR THAT BIRD A LONG TIME. SAYS IT'S GONNA MAKE HIM RICH.
MIGHTY NICE OF YOU TO LEND A HAND.
AND YOU JUST LET HIM GO?
HE'S STILL MY BOSS...
AT LEAST UNTIL HE GETS TO INTERNATIONAL WATERS.
GOD DAMN IT.

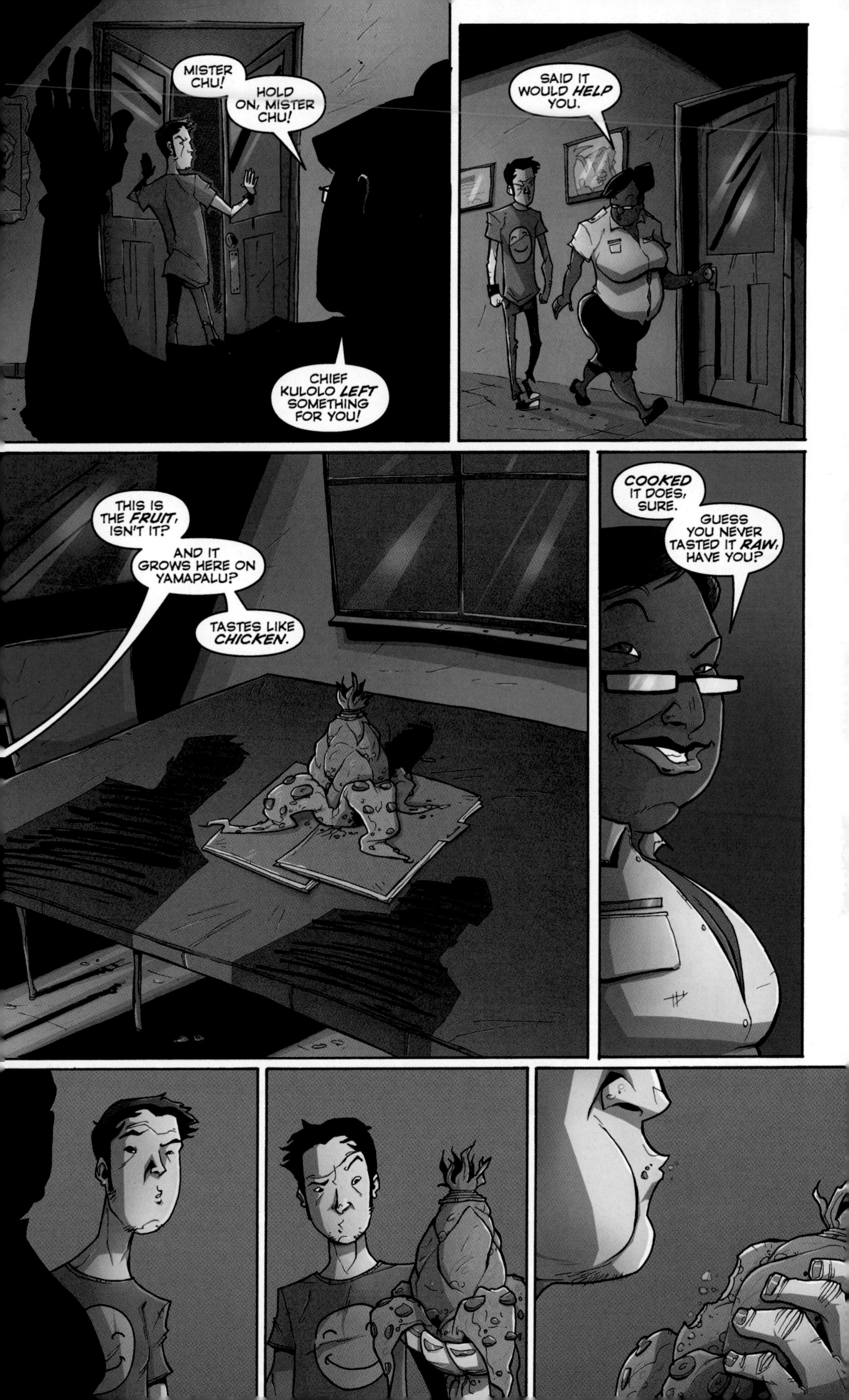
MISTER CHU!
HOLD ON, MISTER CHU!
CHIEF KULOLO LEFT SOMETHING FOR YOU!
SAID IT WOULD HELP YOU.
THIS IS THE FRUIT, ISN'T IT?
AND IT GROWS HERE ON YAMAPALU?
TASTES LIKE CHICKEN.
COOKED IT DOES, SURE.
GUESS YOU NEVER TASTED IT RAW, HAVE YOU?

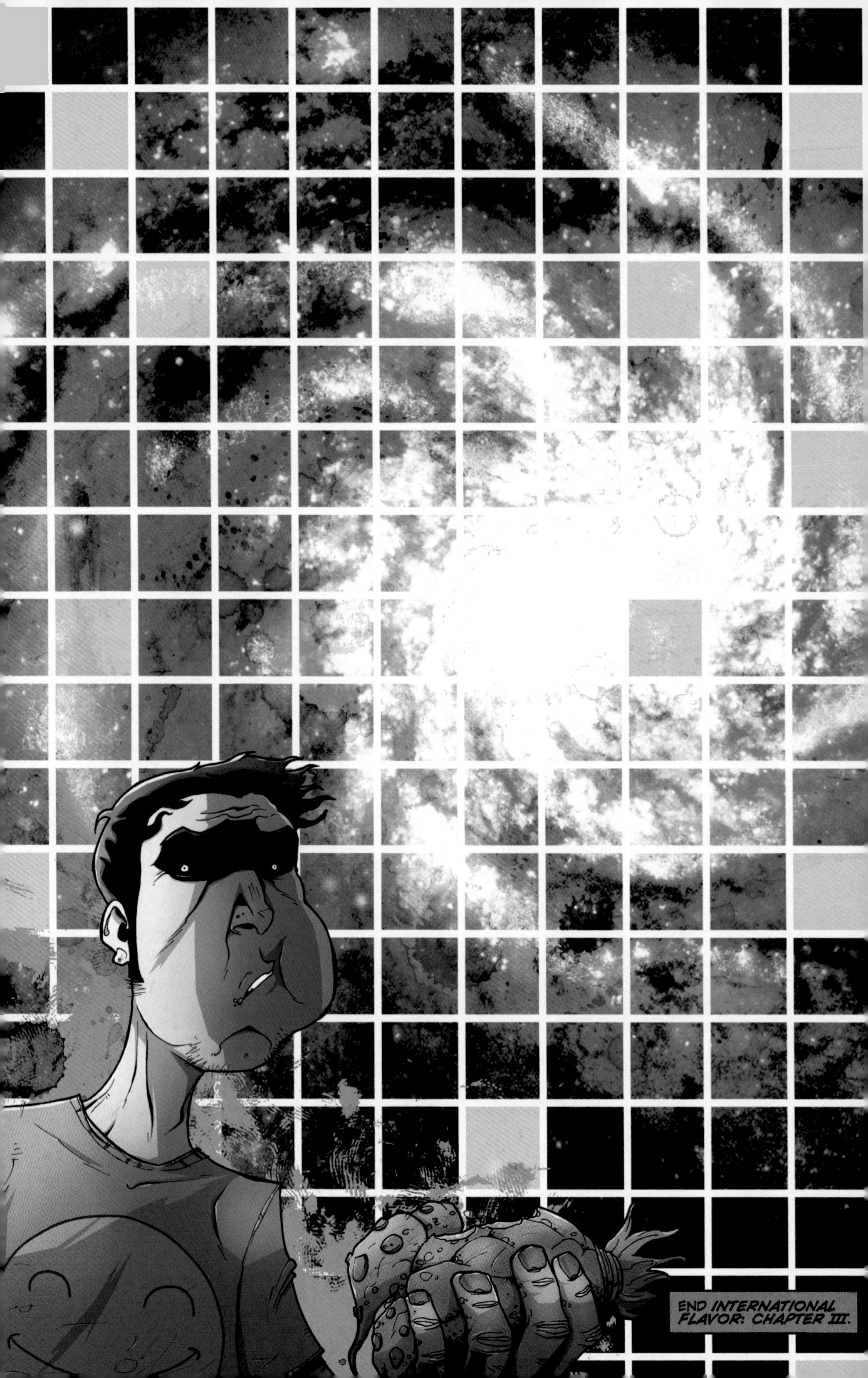
END INTERNATIONAL FLAVOR: CHAPTER III.

Chapter 4

Rob!
10/09

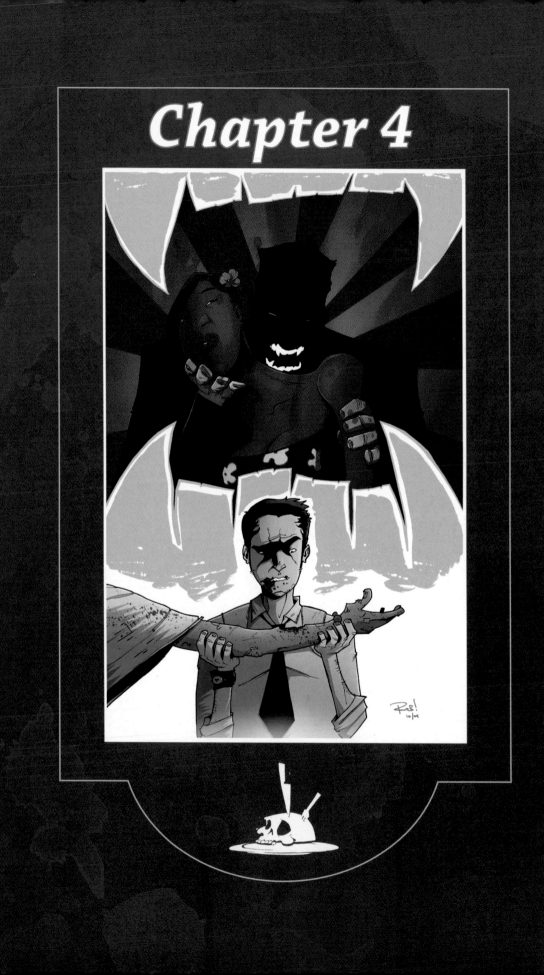

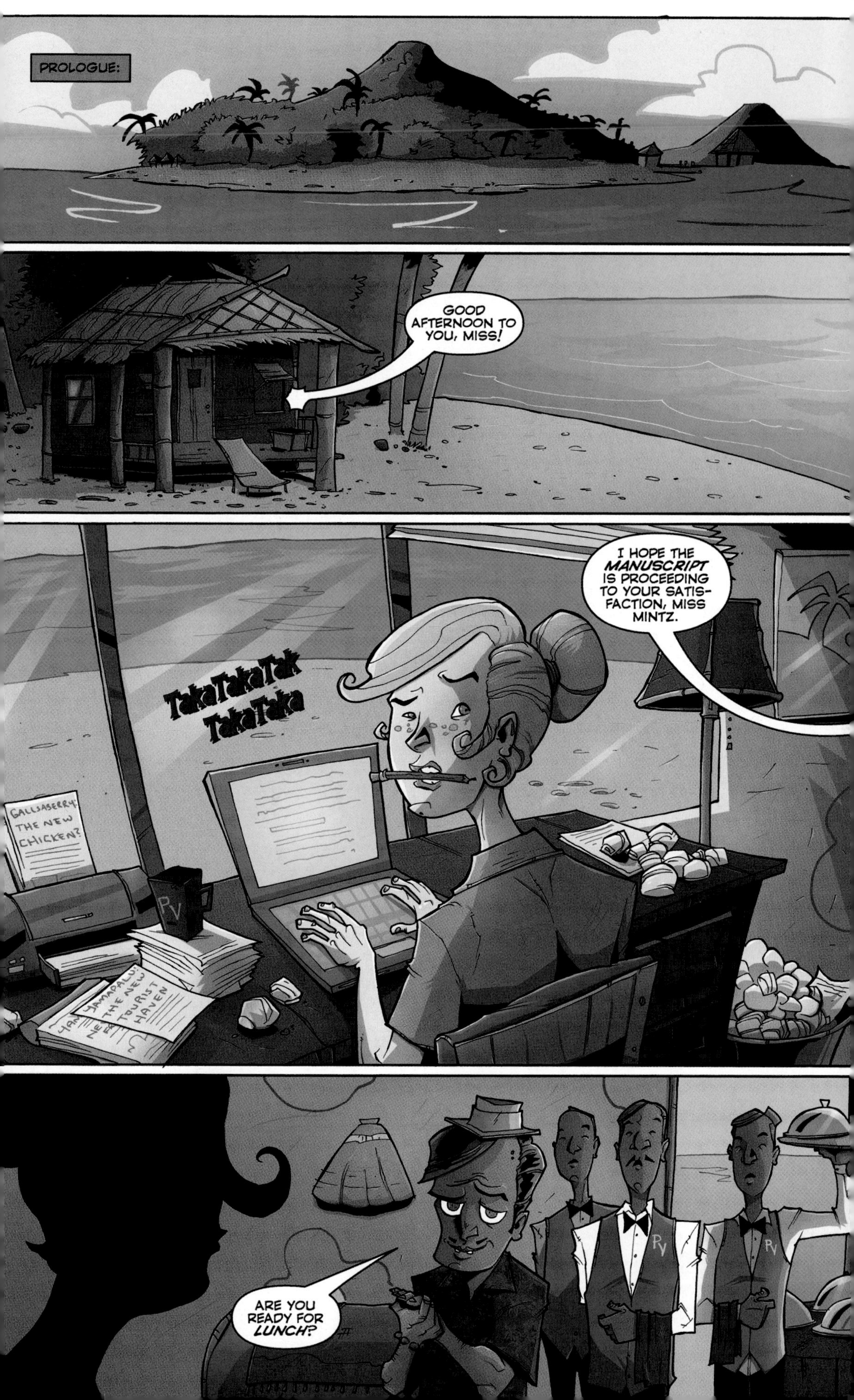
PROLOGUE:
GOOD AFTERNOON TO YOU, MISS!
TakaTakaTak TakaTaka
I HOPE THE MANUSCRIPT IS PROCEEDING TO YOUR SATIS-FACTION, MISS MINTZ.
GALLSASERRY: THE NEW CHICKEN?
PV
YAMAPALU: THE NEW TOURIST HAVEN
ARE YOU READY FOR LUNCH?

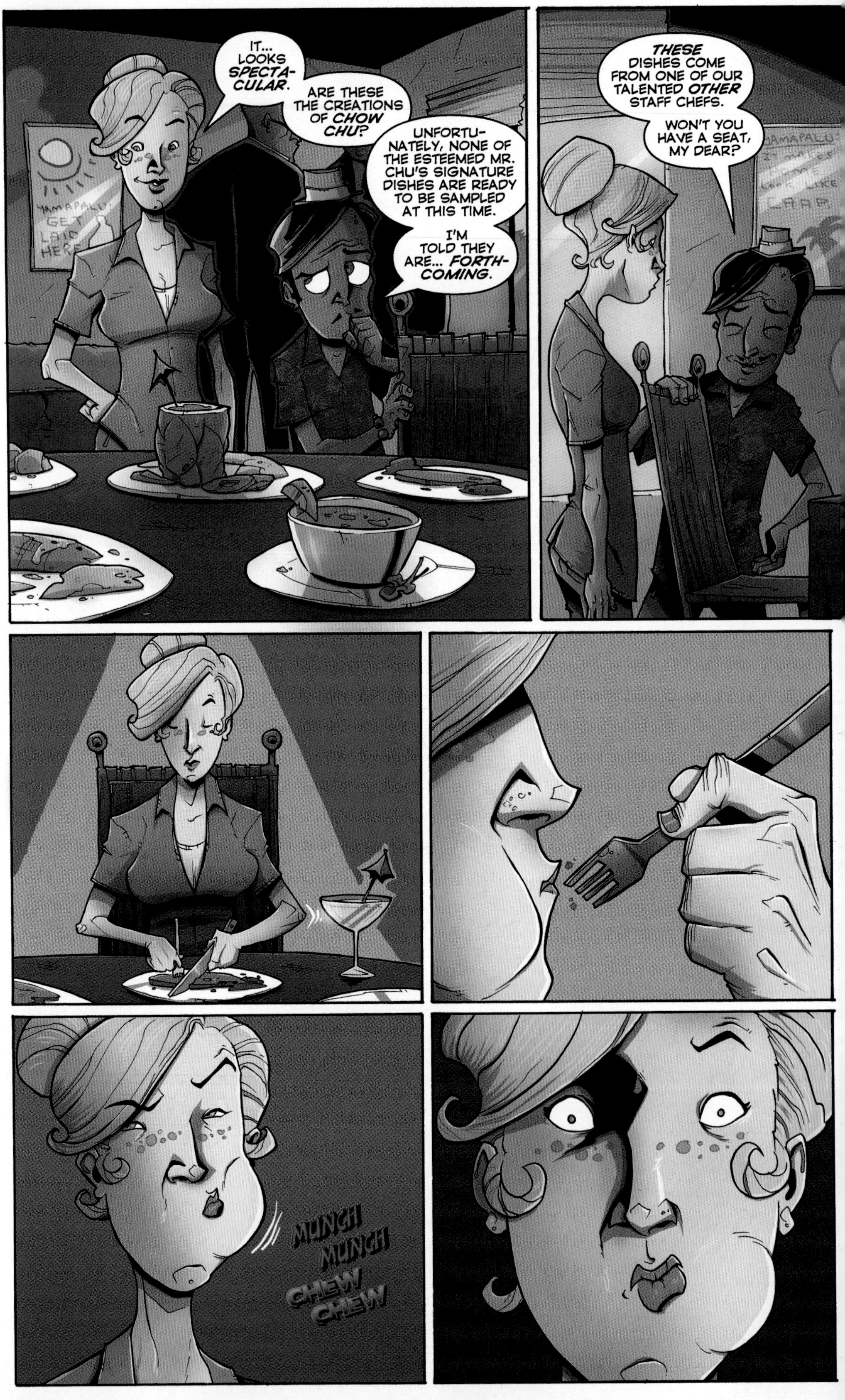

IT... LOOKS SPECTACULAR.
ARE THESE THE CREATIONS OF CHOW CHU?
YAMAPALU: GET LAID HERE
UNFORTUNATELY, NONE OF THE ESTEEMED MR. CHU'S SIGNATURE DISHES ARE READY TO BE SAMPLED AT THIS TIME.
I'M TOLD THEY ARE... FORTHCOMING.
THESE DISHES COME FROM ONE OF OUR TALENTED OTHER STAFF CHEFS.
WON'T YOU HAVE A SEAT, MY DEAR?
YAMAPALU: IT MAKES HOME LOOK LIKE CRAP.
MUNCH MUNCH
CHEW CHEW

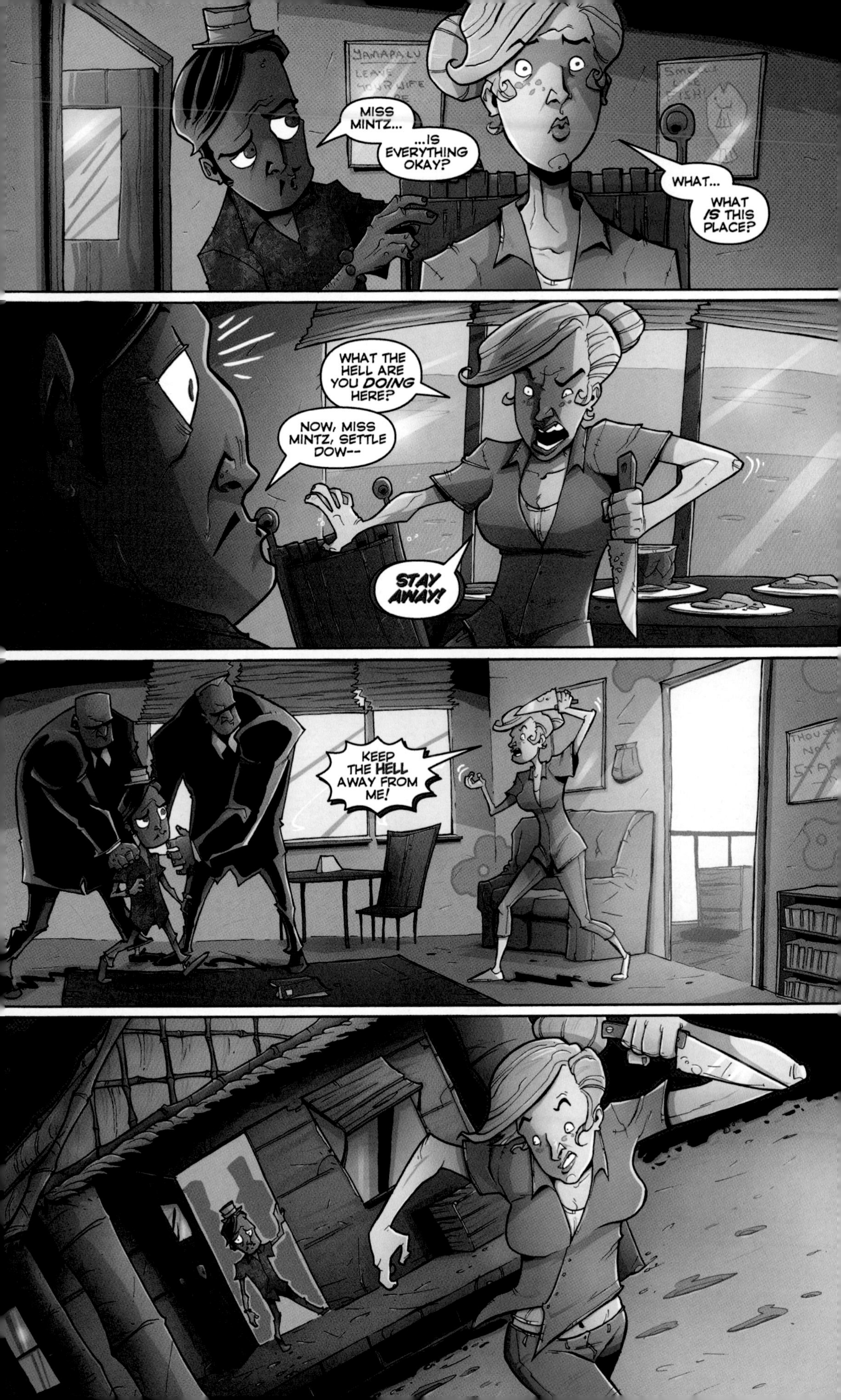

MISS MINTZ...
...IS EVERYTHING OKAY?
WHAT...
WHAT *IS* THIS PLACE?
WHAT THE HELL ARE YOU *DOING* HERE?
NOW, MISS MINTZ, SETTLE DOW--
STAY AWAY!
KEEP THE **HELL** AWAY FROM ME!

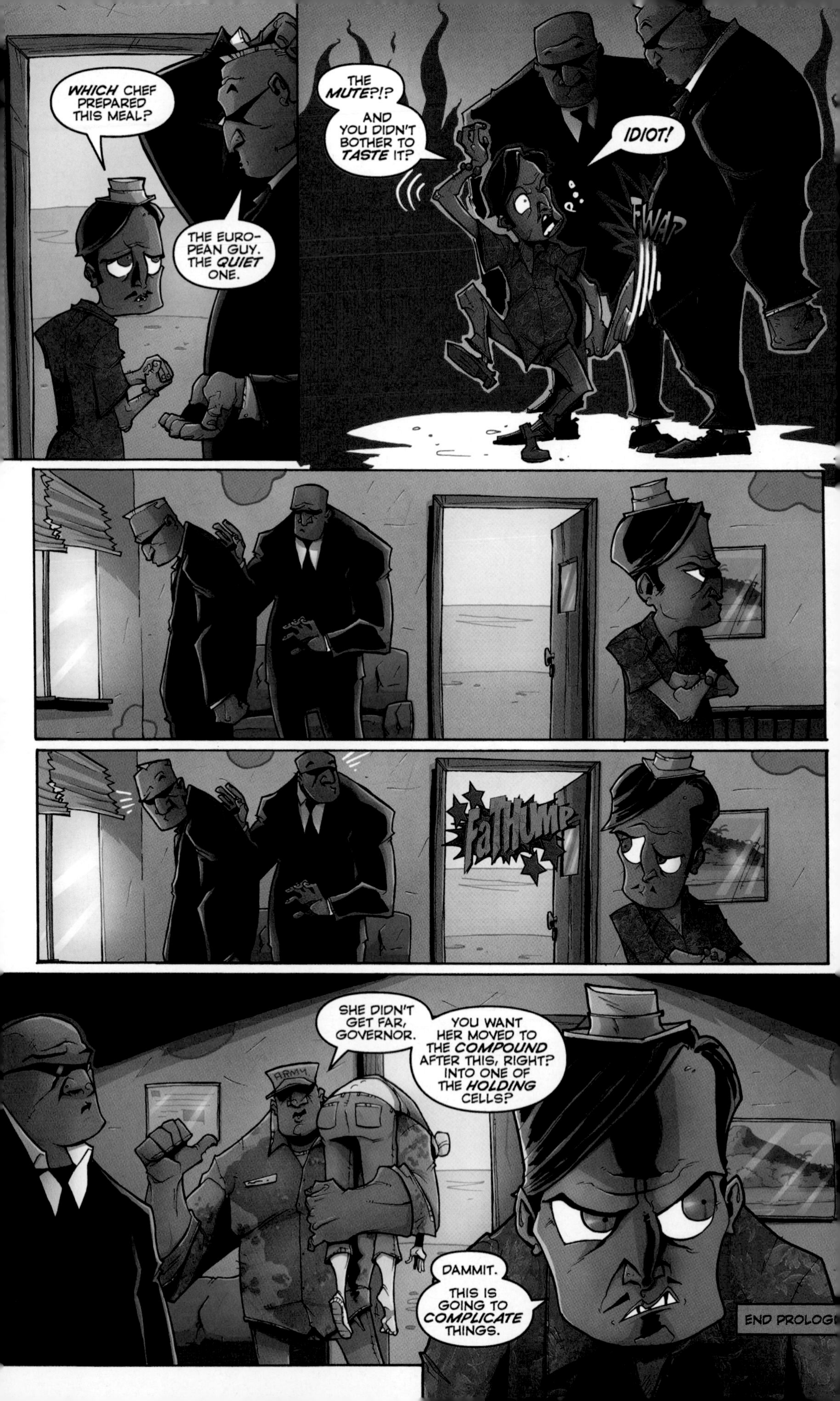
WHICH CHEF PREPARED THIS MEAL?
THE EURO-PEAN GUY. THE QUIET ONE.
THE MUTE?!? AND YOU DIDN'T BOTHER TO TASTE IT?
IDIOT!
FWAP
FaTHUMP
SHE DIDN'T GET FAR, GOVERNOR.
YOU WANT HER MOVED TO THE COMPOUND AFTER THIS, RIGHT? INTO ONE OF THE HOLDING CELLS?
ARMY
DAMMIT.
THIS IS GOING TO COMPLICATE THINGS.
END PROLOG

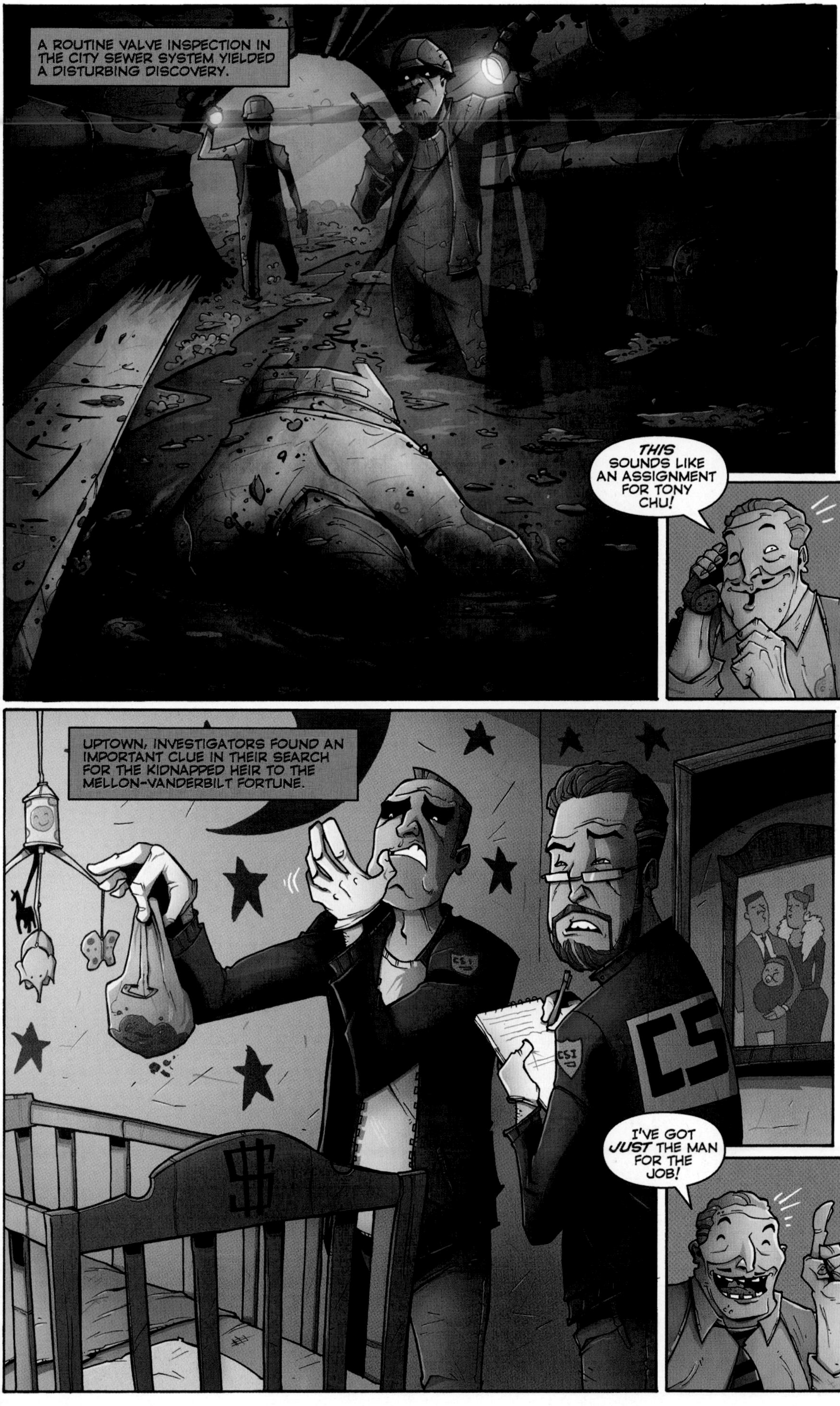

A ROUTINE VALVE INSPECTION IN THE CITY SEWER SYSTEM YIELDED A DISTURBING DISCOVERY.
THIS SOUNDS LIKE AN ASSIGNMENT FOR TONY CHU!
UPTOWN, INVESTIGATORS FOUND AN IMPORTANT CLUE IN THEIR SEARCH FOR THE KIDNAPPED HEIR TO THE MELLON-VANDERBILT FORTUNE.
I'VE GOT JUST THE MAN FOR THE JOB!

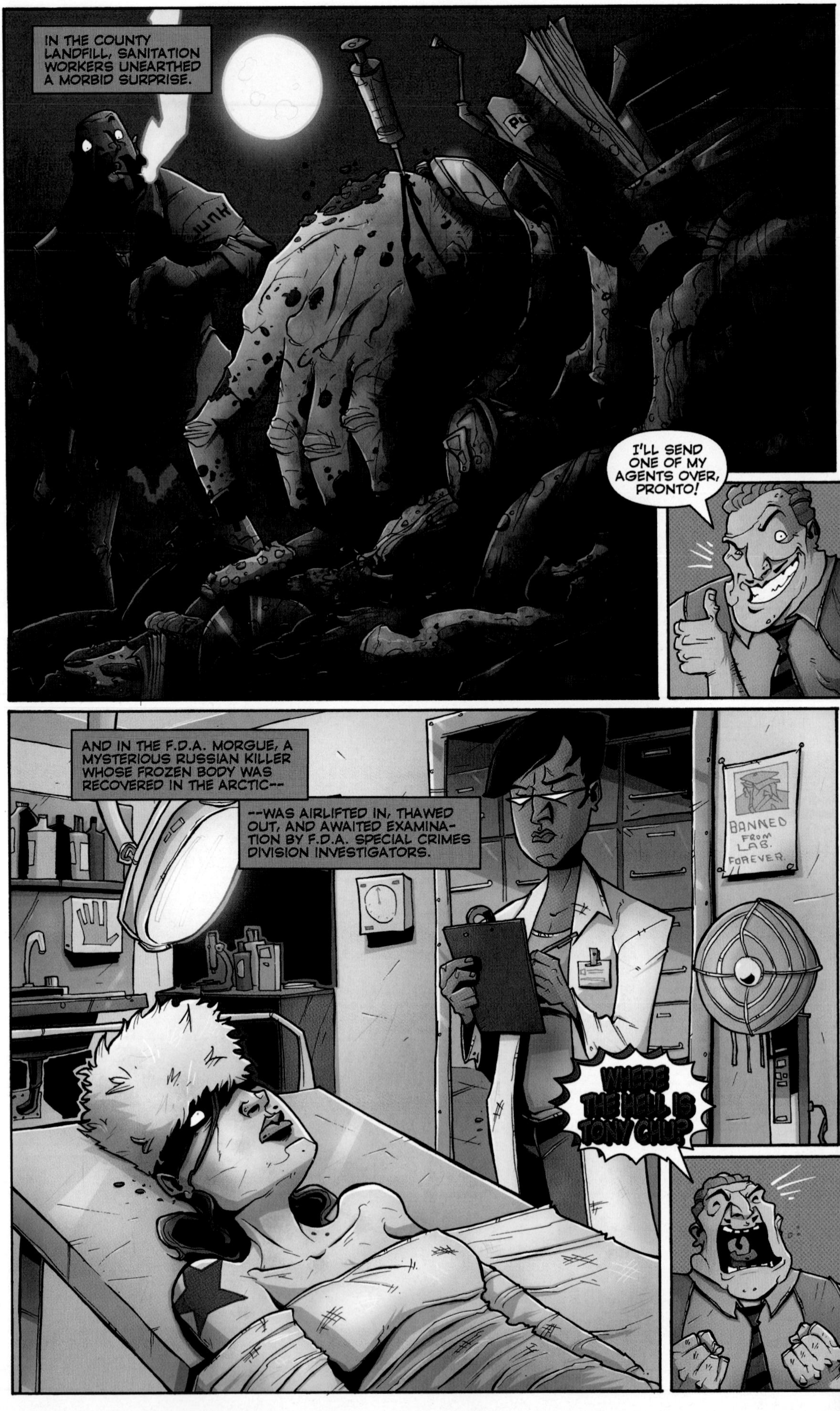
IN THE COUNTY LANDFILL, SANITATION WORKERS UNEARTHED A MORBID SURPRISE.
JUNK
I'LL SEND ONE OF MY AGENTS OVER, PRONTO!
AND IN THE F.D.A. MORGUE, A MYSTERIOUS RUSSIAN KILLER WHOSE FROZEN BODY WAS RECOVERED IN THE ARCTIC--
--WAS AIRLIFTED IN, THAWED OUT, AND AWAITED EXAMINATION BY F.D.A. SPECIAL CRIMES DIVISION INVESTIGATORS.
BANNED FROM LAB. FOREVER.
WHERE THE HELL IS TONY CHU?

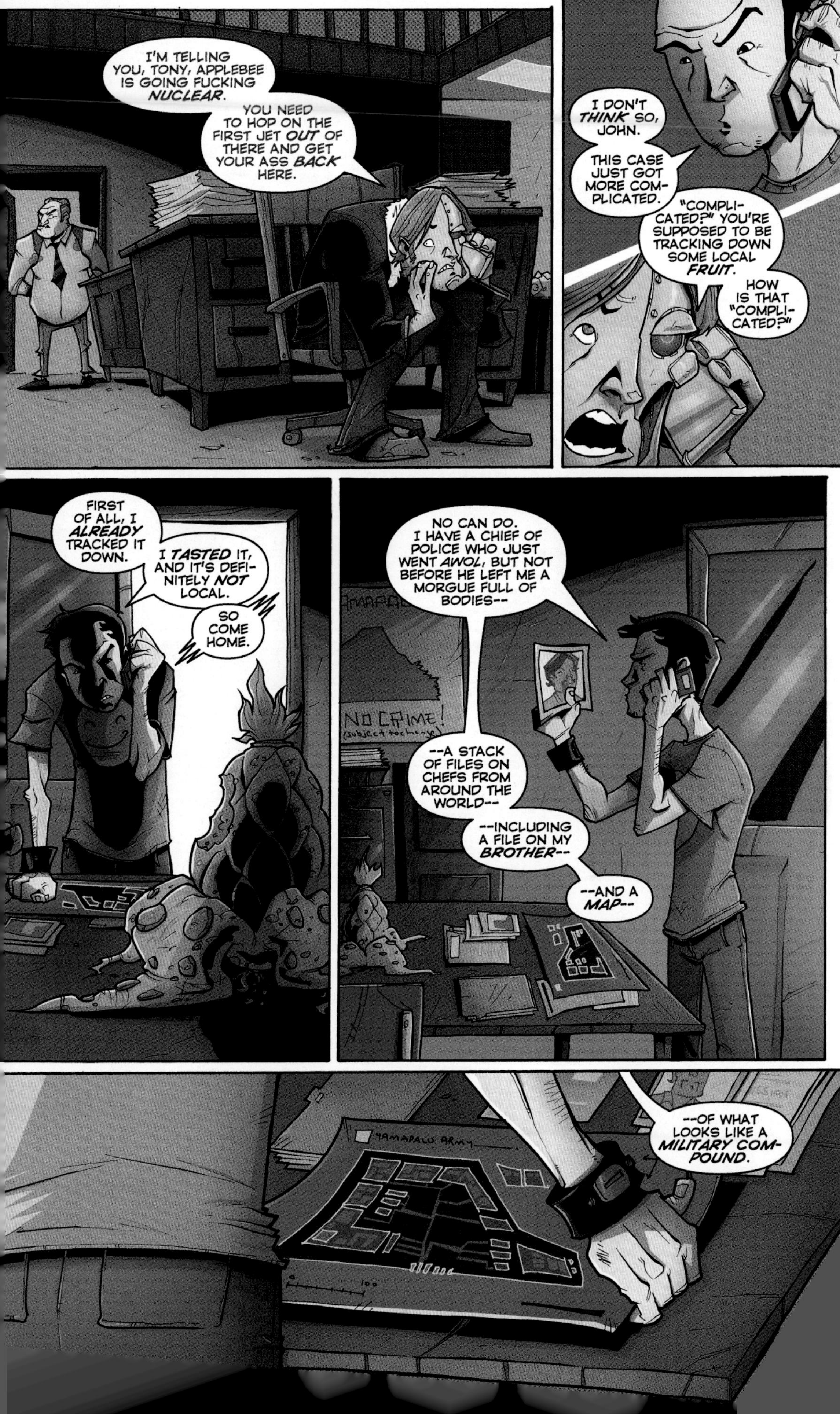
I'M TELLING YOU, TONY, APPLEBEE IS GOING FUCKING NUCLEAR.
YOU NEED TO HOP ON THE FIRST JET OUT OF THERE AND GET YOUR ASS BACK HERE.
I DON'T THINK SO, JOHN.
THIS CASE JUST GOT MORE COMPLICATED.
"COMPLICATED?" YOU'RE SUPPOSED TO BE TRACKING DOWN SOME LOCAL FRUIT.
HOW IS THAT "COMPLICATED?"
FIRST OF ALL, I ALREADY TRACKED IT DOWN.
I TASTED IT, AND IT'S DEFINITELY NOT LOCAL.
SO COME HOME.
NO CAN DO. I HAVE A CHIEF OF POLICE WHO JUST WENT AWOL, BUT NOT BEFORE HE LEFT ME A MORGUE FULL OF BODIES--
NO CRIME! (subject to change)
--A STACK OF FILES ON CHEFS FROM AROUND THE WORLD--
--INCLUDING A FILE ON MY BROTHER--
--AND A MAP--
YAMAPALU ARMY
--OF WHAT LOOKS LIKE A MILITARY COMPOUND.

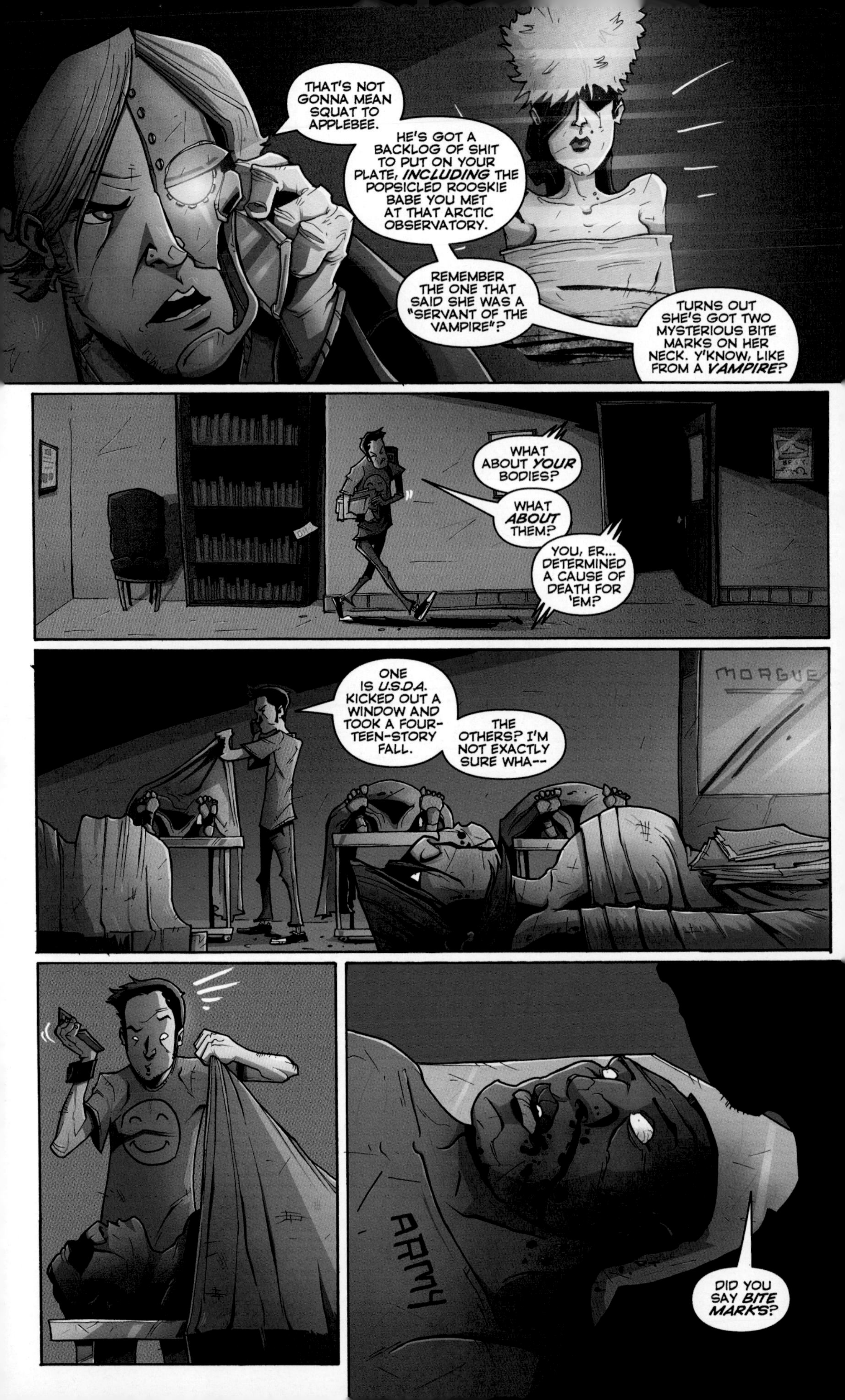
THAT'S NOT GONNA MEAN SQUAT TO APPLEBEE.
HE'S GOT A BACKLOG OF SHIT TO PUT ON YOUR PLATE, *INCLUDING* THE POPSICLED ROOSKIE BABE YOU MET AT THAT ARCTIC OBSERVATORY.
REMEMBER THE ONE THAT SAID SHE WAS A "SERVANT OF THE VAMPIRE"?
TURNS OUT SHE'S GOT TWO MYSTERIOUS BITE MARKS ON HER NECK. Y'KNOW, LIKE FROM A *VAMPIRE*?
WHAT ABOUT *YOUR* BODIES?
WHAT *ABOUT* THEM?
YOU, ER... DETERMINED A CAUSE OF DEATH FOR 'EM?
MORGUE
ONE IS *U.S.D.A.* KICKED OUT A WINDOW AND TOOK A FOURTEEN-STORY FALL.
THE OTHERS? I'M NOT EXACTLY SURE WHA--
ARMY
DID YOU SAY *BITE MARKS*?

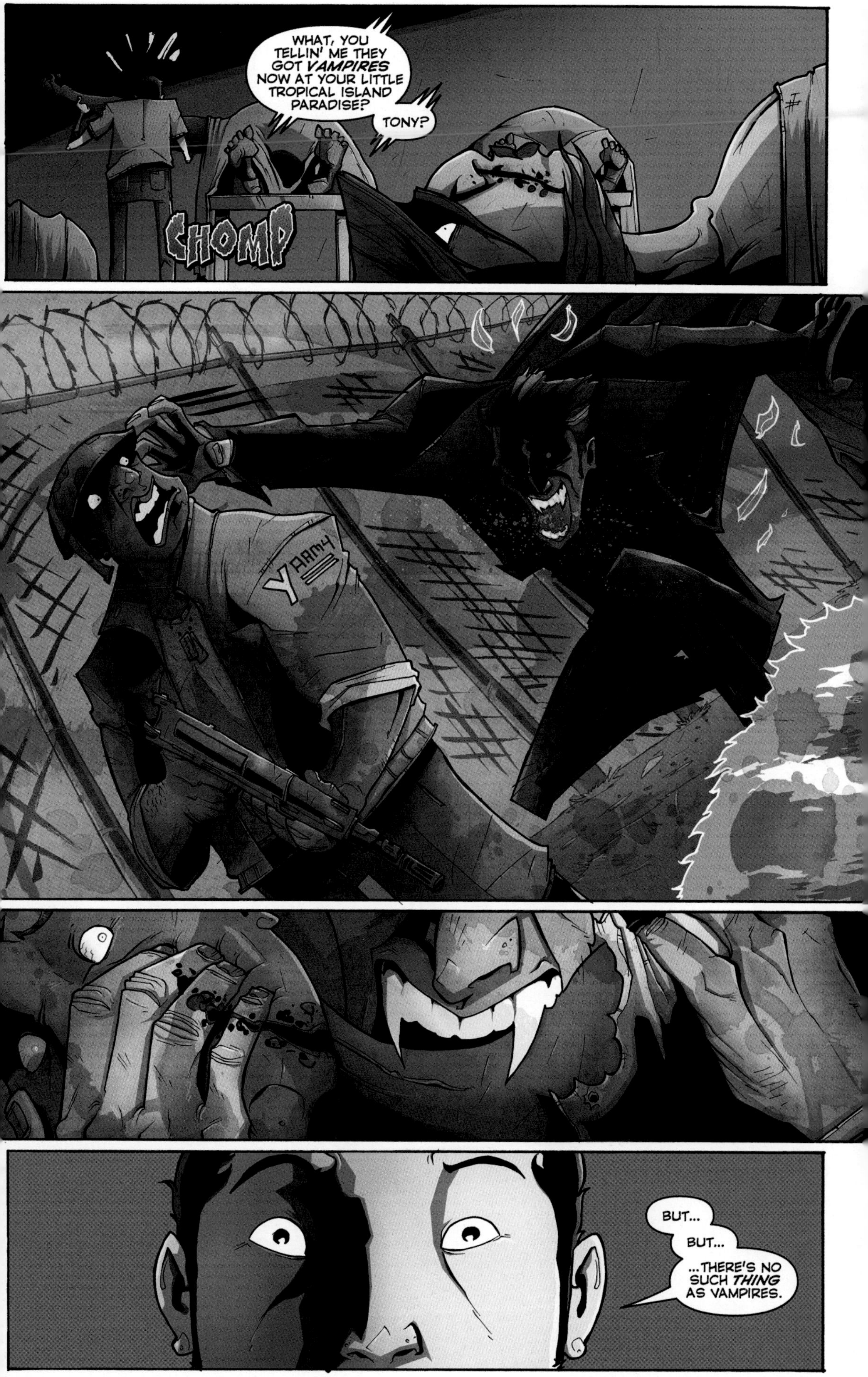
WHAT, YOU TELLIN' ME THEY GOT *VAMPIRES* NOW AT YOUR LITTLE TROPICAL ISLAND PARADISE?
TONY?
CHOMP
ARMY
BUT...
BUT...
...THERE'S NO SUCH *THING* AS VAMPIRES.

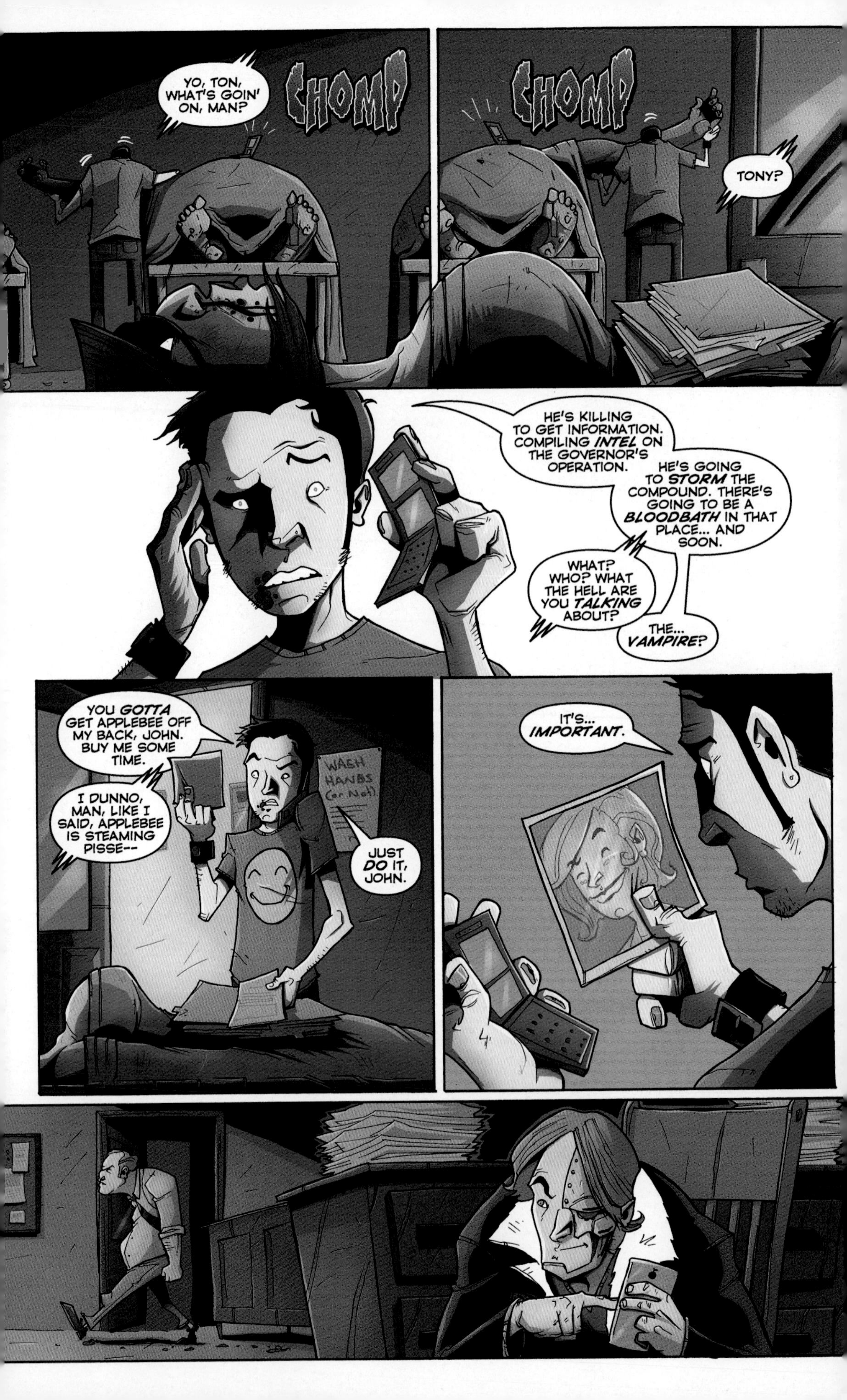
YO, TON, WHAT'S GOIN' ON, MAN?
CHOMP
CHOMP
TONY?
HE'S KILLING TO GET INFORMATION. COMPILING *INTEL* ON THE GOVERNOR'S OPERATION.
HE'S GOING TO *STORM* THE COMPOUND. THERE'S GOING TO BE A *BLOODBATH* IN THAT PLACE... AND SOON.
WHAT? WHO? WHAT THE HELL ARE YOU *TALKING* ABOUT?
THE... *VAMPIRE*?
YOU *GOTTA* GET APPLEBEE OFF MY BACK, JOHN. BUY ME SOME TIME.
I DUNNO, MAN, LIKE I SAID, APPLEBEE IS STEAMING PISSE--
WASH HANDS (or Not)
JUST *DO* IT, JOHN.
IT'S... *IMPORTANT*.

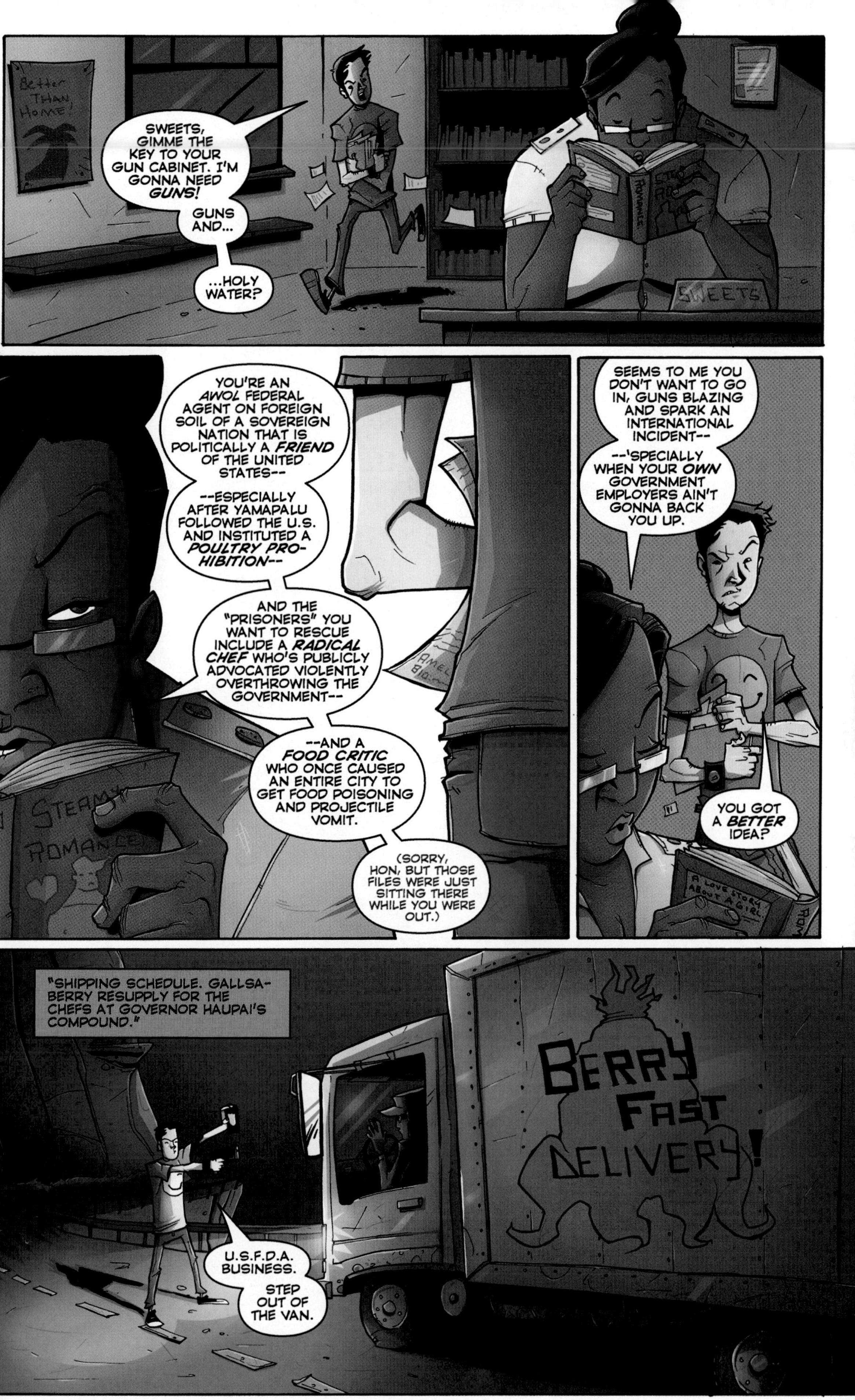
Better Than Home!
SWEETS, GIMME THE KEY TO YOUR GUN CABINET. I'M GONNA NEED GUNS!
GUNS AND...
...HOLY WATER?
SWEETS
YOU'RE AN AWOL FEDERAL AGENT ON FOREIGN SOIL OF A SOVEREIGN NATION THAT IS POLITICALLY A FRIEND OF THE UNITED STATES--
--ESPECIALLY AFTER YAMAPALU FOLLOWED THE U.S. AND INSTITUTED A POULTRY PRO-HIBITION--
AND THE "PRISONERS" YOU WANT TO RESCUE INCLUDE A RADICAL CHEF WHO'S PUBLICLY ADVOCATED VIOLENTLY OVERTHROWING THE GOVERNMENT--
--AND A FOOD CRITIC WHO ONCE CAUSED AN ENTIRE CITY TO GET FOOD POISONING AND PROJECTILE VOMIT.
(SORRY, HON, BUT THOSE FILES WERE JUST SITTING THERE WHILE YOU WERE OUT.)
STEAMY ROMANCE
SEEMS TO ME YOU DON'T WANT TO GO IN, GUNS BLAZING AND SPARK AN INTERNATIONAL INCIDENT--
--'SPECIALLY WHEN YOUR OWN GOVERNMENT EMPLOYERS AIN'T GONNA BACK YOU UP.
YOU GOT A BETTER IDEA?
A LOVE STORY ABOUT A GIRL
"SHIPPING SCHEDULE. GALLSA-BERRY RESUPPLY FOR THE CHEFS AT GOVERNOR HAUPAI'S COMPOUND."
BERRY FAST DELIVERY!
U.S.F.D.A. BUSINESS.
STEP OUT OF THE VAN.

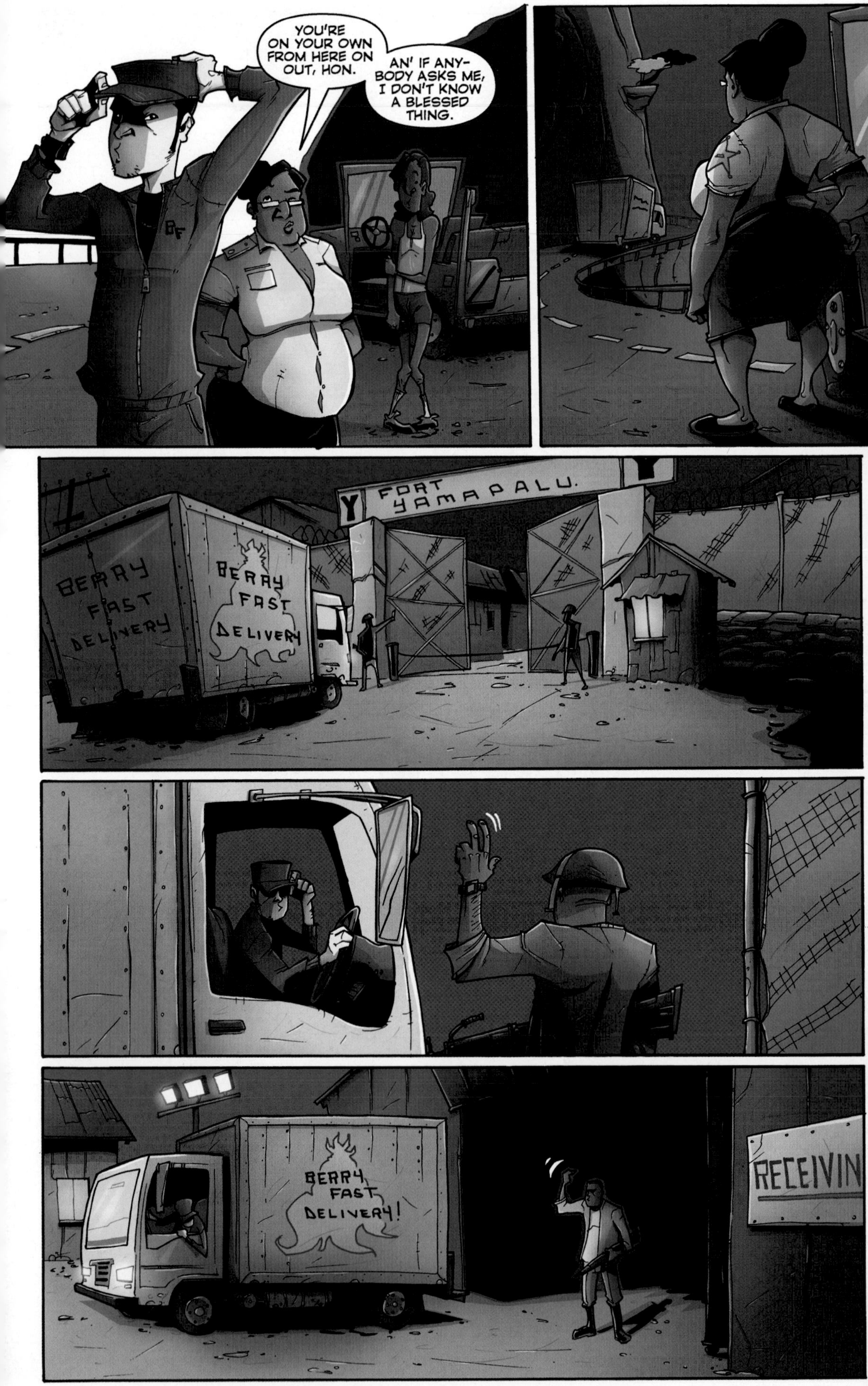
YOU'RE ON YOUR OWN FROM HERE ON OUT, HON.
AN' IF ANYBODY ASKS ME, I DON'T KNOW A BLESSED THING.
FORT YAMAPALU.
BERRY FAST DELIVERY
BERRY FAST DELIVERY
BERRY FAST DELIVERY!
RECEIVIN

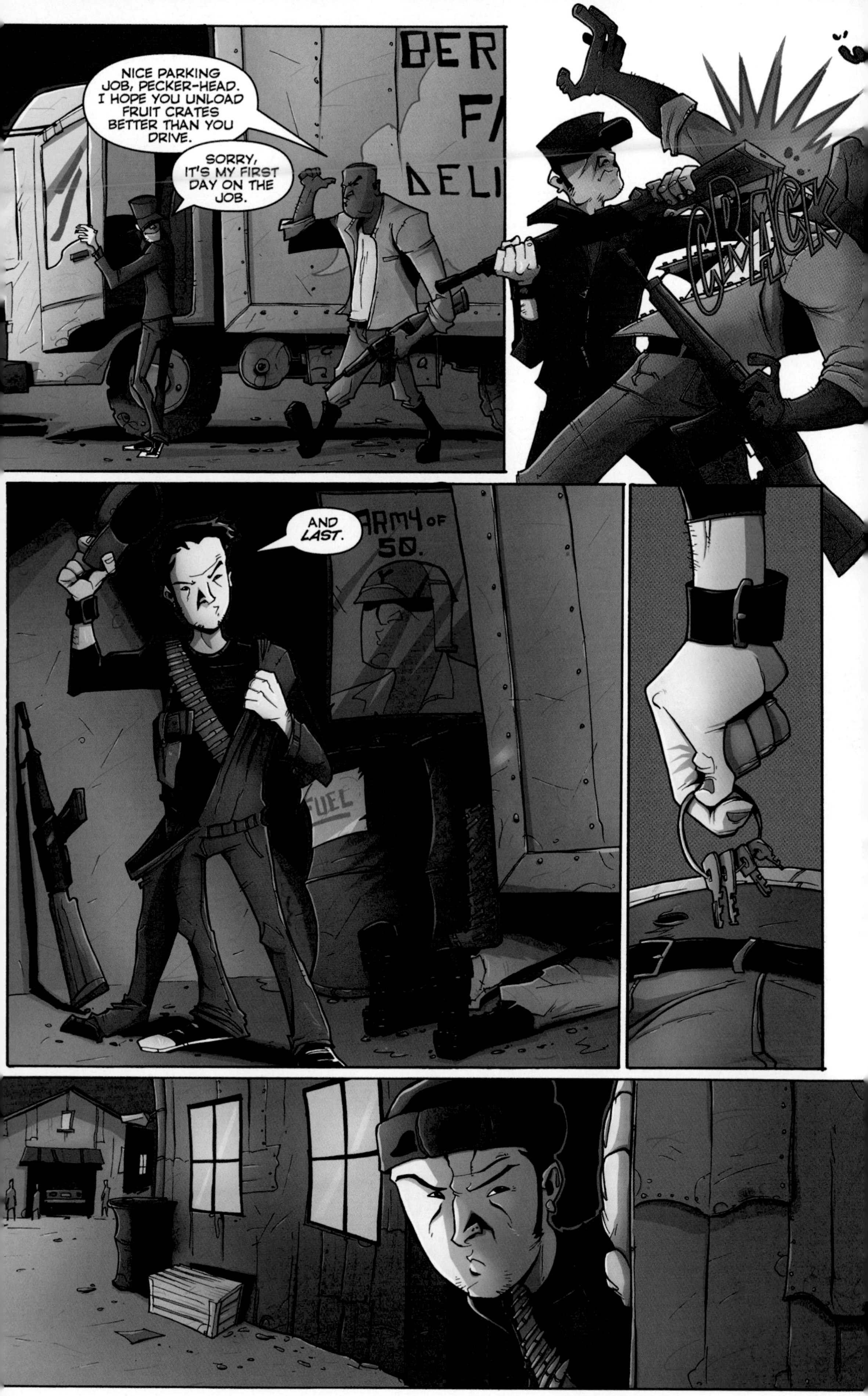

BER
F
DELI
NICE PARKING JOB, PECKER-HEAD. I HOPE YOU UNLOAD FRUIT CRATES BETTER THAN YOU DRIVE.
SORRY, IT'S MY FIRST DAY ON THE JOB.
CRACK
AND *LAST*.
ARMY OF 50.
FUEL

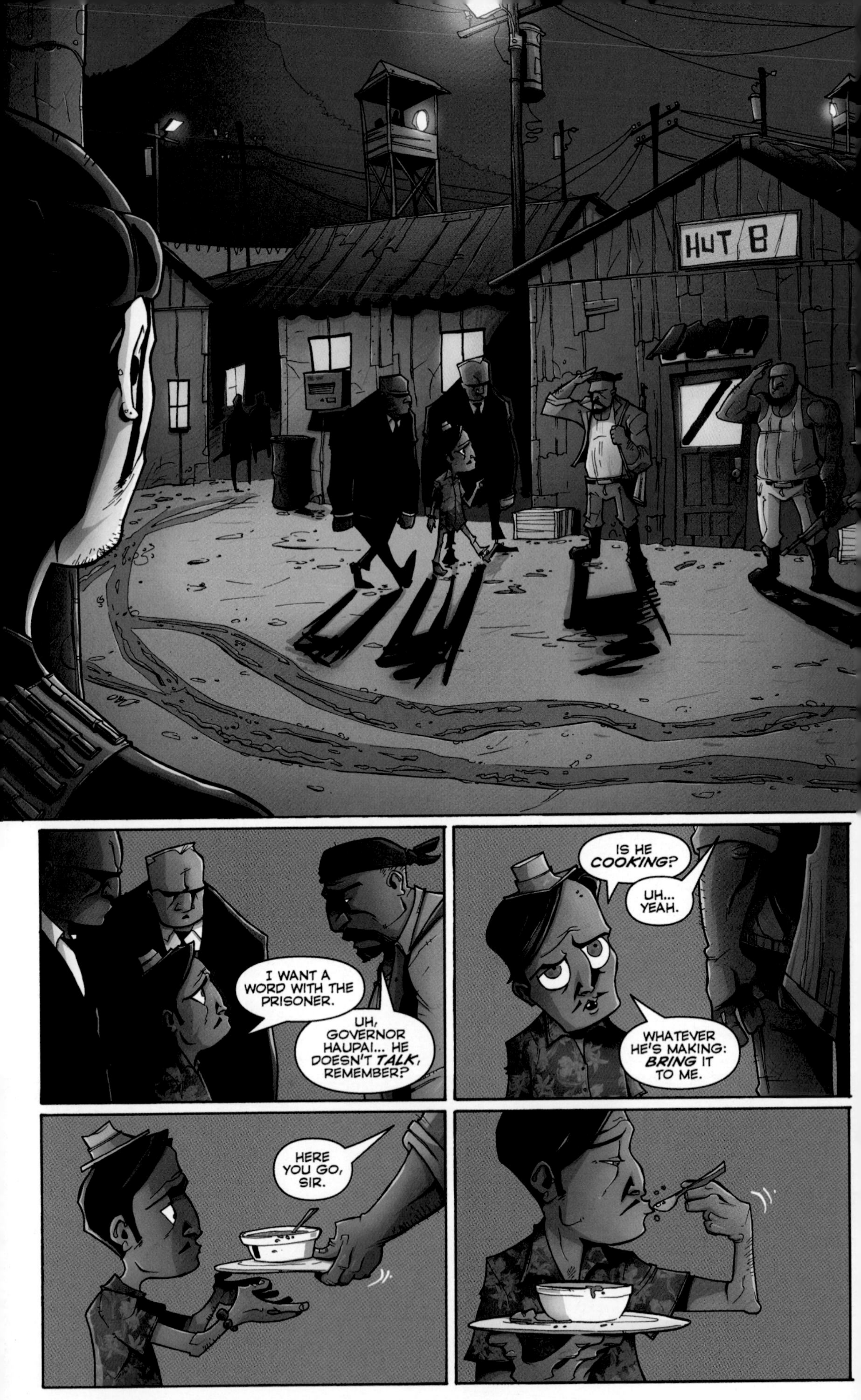
HUT B
I WANT A WORD WITH THE PRISONER.
UH, GOVERNOR HAUPAI... HE DOESN'T *TALK*, REMEMBER?
IS HE *COOKING*?
UH... YEAH.
WHATEVER HE'S MAKING: *BRING* IT TO ME.
HERE YOU GO, SIR.

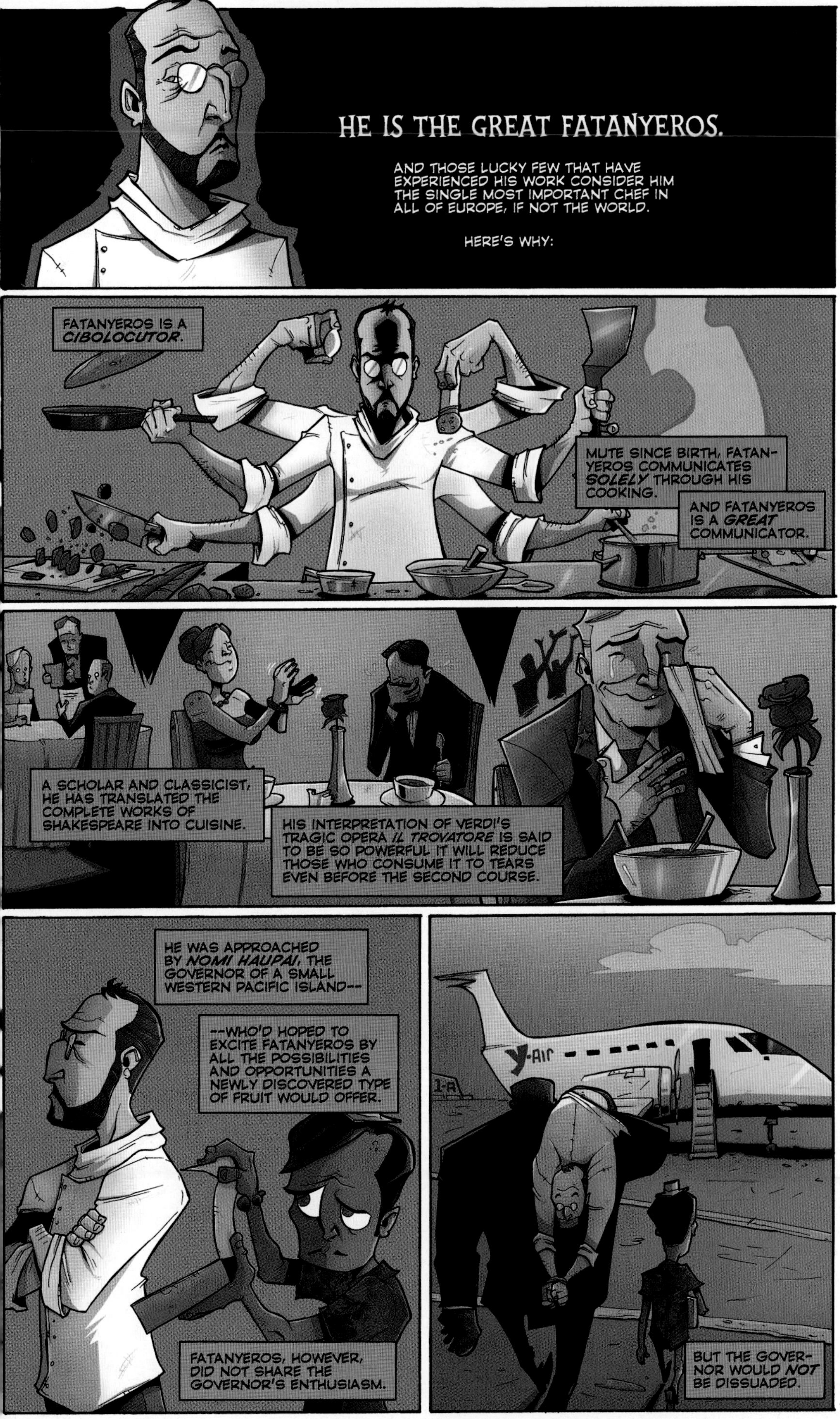

HE IS THE GREAT FATANYEROS.
AND THOSE LUCKY FEW THAT HAVE EXPERIENCED HIS WORK CONSIDER HIM THE SINGLE MOST IMPORTANT CHEF IN ALL OF EUROPE, IF NOT THE WORLD.
HERE'S WHY:
FATANYEROS IS A *CIBOLOCUTOR*.
MUTE SINCE BIRTH, FATANYEROS COMMUNICATES *SOLELY* THROUGH HIS COOKING.
AND FATANYEROS IS A *GREAT* COMMUNICATOR.
A SCHOLAR AND CLASSICIST, HE HAS TRANSLATED THE COMPLETE WORKS OF SHAKESPEARE INTO CUISINE.
HIS INTERPRETATION OF VERDI'S TRAGIC OPERA *IL TROVATORE* IS SAID TO BE SO POWERFUL IT WILL REDUCE THOSE WHO CONSUME IT TO TEARS EVEN BEFORE THE SECOND COURSE.
HE WAS APPROACHED BY *NOMI HAUPAI*, THE GOVERNOR OF A SMALL WESTERN PACIFIC ISLAND--
--WHO'D HOPED TO EXCITE FATANYEROS BY ALL THE POSSIBILITIES AND OPPORTUNITIES A NEWLY DISCOVERED TYPE OF FRUIT WOULD OFFER.
FATANYEROS, HOWEVER, DID NOT SHARE THE GOVERNOR'S ENTHUSIASM.
Y-AIR
BUT THE GOVERNOR WOULD *NOT* BE DISSUADED.

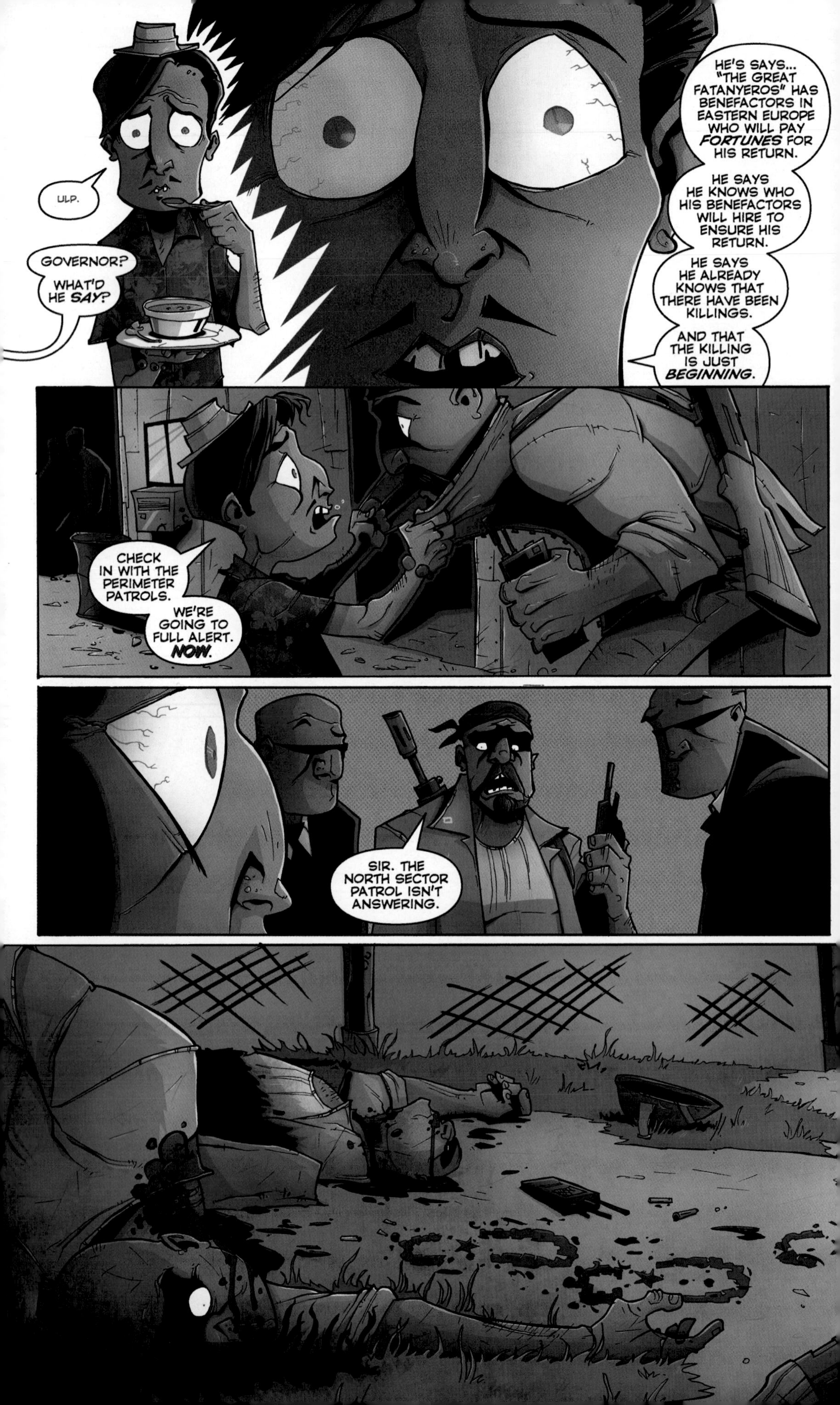

ULP.
GOVERNOR? WHAT'D HE SAY?
HE'S SAYS... "THE GREAT FATANYEROS" HAS BENEFACTORS IN EASTERN EUROPE WHO WILL PAY FORTUNES FOR HIS RETURN.
HE SAYS HE KNOWS WHO HIS BENEFACTORS WILL HIRE TO ENSURE HIS RETURN.
HE SAYS HE ALREADY KNOWS THAT THERE HAVE BEEN KILLINGS.
AND THAT THE KILLING IS JUST BEGINNING.
CHECK IN WITH THE PERIMETER PATROLS.
WE'RE GOING TO FULL ALERT. NOW.
SIR. THE NORTH SECTOR PATROL ISN'T ANSWERING.

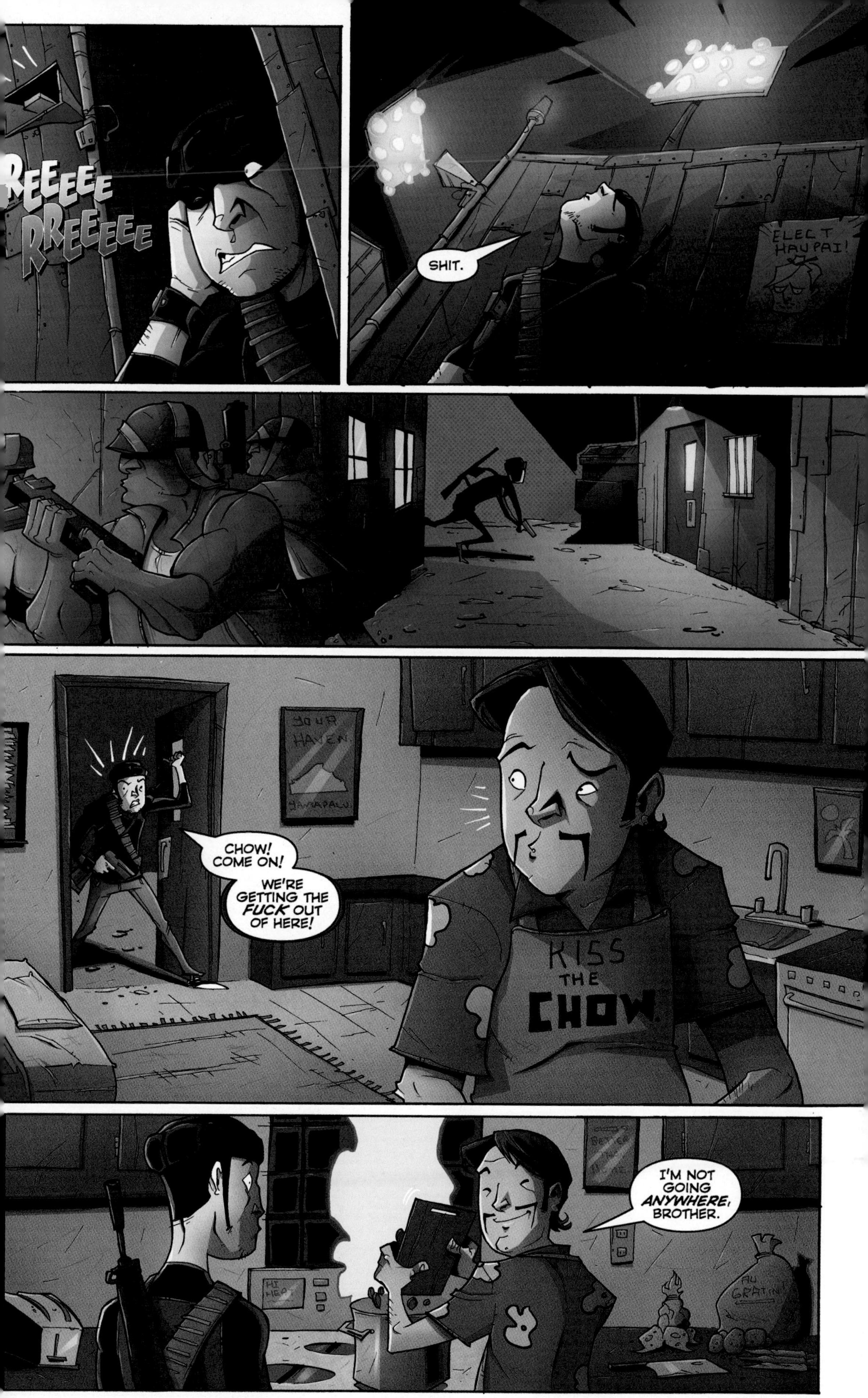
REEEEE
RREEEEEE
SHIT.
ELECT HAUPAI!
YOUR HAVEN.
CHOW! COME ON!
WE'RE GETTING THE FUCK OUT OF HERE!
KISS THE CHOW.
I'M NOT GOING ANYWHERE, BROTHER.
HI HEAT
AU GRATIN

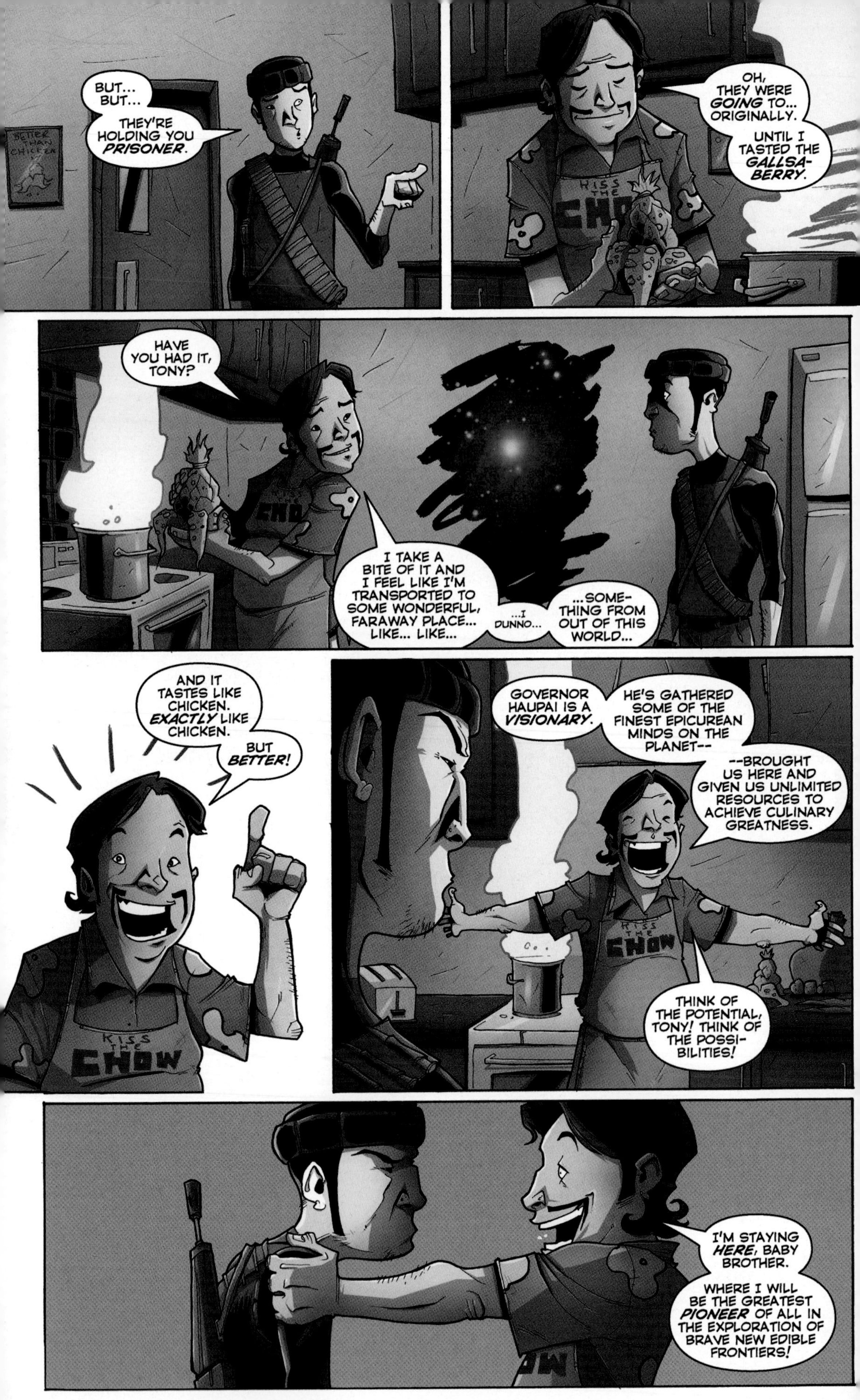
BETTER THAN CHICKEN
BUT... BUT...
THEY'RE HOLDING YOU *PRISONER*.
OH, THEY WERE *GOING* TO... ORIGINALLY.
UNTIL I TASTED THE *GALLSA-BERRY*.
KISS THE CHOW
HAVE YOU HAD IT, TONY?
I TAKE A BITE OF IT AND I FEEL LIKE I'M TRANSPORTED TO SOME WONDERFUL, FARAWAY PLACE... LIKE... LIKE...
...I DUNNO...
...SOME-THING FROM OUT OF THIS WORLD...
AND IT TASTES LIKE CHICKEN. *EXACTLY* LIKE CHICKEN.
BUT *BETTER!*
KISS THE CHOW
GOVERNOR HAUPAI IS A *VISIONARY*.
HE'S GATHERED SOME OF THE FINEST EPICUREAN MINDS ON THE PLANET--
--BROUGHT US HERE AND GIVEN US UNLIMITED RESOURCES TO ACHIEVE CULINARY GREATNESS.
THINK OF THE POTENTIAL, TONY! THINK OF THE POSSI-BILITIES!
I'M STAYING *HERE*, BABY BROTHER.
WHERE I WILL BE THE GREATEST *PIONEER* OF ALL IN THE EXPLORATION OF BRAVE NEW EDIBLE FRONTIERS!

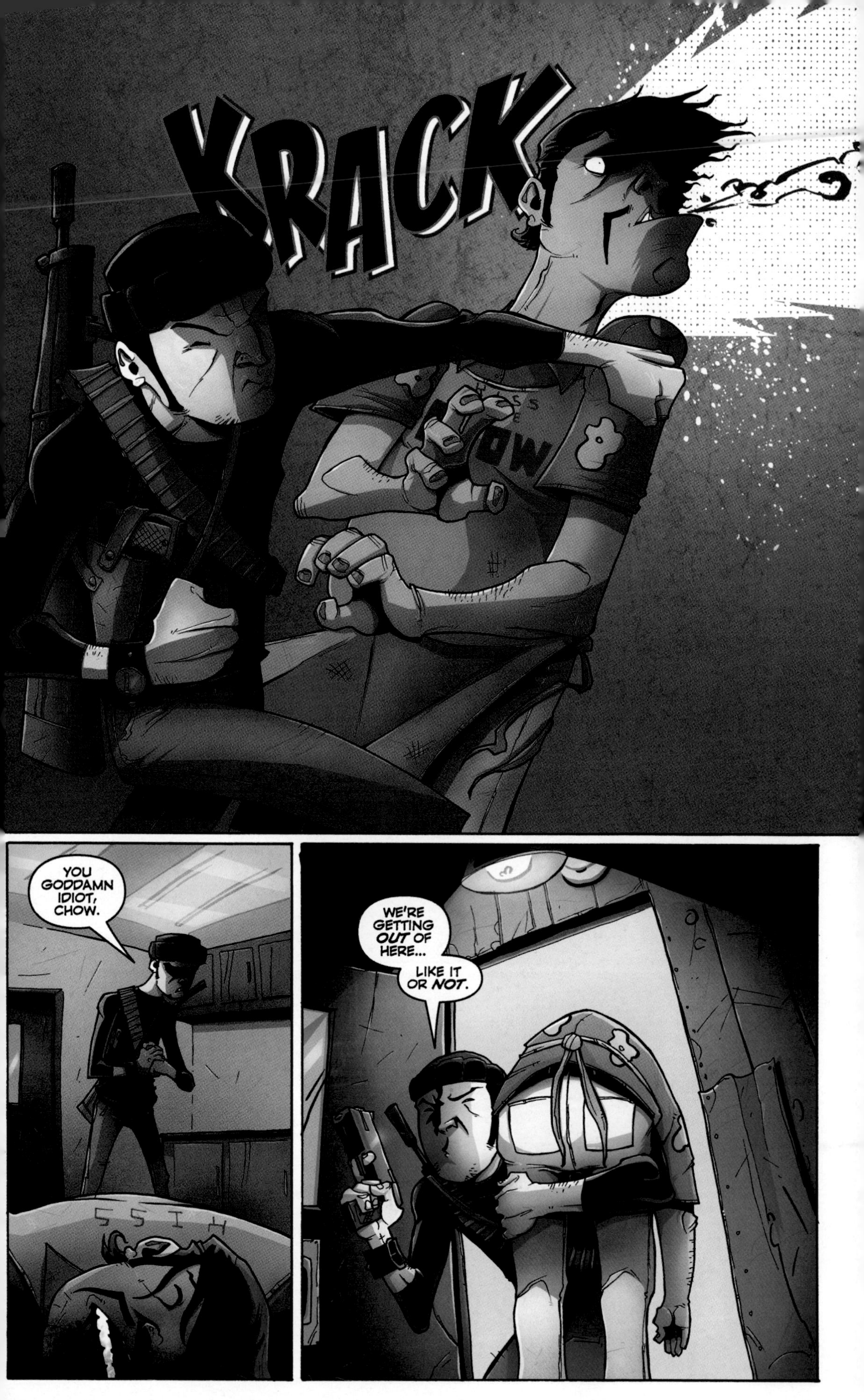
KRACK
YOU GODDAMN IDIOT, CHOW.
WE'RE GETTING OUT OF HERE...
LIKE IT OR NOT.

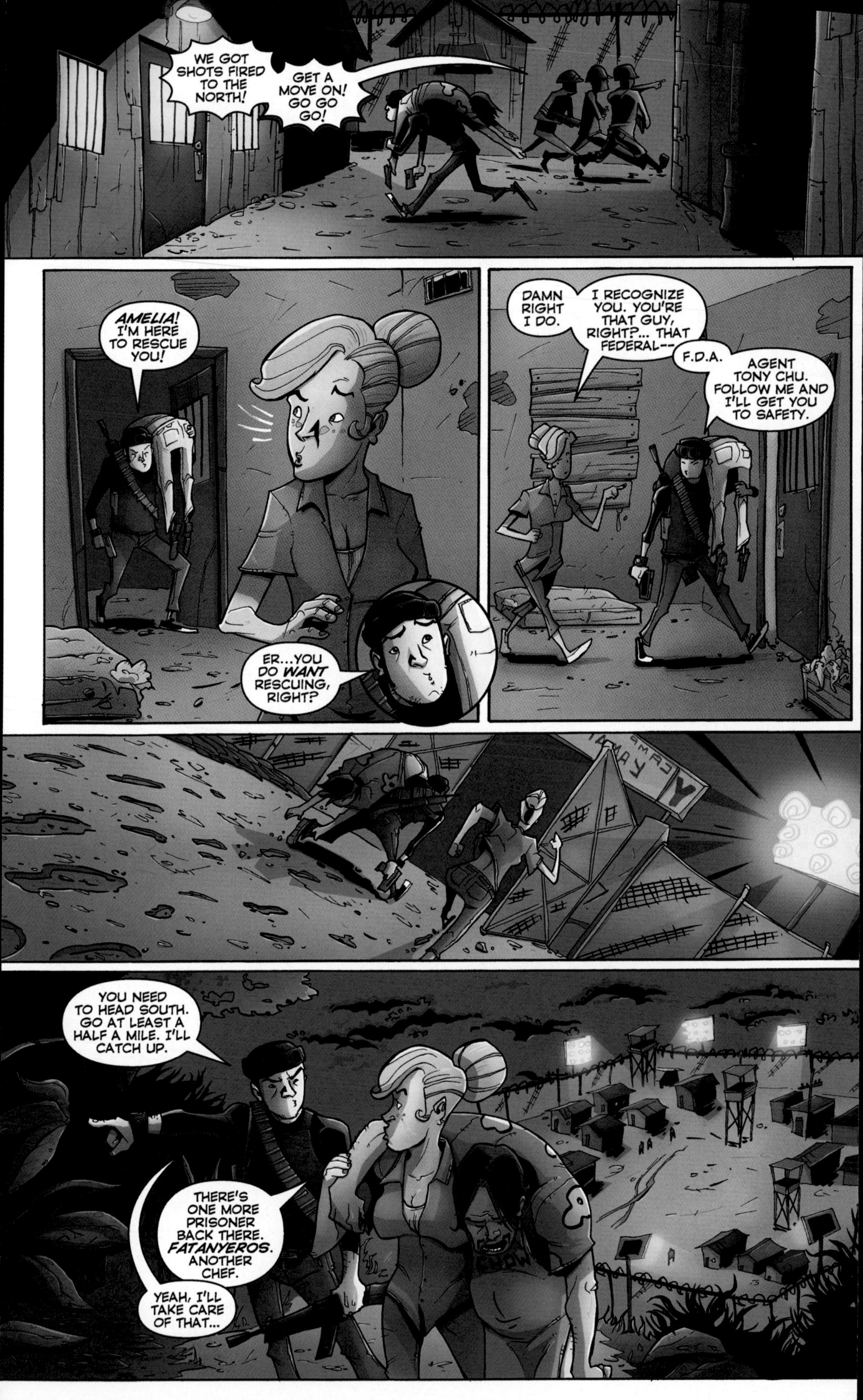
WE GOT SHOTS FIRED TO THE NORTH!
GET A MOVE ON! GO GO GO!
AMELIA! I'M HERE TO RESCUE YOU!
ER...YOU DO WANT RESCUING, RIGHT?
DAMN RIGHT I DO.
I RECOGNIZE YOU. YOU'RE THAT GUY, RIGHT?... THAT FEDERAL--
F.D.A.
AGENT TONY CHU. FOLLOW ME AND I'LL GET YOU TO SAFETY.
YOU NEED TO HEAD SOUTH. GO AT LEAST A HALF A MILE. I'LL CATCH UP.
THERE'S ONE MORE PRISONER BACK THERE. FATANYEROS. ANOTHER CHEF.
YEAH, I'LL TAKE CARE OF THAT...

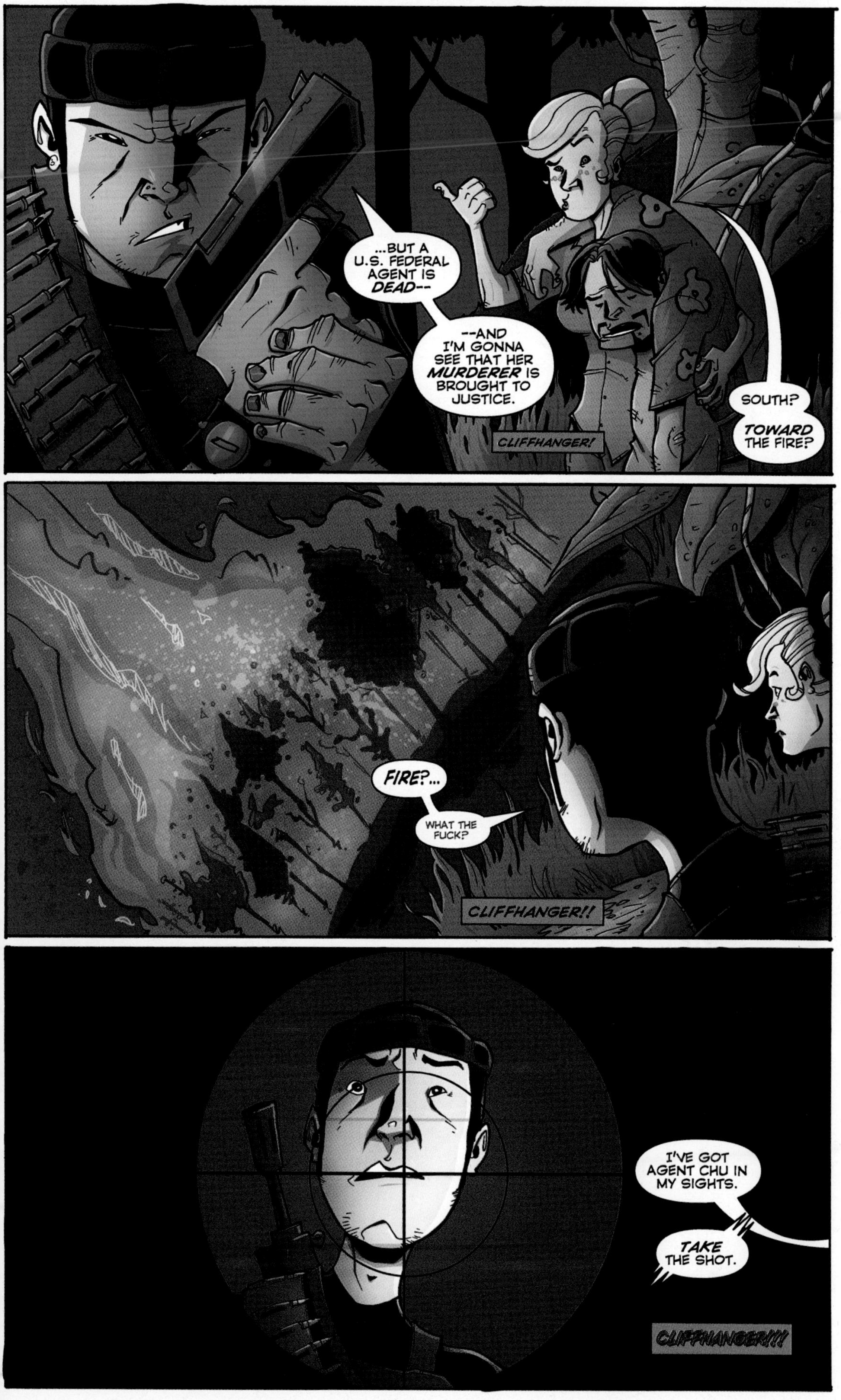
...BUT A U.S. FEDERAL AGENT IS DEAD--
--AND I'M GONNA SEE THAT HER MURDERER IS BROUGHT TO JUSTICE.
SOUTH?
TOWARD THE FIRE?
CLIFFHANGER!
FIRE?...
WHAT THE FUCK?
CLIFFHANGER!!
I'VE GOT AGENT CHU IN MY SIGHTS.
TAKE THE SHOT.
CLIFFHANGER!!!

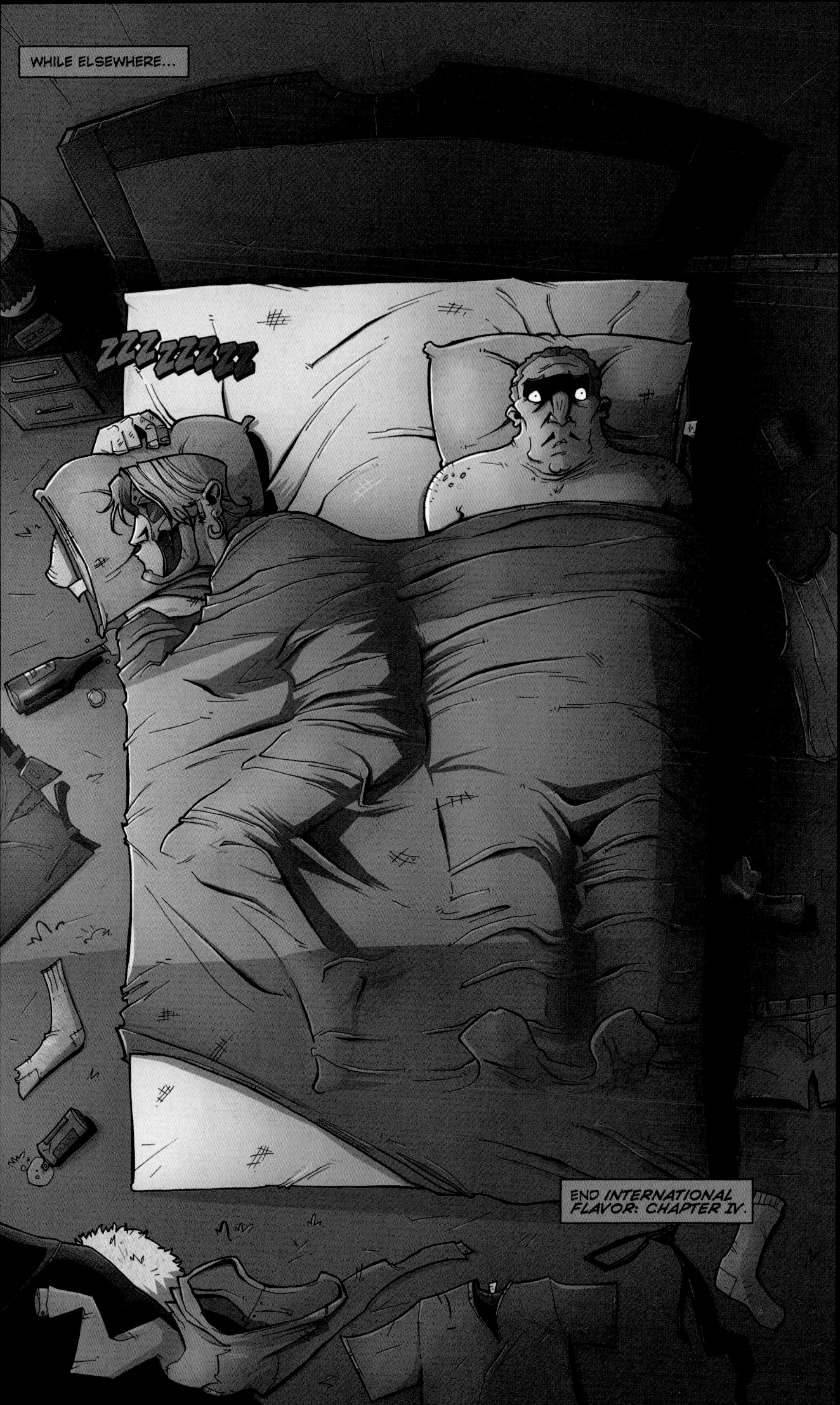
WHILE ELSEWHERE...
ZZZZZZZZ
END INTERNATIONAL FLAVOR: CHAPTER IV.

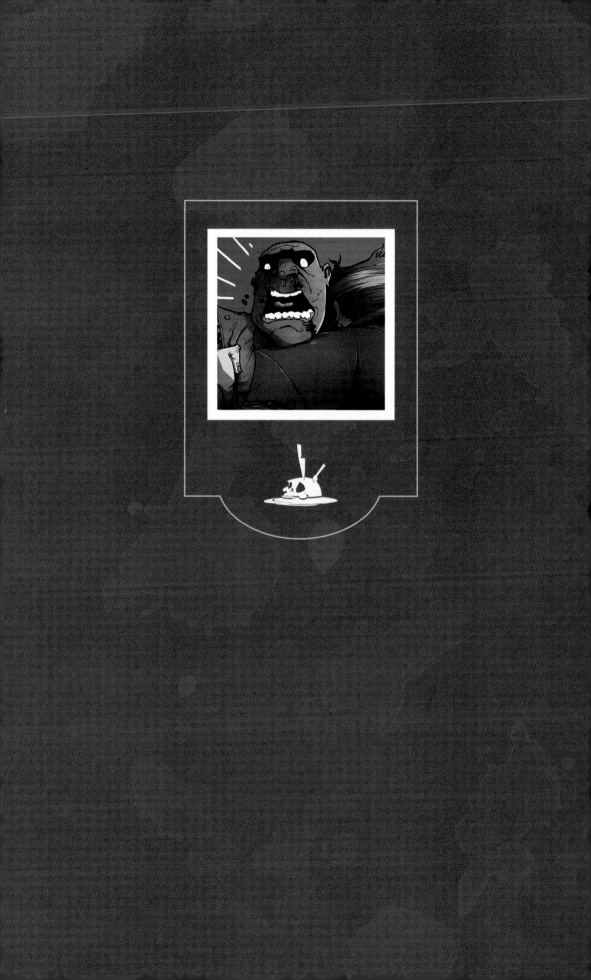

Chapter 5

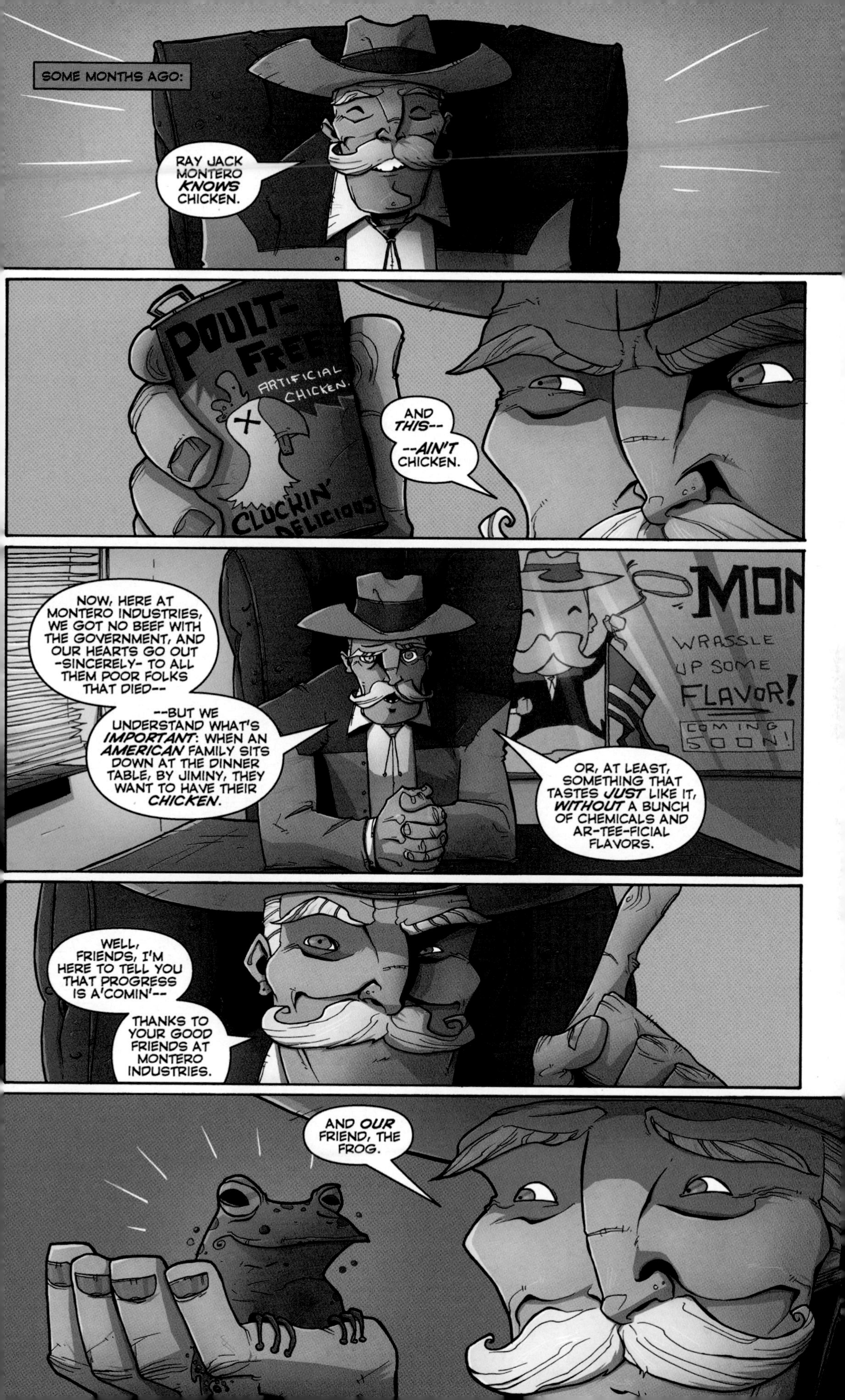
SOME MONTHS AGO:
RAY JACK MONTERO KNOWS CHICKEN.
POULT-FREE ARTIFICIAL CHICKEN. CLUCKIN' DELICIOUS
AND THIS--
--AIN'T CHICKEN.
NOW, HERE AT MONTERO INDUSTRIES, WE GOT NO BEEF WITH THE GOVERNMENT, AND OUR HEARTS GO OUT -SINCERELY- TO ALL THEM POOR FOLKS THAT DIED--
--BUT WE UNDERSTAND WHAT'S IMPORTANT: WHEN AN AMERICAN FAMILY SITS DOWN AT THE DINNER TABLE, BY JIMINY, THEY WANT TO HAVE THEIR CHICKEN.
MON
WRASSLE UP SOME FLAVOR!
COMING SOON!
OR, AT LEAST, SOMETHING THAT TASTES JUST LIKE IT, WITHOUT A BUNCH OF CHEMICALS AND AR-TEE-FICIAL FLAVORS.
WELL, FRIENDS, I'M HERE TO TELL YOU THAT PROGRESS IS A'COMIN'--
THANKS TO YOUR GOOD FRIENDS AT MONTERO INDUSTRIES.
AND OUR FRIEND, THE FROG.

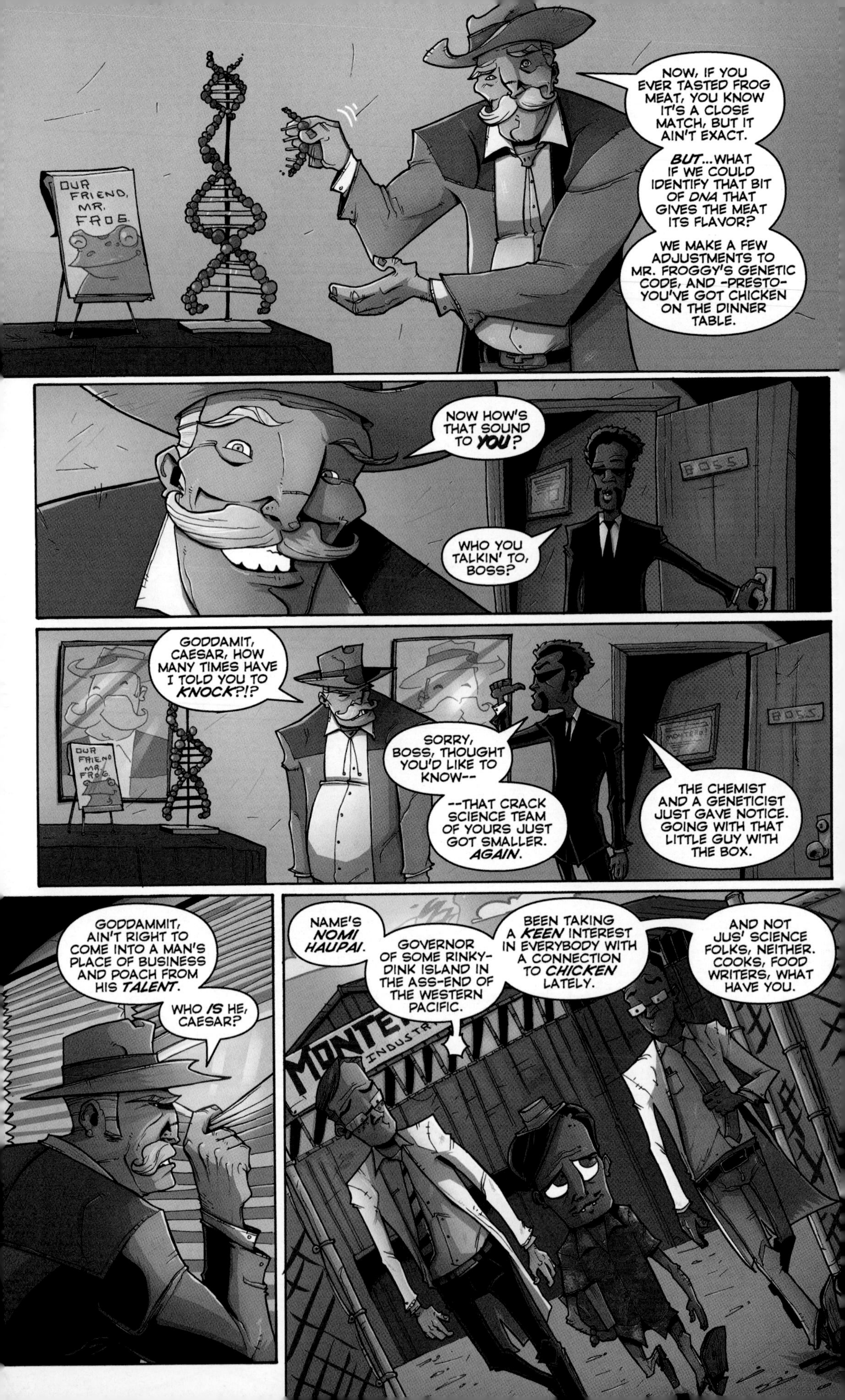
OUR FRIEND, MR. FROG
NOW, IF YOU EVER TASTED FROG MEAT, YOU KNOW IT'S A CLOSE MATCH, BUT IT AIN'T EXACT.
BUT...WHAT IF WE COULD IDENTIFY THAT BIT OF DNA THAT GIVES THE MEAT ITS FLAVOR?
WE MAKE A FEW ADJUSTMENTS TO MR. FROGGY'S GENETIC CODE, AND -PRESTO- YOU'VE GOT CHICKEN ON THE DINNER TABLE.
NOW HOW'S THAT SOUND TO YOU?
BOSS
WHO YOU TALKIN' TO, BOSS?
GODDAMIT, CAESAR, HOW MANY TIMES HAVE I TOLD YOU TO KNOCK?!?
OUR FRIEND MR. FROG
BOSS
SORRY, BOSS, THOUGHT YOU'D LIKE TO KNOW--
--THAT CRACK SCIENCE TEAM OF YOURS JUST GOT SMALLER. AGAIN.
THE CHEMIST AND A GENETICIST JUST GAVE NOTICE. GOING WITH THAT LITTLE GUY WITH THE BOX.
GODDAMMIT, AIN'T RIGHT TO COME INTO A MAN'S PLACE OF BUSINESS AND POACH FROM HIS TALENT.
WHO IS HE, CAESAR?
NAME'S NOMI HAUPAI.
GOVERNOR OF SOME RINKY-DINK ISLAND IN THE ASS-END OF THE WESTERN PACIFIC.
BEEN TAKING A KEEN INTEREST IN EVERYBODY WITH A CONNECTION TO CHICKEN LATELY.
AND NOT JUS' SCIENCE FOLKS, NEITHER. COOKS, FOOD WRITERS, WHAT HAVE YOU.

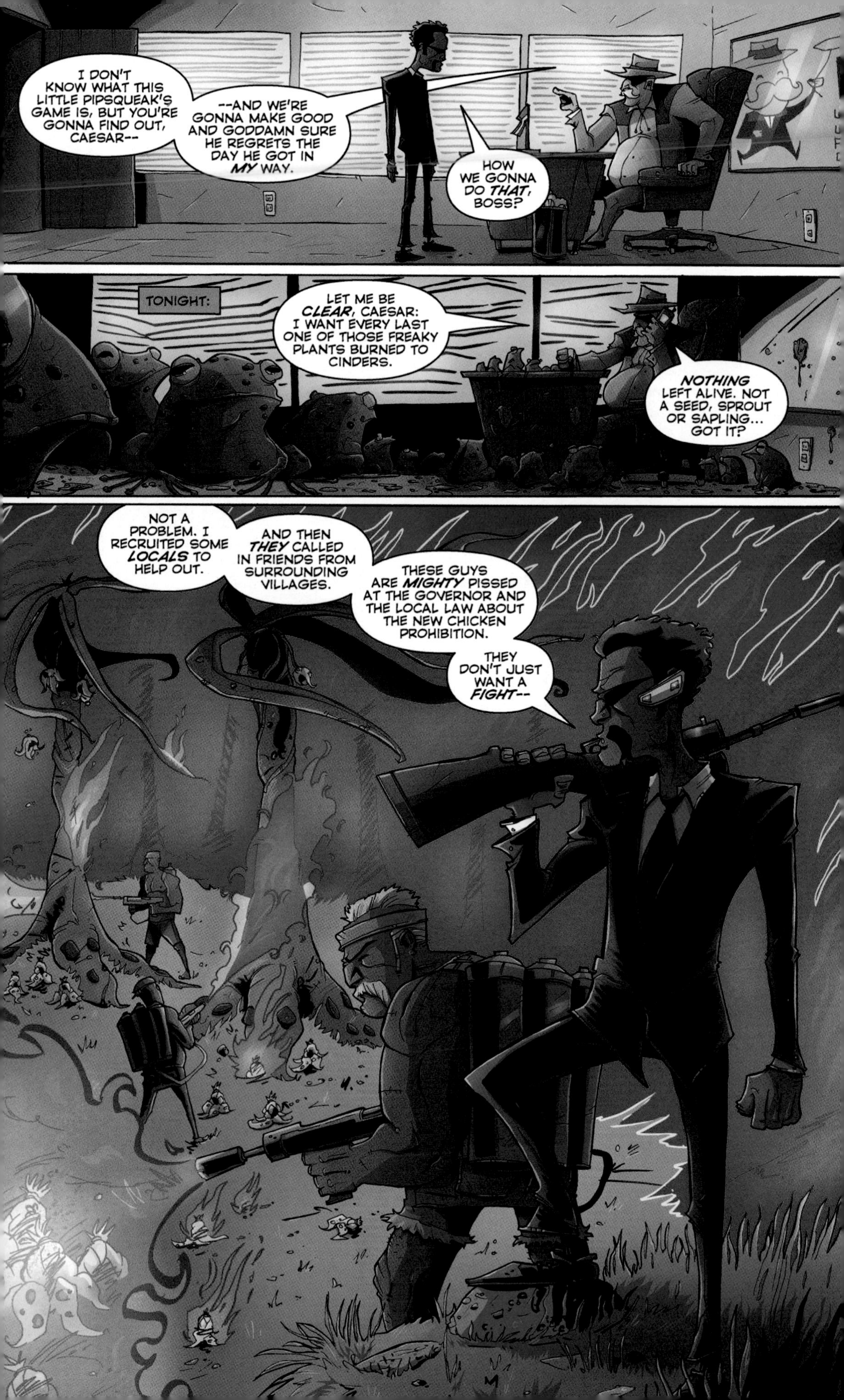
I DON'T KNOW WHAT THIS LITTLE PIPSQUEAK'S GAME IS, BUT YOU'RE GONNA FIND OUT, CAESAR--
--AND WE'RE GONNA MAKE GOOD AND GODDAMN SURE HE REGRETS THE DAY HE GOT IN *MY* WAY.
HOW WE GONNA DO *THAT*, BOSS?
TONIGHT:
LET ME BE *CLEAR*, CAESAR: I WANT EVERY LAST ONE OF THOSE FREAKY PLANTS BURNED TO CINDERS.
NOTHING LEFT ALIVE. NOT A SEED, SPROUT OR SAPLING... GOT IT?
NOT A PROBLEM. I RECRUITED SOME *LOCALS* TO HELP OUT.
AND THEN *THEY* CALLED IN FRIENDS FROM SURROUNDING VILLAGES.
THESE GUYS ARE *MIGHTY* PISSED AT THE GOVERNOR AND THE LOCAL LAW ABOUT THE NEW CHICKEN PROHIBITION.
THEY DON'T JUST WANT A *FIGHT*--

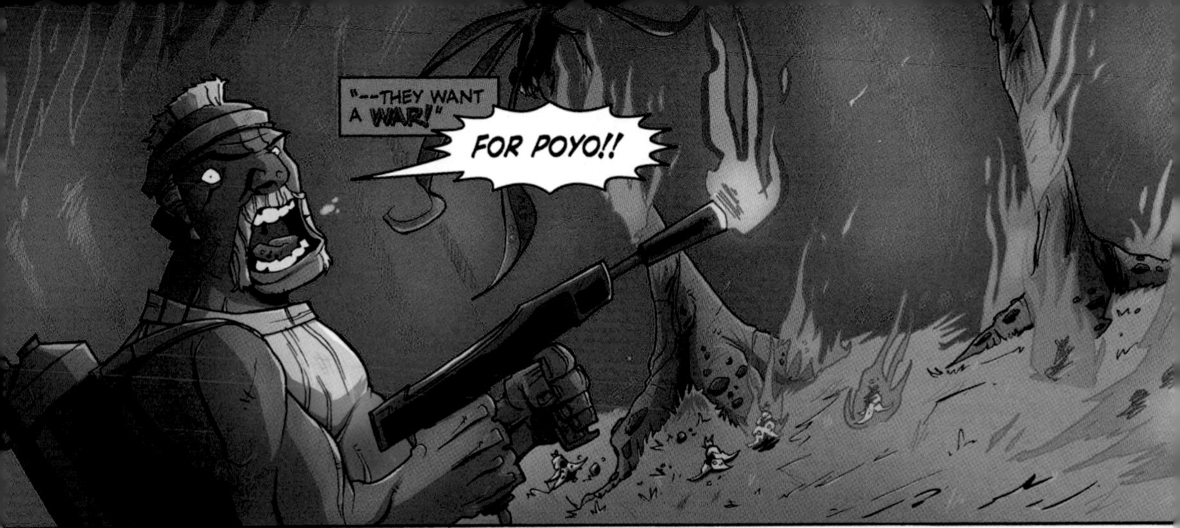
"--THEY WANT A WAR!"
FOR POYO!!
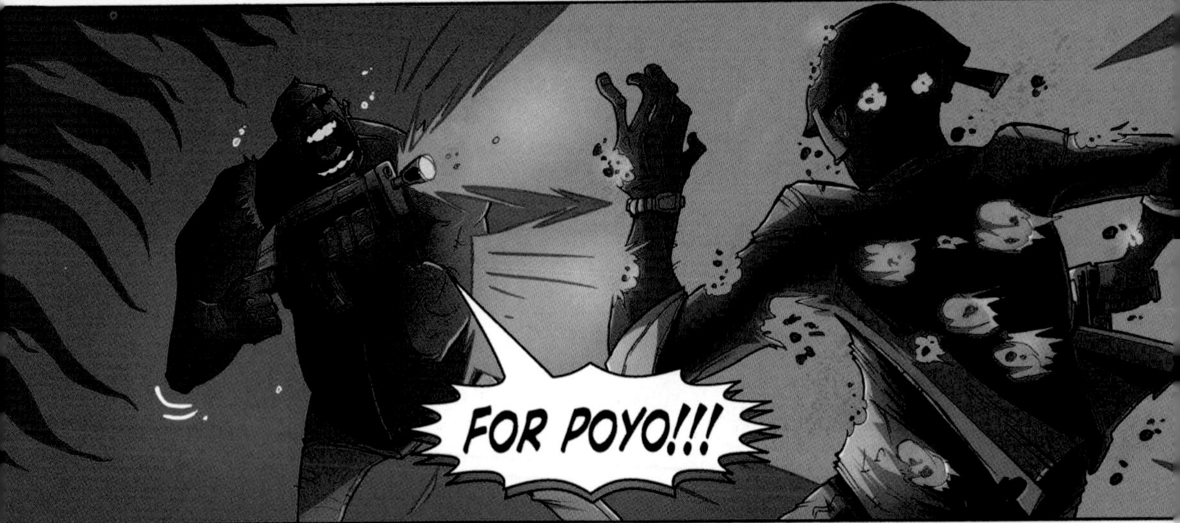
FOR POYO!!!
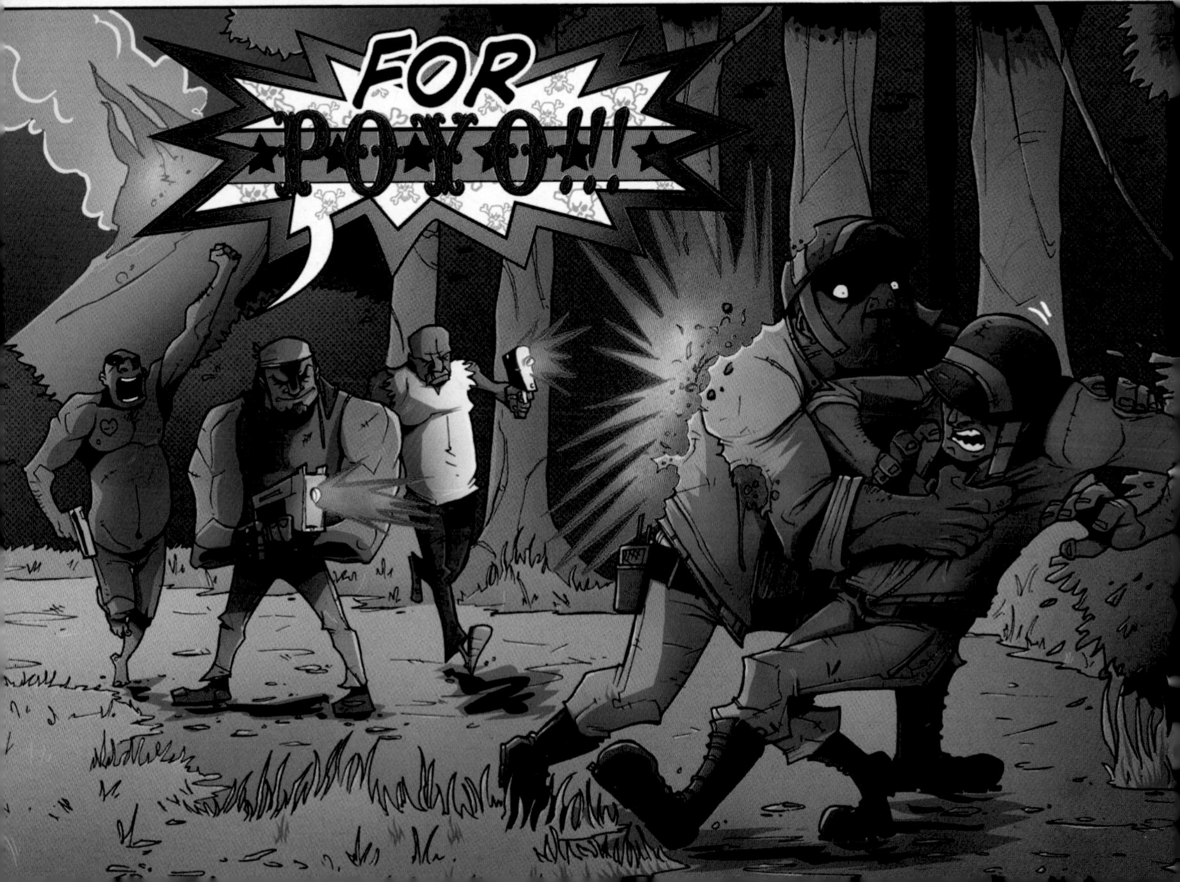
FOR POYO!!!

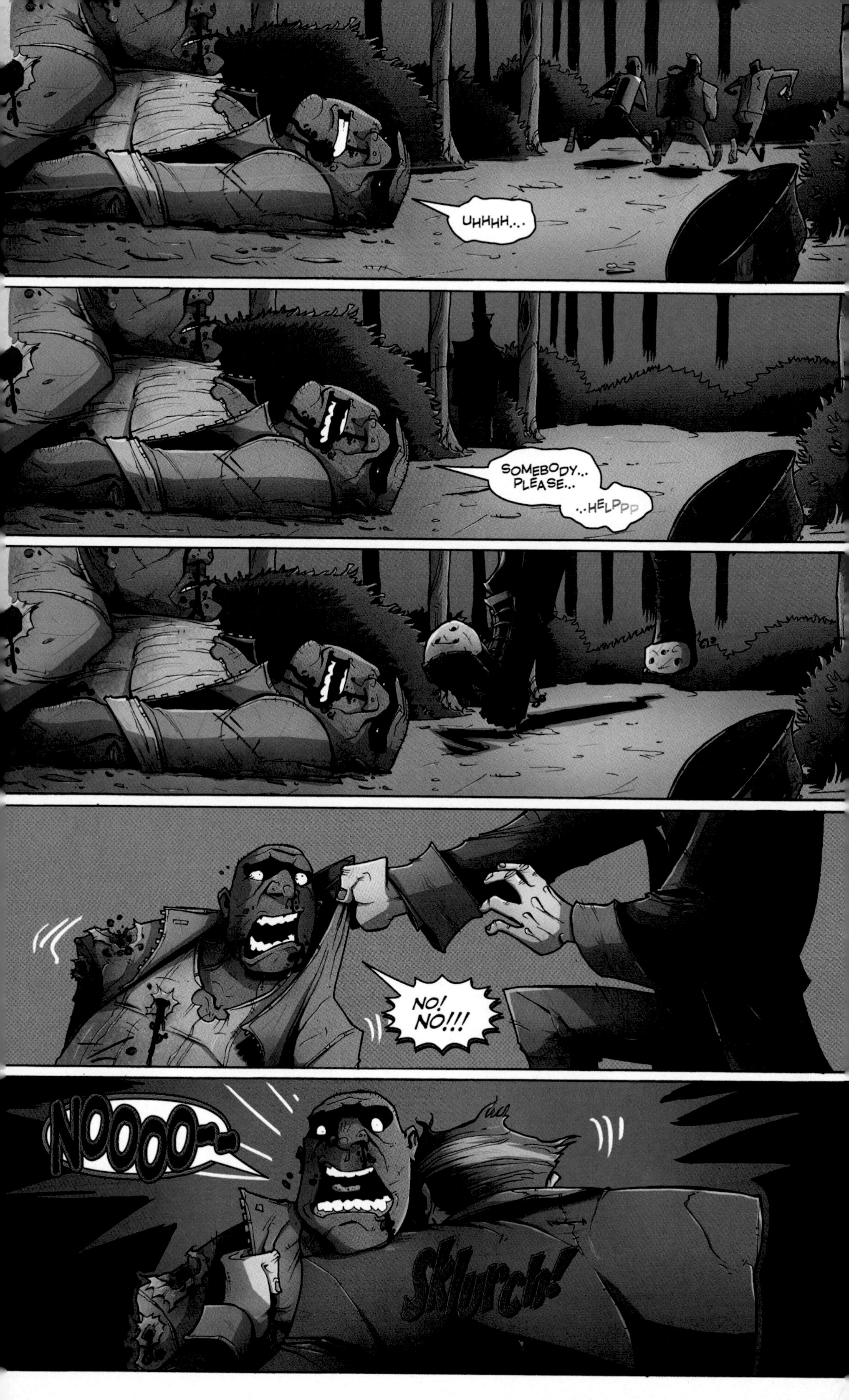
UHHHH...
SOMEBODY... PLEASE...
...HELPPP
NO! NO!!!
NOOOO--
SKLURCH!

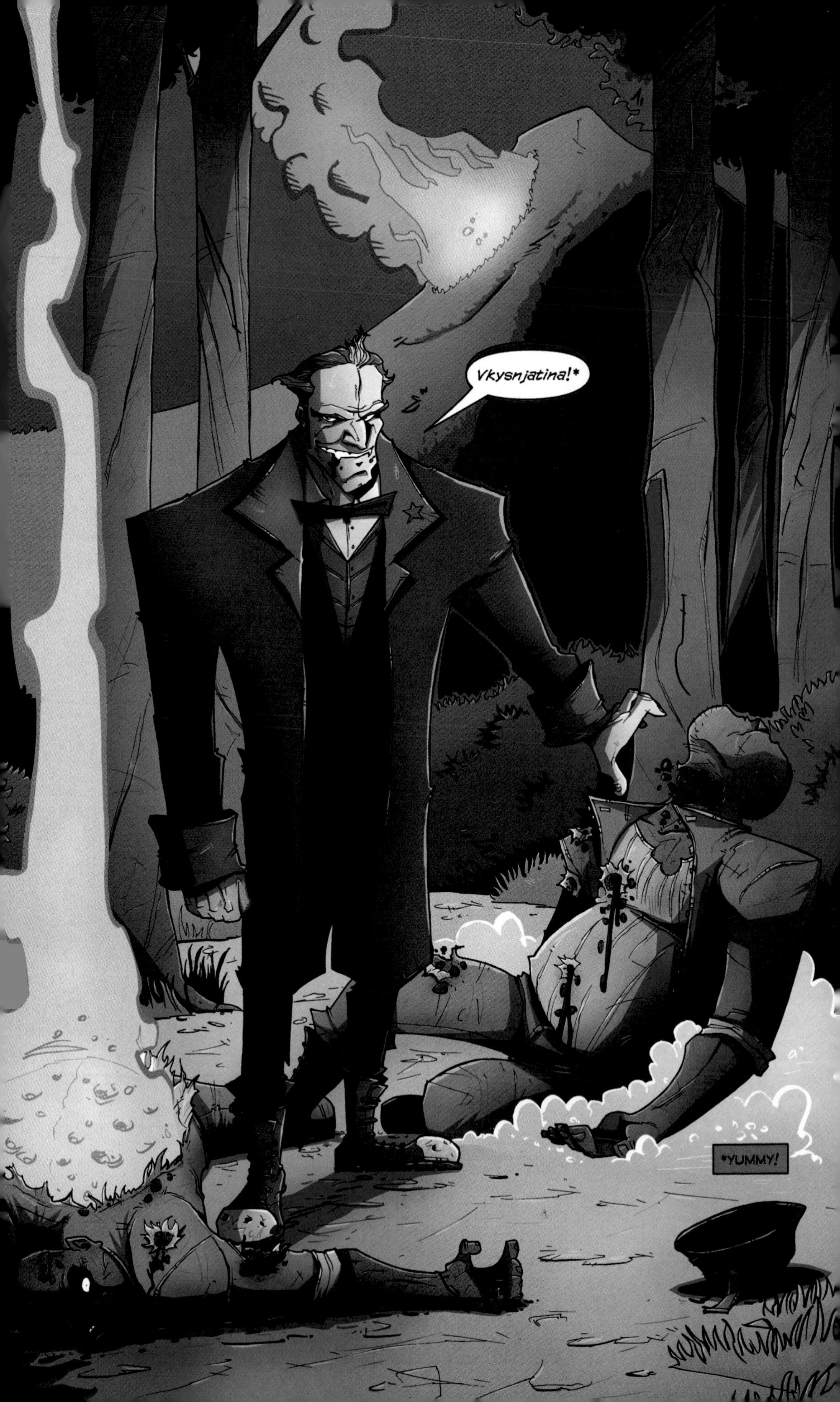
Vkysnjatina!*
*YUMMY!

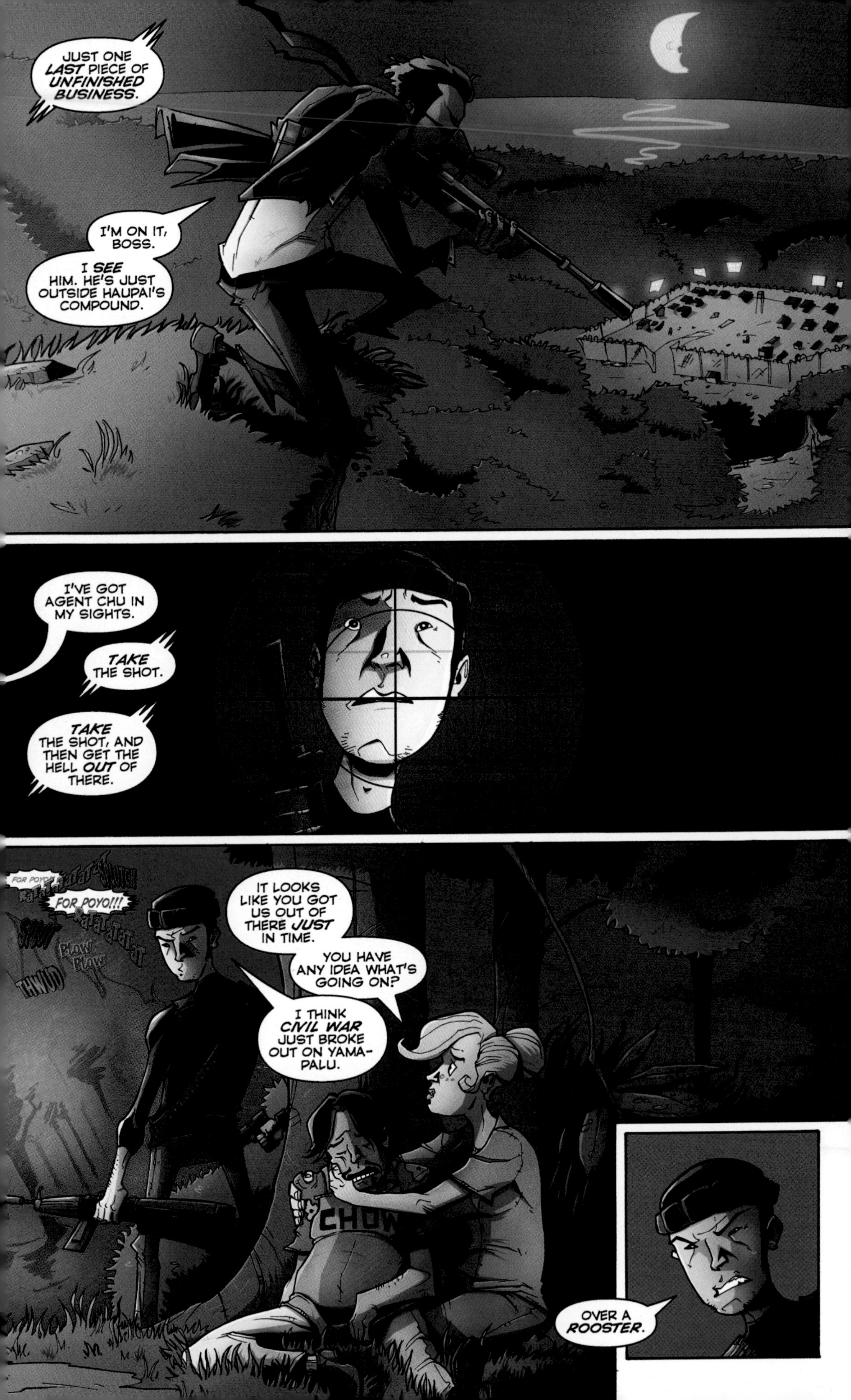
JUST ONE LAST PIECE OF UNFINISHED BUSINESS.
I'M ON IT, BOSS.
I SEE HIM. HE'S JUST OUTSIDE HAUPAI'S COMPOUND.
I'VE GOT AGENT CHU IN MY SIGHTS.
TAKE THE SHOT.
TAKE THE SHOT, AND THEN GET THE HELL OUT OF THERE.
FOR POYO!!!
RaTaTaTaT
Ptow Ptow
THWUD
IT LOOKS LIKE YOU GOT US OUT OF THERE JUST IN TIME.
YOU HAVE ANY IDEA WHAT'S GOING ON?
I THINK CIVIL WAR JUST BROKE OUT ON YAMA-PALU.
CHOW
OVER A ROOSTER.

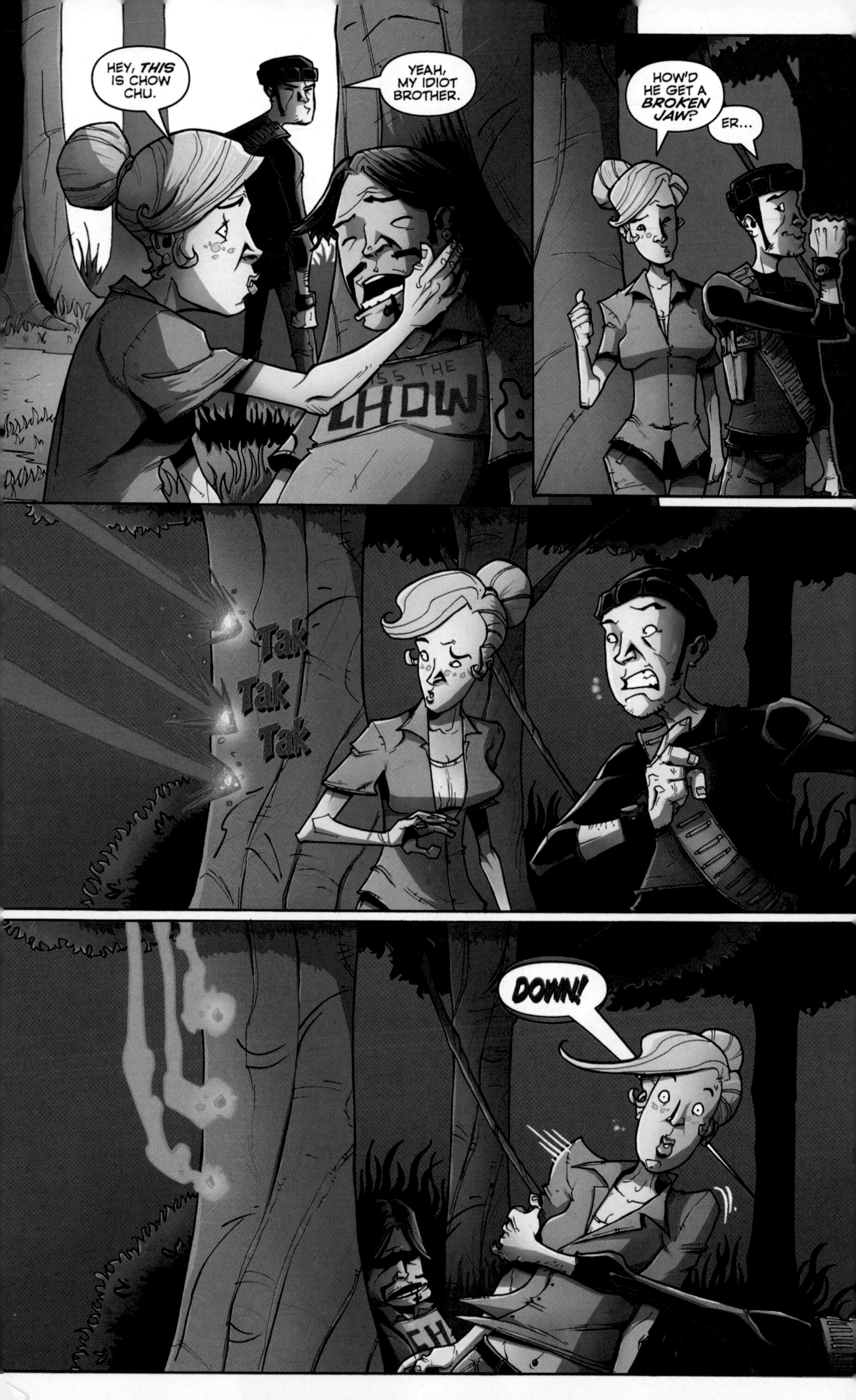
HEY, THIS IS CHOW CHU.
YEAH, MY IDIOT BROTHER.
HOW'D HE GET A BROKEN JAW?
ER...
TAK
TAK
TAK
DOWN!

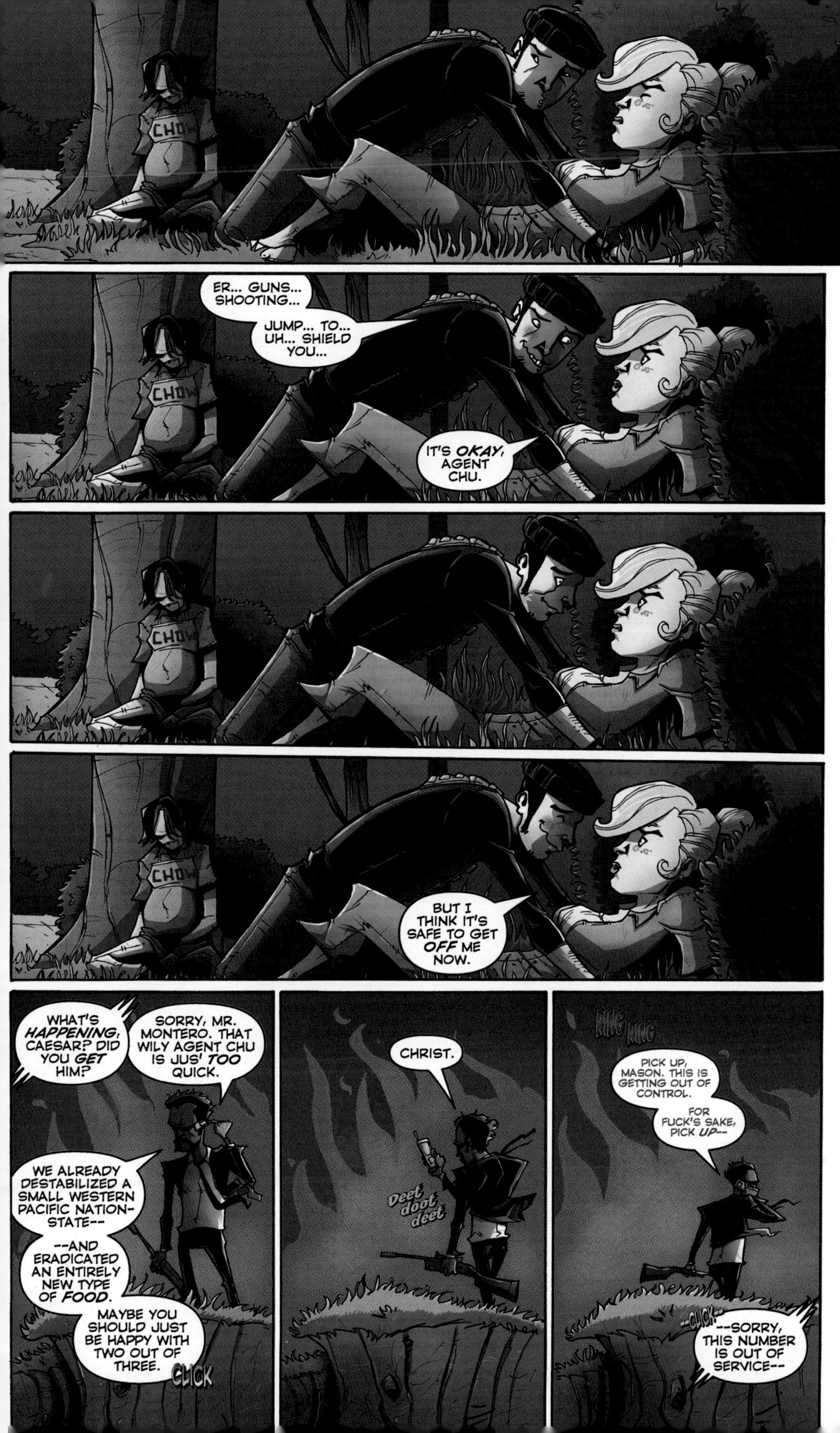

ER... GUNS... SHOOTING...
JUMP... TO... UH... SHIELD YOU...
IT'S OKAY, AGENT CHU.
BUT I THINK IT'S SAFE TO GET OFF ME NOW.
WHAT'S HAPPENING, CAESAR? DID YOU GET HIM?
SORRY, MR. MONTERO. THAT WILY AGENT CHU IS JUS' TOO QUICK.
WE ALREADY DESTABILIZED A SMALL WESTERN PACIFIC NATION-STATE--
--AND ERADICATED AN ENTIRELY NEW TYPE OF FOOD.
MAYBE YOU SHOULD JUST BE HAPPY WITH TWO OUT OF THREE.
CLICK
CHRIST.
Deet doot deet
RING RING
PICK UP, MASON. THIS IS GETTING OUT OF CONTROL.
FOR FUCK'S SAKE, PICK UP--
CLICK
--SORRY, THIS NUMBER IS OUT OF SERVICE--

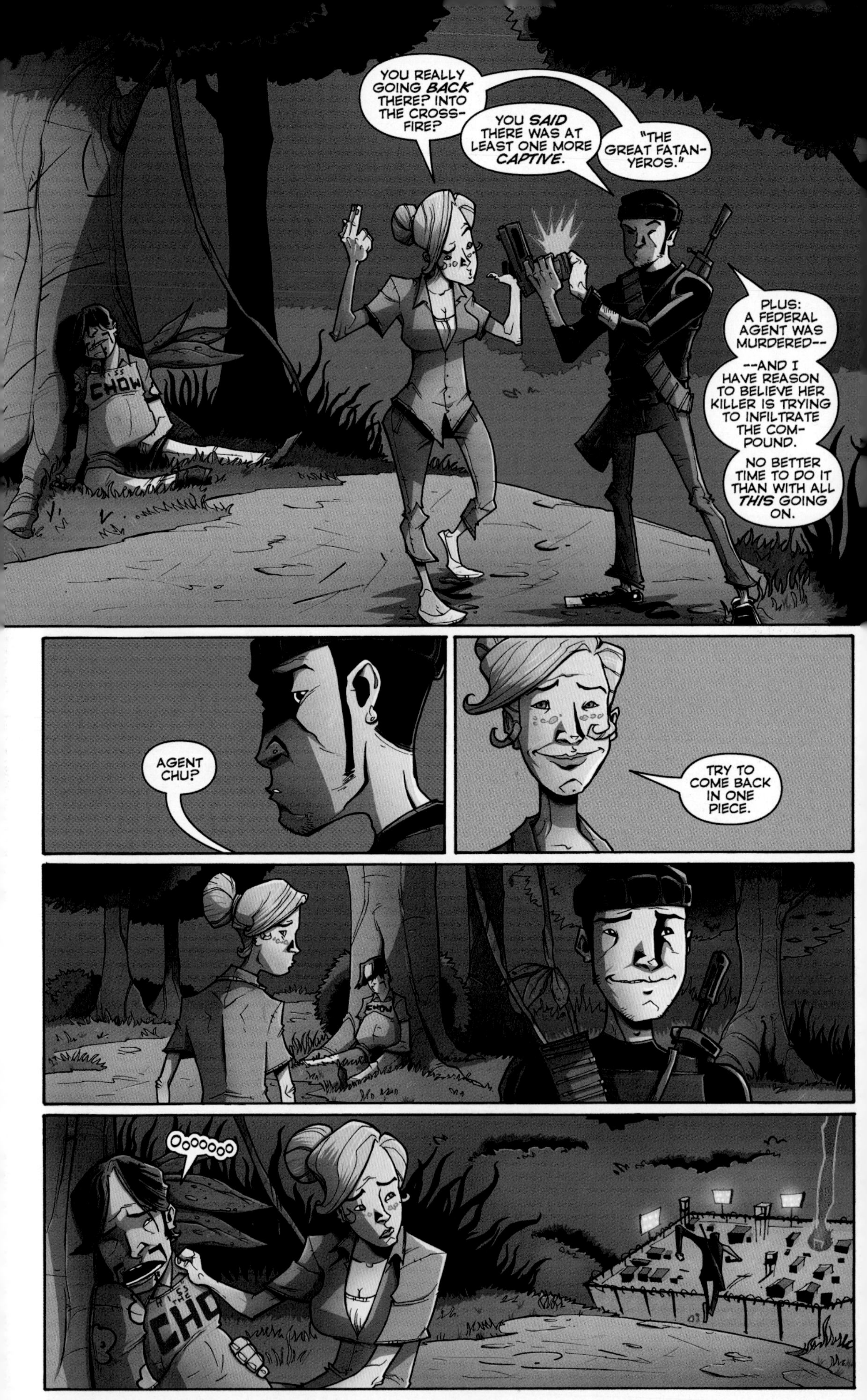
YOU REALLY GOING BACK THERE? INTO THE CROSS-FIRE?
YOU SAID THERE WAS AT LEAST ONE MORE CAPTIVE.
"THE GREAT FATAN-YEROS."
PLUS: A FEDERAL AGENT WAS MURDERED--
--AND I HAVE REASON TO BELIEVE HER KILLER IS TRYING TO INFILTRATE THE COMPOUND.
NO BETTER TIME TO DO IT THAN WITH ALL THIS GOING ON.
AGENT CHU?
TRY TO COME BACK IN ONE PIECE.
OOOOOOO

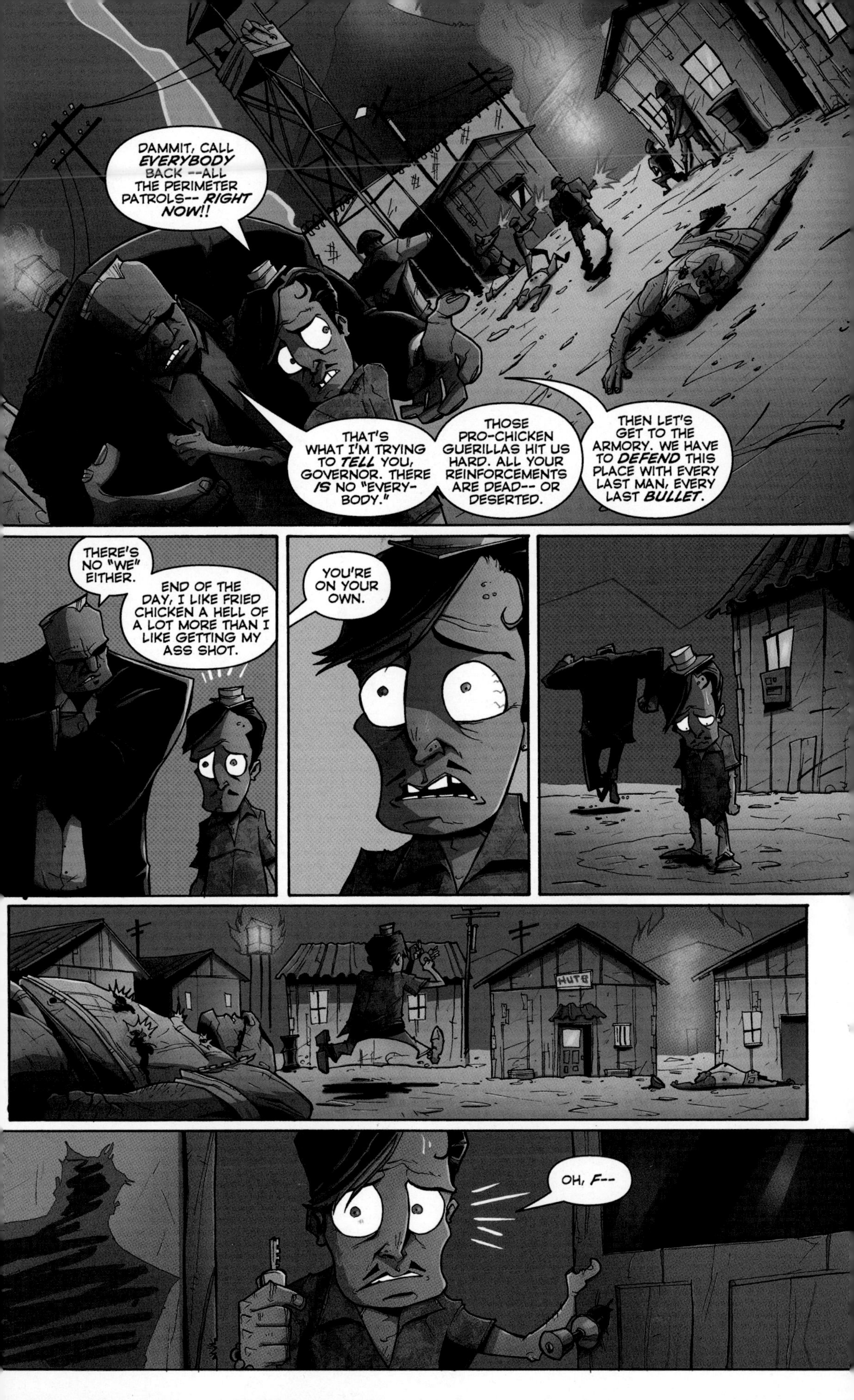
DAMMIT, CALL EVERYBODY BACK --ALL THE PERIMETER PATROLS-- RIGHT NOW!!
THAT'S WHAT I'M TRYING TO TELL YOU, GOVERNOR. THERE IS NO "EVERY-BODY."
THOSE PRO-CHICKEN GUERILLAS HIT US HARD. ALL YOUR REINFORCEMENTS ARE DEAD-- OR DESERTED.
THEN LET'S GET TO THE ARMORY. WE HAVE TO DEFEND THIS PLACE WITH EVERY LAST MAN, EVERY LAST BULLET.
THERE'S NO "WE" EITHER.
END OF THE DAY, I LIKE FRIED CHICKEN A HELL OF A LOT MORE THAN I LIKE GETTING MY ASS SHOT.
YOU'RE ON YOUR OWN.
HUTS
OH, F--

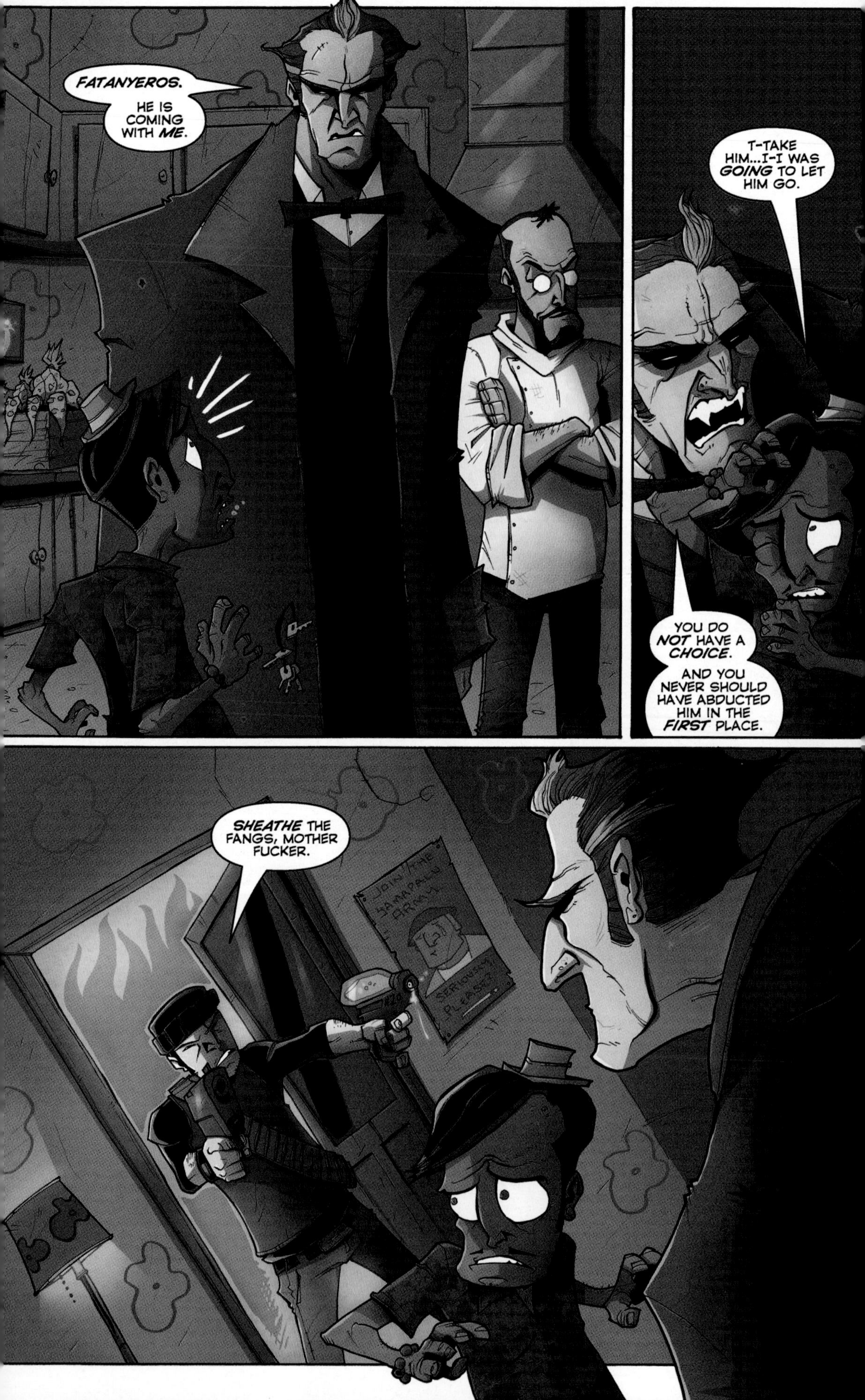
FATANYEROS.
HE IS COMING WITH ME.
T-TAKE HIM...I-I WAS GOING TO LET HIM GO.
YOU DO NOT HAVE A CHOICE.
AND YOU NEVER SHOULD HAVE ABDUCTED HIM IN THE FIRST PLACE.
SHEATHE THE FANGS, MOTHER FUCKER.

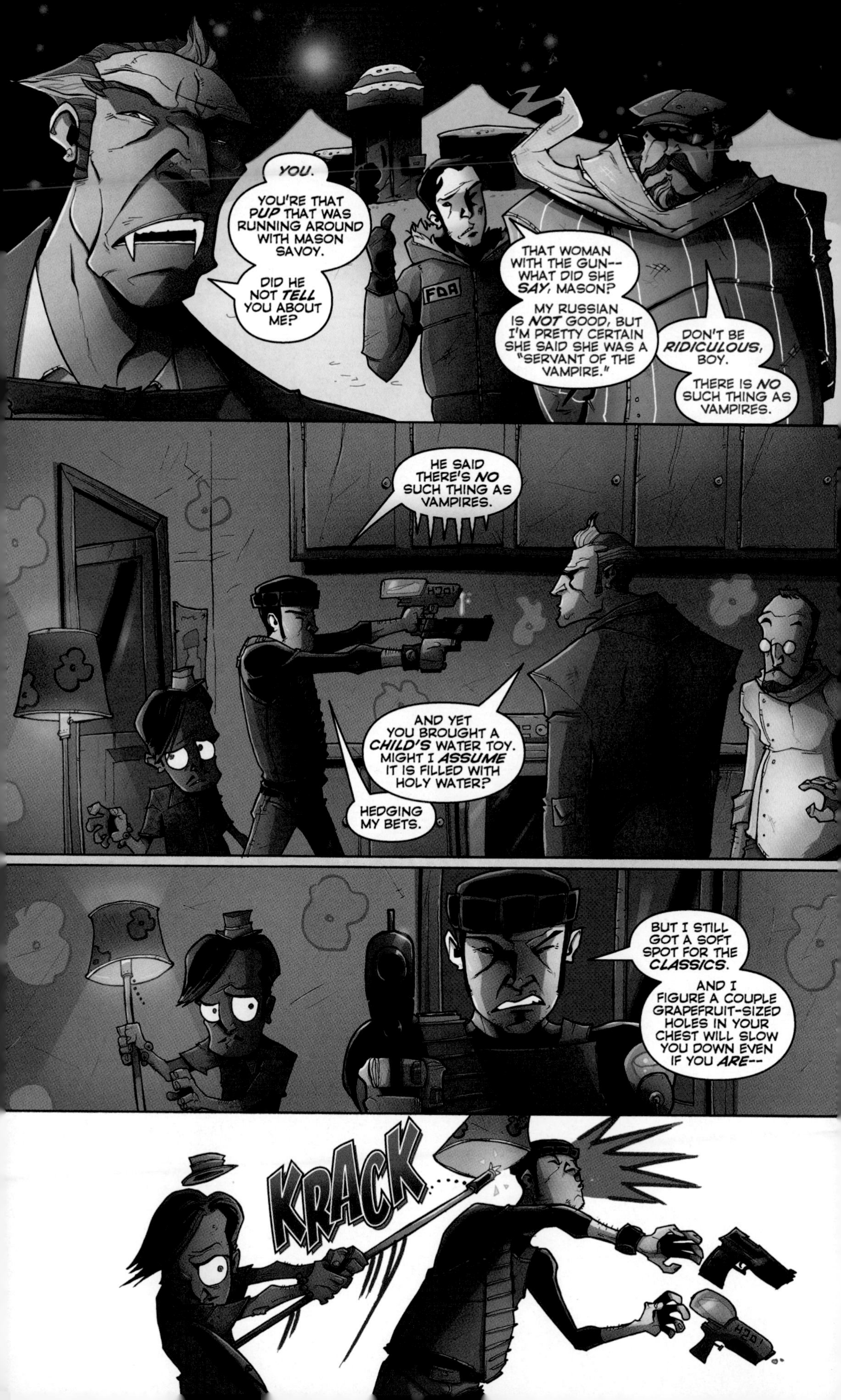
YOU.
YOU'RE THAT PUP THAT WAS RUNNING AROUND WITH MASON SAVOY.
DID HE NOT TELL YOU ABOUT ME?
FDA
THAT WOMAN WITH THE GUN-- WHAT DID SHE SAY, MASON?
MY RUSSIAN IS NOT GOOD, BUT I'M PRETTY CERTAIN SHE SAID SHE WAS A "SERVANT OF THE VAMPIRE."
DON'T BE RIDICULOUS, BOY.
THERE IS NO SUCH THING AS VAMPIRES.
HE SAID THERE'S NO SUCH THING AS VAMPIRES.
AND YET YOU BROUGHT A CHILD'S WATER TOY. MIGHT I ASSUME IT IS FILLED WITH HOLY WATER?
HEDGING MY BETS.
BUT I STILL GOT A SOFT SPOT FOR THE CLASSICS.
AND I FIGURE A COUPLE GRAPEFRUIT-SIZED HOLES IN YOUR CHEST WILL SLOW YOU DOWN EVEN IF YOU ARE--
KRACK

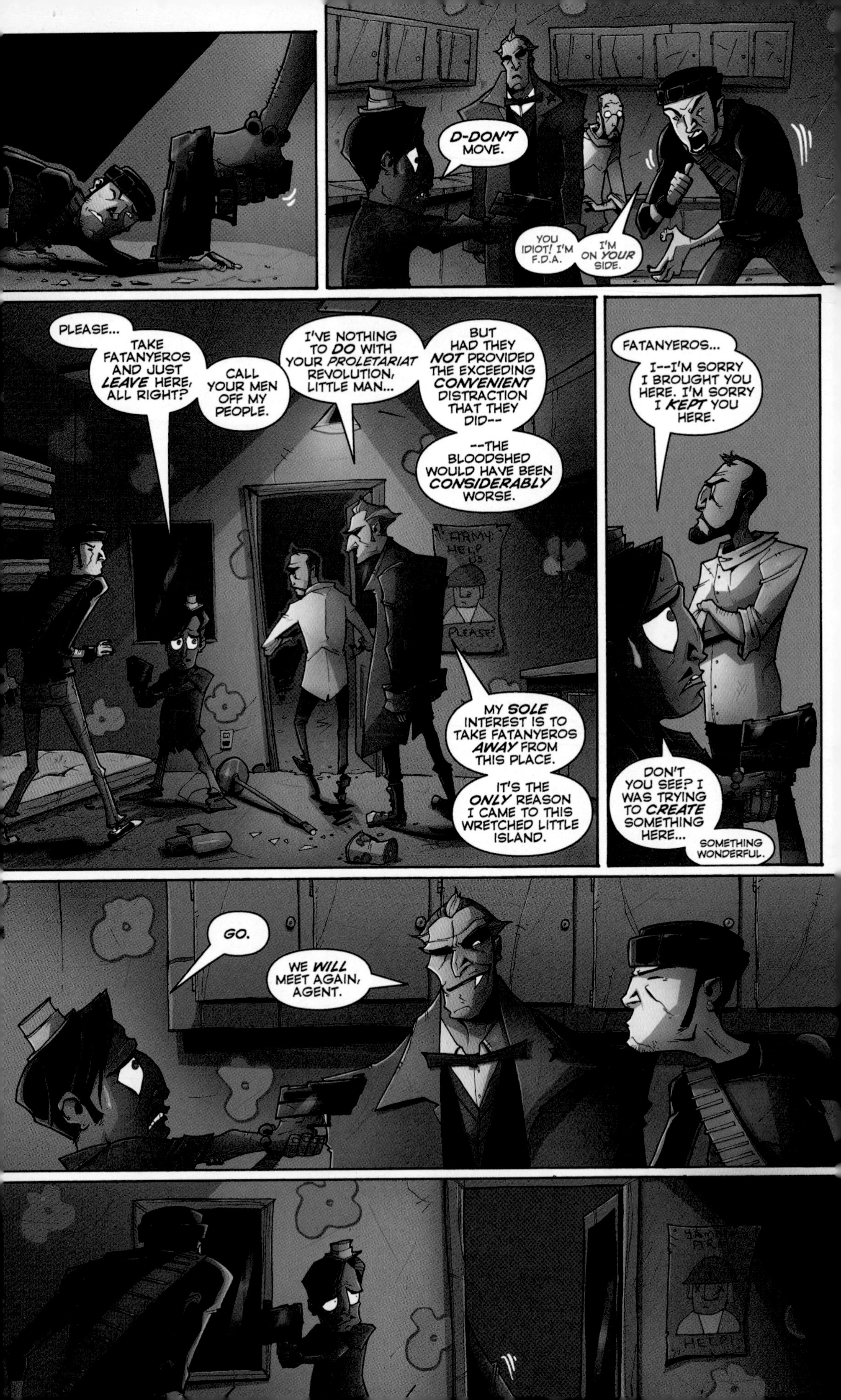
D-DON'T MOVE.
YOU IDIOT! I'M F.D.A.
I'M ON YOUR SIDE.
PLEASE...
TAKE FATANYEROS AND JUST LEAVE HERE, ALL RIGHT?
CALL YOUR MEN OFF MY PEOPLE.
I'VE NOTHING TO DO WITH YOUR PROLETARIAT REVOLUTION, LITTLE MAN...
BUT HAD THEY NOT PROVIDED THE EXCEEDING CONVENIENT DISTRACTION THAT THEY DID--
--THE BLOODSHED WOULD HAVE BEEN CONSIDERABLY WORSE.
ARMY: HELP US
PLEASE?
MY SOLE INTEREST IS TO TAKE FATANYEROS AWAY FROM THIS PLACE.
IT'S THE ONLY REASON I CAME TO THIS WRETCHED LITTLE ISLAND.
FATANYEROS...
I--I'M SORRY I BROUGHT YOU HERE. I'M SORRY I KEPT YOU HERE.
DON'T YOU SEE? I WAS TRYING TO CREATE SOMETHING HERE...
SOMETHING WONDERFUL.
GO.
WE WILL MEET AGAIN, AGENT.

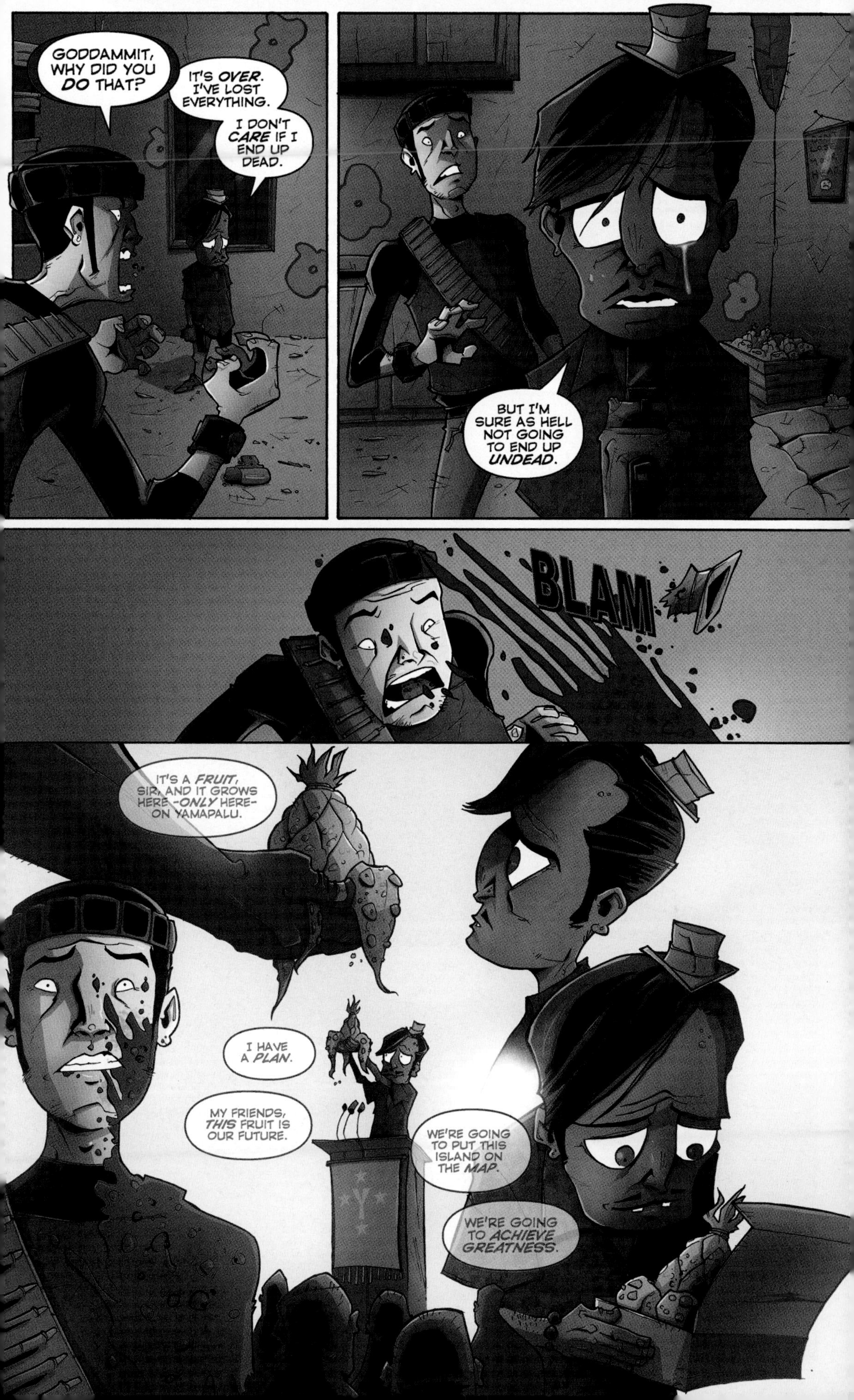
GODDAMMIT, WHY DID YOU DO THAT?
IT'S OVER. I'VE LOST EVERYTHING.
I DON'T CARE IF I END UP DEAD.
BUT I'M SURE AS HELL NOT GOING TO END UP UNDEAD.
BLAM
IT'S A FRUIT, SIR, AND IT GROWS HERE--ONLY HERE--ON YAMAPALU.
I HAVE A PLAN.
MY FRIENDS, THIS FRUIT IS OUR FUTURE.
WE'RE GOING TO PUT THIS ISLAND ON THE MAP.
WE'RE GOING TO ACHIEVE GREATNESS.

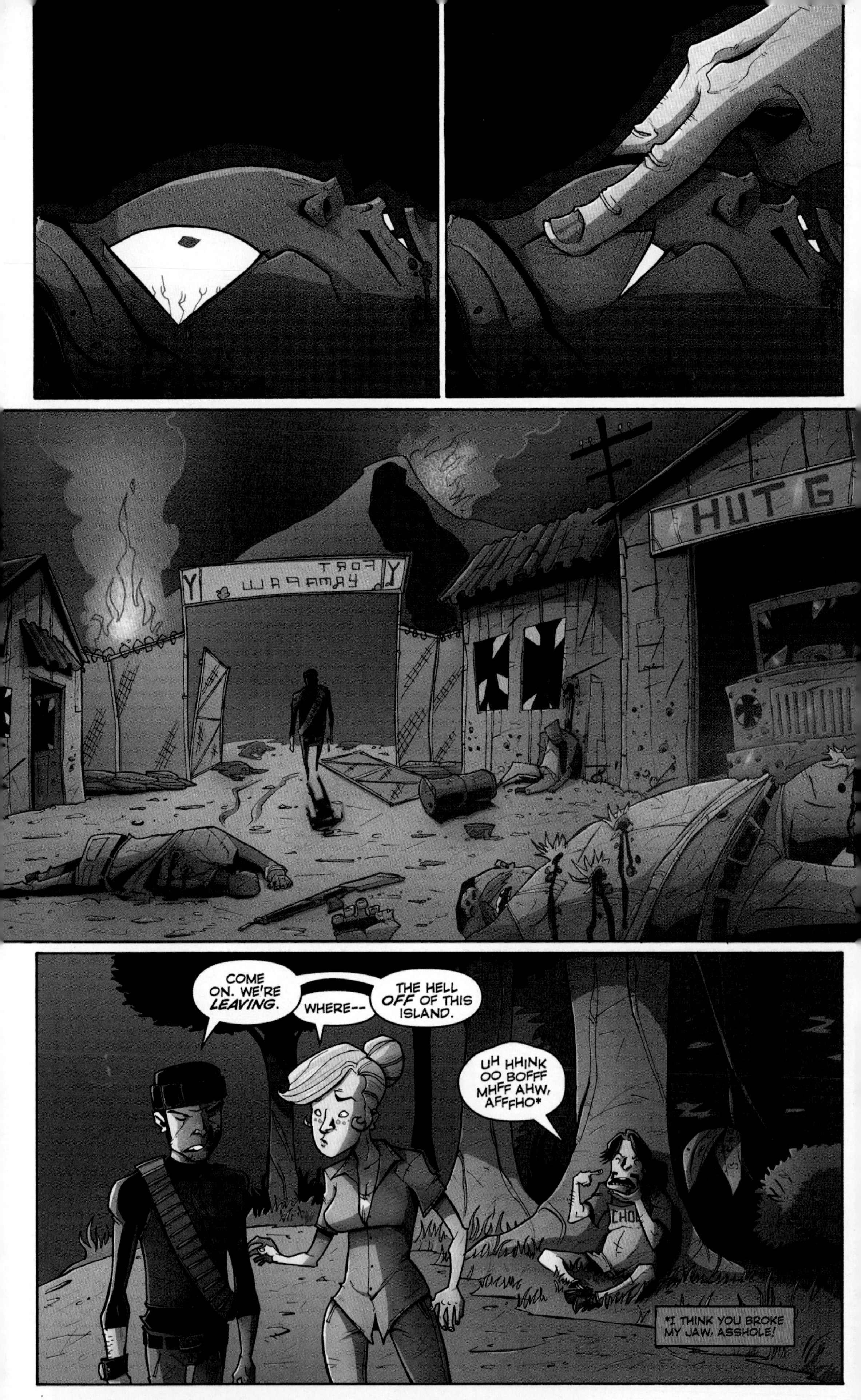
HUT G
COME ON. WE'RE *LEAVING.*
WHERE--
THE HELL *OFF* OF THIS ISLAND.
UH HHINK OO BOFFF MHFF AHW, AFFFHO*
*I THINK YOU BROKE MY JAW, ASSHOLE!

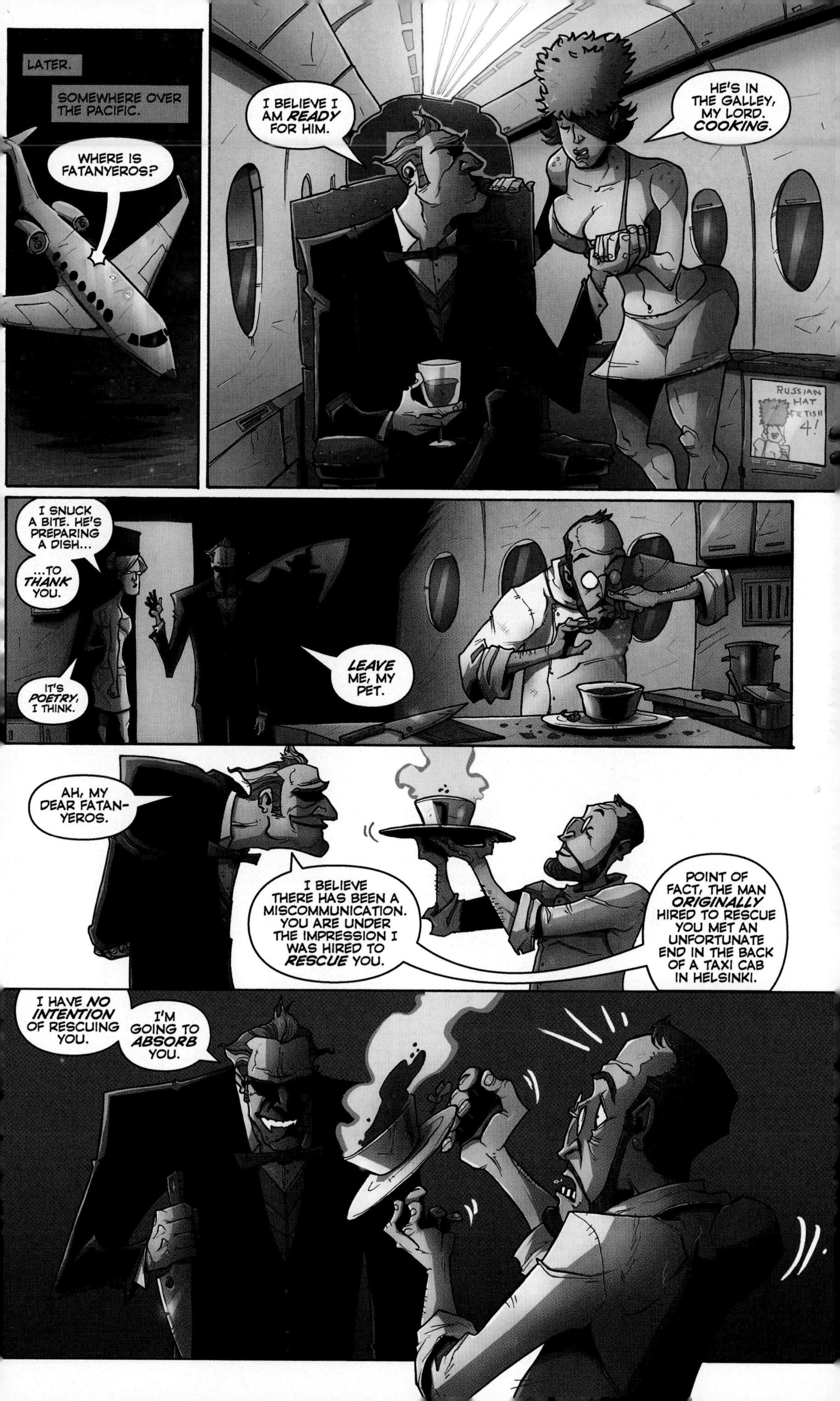
LATER.
SOMEWHERE OVER THE PACIFIC.
WHERE IS FATANYEROS?
I BELIEVE I AM *READY* FOR HIM.
HE'S IN THE GALLEY, MY LORD. ***COOKING***.
RUSSIAN HAT FETISH 4!
I SNUCK A BITE. HE'S PREPARING A DISH...
...TO ***THANK*** YOU.
IT'S ***POETRY***, I THINK.
LEAVE ME, MY PET.
AH, MY DEAR FATAN-YEROS.
I BELIEVE THERE HAS BEEN A MISCOMMUNICATION. YOU ARE UNDER THE IMPRESSION I WAS HIRED TO ***RESCUE*** YOU.
POINT OF FACT, THE MAN ***ORIGINALLY*** HIRED TO RESCUE YOU MET AN UNFORTUNATE END IN THE BACK OF A TAXI CAB IN HELSINKI.
I HAVE ***NO INTENTION*** OF RESCUING YOU.
I'M GOING TO ***ABSORB*** YOU.

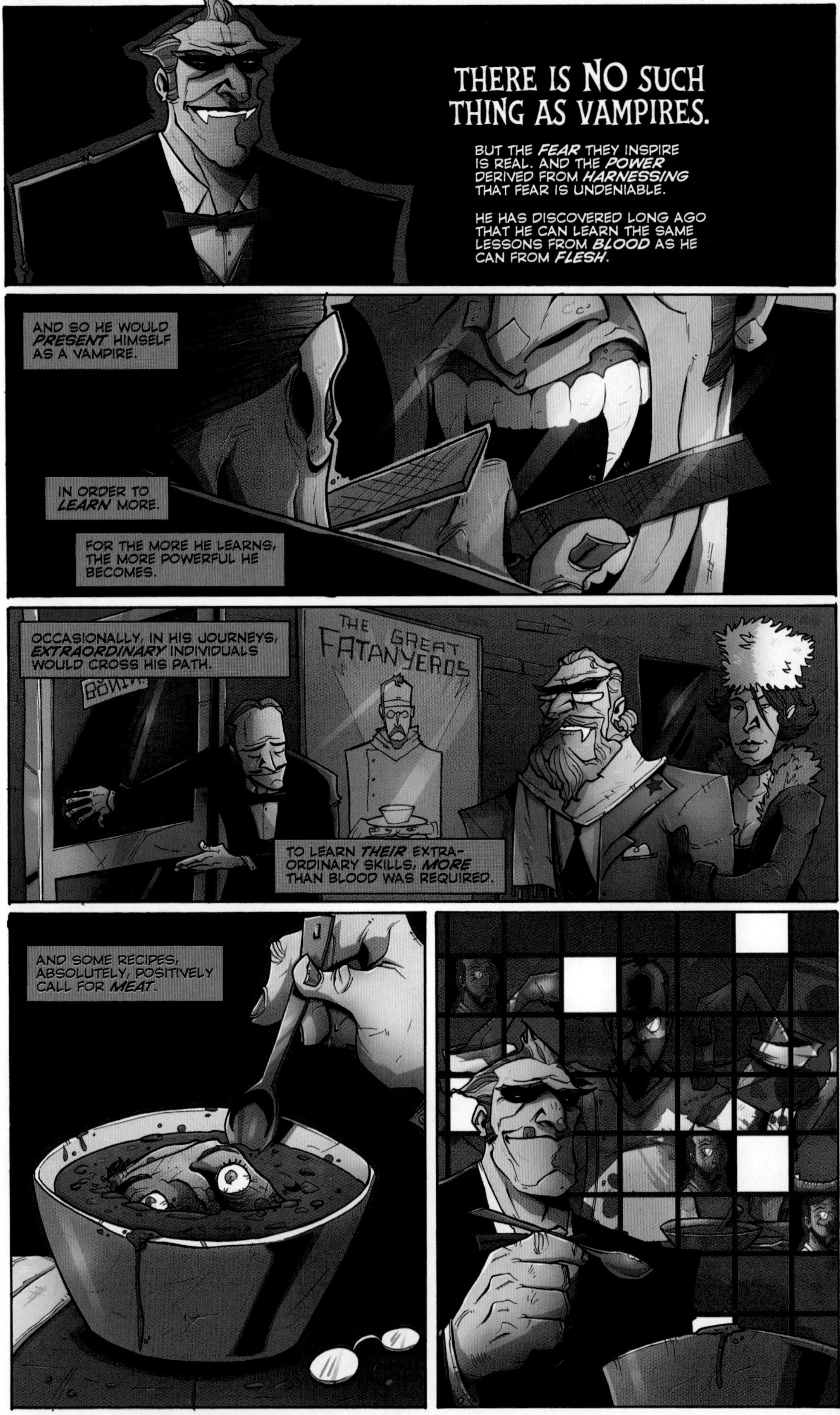

THERE IS NO SUCH THING AS VAMPIRES.
BUT THE FEAR THEY INSPIRE IS REAL. AND THE POWER DERIVED FROM HARNESSING THAT FEAR IS UNDENIABLE.
HE HAS DISCOVERED LONG AGO THAT HE CAN LEARN THE SAME LESSONS FROM BLOOD AS HE CAN FROM FLESH.
AND SO HE WOULD PRESENT HIMSELF AS A VAMPIRE.
IN ORDER TO LEARN MORE.
FOR THE MORE HE LEARNS, THE MORE POWERFUL HE BECOMES.
OCCASIONALLY, IN HIS JOURNEYS, EXTRAORDINARY INDIVIDUALS WOULD CROSS HIS PATH.
THE GREAT FATANYEROS
TO LEARN THEIR EXTRAORDINARY SKILLS, MORE THAN BLOOD WAS REQUIRED.
AND SOME RECIPES, ABSOLUTELY, POSITIVELY CALL FOR MEAT.

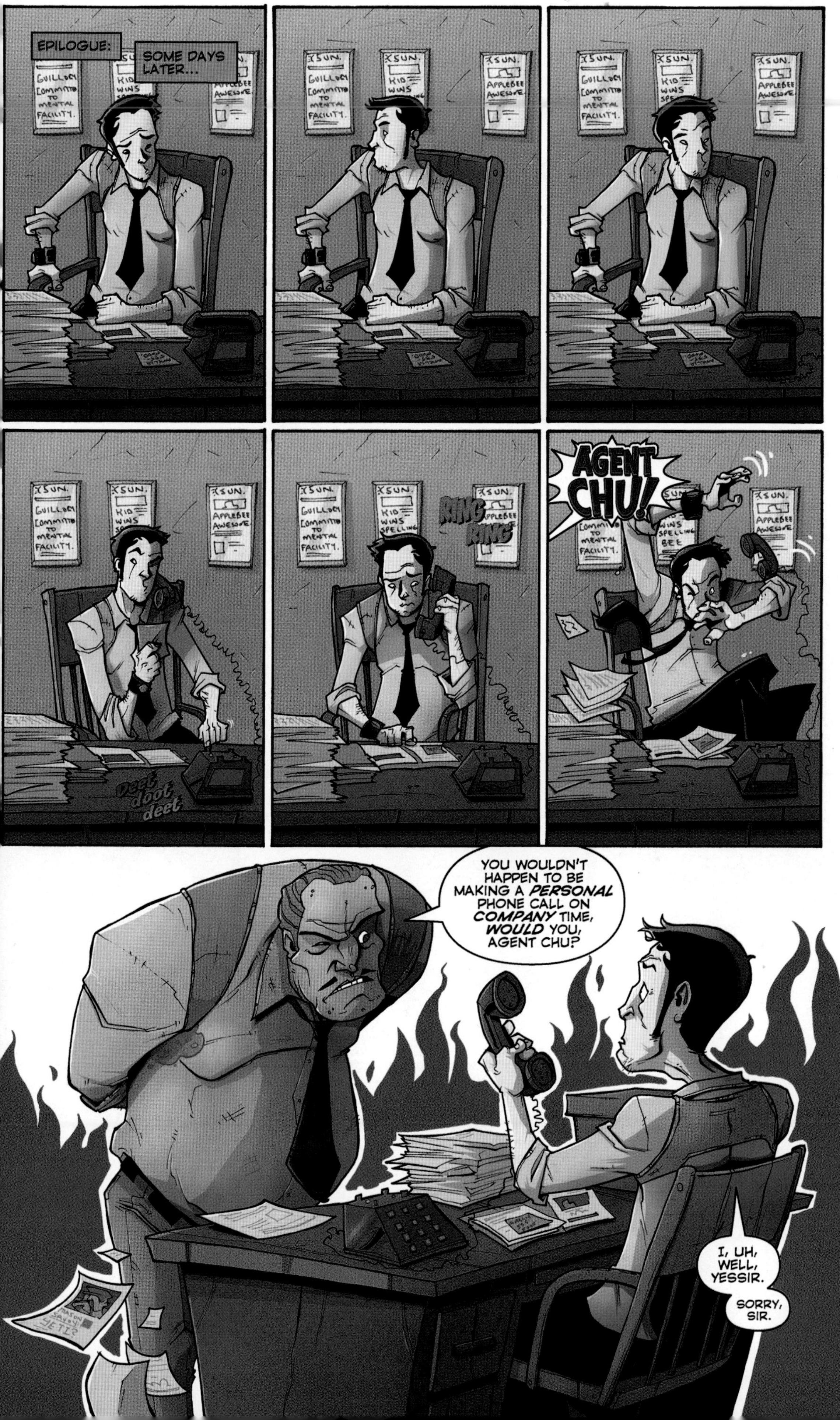
EPILOGUE:
SOME DAYS LATER...
Deet doot deet
RING RING
AGENT CHU!
YOU WOULDN'T HAPPEN TO BE MAKING A *PERSONAL* PHONE CALL ON *COMPANY* TIME, *WOULD* YOU, AGENT CHU?
I, UH, WELL, YESSIR.
SORRY, SIR.

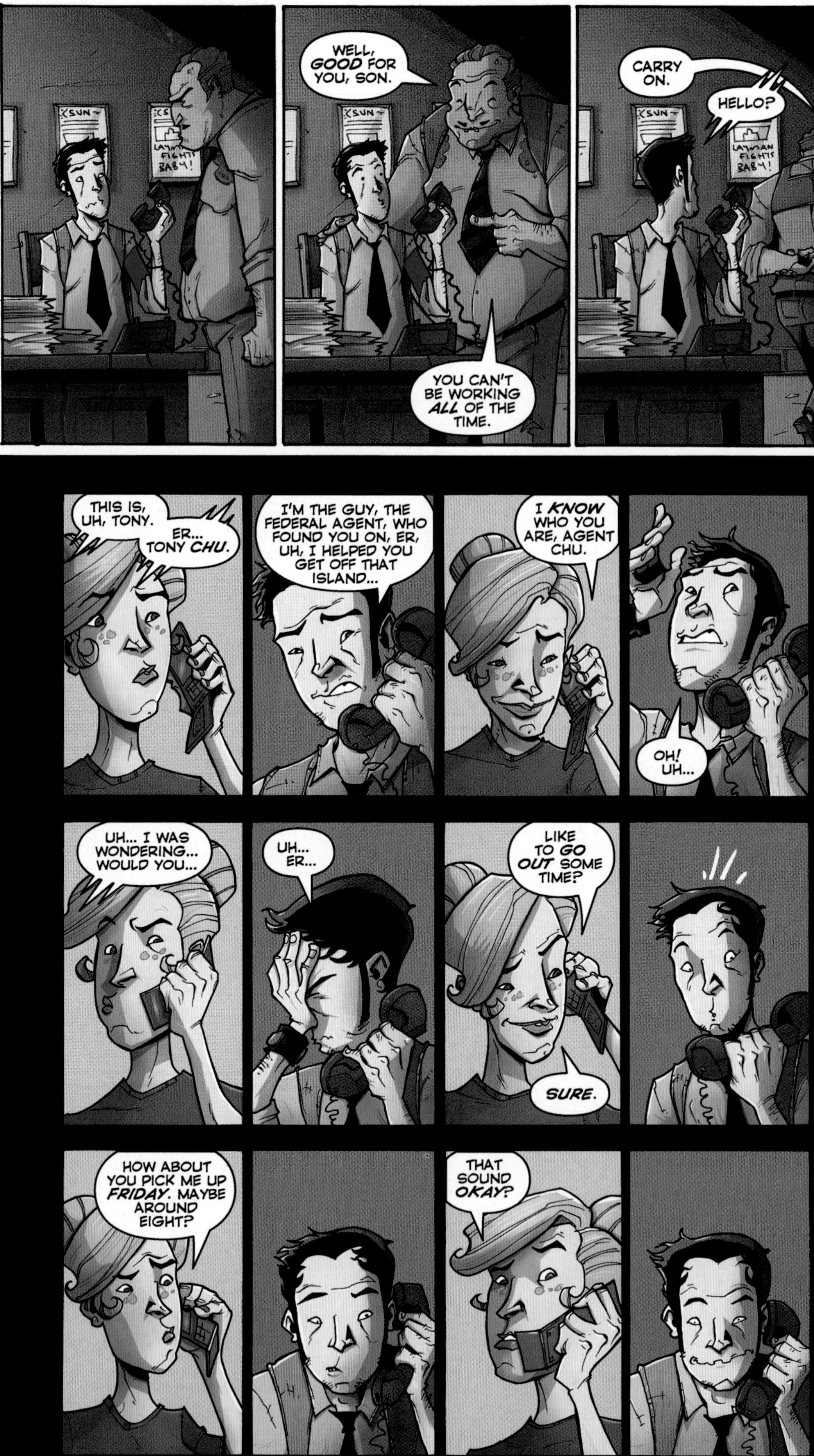
WELL, GOOD FOR YOU, SON.
YOU CAN'T BE WORKING ALL OF THE TIME.
CARRY ON.
HELLO?
THIS IS, UH, TONY.
ER... TONY CHU.
I'M THE GUY, THE FEDERAL AGENT, WHO FOUND YOU ON, ER, UH, I HELPED YOU GET OFF THAT ISLAND...
I KNOW WHO YOU ARE, AGENT CHU.
OH! UH...
UH... I WAS WONDERING... WOULD YOU...
UH... ER...
LIKE TO GO OUT SOME TIME?
SURE.
HOW ABOUT YOU PICK ME UP FRIDAY. MAYBE AROUND EIGHT?
THAT SOUND OKAY?

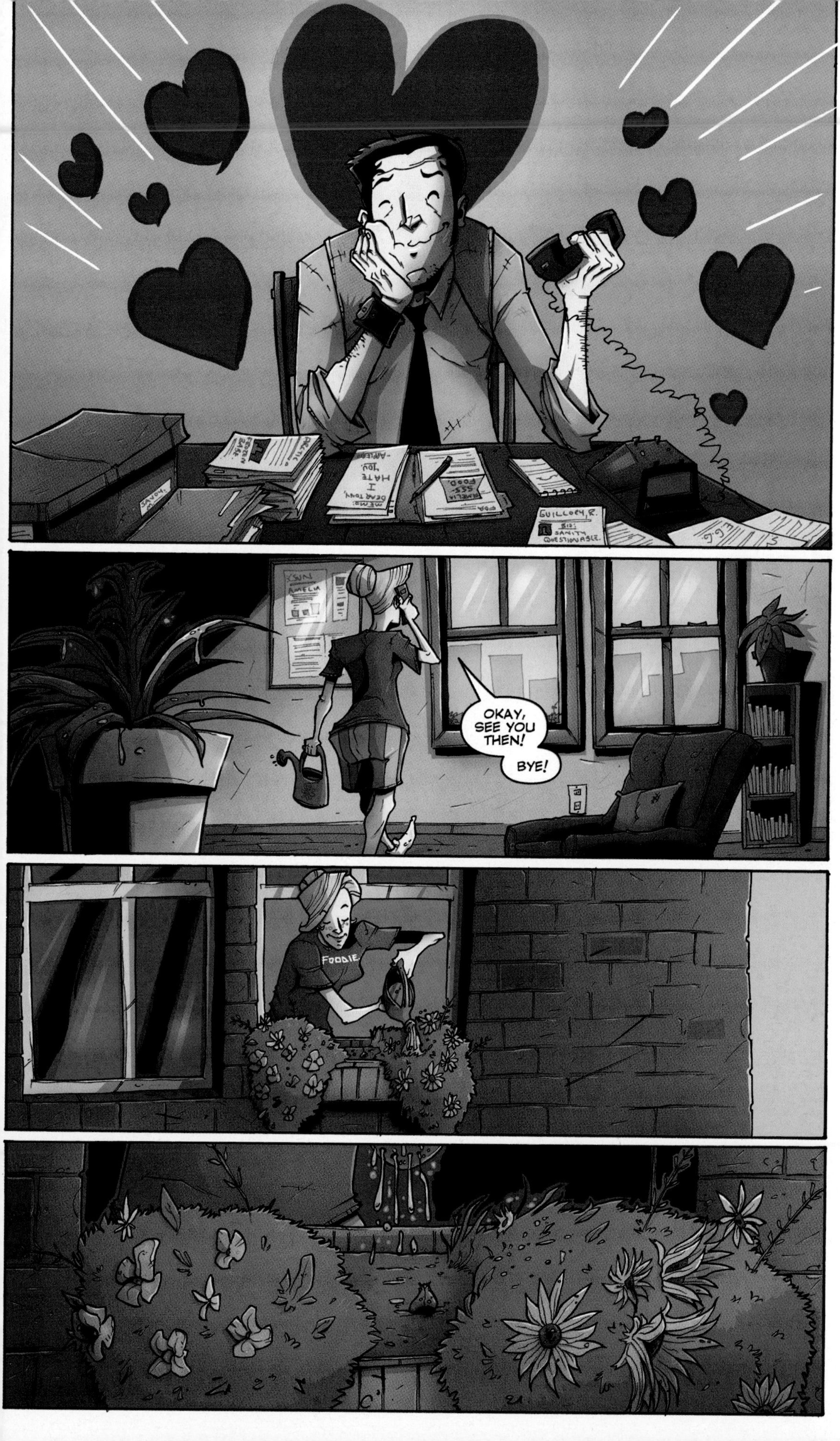
OKAY, SEE YOU THEN!
BYE!
FOODIE

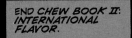

END CHEW BOOK II:
INTERNATIONAL
FLAVOR.

Sketches for The Vampire. I wanted to mix the classic vampire look with a more crazed serial killer. I based his stiffness and angularity on old-school movie slashers, who never were all that mobile, but were always foreboding.

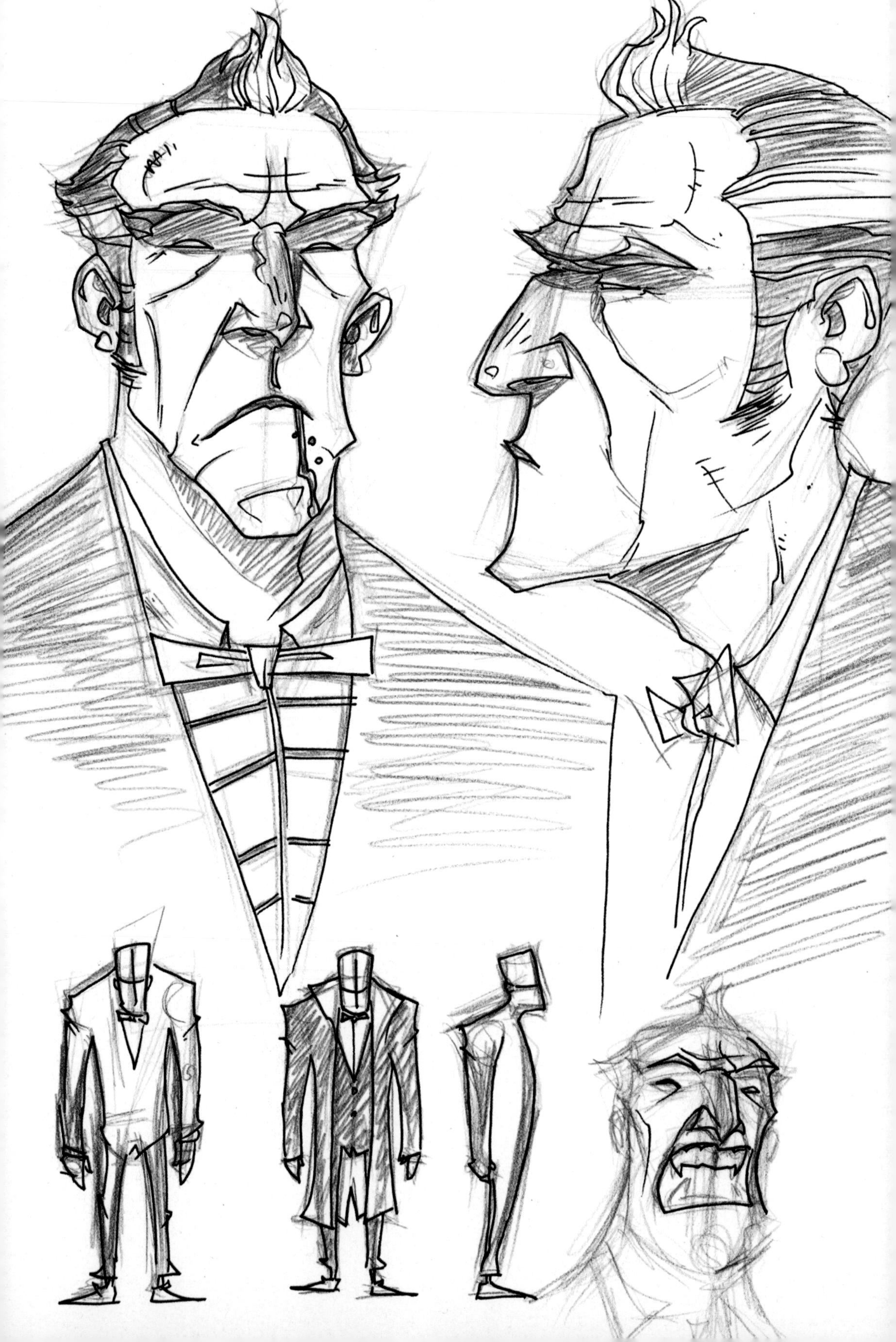

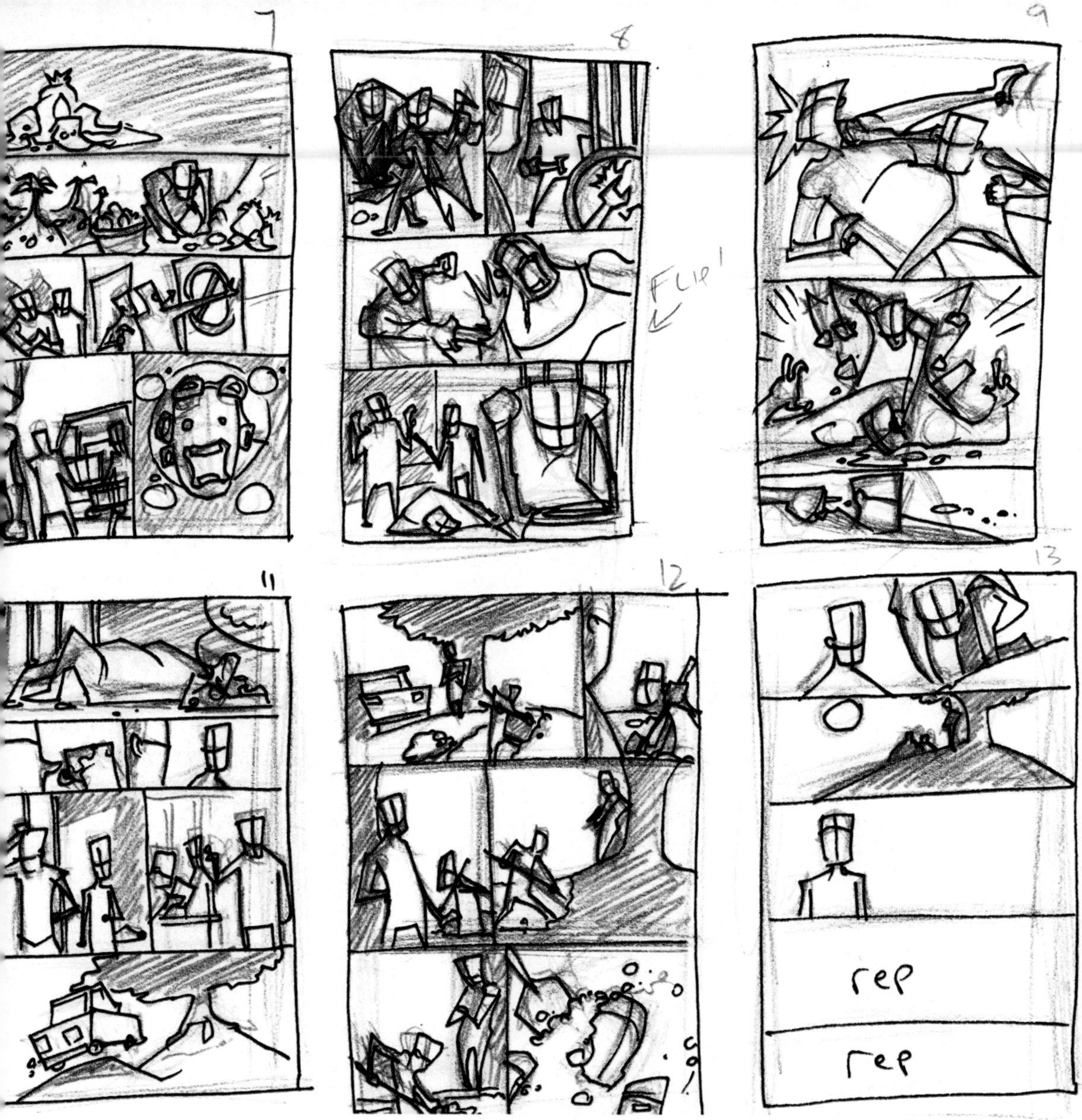
7
8
9
Flip!
11
12
13
rep
rep

Thumbnails for *CHEW #8*. I work out 95% of my design problems at this stage, which is probably why I dread it so much. I focus on gesture, storytelling and pure aesthetic zing. Also, a couple of the icons I wanted to use as design elements in the book. The Gallsaberry icon was never used.

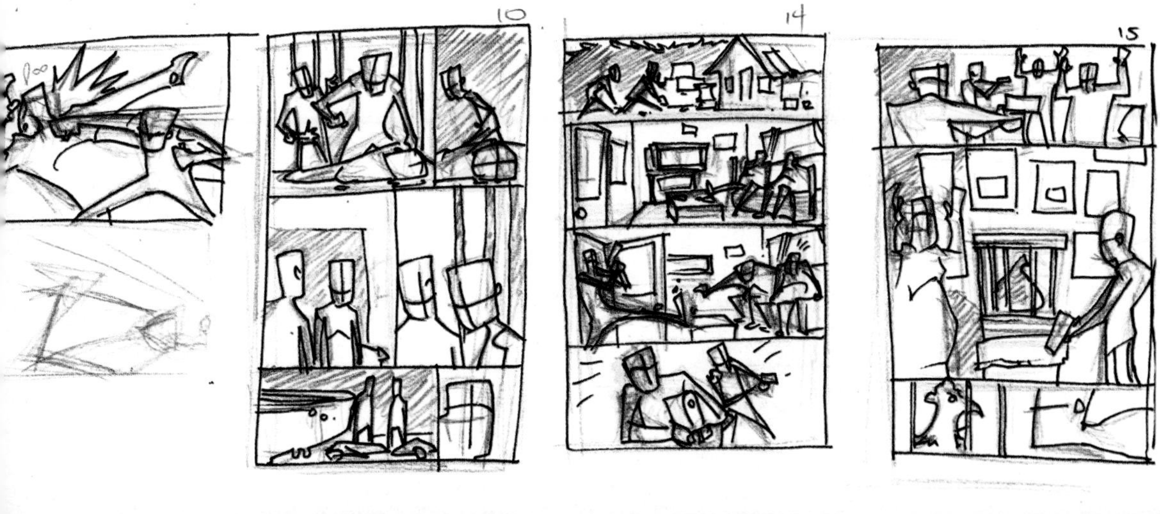
10
14
15

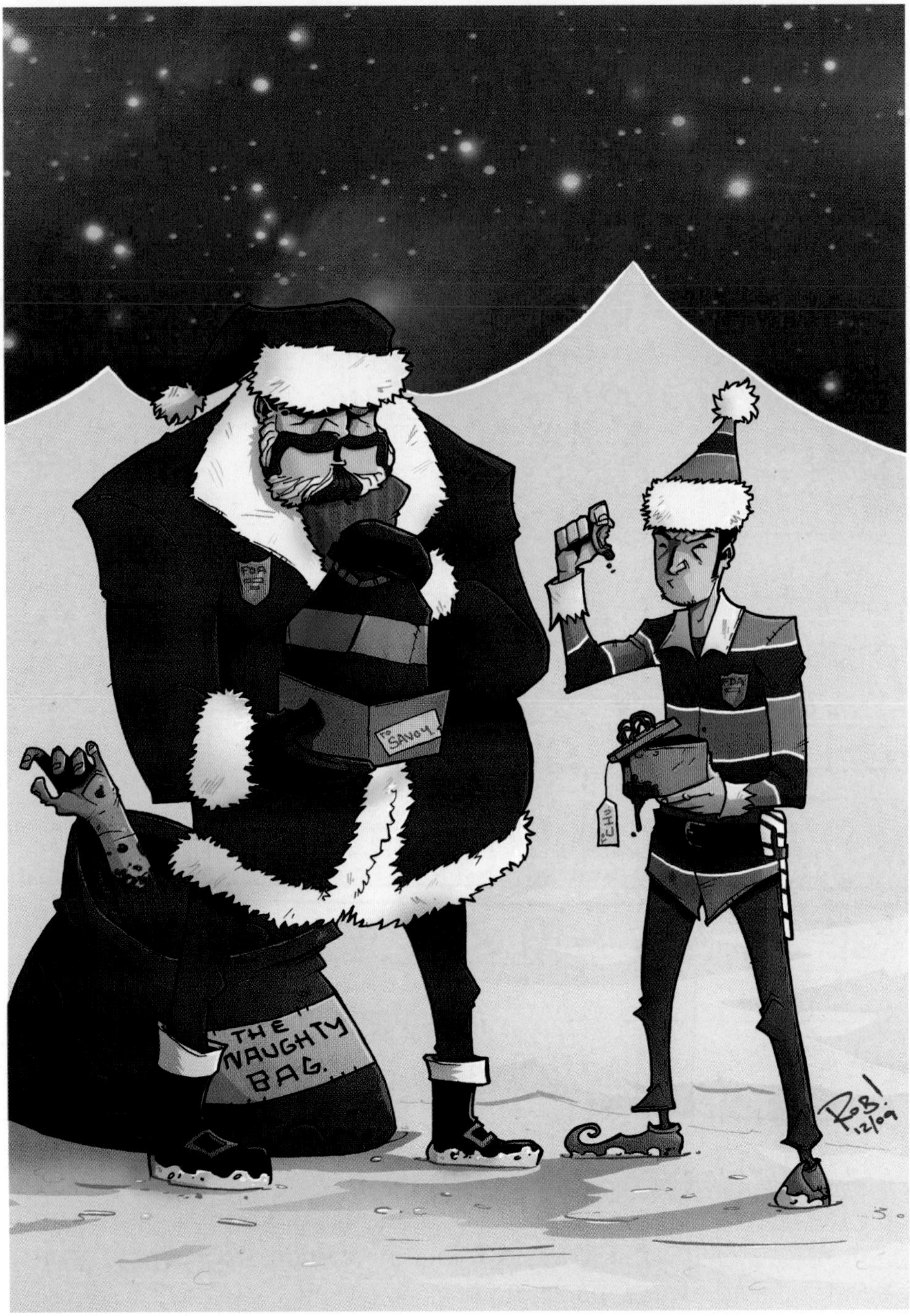
TO SAVOY
THE NAUGHTY BAG.
ROB! 12/09

The 2009 Image Comics Christmas Card, featuring *CHEW*.

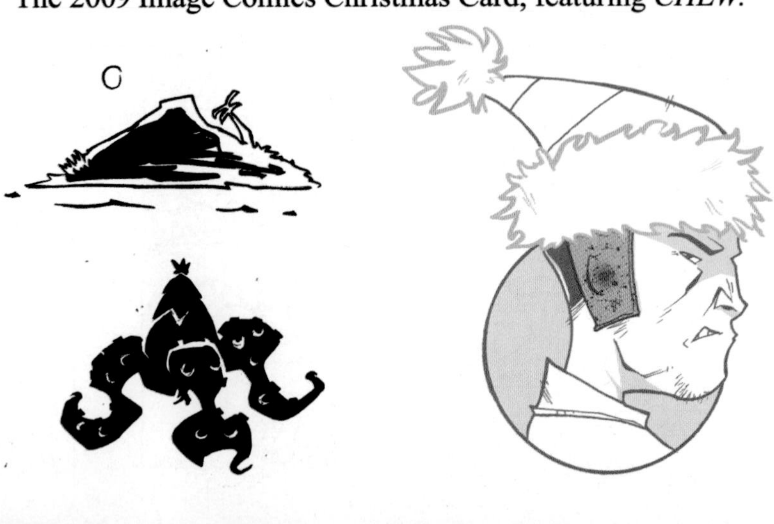